FAILURE OF FISH

THIRD EDITION

Michael Sorbonne Robinson

In Appreciation

The Failure of Fish is a product of diverse influences, including the many friends, acquaintances, and family members who have touched my life. Each has contributed to both my enjoyment and understanding of our world. Not the least of these was my own mother, Rita Sorbonne Robinson. Her ninety-two years of life were largely dominated by an enviable, irrepressible brightness and optimism. Despite what I considered to be the often bleak scenery of her life, there were few times when she was not genuinely happy, and she had a way of lifting others with her dauntless and innocent sense of joy.

This book is dedicated to the mother who inspired me, the weight she placed on excellence, and her encouragement in my literary endeavors.

My sincere gratitude also goes to this book's first readers—Kent Hales, who provided essential feedback and some well-taken suggestions, and Peter Empringham (The Afternet series and Paving Paradise), a fellow novelist and invaluable critic who assisted me in the final editing.

Contents

Billy's Last Journal Entry

July 19, 1983

I woke up this morning feeling weaker. My belly's distended, and my skin's a putrid yellow color. Dr. Simms stopped by, and he told me what I already knew--says "It's just a matter of time." I picked up my old Hamilton 940 from the stainless steel tray beside the bed. It has served me well, and its smooth gold finish feels like a friend in the palm of my hand. I turn it over, remembering the 1911 Christmas when the Murphys gave it to me. Then I stop to read, once more, the inscription on its back. "Time Waits for No Man."

I'm not sure what I hate more—the nausea, or the pain I'd be suffering if it weren't for the medications. The kitchen brought me a light breakfast, but I only got a few bites down before tossing it back up. It seems to me that if a man gets the privilege of a "last meal," he ought to at least be able to keep it down. For the moment, I'm feeling a bit better, so I'm going to write while I can.

I've noticed that many old folks feel a need to review the past. It's obvious now that I'm no different. Several things stand out when I think of my earliest conscious memories and the thoughts that accompanied them.

For instance, I sincerely believed that I was special, always so sure that bad things could happen to others but not to me. I guess every kid feels the same way. Now I know I was very naïve, and that virtually no one escapes those surprisingly predictable--and remarkably malicious--things that life does to us. Ahead are weathered grave stones, neatly cascading across an expanse of earthworms and grass. That's enough to shrink any ego to size. It certainly eliminates any notions that I was so different from everyone else.

When I look back at my early years in Stella's Cove, my world seemed almost magical. It was a place of storybook beauty, where I watched falling stars exploding off the face of the Gavins Glacier as the moon threw down a shimmering shaft across the sea. (I know—I may be guilty of some purple prose, but it really is a challenge to describe things so stunningly beautiful in ordinary words.)

When Dad died, the dream was suddenly gone, and I remember being so depressed that I silently wished my life would end. Now I know that I wasn't alone in that. Lots of boys have lost their fathers, and I've come to understand that my pain was no greater than theirs. That event took my naiveté and innocence, and I've been stuck, ever since, in the tenacious discomfort of reality.

I have considered, with brutal honesty, the fragile margin between the real and the imagined. In particular I've scrutinized those things I'd accepted as a child, without question. What I've discovered is that nothing in Stella's Cove was ever perfect. The strains of majestic hymns, tearing across the serenity of our town from the old Methodist Church, failed to deliver the message of Christ's love; Mother, though I'd told her so many times, "You're the best mommy in the world." was morally flawed and emotionally unstable; and the dream of a bright future for Stella's Cove had proven to be only momentary and elusive, flaring brightly, like an oil lamp as it exhausts its final drops of fuel.

And yet, with age I've realized that one doesn't need perfection in order to be happy, and that life's most dismal moments are effaced by a few stunning and profound revelations of truth. Finding Celeste was one of those, when love and understanding removed all barriers. Another was that moment when I pressed my lips to Elizabeth's tiny cheek, instantly changing everything I'd previously believed about love. George Murphy's words of kindness were yet another, when he first reached out to me, "You're Billy Potter, aren't you? I was sorry to hear about your father." My friend Burdett's mischievous smile still both warms and haunts me. So does the fateful arrival of the new school teacher, the angelic Miss Hardwicke. She inspired me to strive for excellence, and her presence tore at the foundations of our town.

Life has gone by so quickly. (For one who dislikes clichés, I seem to be stuck with some extremely trite words.) I wish I'd begun my compilation of Stella's Cove's history years sooner. Some of the details have probably been skewed by my imperfect memory—particularly the depictions of certain unrecorded events which relied only on the oral accounts. The Arnold University Press--publisher of my university thesis, "Carnivorous Sheep," has agreed to publish my book as a work of historical fiction, but I won't be around to see it in print.

Overall, I have few regrets, and it's been a good run.

Billy Potter

Beginnings

Nobody could say how long the glacier had been there, but there was one thing the townsfolk of Stella's Cove never seemed to question: the glacier's looming blue spires, though looking like steeples on a dazzling glass cathedral, were regarded as a foreboding of tragedy. That was true from the days the first trappers set foot where Muir Creek met the salty waters of the Pacific, and it remained so, even during the periods of rich prosperity--the most recent of which brought fresh paint, washing machines, electric lights, and new roofs to my town.

Though the glacier's advance was sometimes as little as a foot per year, the steady delivery of deaths and economic disasters were a reliable expectation of its presence. The massive behemoth was heralded each day by the long shadows it cast, falling silently across the town like mute, gray trumpets announcing the sun. But the sun only provided disappointing moments of glory, for it usually made only a short appearance as it climbed over the east side of the coastal mountains, only to be masked by the typical shrouds that blotted out the light and sucked the shadows back into the ice.

With similar predictability, the Stella's Cove population flocked to church every Sunday. But my perception, except during my youngest years, was that the religious dedication of the town was dictated much less by a love of God than by a fear of divine punishment. In retrospect, even the fear of punishment had been an ineffective motivator.

Dominated by superstition and religion, the people of Stella's Cove were largely entitled to their paranoia, for, like the instability of the glacier that hung menacingly over it, the town of Stella's Cove was always on a precipitous footing.

A beautiful place that every visitor described as "heaven," the town was, in fact, no more eternal than the blue spires at the Glacier's tongue, which sometimes lasted for months--even years--then ultimately crashed to the stream bed below, scattering shards of glassy blue fragments down the narrow canyon. There was always a delicate balance between nature and economics; a thin line between life and death--both literal and figurative; and there was a distinct and disturbing dissonance between reason and religion, faith and actions, that haunted the history of my town.

There's a passage in the Bible that predicts a time when the lamb and the lion shall lie down together, but, in Stella's Cove, the sheep were the ones with the teeth and were no better than a pack of wolves. Guided by their Rev. Miles Cromwell, the townsfolk were the product of mob mentality and the misguided notion that the chosen people could do no wrong. While the flock saw its duty as preserving the purity of the community and purging evil from its midst, it forgot, in its piety, the most essential teachings of Christianity.

As I look back on my five years away at the university, I'm reminded of a course I took in music history and appreciation. Of all my electives, that class was my favorite. When I heard the classical music that flowed from the minds of Mozart and Beethoven, there was a gentle, warm swelling in my heart, and I understood immediately the indelible imprint their music had left on both their contemporary audiences and the generations that followed. The music spoke directly to my soul and left me with a tingling sensation that felt, as I could only imagine, like the touch of an angel, or the gentle surge of electrical current running throughout my body.

I was fascinated, as well, by the less traditional works of the so-called avant garde composers--those outside-the-box geniuses who rejected the traditional harmonies and tonalities, creating works that sawed and grated at the ears and minds of their listeners. Their compositions were unsettling and unpleasant—anything but melodious--yet they always ended with the same profound confirmation: Pleasure is the absence of pain. I experienced a sense of both relief and joy when the final resolutions bonded the music together with a sense of harmony and grace. Unlike those avant garde symphonies, the dissonance of Stella's Cove never transitioned to harmony, and the pleasant expectation--that all would be finally resolved--was regularly dimmed by yet one more sour and tragic happening.

Doomed by its over-zealous trappers, and then, by the driving and breathless greed that quickly depleted the rich placer mining claims, the businesses, buildings, and fortunes, spawned by the whirlwind booms, were blown away by the same storms that brought them. For, it had been runaway enthusiasm over the area's natural resources that so indiscriminately depleted both the fur animals and the gold. Those two disasters each brought a screaming silence to Stella's Cove, the remaining residents totally mired in the despair that buried their town.

Despite what appeared to be its economic end, there would be yet one more boom in Stella's Cove, B.C. I was there when it started, and I was there to see the events that followed.

A Sad Journey

There's a light fog scrolling over the Vancouver waterfront as Celeste and I haul our bags up the gangplank to the Aniak's deck. The well-varnished mahogany planking is slippery from the cold, overnight condensation, and a young deckhand warns us and our fellow passengers, "Be careful, folks. The decks are slick." But it's already too late.

Despite his warning, Celeste's right foot slides precariously as she steps from the gangplank to the boat's deck. Dropping the carpet valise I'm carrying, I reach for her upper arm to arrest her fall, but her other foot, desperate to regain a firm footing, also slides, and she falls with an indelicate thud. During our years of public schooling in Stella's Cove, she was always willowy and light. Now petticoats cover her shapely figure as she smoothes her skirt and rises to her feet, laughing over the awkwardness of her fall.

The deckhand rushes toward us to steady her, inquiring with great concern, "Are you all right, Ma'am?" Before Celeste can answer, he has picked up our two bags. "I'll stow them in your cabin," he offers, "and I'll pull them out for you when we get to your destination. By the way, where are you headed?" Celeste and I speak at the same time, "Stella's Cove, but," Celeste adds, "I'll be continuing on to Eagle City." There is a noticeable change in the man's countenance at the mention of our destination, and his friendly smile turns, almost instantly, into a vague frown. "Stella's Cove, eh? That's too bad."

The deckhand is slightly built, blonde-headed, and sports a more than ample mustache. While mostly well proportioned, his looks are marred by a pronounced under-bite--so prominent. In fact, that I do a carefully concealed double-take. His lower teeth and chin protrude at least an inch beyond his upper lip, and he seems to have significant difficulty in the enunciation of his words. I consider, for a moment, that his broad mustache was likely grown to soften the appearance of his abnormality, which hints to me that, somewhere, back on his family tree, there must have been a pelican. He's wearing a shirt with broad, horizontal red, white, and blue stripes, and a pair of stunningly white pants, which drape over his skinny frame. "That town is going to be a ghost town soon," notes the deckhand with a look of knowing resolution. "Everyone's trying to leave."

"Yes, we know," I assert, "We're both from there, and we were there when it all happened." There is recognition in the deckhand's face, and his expression turns to a sad, wistful, look. "I felt awful when I heard what happened. Harry Mills was my friend. I used to find books for him at our other ports of call. Sure, I'd heard about the Eagle City story." the deckhand recalls, "Who hasn't, but I never believed it. There couldn't have been a finer man. He loved people and everyone could feel it."

Celeste has obviously survived her fall without the slightest injury. She smiles sweetly at me, presses her cold, wet hands against my cheeks in a teasing way, then gives me a warm, gentle, well-reciprocated kiss. It is not a kiss of passion, rather a punctuating moment when appreciation and love are conveyed through a connection of the eyes. The young deckhand sets down our bags for a moment. He smiles, then claps briefly, and remarks one more time about Celeste's fall. He says it with a wink, "I told you it was slippery."

As we kiss, I notice two matronly ladies eyeing us with the imputation of impropriety, but neither Celeste nor I feel the least bit self-conscious, for her own father and mother were never shy about outward affection, and neither of us feels bound by the formalities of strict convention. I've known Celeste since our early days at the Stella's Cove School, so ours is a love born of long time respect, and our relationship has become more intimate, only as we've considered our new life in a different place and the family we intend to have together. There's a slight tug of surface tension that seems to hold Celeste's lips to mine, but the moment ends as the wetness of the air slides between our faces. I glance at the two matronly ladies. It is fairly obvious that the pair have disapproved, and I simply choose to look away from their irritating stares.

The crew is now in position to cast off, and the boiler has

created enough steam pressure that the automatic relief valves are rhythmically puffing steam, accompanied by a shrill hissing. The Captain pulls the lanyard above him, blows the boat's whistle three times, and the dock lines are released. There's an instant, unison movement that seems almost orchestrated, as the passengers move to the starboard railing to witness the finality of the departure. There are shuddering rumblings as the propeller pulls the stern away from the dock, and, after the bow has cleared the last piling and we're about two hundred feet away, deep green whirlpools spin in our wake. There are additional rumblings and vibrations as the Captain adds power, and the Aniak slowly moves ahead, creating a foamy white tail in its path. A look of satisfaction floods the other passengers' faces as the boat moves toward the channel, but I have a feeling of unpleasant apprehension, understanding that every moment is bringing me closer to Stella's Cove and the persistent memories I wish I could forget.

The impressive profile of Vancouver disappears in a blanket of mist. One moment the city was there, still vivid in our sight, but now it is as if someone has shut a Venetian Blind behind us. I am reminded of the concept, that faith is the belief in things not seen, for the vestiges of my early religious education are still very much a part of my mind. Mother told me a thousand times, "Billy, faith is the greatest virtue, for there is so much more out there than what we can see with our own eyes. God wants you to get to know him, but believing is the only way."

For a moment I'm reminded of how it is faith and reason, together, that allow us to accept, as fact, that the sun is still out there in the sky, even when it's obscured from view by the clouds or the shadow of the earth; how there are deer, everywhere in the woods, yet they most often elude our vision; and how the sea, though appearing as a flat surface, pressed by the pale sky, is simply a blanket that hides an amazing array of life, currents, and sunken treasures. Acutely aware of the almost instant disappearance of Vancouver, I muse for a moment. "Is it really there?"

Taking advantage of the long summer days, the Aniak Captain has announced that we will average 120 miles per day, and that the first night will be spent at Pierre's Cove. The boat is mostly quiet as it glides through the water, but any changes in power and direction are, each time, accompanied by some pulsing vibrations, which cause a low frequency rumble, and rattle anything that isn't bolted down. As the boat approaches the main channel marker buoy, there's a large freighter crossing our path, with what looks like, Chinese characters on its bow, and we are forced to slow to an idle. The ship is huge, and it takes a few minutes for it to pass. I find myself feeling impatient, although I'm already feeling angst about our arrival in Stella's Cove.

I notice that the freighter is loaded with coal, towering from its deep hold, creating large mountains of black that loom well above the ship's gunwales. For a moment I'm imagining how such a ship maneuvers when the seas are rough, and wonder how much of a wave it would take to capsize the vessel--first causing its massive load to shift, moving the ship's center of gravity to one side or the other, and then causing its heavy cargo to roll it upside down. At the same time, I imagine its crew frantically floundering in the coldness of the waves and praying for a rescue that will never come. I am right there, struggling with the anguish of a drowning man-- fearing the fates of a wife and son left to fend for themselves. Since Father's death, I have not been able to watch a ship in the distance without considering his last moments. I understand that such thoughts are both unproductive and damaging, so I silently chastise myself: "Don't do that, Billy…" and there's a pause before I complete the thought, "There's nothing you can do to bring him back."

Having cleared the harbor and the congested traffic of Vancouver, the Aniak turns north, shuddering, once more, as the Captain adds power and brings the boat on course. Passage to Stella's Cove from Vancouver takes the better part of four days. Though the distance could easily be covered in half the time, the duration of the voyage is increased because the steamboat cannot operate safely at night in these waters. The coastal islands and narrow channels, dictate that the Aniak will be docked each evening at safe harbors along the way. After Pierre's Cove, it will be McLaughlin's Landing, and the last night will be spent at Bourne River, which is the next town south of Stella's Cove.

Though our captain has spent almost forty years at sea, the Aniak's owners require local pilots for each leg of the voyage— pilots who specialize in the complexity of navigating such a difficult and dangerous route. There are islands everywhere, and the pelican-billed crewman remarks to us, "The boat could easily go aground; there's a maze of hidden, unyielding geological structures below the surface, straddling our course only a few hundred feet off either side…Gotta have a good pilot." In all the years that I'd seen the Aniak come and go from Stella's Cove, I'd never considered the perils that were faced on each voyage, nor the specialized competence such a passage requires.

Luckily the seas are calm and the air is a gentle fifteen degrees Centigrade, a typical temperature for this time of the year and the early hour. It is not the temperature that has chilled us--but the effect of the cool, relative wind as the Captain pushes the throttle to full power. The ship shudders once more, until its normal cruising speed has been reached, then settles down to a smooth purr as the forces of resistance and thrust finally come into balance.

Bundled in Sou'westers, we're enjoying being on the deck, but our comfort doesn't last for long. Our sightseeing is interrupted predictably throughout the day by more visits to the salon. At noon, Celeste and I choose to have our lunch on deck, but, noticing that our teeth are soon chattering like a military drum roll, we go back inside.

Before dusk, the Aniak puts into Pierre's Cove. Besides the array of fishing boats that dot the harbor, there's little to look at—a few humble homes, a line of fisherman shacks along the water's edge, and a large green building that sports a painted sign. "Marvin's Marine Repairs and Fittings." Since no passengers are embarking or disembarking here, the Captain has tied-up to a line of pilings several hundred feet from the dock.

"I really hoped we could go ashore." There's a look of resignation in Celeste's face as she says it. "I know there's probably nothing exciting to look at, but it's just that I'm already tired of the sea, and I'd like to stand on solid ground." I wish that I could say something encouraging, but I'm forced to simply commiserate. "Me too." Celeste's disappointment seems soothed by a glass of wine and a surprisingly tasty supper of halibut and chips. Afterwards, we linger on the deck for just a moment, wrapped in each other's arms under a generously jeweled sky, then climb the companionway to the boat's upper deck and the little cabin which will be ours for the next three nights.

I have not scrimped on our accommodations. It is the best the Aniak has to offer. The relative luxury of our cabin was provided by several extra shifts on my bar-tending job, along with a "graduation" contribution from Celeste's father, George. Our cabin is number six and it has a large window next to the door, which allows us to sit on the bed and watch the coastline streaming by. I was careful, when I made the reservation, to be sure that our quarters were on the starboard side, with an unobstructed vista of the passing scenery. Today, there is little to see; every now and then a fir tree or mountain is revealed by a wink in the fog, but it is the gentle, damp, scrolling shroud that mostly dominates our views.

The night is quiet, and Celeste and I have a gentle evening, snuggled up together in a down comforter, provided by the Aniak for each single berth. It is not the most romantic of accommodations, but we both understand that the ship's layout is typical and that only the largest liners have beds large enough for two. My back is pressed firmly against the mahogany bulkhead, and Celeste's neck is a perfect fit for my outstretched left arm. Lulled to sleep by the gentle rocking, Celeste's breathing turns to a kitten's purr, and then we are both quickly submerged in oblivion.

The sound of sea birds wakes us at around 5:00 a.m. Something's not right. Though Celeste gives me a warm good-morning smile, I am immediately confused that there is someone else's arm around her neck. It's not mine. I reach over and carefully follow the stray limb; I am relieved to find that it is attached to my own left shoulder. It takes a minute or two of stretching and massaging it before sensation returns—first the tingling and numbness, and everything is back to normal again. We dress, then descend to the salon for a cup of coffee and some batch-made mush.

After eating a bowl of the gooey gruel, I can see why crew members had traditionally been provided a daily ration of mildly alcoholic grog in an attempt to make their lives more bearable. The gruel has the consistency of wood glue, and I have visions of craftsmen daubing the sticky slop over the mating parts of a mortise and tenon joint and carefully pressing the pieces together with a clamp. "No doubt," I consider, a resolute, muted smile curling on my lips, "the joint will never come apart." My mother's gruel was never great, but the Aniak's is barely edible.

The view is stunning as the sun rises over the crest of the coastal mountains, and, with breakfast over, we spend the following hour leaning against the deck railing and taking in the beauty of the coastline.

The next two days are just a blur of green, gray, and granite, except for a few minutes of excitement when the sea rises violently and its crests explode against the sky. Only a few minutes into the short, violent gale, there was a loud crack. It sounded like a pistol shot. The passengers on deck all turned in staccato unison, just in time to see the Aniak's main stack, first shudder, then veer to one side, banging noisily as it flailed against its base. There were gasps, and people near the stack ran for cover. Moments later, one of the deck hands climbed up to inspect the damage, then reported to the captain. "We've sheared the portside bolts. The stack is barely hanging on. We're going to have to stop and secure it, or we'll sustain even greater damage."

Captain Nordstok deployed the Aniak's anchor and shut down the engine to allow the stack to cool. "I'm sorry, folks," he apologized, "but we're going to be stuck here for a while." The Aniak sat there, weather-vaned into the wind, waiting for the blow to ease. Luckily it passed quickly, and the repairs were commenced. It took all five members of the crew to lift the stack back into position, but, less than an hour later, the failed bolts had been replaced, the anchor hoisted, and the trip resumed—this time at an even faster pace. No one had been happy about the delay, and especially the dead-ship-bobbing motion that brought a wave of seasickness to most of the passengers. Celeste had been one of them—her complexion closely mimicking the green of the sea-- leaning over the railing and feeling miserably un-ladylike.

At McLaughlin's Landing, once more there are no passengers being dropped off or picked up, so the Aniak is tied up offshore. By time the boat finally docks at Bourne River, we are both tired of the sea, so we go ashore and walk around the town. Like most B.C. towns, Bourne River is dominated by its oldest and grandest building, so it is a Methodist church that lays down a sprawling shadow, hundreds of feet long, as a peaceful, unhurried, summer sunset takes its reliable pause upon the sea. At these northern latitudes, the nights are short this time of the year and sunsets persist long into the evening hours.

Just east of the church is a little, grassy square with four, cast-iron park benches, a large bronze statue of Edward E. Bourne, standing on a granite base engraved with the words, "Pioneer and Visionary", and a fountain with three Orcas, arching toward a shallow pool. Except for us, there is no one enjoying the serenity of the moment, and we have it all to ourselves. "It's a shame," I note to Celeste that the stone Orcas have so little water pressure--just seems that something so beautifully sculpted shouldn't be neglected. Celeste delivers a dim smile. "It seems to me that Bourne River's story is like many others," she observes, "where towns proudly grow, maintaining their grandness for a time, and finally suffer a slow attrition of their glories." My mind settles, for just a moment, on Celeste's words. The thought crosses my mind, that her observation was a bit overdone. She has a way of turning common reflections into poetry. Sometimes it charms me, but not always.

For a moment, I visualize a more bustling Bourne River during that time when its residents flocked to this little square, socializing and relaxing during the lingering sunsets of summer, then nod in agreement. I try to visualize the Orcas' joyous streams spouting skyward, in contrast to the anemic dribbles which now spill from their mouths, leaving streaks of slimy algae on their shaded undersides. Pollywogs frolic below in the stagnant water, unaware of their imminent changes and what they will become tomorrow. For a moment I find myself considering how those creatures, in their metamorphic suspense of adulthood, have much in common with me. I am acutely aware that, though an adult, I am still in the process of my own maturation.

As we stand there, taking it all in, Celeste says she'd like to sit for a while, so we settle into the bench that has the best view of the sunset. The thought of Celeste leaving me in Stella's Cove and continuing on to Eagle City is almost frightening. I am already feeling stress over my one-month layover and those long weeks as Mother's guest. Except for incarceration in a provincial jail, I cannot imagine a longer month than the one I am about to live, for I have a glum premonition that Mother will plague me with her religious harangues, a grating echo of my childhood years.

Celeste has noticed the look of dismay on my face. "Sweetheart," she offers, "you should make the best of your stay in Stella's Cove. It's only one month." Her soothing voice temporarily buoys my spirit, and she concludes, with enough resignation for the two of us, "You just need to find a way to enjoy this time with your mother."

I am overwhelmed by a conflicting mix of emotions. I love Mother; of course I do. I'm forced to momentarily consider that I am some sort of ingrate, and that I should have more appreciation for the woman who bore and raised me. I try to consciously purge the negative thoughts, but I'm still left with a feeling of discomfort and the awkward anticipation of what I will do during my visit. Except for the sporadic moments of familial, childhood joy, her interactions with me have been largely dominated by her preoccupation with saving my soul, and there is still a constant din inside my mind, reminding me of the chidings and exhortations which were so regularly inflicted.

Now I'm imagining what each day will be like in that sullen derelict of a town, and I consider how much of it will be in lonely quiet, particularly each evening, after Mother has her typical, ration of whisky. I've not been able to have many meaningful conversations with her since Father died, and I understand that some of it was my fault--because I was not able to appreciate just how deeply she mourned--believing that her loss was much different than my own. For, while I was cast about like a rudderless ship, failing to have any sense of my final destination, her life merely continued. Today I understand--that a mother cannot simply stop in her tracks, no matter how great the tragedy. Her tasks had not been deferrable, nor had there been recesses or summer vacations to provide her with moments of respite.

But there was that episode, a horrifying break in which Mother tried to escape the loneliness of her loss, seeking the company and companionship she missed so much. While maturity has altered my view of that moment, the long-festering memory of Mr. Merriman has troubled me ever since the day I'd interrupted them with my unexpected return from my chores at the Murphy home.

During the month at Mother's, I will be counting the hours until the Aniak makes its next run up the coast and when Celeste and I can be together again. Returning to our stateroom, we settle into our final night, the tiny ripples of the sea gently nibbling at the Aniak's mahogany hull.

It's another calm morning. The Aniak returns to the sea at daybreak, and, only a short time later, Celeste points toward a distant specter in the mist. "There it is," she says, "It's Point Fay." A large lighthouse pokes its weather-vaned roof into the sky, seeming, for just a moment, to skewer the mountains which rise above a flat, thin layer of cloud. It stands there like a huge exclamation point on the long spit of land that reaches into the sea, and announces that the Stella's Cove harbor is only two miles ahead.

I can't help but thinking, that Celeste must be somewhat upset by the sight, for, on the point, a few hundred feet from the lighthouse, there is a large home, standing all by itself. It is the home where Celeste lived throughout her childhood and that the Murphy family abandoned only seven years ago. She glances up at me, then looks back down toward the deck. "Daddy never told us we were leaving until the night before. I never anticipated it." I place my arm around her back, press her head toward me gently, and kiss her through her auburn locks. "We'll make this day a good one," I remind her, "Let's try to remember the happier times we had in this place." When I consider what I just said, I am momentarily stumped by the naiveté of my own advice. There's no question; both of us have good memories of home, but they are almost inaccessible, virtually eclipsed by the understanding that some of the people we loved the most are no longer alive.

As the Aniak rounds Point Fay, we are both filled with awe at the bright sapphire behemoth that towers over the town. The Gavins Glacier stands in silence, arrested in its travel by the narrow canyon below, looking much like a sparkling sapphire clenched in a buxom queen's cleavage. Though it is only the blue face that announces its prominent presence, its white body extends for miles beyond, merging into the large mountains which separate Stella's Cove from its nearest neighbors to the East. Celeste does a few oohs and ahs at the beauty before her. She and her family left more than a year before I did.

"I'd almost forgotten just how beautiful this place is." she reflects, then pauses for a moment, a look of sadness immediately replacing her awe. "I wish," she laments, "there was some way for me to look at it without all the bad memories."

———

During the eighteen years of life I spent in Stella's Cove before college called me away, I'd never seen this particular view of the glacier. With the superior height of the Aniak's deck, I'm able to see far more of the grand setting that frames the town— much more imposing than the views from those barely-offshore dories on those occasions when my father took me fishing.

I find myself confronted with a clear perspective of time, movement, and nature's purposes. I'm not sure I've ever even thought about it before: I am considering what the glacier has meant to my town. There's a sudden realization; the glacier has performed its duties well. It guards the town; it's the source of Stella's Cove's plentiful fresh water; it is a picture that hundreds have sought to see during the more than fifty years since the area became inhabited; it insulates the town from the outside world, effectively blocking the gentle canyon which might have allowed a road from the B.C. interior; and it has done its share of undertaking over the years, interring scores of those who dared to challenge its formidable power, and failed to heed the hazards.

"I'm glad we're here," Celeste whispers. "It will be good for you to see your mother and good for her and me to get acquainted." Though our wedding is planned for only one year from now, Celeste has never met my mother before. The couple hours she'll spend with us in the Cove today, are important, and I'm hoping Mother will be civil. I am comforted in knowing that Celeste will remain only a couple of hours--just long enough to get acquainted with Mother before the Aniak departs for its continuing run up the coast.

————

Captain Hans Nordstok, standing in the wheelhouse with his pressed uniform and snappy cap, calls for hands on the starboard side, and three sailors in their horizontal-striped shirts make their way toward the coiled ropes and the cleats that will hold the steamboat firmly to the dock. The Captain has made this same approach into Stella's Cove hundreds of times, but he is still cautious of the tightness of the channel, and the shallow bar that can ground a ship until the next high tide.

I have an uncomfortable feeling inside me, recounting the events which so thoroughly dashed my community's dreams, and I find myself contemplating, especially at this time when commerce has died and the financially-broke are all who remain, that there is no real purpose for the presence of the few folk who stand on the dock as we approach. I conclude that it must be the mere force of habit--a perfunctory mandate that silently bids the curious to be there.

I notice Captain Nordstok reaching for the tall, well-polished brass lever in front of him. He grasps its whale-bone grip, and pulls it toward him. There is a noticeable reduction in thrust, and the steam engine settles to an idling lope. The Aniak glides for a few hundred feet across the mirror-perfect surface of the water, noses sharply toward the dock, and then takes a hard left, finally reversing its engine as the rudder goes all the way to the right stop, and progressing sideways until there's a light touch against the evenly-hung frayed-rope fenders.

There are several people standing on the dock, none of whom are stevedores or hired help. Instead they are the typical menagerie that appears every time the coastal freighter makes its scheduled stop. Back when trapping created wealth in Stella's Cove, there were dozens of workers waiting for the boat to arrive, and, when the discovery of gold brought an explosion of growth, it was obvious, from the number of people at the dock, just how much the instant prosperity had changed the town.

When George Goodwin Murphy found that the area, only three miles north of town, possessed the possibility for a deep-water port and hydroelectric power, it had become the town's third bonanza. The furs and gold had created the town's first two booms; they were easy pickings. But it was only Murphy's vision, creativity, and dogged tenacity that resurrected the town from the second financial disaster.

Murphy, introduced the town to its third age of prosperity, creating an influx of people that, at times, looked like the hordes on a pilgrimage to Mecca. Everyone who wanted to work was employed; the town's taste for inexpensive whisky evolved into a preference for Scottish single malts; textile finery dotted the pews of the Church each Sunday; Stella's Cove women learned to love good perfumes, and found that lye soap was not the same as the shampoos which were pouring in from New York; and, when the plate was passed at the Methodist Church, there was competition between the townsfolk to conspicuously exceed the donations of the others.

But there was also a flip-side to the new surge of prosperity and the growing importance of material possessions. The townsfolk's' religious piety had also burgeoned, and there was a general understanding among the residents of Stella's Cove that God was finally blessing them for their goodness.

Since the arrival of mail and goods has been both the marking of time and the provision of necessities, there has always been an accepted ritual of meeting the Aniak when it docks, and virtually anyone who didn't have an immediate, non-deferrable task took the time to be there.

But it is not the same now. There is no Mayor to greet the ship, no key to the city being ceremoniously awarded to some questionably important dignitary, and there are no books for the defrocked Rev. Harry Mills, who offered good money for any quality reading materials the Aniak crew could round-up during its stops at the various ports along its established route. With its more-or-less predictable schedule, the Aniak had been serving the small towns along the coast for many years, in places that lacked roads to the interior and could be reached only by the sea. From Kokeemah Bay to Pierre's Cove and all the way down to Vancouver, the steamship was a lifeline for the isolated villages along British Columbia's Pacific coast and the tiny settlements that dot the cold expanses of the Alaskan Gulf.

During the best of times, residents excitedly met the steamboat, anticipating the delivery of new treasures and lifetime dreams that shipped from the catalogue store--the newest creations of industry and science, parading from the Aniak to the Stella's Cove dock. For one, it was a new washing machine; for another, gold-set diamond earrings that came all the way from Tiffany's in New York. There were French perfumes and exotic soaps, and there was an endless supply of fine wines and liqueurs. Though, during that time of plenty, most of those items were already common in larger communities, they were, nevertheless, the realization of formerly unattainable dreams for the people of Stella's Cove.

While the town's first trappers became rich from the plentiful supply of fox and mink, the general lack of sophistication, in both the trappers and their families, had little effect on their lifestyles. Like the handful of Indians in the area, their choice of materials for clothing came from the animals they trapped and hunted. The lye soap, tallow candles, and patchwork quilts were good enough for them. Dominated by matters of simple need, the trappers' wives, somehow, largely avoided the new luxuries they could have easily afforded. Consequently, except for a few who were inclined to ostentation, the buying habits of the townsfolk changed little during that first boom. But the second boom transformed the community.

It was the discovery of gold in Muir Creek that made one of its residents the richest man in British Columbia, and it was that boom which created an immediate taste for luxury.

Willis Fox, discovered gold in Muir Creek, and he proved himself to be one of the town's finest citizens. Though wealth is often a big contributor to the downfall of men, Fox would be remembered as a man who loved mankind and judged no one. By all accounts, wealth never infected his heart, and that was to his ultimate credit.

The "Reverend" Fox created a meaningful unity in the town, and though he was an accidental imposter in the local Methodist Ministry, his sermons promoted something which was later lost when a real man of the cloth replaced him. That "something" was humanity--the most basic conscience and regard for others that all mankind should possess. Willis Fox knew that no man can be in a position to judge others, and his broad acceptance of his imperfect fellow men reflected his understanding that he too had faults. It was his goodness that gave him a wreath in the history of our town. I realize that few of those who knew him are still alive, and, I lament that, despite his legendary kindness toward others, his example of compassion and understanding didn't outlive him in Stella's Cove.

Within only a few months of Fox's discovery of gold, the population explosion had created a real town, and, at the peak of its growth, Stella's Cove soared from a handful to over two-thousand people.

Except for the original Muir and Gavins log cabins, the Methodist Church outdated everything and was the unmistakable man-made landmark of the town. With a chapel designed to hold over five-hundred and a steeple that towered seventy-four feet above the sea, it was the center of both religious and social activities for over fifty years. It was "Reverend" Fox who, at an exorbitant cost, remodeled and expanded the original, little church that was built during the trapping boom, transforming it into the grandest Methodist Church in all of B.C. Since then, Fox's generous endowment of a perpetual maintenance fund has kept it in the best of care.

No one was really sure who, exactly, the Rev. Willis Fox had been, but there was no question: Both, his stellar memory and his money would speak many years after his voice was silenced by cancer, and his contribution to the town would always be there.

When Will They Ever Learn?

It's June 3, 1918, and I turned twenty-four just one month ago. The war in Europe, which has taken my best friend's life, still rages. Casualties and deaths have reached staggering numbers. There is talk that it will soon be over, but that talk seems to contradict the growing weekly tolls. Every headline betrays the reality that things will likely be getting worse before they get better. The world has found a new curse word, and the Germans will be hated for years to come.

I just received my Master's Degree in Psychology from Arnold University, and, only a week ago, I proudly walked in my cap, gown, and red hood, to the commencement podium. The competition at Arnold had been intense, but when I felt myself flagging under the heavy scholastic load, I always thought of Miss Kimberly Hardwicke and the short tenures of both her teaching career in Stella's Cove and her life. For it was she who changed me from a dunce to a scholar, providing the needed faith and confidence I had gone without for so long. Though she was gone forever, I wanted to remember her as the catalyst for my own achievement. And the truth was, there was a part of her in every paper I wrote, every assignment I completed, and every effort that lifted me from mediocrity to excellence.

My Master's thesis addressed a fascinating but disturbing phenomenon of society--when the consciences of individuals are forfeited to the rising emotions of an angry group. I entitled it "Carnivorous Sheep: An Analysis of Mob Psychology," and it was published by the Arnold University Press. Along with the honor of publication, there was a small cash award and the promise that, if it went into a second edition, royalties would follow. The initial run of 1,000 books was quickly absorbed by other universities as an informal textbook on the subject of mob psychology, and I am anticipating that "Carnivorous Sheep" will be moderately profitable.

Though graduating only second in my class on my Bachelor Degree, I was number-one on my graduate studies. Chosen to deliver the valedictory address, I pondered the importance of the honor and spent hours considering what wise words I could provide to my classmates. After many hours of soul-searching contemplation, I understood that there was one inspiration in my life which prevailed over all others, so I included Miss Kimberly Hardwicke in my valedictory message:

"We all have our heroes and it is of the utmost importance to remember those we admire and wish to emulate. I was the classic low-achiever only a few years ago, when an educator resurrected me from my own ashes and helped me to become a Phoenix. A new school teacher made the difference," I noted, "and it is to Miss Kimberly Hardwicke that I dedicate my words today. Find heroes in your own lives, as you embark into your careers, and use their inspiration in creating your own success."

I sent applications to a number of employers, and the response was exceptional. Accompanied by my transcripts and the glowing recommendations of George Murphy, the Dean, and others, employers were enthusiastic. With a choice of five different jobs, from Vancouver to Yellow Knife, I decided to bring my success back to the same general area where my life began. Of course, there are no jobs in Stella's Cove, and, even if there were, the town would be a constant reminder of its darkest hours.

Maybe, if George Murphy had not left the population in such a hopeless economic ruin, I might have considered my hometown despite its past. When I think about it, I have mixed emotions on the coup de grace George so suddenly lowered on the town, and I sometimes think there might have been a better way for him to show his disgust for the united bad behavior of its residents, without total economic destruction.

But, when I reflected on George's decisive and brutal reaction to the rude treatment and carnival-like spectacle of the bodies of Miss Hardwicke and Rev. Harry Mills, I could understand his wrath completely, and I certainly shared in his loathing for those responsible.

I'm really happy about the opportunity in Eagle City, for, though a much larger town than Stella's Cove, it still very much resembles the same scenery that I love. To me it's a matter of tossing out the bad while saving the parts that I savor. I'll be working for the Provincial Social Services, and though the pay is going to be mediocre, it is a position of relative prestige. I've been named the new Area Director, and I'll have five other professionals working under my supervision.

During the last few months of our jobs search, it became a growing concern that Celeste and I might become separated by the inconvenient geography. For, graduation would mean moving on, and we both understood the futility of being divided by a gulf of time and distance. Despite the worry and what-ifs, luck has been favorable. Celeste and I were elated when she was able to find a teaching position in Eagle City. We're both looking forward to having a home and family together.

My five years at the University were an awakening, for so much had gone on during that time, including the dark tragedy that is still taking so many lives in Europe. Over 46,000 Canadians have been killed in action, and that is only a miniscule percentage of the total loss of life. I feared, during the campaigns of 1917 and 1918, that I would end up like Burdett Scott, a fellow Canadian who was my roommate for my first three years at Arnold. Without George Murphy's wise advice on filing an educational deferment request, I could have easily found myself with the same conscription letter that both changed and ended Burdett's life.

———

Reviewing our amicable relationship, I cannot say there's anything that could have made Burdett more perfect. He had a fun sense of humor and almost always found a unique and clever way of saying things that left his friends in hysterics. But, despite his funny-bone, most of Burdett was serious, and his obvious diligence in his studies showed that his greatest commitment was to the realization of his well-defined goals. He was clever enough to be a comedian, but it was his chosen isolation from the distraction of social detours that kept him mostly quiet.

When Burdett wasn't in class or doing his labs, he was always sitting at his little desk, preparing for tests or writing a paper that wasn't due until the following week. While others procrastinated, he kept himself well ahead of deadlines. His light was typically on until after midnight, and I could not understand how he held to his merciless schedule. His life was one of work, and he never took time for parties or the night life that seemed, at least to me, to be an essential ingredient in the life of a university student.

Burdett stood six feet tall, and had curly brown hair that rested on his protruding ears and looked very much like one of those typical Russian fur hats. He had unusually bushy eyebrows, and his narrow face was accentuated by a strong chin. Burdett was a neat dresser, and though he did not come from money, he took obvious pride in cleanliness and presenting himself well.

While not a stunningly handsome man, Burdett had a smile that was always there, and, though not intentionally, he attracted his share of attention from the girls at school. Occasionally he talked with them and I even saw him flirting a time or two, but everyone easily saw that he was a man with a mission, and that he consciously steered away from anything that would be a distraction from his goals. Burdett's smile was not one that sought the notice of others. His wide lips, with their perpetual curl, suggested more a sense of general pleasure in life, and it was a certainty: He was a very happy young man, for he realized that he could just as easily have ended up being a day worker, sweating over equipment at the lumber mill in the town where he grew up.

Burdett's home circumstances were anything but ideal. His father was unable to work because of the ravages of multiple sclerosis, and his mother tried hard to fill the financial void that was so pressing in their lives. When other boys received toys for Christmas, Burdett understood that his two new pairs of socks would keep his feet warm over the next year. Most of his clothes were purchased from second hand stores, but he learned at an early age how valuable a good pressing could be to the appearance of a shirt or pair of pants. His mother attended to ironing tasks, as her busy schedule allowed, but Burdett always took it upon himself to create sharp creases in his clothes. It may have been a bit obsessive, but his attention to ironing, even after his mother did what she considered to be an adequate job, helped to give him a sense of pride among his peers. He never left home with a rumpled collar; his sleeves always had a perfect crease; and no one could have ever known that his wool trousers did not come from the finest store.

Neither of Burdett's parents, Ryan and Bertie Scott, had been educated past the ninth grade, so their own options were greatly limited. His father's sickness ensured that the family's circumstances were not likely to improve. While still at home, Burdett was constantly confronted with the success and wealth of others, and he dedicated his life, largely, to the task of rising above his family's meager circumstances.

When Burdett graduated at the top of his high school class, he was troubled by, what he believed to be, the dead end he'd dreaded and so abruptly reached. His struggling family could be of no financial help. There were children still at home, and his mother's work at a garment factory was inadequate to meet the family's growing financial needs.

Unless Burdett worked for several years, carefully saving what he earned, there would be no college for him, and he would never get a veterinary degree. But the prospect of an interim job for the purpose of funding his education, created a perplexing risk. He had seen others with big ambitions settle for jobs far beneath their capabilities, and he realized that whatever work he chose, in order to save for his future education, might well be a trap from which he could never emerge. He knew that, despite lofty ambitions, people were often forced to accept an end that was far short of their goals. Getting stuck somewhere, in a marginal job with no real future became Burdett's greatest fear.

Appreciating his work ethic and proven intelligence, a small accounting firm offered Burdett an apprenticeship in bookkeeping, and he worked for a few months after graduation from public school, learning, in a few weeks, the accounting methods that would have taken others years to master. But Burdett felt nothing encouraging in the accounting office, and he could see a life of frustration and mediocrity looming before him. In an amazing stroke of generosity and luck, Burdett's frustration suddenly changed.

When his Uncle James, from Edmonton, came to visit, understanding that it was just a matter of time before Burdett's father would succumb to his lingering illness, James took a special interest in Burdett's future. Feeling appalled by the prospect of wasted talent, and learning that Burdett hated his job, he inquired, "Burdett, what would you do if you could choose any career?" There was no moment of demanding thought, no question in Burdett's mind. He understood that Uncle James's question was only about dreams, and he also knew that his family's penurious existence could not get him what he wanted. Burdett answered anyway.

"I would be a veterinarian." Burdett said it with both futility and conviction. He loved animals, and both family and friends recognized his unusual talent with dogs and horses. Looking at Burdett with kind eyes, James silently reviewed his own life, noting how luck is either a blessing or a curse. For he fully appreciated that his own successful career in banking would have been impossible, were it not for his own family's successful lumber and paper business and some fortuitous serendipity along the way. Though Uncle James's father had always assumed his oldest son would be the general manager of the Scott Forest Industries sawmill, James made it clear that his father's blueprint was not his personal ambition.

For a minute or so, Uncle James seemed disconnected, with his eyes staring blankly at the old clock on the wall, and Burdett understood that James was roaming, temporarily, in another place and time.

It was easy to detect when Uncle James's journey in time was over, for he now wore a gentle smile and his kindness radiated like the iron stove on a chilly day. "Burdett," Uncle James spoke "I know that you could do it on your own, but I hate to see you stuck with the drudgery of spending years trying to save enough for school, while losing these youthful years on a late-starting career." Uncle James continued. "I will pay all your expenses to go to college and veterinary school, and…"

And, as an afterthought, Uncle James added. "All I ask in return is that you use your success to help others achieve their dreams." Burdett had never seen his Uncle emotional, but, when Uncle James finished presenting his offer, his eyes watered, and he turned momentarily away. In an unusual show of emotion, tears welled in Burdett's eyes too, and he hugged his uncle in a way he'd never hugged before.

Burdett told me that story when we first became roommates, and, when he'd finished the account of his uncle's generosity, my eyes were wet too.

I'd returned one afternoon during our third year at Arnold

to find Burdette sitting on his cot. When he looked up at me, I could see an unmistakable look of bewilderment, so I knew something was terribly wrong. "Here," spoke Burdett "you can read it yourself." And he handed me a letter, which was written in an unmistakably feminine hand. I didn't even get to the end of the first sentence before I noticed I was choking up.

"Dear Burdett, It is difficult for me to tell you this, because I know your love for your Uncle James. The doctors have diagnosed a tumor on his brain, and they are not giving him very much time. Please just attend to your studies, and pray with all the faith you have that the doctors are wrong. Love, Aunt Beatrice."

Burdett was visibly shaken by the letter, and, though he did not take much stock in religion and superstition, I saw him, every subsequent night, closing his eyes, for a minute or so, his head bowed and his lips pursed in deep concentration. He admitted to me, "I don't know that it can help, but I am concentrating on Uncle James's recovery."

It was only five weeks later that a telegram arrived from Edmonton. "Dear Burdett, Your uncle passed away this morning. One of his last requests was that you continue your education and make him proud. He has provided for the continuation of your studies, and there will be more than enough to finish your Veterinary Degree."

Burdett was inconsolable, and, for the first time, he failed to attend his daily classes. Making hasty arrangements to sell his favorite possession--an old violin that he'd played in public school--he left two days later, by rail, to attend his Uncle's funeral.

School continued to go well for Burdett, and except for breaking his stride at that one tragic moment, he remained one of Arnold University's best students. His life returned--despite the loss of Uncle James--to reflect Burdett's personal excellence. Everything was going stunningly well, until September of the following school year.

I remember that afternoon, when I returned from my classes and four hours of library research, only to find Burdett sitting at the little desk on his side of our dormitory room. He turned to me, and I immediately noticed his eyes were red, and there were little white streaks below each eye, the salty residue of sadness. I assumed that there was news of another death in the family, and that it was probably his father's, and I hurt to think that his life was being marred by yet another tragedy. "Burdett," I asked sympathetically, "Is it your father?"

Burdett turned toward me, his head shaking back and forth. "No, he answered, it's not that." and for just a moment I found my own burden lifted in profound relief. Holding up an official looking paper, Burdett's face had the unmistakable look of pain. "I'm officially a conscript," he murmured, "and I'm not going to be able to finish school. I received this notice that I am to report to Valcartier Military Base in Quebec, and I am ordered to be there by the tenth of October. The Government sent me a bank cheque for my travel."

I glanced at the calendar, and the fifteenth was only three weeks away. Trying to use the most compassionate words, and understanding that, at least for now, his educational progress was sidetracked by an unfortunate turn of events, I comforted him as I could, and, when his mood brightened up a bit, I suggested that we go out for a drink that evening. Burdett agreed. Under typical school circumstances, Burdett would not have said yes, but he was understanding that his immediate goal was indefinitely and involuntarily deferred, and that it made no sense to languish in a maudlin state.

It was at that moment, that I understood, for the first time, just how insulated I remained from the tragedies of my world. I vaguely knew that misery was everywhere, but I also appreciated that it was never right here. Well, now it was. Though the World War had seemed so far away, suddenly the Huns were breathing down my neck, and I became acutely aware of their threat to the free world. For the first time I was thinking about all the young men, who, less privileged than I--and still struggling with their pimples and puppy love--became fodder for enemy gunfire. British Canadians rallied for their mother country--which was the nightly target of German bombs--understanding that England was in one of its darkest hours, and over 100,000 Maple Leaf troops were mobilized to stop the Germans.

By 1917 over forty thousand Canadians had lost their lives on the other side of the world, and though British Canadians heartily supported the war--at least initially--the Government failed in attracting a steady supply of willing volunteers. The implementation of a draft was dreaded by all--especially Prime Minister Robert Borden. In fact, Borden promised, publicly, that the government would not use conscription to bolster the military forces, but that promise soon became shaky and the need for a draft became a categorical imperative. Borden lost sleep for several days before making the announcement. Tensions with French Canadians had been growing for years, partly fueled by Ottawa's decision to force the use of English in all public schools, and the decision to pass the draft law was the last straw in what many of them viewed as an endless string of unfair and prejudicial affronts.

On May 18, 1917, Borden stood on the plaza in front of the Ottawa Parliamentary Building, faced the rubber-band-suspended microphones, and created echoes that would be remembered in the history books. "My fellow Canadians," he soberly spoke, "As you all know, the War in Europe is raging, and the death toll of Canadians and their allies now totals in the millions. I have been reluctant to make a decisive move, and it has been my promise in the past to avoid the matter of military conscription. And yet, we cannot do our share as Canadians, if we refuse our friends the help they need in defending their freedom. It is with the solemn understanding that our effort is necessary to bring this terrible war to an end, that I have, this morning, signed the Military Service Act."

That act became law the following month, and there were two days of rioting in Montreal. The tramway tracks were ripped from their ties. Store windows were broken, and soldiers attacked. Quebec City also saw violence, and, in the end several civilians lay dead. Despite the deaths of over 1,300,000 European French, the French Canadians never rallied to the cause of their distant brothers. A major clash occurred when soldiers arrested a French Canadian for failing to register for the draft, and, in the end, only a few French Canadians actually fought for their country in the First World War.

The new policy made the government unpopular, but it was the French Canadians who flatly balked and disobeyed the edict of conscription, reasoning that, though other Canadians had a duty to help the Crown, it was not their war, and so, they wanted no part of it. The reality was that France's losses were some of the greatest in Europe, and French Canadians should have answered the call. The political skirmish that followed came close to a civil war in Canada, and the visible and hateful schism, which had always been there, intensified and raged between the two sectors of our Country.

During the three years of war, which had already caused the greatest human losses in history, I never knew anyone in the military. The small crop of young adult males in Stella's Cove, numbered only five at the time of my graduation from public school, and I couldn't help thinking that the loss of Canadian lives, alone, was already many times the size of Mother's whole community—almost twenty times, I counted, greater than Stella's Cove's peak population during its most prosperous time. The thought of Burdett's involuntary departure was shocking to me, and I wished that, by some small change of fate, he could remain my roommate until I completed my studies at Arnold. He wasn't just a roommate, for he had become my most trusted friend.

After having a light dinner in the cafeteria, Burdett and I headed to Duffy's, which was a favorite night spot for Arnold students. We sat down and ordered drinks, chatting on pointless nothings while sizing up the action. The whisky had not even arrived at the table, when a dazzling, red-headed coed walked up to our table. (I actually worried, for just a moment, that Burdett would suspect I'd put her up to it. The timing was so unexpectedly impeccable.) It was actually a bit demoralizing to me that she didn't even turn her eyes my direction, but immediately struck up a conversation with Burdett.

I thought to myself how fortunate it was for him to be temporarily lifted from his pain. "Hi," she said in an almost seductive tone, "Haven't I seen you in the Physiology Lab? I'm Amy LeGrande." I couldn't help but notice that her hem was a bit high, and that her legs were both shapely and slim. She had an impish smile, a bit too much makeup, and her green eyes looked like those an illustrator had painted for a magazine cover. Her complexion was blemish-free—perfect, and the second button of her blouse was unsecured, revealing a plunging line that disappeared below.

I rose from my chair and offered it to her. "Please have a seat." and she obliged me with a polite "Thank you." Burdett got up, grabbed a chair from the other side of the bar, and dragged it to our table--asking Miss LeGrande if she'd like to join us for a drink. She nodded with a sincere look of pleasure on her face, "I would love to." and Burdett hailed the barmaid, who almost immediately stood at our table.

"What will you have?" asked the barmaid, and Burdett and I indicated that we'd already ordered. Amy sat for a moment, looking as if she was considering the choice with great gravity. "I'll have a whisky," she spoke, "and I'd like it straight up." Burdett looked at me in shock, and I swallowed--probably too conspicuously--when I heard Amy's selection.

Girls did not drink whisky. It was considered a man's drink and was generally too harsh a taste for the fairer sex. But there were certainly exceptions to that silent rule--like old Mrs. Crump, my mother's neighbor, and though my mother still didn't know that I knew, Mother also drank whisky to dull the sadness of my father's death. Rev. Cromwell wrote me a short note during my second year at Arnold. "Billy," it read. "I realize that you have embarked on your own separate life, but I feel it is my responsibility to let you know that your mother has taken to drinking during your sojourn away at school. I believe the problem is getting to such a level of severity that a doctor of appropriate qualifications should be engaged to assess her condition. Please do whatever is within your power to help free her from this addiction, Sincerely, Rev. Cromwell."

The letter didn't surprise me, for I had anticipated that, in my absence, the drinking was going to get worse. Notwithstanding Rev. Cromwell's concerns, I was far too familiar with Mother's stubborn responses to my suggestions in the past, and I found it unlikely that she would heed anything I said. I think it broke Mother's heart to see me leave, for there was a tearful goodbye as I headed south five years ago.

It was Mr. Forsythe, one of Father's old friends, who told me in the kindest way, "I think your mother is having a problem with alcohol. Maybe you can help her to taper off a bit." He'd said it just a few days before I boarded the Aniak for Vancouver, and the trip to Arnold University, but I didn't believe I could have any influence on her decisions, for she looked at my departure--I believed--not as my advancement into the world, but as a dereliction of my duties as a son. At least, that was my perception, and her laments, as I left, betrayed her resentment of my decision to go. I had discovered the bottle, carefully stowed behind the tin of flour in our kitchen cupboard, and knew that it was not something left over from my dad. Yet, in a way, the whisky she drank was very much about Dad and me.

In a few minutes, the waitress reappeared with the straight-up whisky for Amy, and she and Burdett seemed to hit it off immediately. I had a guilty suspicion that Burdett's present mood was making him more vulnerable toward her advances, for it occurred to me that Amy herself was likely off balance from some failed relationship, and that romance was a veiled threat that neither of them should be facing. I sat there with my drink, observing their faces, and, though I was missing most of their words, I was aware that a nice rhythm of conversation was bouncing across our table. . There was a part of me that wanted to take Burdett aside for a word of friendly caution, and I actually formed the short warning in my mind. "Burdett," I would offer, "she's awfully forward." But the smile on his face dissuaded me. My suggestion of going out for the evening had been a winner.

At Duffy's there was a pathetic ensemble playing Celtic music that night. The fiddler was the worst part of it. His scratchy tones were almost unrecognizable, and his defective bowing was catching strings that were obviously not intended. There were even moments when his fiddling seemed to hit an invisible wall-- ones in which the sound simply ceased, and, after sufficient observation, I determined that those abrupt voids were being caused by his long, scraggly beard getting caught in the strings. But the worst part of it was his apparent tone-deafness, for the notes he played were a half-tone apart from the guitar, which seemed to be relatively in tune, and the guitarist, a neatly groomed frat boy who looked totally out of place in the group, was making grotesque faces in response to each sour note. It was clear to me that the lady playing the hammered dulcimer was also stone-deaf, and it sounded like she too was playing in a totally different key. I couldn't help but notice that others in the bar were showing a painful disapproval of the performance, for there were regular cringes and vigorous contortions of their faces, and a few rudely put their fingers in their ears when the worst dissonance prevailed. It was bad--really awful--but it didn't dampen Burdett's obvious fascination with little Miss LeGrande.

For almost two hours I sat there by myself watching the pair dance, ordering several more drinks in my now despondent condition, and occasionally noting how Burdett's new and casual acquaintance was turning into a much more compelling interest.

Burdett was feeling no pain, and the specter of facing Army service seemed entirely obliterated by the whisky and the provocative pressure of Amy's body next to his. During the slow dances, Amy moved her left hand from his shoulder to his neck, and there was a sense of familiarity that seemed to be much older than the sudden introduction that had occurred only two hours earlier. By nine-thirty, Amy had her cheek next to Burdett's, and at about 9:45, I noticed that their lips touched for a moment.

I was bored. No one paid me any attention--except for the barmaid who was cultivating me for a healthy tip. Each time she leaned over the table to straighten things up and refresh my drink, she lightly brushed her body against my shoulder in a way that, at first, conveyed no obvious intent. It was only the repetition of the familiarity that made it so obvious to me. Once or twice could have been totally innocent, but there was no question that her behavior was meant to tease. She did it over and over, and I found it harder, with each successive drink, to restrain myself from a glance at the second button of her blouse.

I actually took the time to scan the bar for girls that might interest me, but the few who were obviously not tied to a particular guy, were overlooked for the same reasons as mine. Too frumpy; too heavy; too much makeup; a vacuous look or an over-done and obnoxious giggle. I found no amusement during those hours, except for the barmaid's flirting, and I was now finding the evening interminable. I kept wondering to myself, "Can I find some way to leave without having Burdett feel that I have abandoned him, even temporarily, at such a difficult moment in his life?"

I consciously accepted my own boredom with the understanding that we had come there, that night, for Burdett--not for me--and, specifically, to improve Burdett's mood. It was certainly working, and I was happy Burdett was having such a great time. Yet I still found myself mulling over my possible exit strategy, understanding that I would have to assign blame to something beyond my control, carefully choosing words that would convey   a) how tired I was b) how my headache was intensifying c) how I had a 7:30 class the next morning d) how I'd suddenly remembered I had a paper due. As it turned out, I was not forced to make any decision on the duration of my stay at Duffy's. Burdett came back to the table for just a moment, around 10:00, apologizing for leaving me by myself, and announcing, "I guess we're leaving, old pal, and I probably won't see you again tonight."

Whatever happened that evening, Burdett didn't share it with me. As that night connected with the following day, I did not see him, and almost a week passed before he came back to the dorm. I suspected that he had already withdrawn from his classes to accommodate his upcoming departure, which was the appropriate course of action under the circumstances.

Burdett returned six days later, looking happy and relaxed, declaring, "I have a little announcement. Amy and I are getting married before I leave for the Army. We're in love," Burdett added, "and we'd like you to be our best man." Less than one week later, Amy and Burdett were married at the Courthouse, where a magistrate sealed their love with an official stamp as I looked on.

Burdett's mother, though irritated and uncomfortable with her son's hasty decision, sold the silverware her grandparents had left to her, and paid for the couple's weekend at the Chateau Benoit, a posh resort which was out of reach to most ordinary folks. Burdett remarked to me, with a tone of genuine guilt, about the obvious excess his mother had provided to the couple, and told me he felt sad that the money hadn't been used to help his struggling siblings.

After the wedding, I saw Burdett only one more time, when he appeared at the dorm, collected his belongings, sold his textbooks at the Arnold Book Exchange, and left for military service.

Burdett was never replaced as a roommate, because dormitory assignments were made for the entire school year. Each time I studied at my little desk, I could not help but thinking of the one across the room that sat empty. Though his presence there was dominated by an endless commitment to school, I found myself acutely aware that his smile and gentle laugh were gone.

I heard nothing from Burdett for the next three months,

but a brief note, sent from Valcartier Army Base, Quebec, told me that he was doing well. It was no surprise that he was the star of his basic training unit, and that his superiors pondered how his exceptional intelligence could be most effectively employed. After spending six weeks at a special military Veterinary Technician School, he was working with horses and loving what he did. For him, the disappointment of having been called away from his education was offset by the interest he took in his new job, and he understood that his work could provide valuable experience for his temporarily sidetracked veterinary career.

Burdett's note included the news that he was advanced to the rank of sergeant--something unheard of for a newly graduated trainee--but he also admitted that his pride in service was marred by his immediate reassignment to the Canadian Forces overseas. Burdett would be attached to the Canadian Cavalry Brigade at a place known as the Hindenburg Line, a defensive, fallback position for the German troops, who had been routed at Somme. An elite group, the Canadian Cavalry Brigade would become one of the most decorated units in the War.

While his veterinary responsibilities appeared, at first, to be providential, it would actually be Burdett's love of animals that continually haunted him at the front. Veterinary Technicians attended to wounded animals, and there were only a few equine casualties that could be saved. Unlike people and even dogs, horses were surprisingly fragile, and their size and weight made it virtually impossible to immobilize them for the purpose of recovery--particularly recovery from leg injuries or major surgery. When assigned to the CCB, each Technician was provided with the essential veterinary supplies: a pack of compresses and dressings, an assortment of liniments and ointments, a twitch for use in controlling a hurt animal, and a 1911 Colt .45 caliber pistol.

Unlike the few stubborn and unruly ponies Burdett rode in Bourne River, the cavalry horses were all trained to perfection. They had one purpose--just one purpose, and that was to carry and protect their riders at the peril of their own lives. The horses were taught to return when their riders were thrown, since the horse, in such a situation, would be the wounded soldier's only transportation to safety. They were taught to respond to their soldier's particular call--to decipher the voices of their riders, even when the din of artillery drowned all other sound. And they were taught to lie down, on command, as shields against the machine gun fire that was now dominating the war. Burdett suffered every day from the pain he both witnessed and terminated, and found himself waking in cold sweats from the nightmares which continued through the daylight hours, to the echoing cries of the animals he was unable to save.

After putting down a large bay gelding, whose front legs were severed at the fetlocks by German fire, Burdett vomited his C-Rations and cried. The gelding tried twice to rise, and howled in pain as his remaining stubs bore the weight. Almost worse, Burdett noted the deep defeat in its large brown eyes, which seemed to beg for the final relief that only a man with a gun could provide. Burdett did not know how he could go on, watching soldiers and their animals being sacrificed en masse. And though he somehow managed to survive his first month on the front, it was necessary to use his Colt on thirteen more animals. After the first few days, each shot seemed to connect with the last one, and he found himself nauseated after each act of human compassion and duty.

One morning, after a particularly quiet mess of "C" Rations and coffee, Burdett cleaned and loaded his Colt, noting how the cartridges being pressed against the spring-tensioned magazine follower, were like little soldiers lining up for duty. He snapped the clip into the Colt's grip, hitting it sharply with the butt of his hand to make sure it was locked into place, then holstered it at his side. Though he'd never even dabbled in poetry, nor ever considered the proper construction of verse or prose, he penned his first and only poem in his diary. All he knew was that the lead bullets that spoke from his Colt were simply the gray messengers of death.

"Gressenger"

Fall in line, oh, Gressenger,
ahead of pressing follower,
anointed to your duty.

Snapped into the young Colt's grip,
and pressed against your brass-clad friends,
as comrades, wait the moment.

'Tis you who must deliver
cold, grey messages to pain-wracked minds.
Loudly announced and swiftly sent,

your only message: "Peace."

Burdett counted each day, calculating how many more he'd endure before the bad dream was over. It was February 3, 1918, and dark, wet clouds blanketed the battlefield, creating a visual hush amid the battle din. Burdett's uniform and face were spattered with blood from his point-blank deliveries of death, and, as the quiet of evening fell across no-man's land, he fell asleep in a state of utter exhaustion. The six cavalry horses still remaining were placed behind a small hill, tied together in a string, but, sometime in the night, the animals became loose--still tied together as they became entangled in barbed wire only a hundred feet or so ahead of the Canadian line.

It became clear that the Germans often fired directly at the horses, understanding that, in so doing, the cavalry soldiers were left without escape or cover. Burdett heard a report and saw a gut-shot horse, writhing on the ground. More shots followed, and all hit their marks, but none of them were instantly fatal, and each fallen animal thrashed about and cried out in fear and pain.

Burdett, in a frantic effort to end their suffering, ran to the horses. As the Germans concentrated their fire on their new target, Burdett drew his Colt, carefully dispatching peace to the first five animals. Bleeding from a chest wound, and with his right hand partially blown away, Sergeant Burdett Scott picked up his pistol with his left hand, looked into a pair of deep, brown, hopeless eyes, and pulled the trigger once more. There was no glory in his effort, for, like the horses, Burdett also fell and never moved again.

It was Burdett's dying father who sent me the letter. As I returned from my classes, I noticed an envelope under my door and picked it up. The postmark was difficult to read, for either the stamp had been too dry or the postal clerk had struck it too softly. Squinting, I was able to make out only the word "Bourne," but I could not make out the date.

The return address was very clear, showing that the letter was from Ryan Scott in Bourne River, B.C. I understood, at once. This was the letter I dreaded, and I tried to slow its delivery, first tapping the end of the envelope against my desk, holding it up to my desk lamp, carefully verifying that there was empty space along its end, and carefully slitting it open with my penknife. Pulling the letter slowly from its sheath, I unfolded it, noticing the momentary cessation of my breathing as I fearfully lay it beneath the lamp. It read:

"Dear Billy," "Burdett was awarded the Victoria Cross today. It was a posthumous ceremony, and we will all miss him terribly. He has told us, in the past, what a fine young man you are, and what a good friend you have been to him." It was signed, "Ryan Scott." An explanation of the circumstances followed, and Burdett's father included a second sheet of paper on which he'd drawn a pencil sketch--a facsimile of the medal, explaining that King George V, a great lover of horses, personally recommended Britain's highest military honor to his son. Mr. Scott also included yet another half page, which appeared to have been torn from a small diary. On it was Burdett's first and only poem, "Gressenger," and I could barely read it for my tears. The letter itself looked as if the pen that wrote it had left large splotches at several points across the page, but then I realized it. Those splotches of ink were from a father's tears.

I cried openly when I read the letter, but, without a roommate, there was no one there to hear. I had not fully appreciated just how much affection I had for Burdett, and I was unable to go to class for the last two days of that week. I was thirteen when my father died, and his passing hurt me deeply. I did not believe that any loss could feel so great. But it seemed that Burdett's death now brought me to the low point in my life-- not because his death was more significant than my father's, but because maturity brings a greater awareness of devastating pain.

Late one night, I returned to the dorm from my bartending job, only to find Burdett sitting at his desk. He turned to me; his face glowed with its typical, broad smile. I couldn't hide my amazement; there was no effective way to mute it, and I was aware that my chin had dropped and my mouth was wide open.

"Gosh, Billy," he laughed as he said it, "you look like you've seen a ghost. I leave for just a few days, and you go weird on me."

I stammered briefly, and then it hit me; the whole thing had been a bad dream. "I just had the most realistic nightmare, Burdett. It's really strange, the stories our minds are capable of fabricating." I didn't elaborate on the details, because I suspected the revelation of my dream would be upsetting to him.

But Burdett pressed me. "Tell me about it, old pal."

"Well, in my dream you got called up by the Army; you met a girl, got married, ended up in France and died there. It wasn't the typical disjointed nightmare. The realism was remarkable—names, places, dates, and a story-line worthy of a novel."

"No wonder you're upset about it." Burdett's face held an unmistakable expression of pain as he spoke. It was a look of sadness and compassion. "The part about the war is not so surprising. We've been mighty lucky not to find ourselves in some trench in Europe. Lots of other chaps haven't had our good fortune." Then he added, "Nightmares don't get any worse than that."

Suddenly, Burdett smiled--something totally incongruous, considering the gravity of our conversation--then added, with a wink, "Actually, the part about the girl wasn't bad at all. Jolly good!"

I was unable to drop the subject. "The dream had so many interesting twists, right down to you becoming a veterinary specialist, dealing with injured horses. I had never even considered that such jobs were available in the military." As I recounted the details to Burdett, I found myself swamped with a confused, disturbed feeling. Nothing was making any sense. We were happily bantering away, when I heard some kind of a bell. "Hold tight," I suggested to Burdette, "while I figure out where that sound is coming from."

Confusion transitioned to clarity. My alarm clock read

6:00 a.m. The door on Burdett's wardrobe was open, and there were no clothes on its stingy rod. His bed was empty, a stack of neatly folded bedding and a bare pillow lay at its foot; his desk showed no signs of study, but mine had its usual clutter—a pile of books and papers, topped-off with the pencil sketch from Burdett's father, and the handwritten poem, "Gressenger."

In time, I would find myself reviewing that nightmare in a totally different light. It had been so stunningly real. Typically I found it easy to differentiate between fantasies and real experiences. But that dream had been so different from any other. I'm happy I was able to visit with Burdett that one, last time.

———————

A few months later I saw Amy LeGrande Scott. I was walking along the President's Way and noticed her a few steps ahead. "Amy," I started, "it's me, Billy." She turned momentarily and I started to say how sorry I was about her loss. She looked at me with a sad recognition, but didn't say a word. I couldn't help but noticing that her face seemed a bit fuller than I'd remembered. In the place of her willowy, petite frame, there was a loose-fitting dress cascading over her rounded tummy. She paused for just a moment, as if contemplating whether to speak, then walked slowly away, choosing, for that moment, not to revive the pain. As I watched her disappear into the Science Building, I wanted desperately to tell her how sorry I was about the tragedy at the front. At the same time I was feeling another emotion, one that softened my sense of loss. I knew that Burdett's greatest happiness in life had come from his time with Amy, and my heart was warmed by the understanding and sweet pleasure that the baby would always be theirs.

Comfort of Friends

After Burdett's death and his father's sad letter, I felt a sense of futility, understanding that much of life is about random events over which we have little or no control. Burdett's conscription into the service was one of them; my acquaintance with George Murphy also; the meeting of my father and mother; and nature's lottery of conception was one of them too. It frustrated me to have such a clear view that random happenings change everyone's lives, every day, and that, though our choices in dealing with them influence the future, our capabilities cannot anticipate the steady flow of randomness that will surely follow.

In addition to the sense of futility, I found myself angry-- angry that a grownup world was actually too immature to resolve the childish squabbles that led to war and the deaths of so many fathers' sons. I sorely lamented that Burdett's life was likely wasted, merely merging with an endless trail of flesh and bone that littered the history of mankind, largely because there will always be those who never grow out of their bullying and greed. He was dead and millions of others had met the same end, and I knew that, at some juncture in time, the Germans would be stopped and the bloody war would finally end. But there was no question about it. Someone, for utterly selfish reasons, would start another war. This one was an unimaginable devastation. But it wasn't going to be the last.

Burdett's death made it hard to concentrate on my studies. He was the one who heard my most personal words of both elation and disappointment. So I turned to the only other real friends I had--the George Murphy family. We were very close during their last years in Stella's Cove, and, though I worked odd jobs at the Murphy home, to bring in some extra money, I always knew that my biggest reason for being there was George's gentle kindness and his sense of my need for a father.

I made the trip, during spring break, to the Murphy's home in Vancouver. It wasn't like I was simply reappearing in their lives, for every month I faithfully wrote them a note of my progress at school, and there was always that immutable understanding that I would not have been at the University except for George Murphy's kind generosity. My long separation from the Murphy's created a yearning, but, because I worked as a bartender during my semester breaks. I never left Arnold during my first four years there, because I understood that, while George seemed happy to pay all my expenses, it was a show of my appreciation to carry some of my own financial load.

The month before spring break, I dropped the Murphy's a note that I'd like to visit them and that I had about a week of break, starting with April 16th. As a P.S., I tacked on an extra note: "If you have any chores that need to be done, I'll be happy to do them. Love, Billy." They wrote back, and their letter encouraged me to stay for the whole week. They too tacked on a short P.S. "Lucky timing," it read, "since Celeste's spring break is at the same time. She's just finishing her teaching certificate, and she'll be so happy to see you." I found my mood suddenly changing. I was so excited about the visit.

The tone of Murphy's postscript seemed to acknowledge what I already believed--that Celeste had a lingering interest in me that mirrored what I was feeling. Maybe I was reading too much into the note, but I couldn't wait to see her, after almost four years of only space and the mail system between us. She was the girl I thought of when I allowed myself romantic daydreams. There was no question that she was a smoldering interest which always burned in my life, and that had been true since the first time I'd seen her at the Stella's Cove School.

With renewed enthusiasm, I aced all my classes, and, several weeks before the end of the quarter, I already knew that I'd be at the top of the Dean's List again.

Over the years, I would read "Gressenger" many times, trying to glimpse the last and precious thoughts of my friend. Like the loss of my father, it would always be there, but the death of someone should not cause anyone else's life to stop, and Burdett would have only wanted for my happiness and success. The healthy change in my focus brightened my mood, and my mourning was largely displaced by the anticipation of visiting with my special friends, the Murphys, and my wishful expectations of love.

As spring break approached, it was hard to concentrate on my studies. I longed for a hug from my sweet benefactor, and for his empathetic words. When I spoke with him during my chores at the Murphy mansion in Stella's Cove, it felt almost like Father was back in my life, and though I fully understood that fathers cannot ever be replaced, George was the role model of what a father should be--and, largely, what my own father had been.

On April 15th, after finishing my exams, I hurried to the station, and the countryside was an indefinite blur as the train proceeded north. That was more than a year ago, and the visit had no disappointments.

The gentle bump of the Aniak against the dock fenders, light as it was, has jarred me from my reflections of the spring break visit with the Murphys. Celeste is going to be continuing on to Eagle City after a short, layover visit with my mother, while I remain for a month. Initially I planned on only that short introductory visit, and I'm not sure why I chose to extend my stay. I certainly don't enjoy Mother's company, and I don't have any desire to spend a month butting heads with her—something I consider to be almost inevitable. I have the uncomfortable feeling that there's unfinished business for me here; I need to come to grips with the tragedy and find some way to absolve myself of the nagging, lingering guilt that's been eating at me all this time. Sure, I was only a boy, and yet I've not been able to forgive myself for my silence. If I had only possessed the courage to speak out, someone might have listened, and maybe the tragedy could have been averted.

The next time the Aniak heads north, I'll be on it, anxious to rejoin Celeste. That spring break visit with the Murphys after Burdett's death permanently changed my friendship with her. Since then there has been a perpetual romance and the understanding that we will be spending our lives together. When we said goodbye and headed back to our final college classes, she looked at me happily. "I'll go wherever you go." She'd said it with a reassuring tone, but there was a tacit understanding that circumstances might not allow it. In a continuing run of good luck, she too has secured a job in Eagle City, working as a teacher for grades 6 through 12. Her contract is to begin only three days from today.

I think about my aging mother. She is now nearly seventy and has been experiencing some health problems, and I feel certain that it is her drinking that's responsible for her waning vigor. I have been warned that she may be drunk at any time of the day. Though Celeste is anxious to meet Mother, I am facing the moment with trepidation, imagining the gushing, slurred words, and Mother's footsteps as she staggers to open the door.

I have come to understand, after my college biology and physiology courses, that virtually all creatures and plants go through a reproduction frenzy right before the permanent injunctions of, first infertility, and, last, the cessation of life. I was a late-life baby. It wasn't that my parents hadn't tried. Mother and Father desperately wanted a child, but for over twenty-five years, they'd come to accept that it was simply not going to happen. Mother has often told me that she and Father considered her pregnancy, at age forty-five, to be a miracle, although that romanticized account fails to ring true. For "miracle" is not a word Father would have ever used, and he would have politely described it as a chance event. I am one of those accidental children, born out of nature's compelling need to perpetuate the species, and I feel fortunate that some accidents turn out for the best, understanding that the incidence of congenital physical and mental abnormalities are high when mothers are too old.

Dorothy Blethers' son was not so lucky. He was severely congenitally impaired and had the mental capacity of a young child. "Mongoloid" was the pronouncement by the Vancouver doctors who'd examined him. Considering the luck of the draw and the age of my parents, I could just as easily have been another Denton.

A year after the death of Rev. Mills, and Denton Blethers' horrifying postmortem violation of Miss Hardwicke, Blethers sexually assaulted two local girls. The RCMP investigated, and a circuit judge found him guilty. Because of the boy's diminished mental capacity and the fact that the acts were limited to fondling, the judge gave Blethers a two-year sentence. In the same breath, the judge suspended incarceration and remanded him to the custody of his parents.

The generosity of the judge, in retrospect, was a terrible mistake. Denton raped another girl a short time later, forcing her down as she walked along a forested trail, tearing off her knickers, and having his way with her. As she lay there, bloody and half-clothed in the trail, Blethers ran off, laughing and hee-hawing like a jackass. No one else was laughing, and there were several parents who wondered, waiting, what would happen to the boy, who was then twenty-four years old. For, though mostly unreported, there were a total of seven girls in town who had been either assaulted or improperly touched.

After the violent, forest rape, the RCMP questioned Blethers again, and decided to charge him with both rape and lewdness, as his acts were those of a repeated offender. Though he was probably not culpable for his crimes, it was also understood that he was a severe menace to the community. The RCMP told his family that Denton Blethers would most likely be sent to a facility for the criminally insane, because any court hearing on the boy's mental capacity and state of mind, would be certain to block the possibility of him being sent to a regular prison facility. Once again, Blethers was remanded to his parents' care while awaiting trial, as there was no suitable facility for temporary custody, and his parents posted their own home as bond. They were given strict instructions not to allow the boy out of their sight.

It was Josh Smithers, father of that last, violated girl who ended it all. I have never told anyone else about this, for Rodney Smithers, a friend of mine at school, had confided in me. Any revelation of the story would have caused the Smithers family endless pain. Finding Blethers peeping through a neighbor's window the following night, Mr. Smithers had bludgeoned and gagged Blethers, dragged him into a grove of firs, and put a bullet through his brain.

The sleeping residents of Stella's Cove had re-positioned themselves on their pillows and pulled their comforters about their faces, following the distant and faint pop. There would be no more sexual assaults in the community. The RCMP investigated the murder, and, while several of the townsfolk were questioned on the sad event, no charges were ever filed. There were no confessions, no witnesses, nor any damning evidence to support a government indictment. And, so, there was no trial, no hearing, and no one in Stella's Cove seemed to fret that the poor boy had not been responsible for his crimes. Rev. Cromwell addressed the tragedy briefly in one of his weekly sermons, acknowledging that the boy's death was very sad, but adding, "Despite the terrible tragedy of Denton's death and the great loss to his parents, justice has been served." As shining examples of Christianity's absence in Stella's Cove, Dorothy and Edgar Blethers nodded in agreement with the preacher's words, for, despite their grief, even they did not question the fairness of the outcome.

The ultimate fate of Denton Blethers made me more empathetic about chance happenings. As the child of aging parents, Blethers' lot could have been my own. Luckily I had no congenital abnormalities, yet I also understood that my early life would have been different, had my mother and father been younger. I regret, now, that there was, at times, a hint of my embarrassment over my parents' age. And though it was not a constant theme, nor had I ever articulated it to my dad, I felt some jealousy when I saw youthful fathers doing strenuous activities with their children.

While Father did his best to keep up with me, he could not match my confident stride and youthful vigor, and I am feeling regret now, that I didn't slow a little to compensate for the inevitable effect of his age. Father loved the little canyon that rose eastward toward the glacier. Most Saturdays greeted Mother as a work day, when laundry, ironing, and cleaning kept her a virtual slave of the home, but Father always took me hiking, as the weather allowed, and he never stopped saying, "Isn't this beautiful!" It was so predictable, and, though so often repeated, Father meant it every time he said it. There could not have been a father who promoted a greater love of natural beauty.

During the warmer months, when the sun shone almost perpetually through the night sky, Father and I hiked that canyon a thousand times, and he always sat down on the same rock, just a stone's throw from where Muir Creek rushed from beneath the towering blue ice.

Long after Father was gone, I continued my hikes to the glacier, as my busy life allowed, and I always sat on that same rock we had shared. But, my solo outings became progressively more difficult, largely because I could not go there without hearing our conversations and experiencing my sorrow over and over again. The hikes were a routine, but Father added additional excitement to my life by the variety of one other essential activity. After all, what kind of father doesn't take his boy fishing? He knew that I loved it--grabbing the fishing poles and bait, and casting off the end of the dock. There were times, too, when he'd borrowed a dory from his friend, Jerry, and rowed to the end of the jetty. I particularly loved those little forays into the sea, for they provided a view of the Gavins Glacier that was not possible from the town.

As Stella's Cove is situated at Canada's western shore, and there's little between it and the islands of Japan, it is surprising that we didn't fish more frequently. There was one thing that deterred us from doing so, and I came to appreciate that my father was a gentle man and that he loathed having to kill the thrashing catch. I understood that, as unpleasant a task it was for him, he only did it because I needed some variety in my life.

Once, I hooked a fifteen-pound sea bass, and the pole, which was propped at the edge of the dock, suddenly lurched toward the water. Father and I both grabbed for it, but the pole stood on its tip as it hung over the final board at the dock's edge, then tumbled about six feet into the water. In moments, Father had his shoes pulled off, and, before the cork handle of the fishing pole had sunk beneath the surface, he was in the water too. Ducking below the surface, and finding the sinking pole, he retrieved it and swam to the water's edge.

I can still remember the excitement, for I had never before seen my father swim. The cold water of the Cove was something I always considered uninviting since the three swimming lessons I'd suffered through back when I was six years old. Because water was everywhere, my parents hired Delsey Farmer, a neighbor who had once been a competitive swimmer, to teach me the basics of water survival. That was all it was. There was no breast stroke, no Australian crawl, and I certainly never turned over on my back. The water left me blue after each session, but I was successful in learning what was called the "doggy paddle," and I could swim to the end of the dock and back. After the third lesson, Mrs. Farmer told me, "That's all you need to know. It isn't fancy strokes that save people's lives, and you're never going to drown."

Father's plunge into the cold depths saved the precious fishing pole, and at the end of its hundred feet of line was that grand fish. Climbing from the water, and shivering as he slogged back to the dock, Father grabbed a large rounded stone, lay the bass on the edge of the dock, and struck--closing his eyes just before the impact. His aim was good, and the fish lay there, beautiful and still. That bass became several of our family's tastiest meals, and I will always smile at the thought of my father, fully dressed and dripping wet, standing there, laughing on that dock.

I couldn't help but wonder why a man who spent so much of his life as a commercial fisherman seemed so sensitive to the dying fish, and I asked him once why he closed his eyes as he struck the fish into oblivion. "I hate killing them." He responded. "Every time I club one, it hurts me to do it." For the moment after he'd spoken, I was shocked at his squeamishness, but further consideration gave me a sense of pride in my father's sensitivity. I guess, on the trawler, that he'd not seen the fish as individual lives. They were, collectively, a catch, and there was something impersonal about the process of pushing a net-load of fish onto the pile of ice in the trawler's hold.

With my own maturity, I came to appreciate that Father did his best to share activities with me, but age was not his friend. Besides his lungs, ravaged by his years of smoking, his right hip always ached, and his only relief seemed to come from the heat of the cast iron stove. It was a fact that, though aging and aching, he did his best as a father. As I think of him there's a happy warmth spreading through me, like rays of a summer sun bursting through a break in the clouds.

As more recollections flood my mind, I know that this visit is an important event in my life. I find myself momentarily sad, understanding that Mother will not live forever and that all children are destined to become orphans if they live long enough. I spend a moment wondering what terminal malady will take her, and I worry that there will be no one there to care for her in her dying days. She has been so strong and endured so much. Time has helped me to understand just how hurt Mother was by Father's absence, yet she has never allowed herself to complain and has generally borne her trials with a quiet and resolute stoicism.

The most obvious sign of her sadness has been the whisky, which seems to take the edge off her silent suffering and allows her to make it through the solitude of the evening hours. I have come to appreciate how difficult it must have been for her--trying to adopt the duties of a breadwinner, while attending to household responsibilities and the needs of an adolescent boy. For a moment I'm finding it hard to know what touches me more deeply. Is it the father who tried so hard and was lost too soon, or is it the mother who bore the aftermath and determined to go on?

I know that Mother is now among the poor, and that the government cheque is her only income. While George Murphy remained in the Cove, her life was better--a time when there were no worries over the bills, and during which she'd even considered the possibility that she'd have another man in her life. But, during that year I left Stella's Cove for the University, I'd noticed her deepening depression and the doldrums which left her like a ship with full sails and no breeze to move her forward. And I frequently saw her in such motionless states, quietly considering the good times that were all gone.

My psychology studies have greatly expanded my understanding of deep, personal loss, and I am much better able to appreciate the inertia that ruled Mother's most hopeless days. In the weeks before I left for school in Seattle, I had noticed how she fiddled, almost continuously, with a pearl necklace she'd always worn around her neck. It was the nicest gift she would ever have and the most expensive gift she'd ever received. A distant smile would come over her, and I understood; she was remembering the day when Father offered it from his open hands, at a time when the sun still shone on our lives.

Fellow Travelers

I'm leaning against the Aniak's railing, quietly speculating on how Mother will receive Celeste as her future daughter-in-law. During the voyage I have not dwelt on it, but my education-- particularly its focus on the underlying motivations of behavior-- has made both the actions and attitudes of people more transparent. I have no doubt that Mother will try her best to mask her feelings, but no matter how good-intentioned, she will surely have some concerns over my betrothed. I find myself asking questions. How will Mother feel about Celeste—will she view her as creating a greater schism in our relationship? Will Mother view Celeste as a competitor for my affections? Will she view Celeste as a nail in my spiritual coffin, when another agnostic becomes my steady ally? I am actually dreading their meeting, understanding that the answers may not be the ones I prefer to hear.

My thoughts turn from my immediate apprehensions to a kaleidoscopic review of Stella's Cove's past. I'm puzzled a bit by my compelling, almost obsessive, need to find some kind of reason in the cyclic fortunes of my town, and I even question myself, "Does this kind of self-torture fall into a clinical diagnosis?" It's such a depressing subject, but I find myself constantly reviewing the boom-bust history. The town was virtually abandoned when the fur animals were gone, and there was no reason to believe it would survive. It was the cry of "Gold!" that turned more heads than the town could accommodate. Just like the failure of the trapping industry, the gold rush, too, ran its course, and the town suffered yet another swift and staggering economic death, and a mass exodus of its people.

Without jobs and cash, poverty fell across the town like the shadows cast by the coastal hills. Through those bad times, there was only one thing that survived. The beautiful church that Willis Fox so generously funded was always there, and there was no time, even when the community was a silent ghost, that Fox's perpetual maintenance fund did not properly maintain it. While the town may have shown a profound deterioration during the bust economic sieges, the church was always perfect, and anyone seeing it would have believed it was only recently constructed.

The Town Hall was another story. Merely the living room of one Town Councilman, it did not have a position on the list of major surviving landmarks. Its worn rugs and sooty ceiling were never replaced, and it still bore, the last time I saw it, the understanding that it is only God's buildings that remain important over a period of time. The Town Hall's owner abandoned the home when the final prospects of economic success were so summarily erased, and it stands there, unoccupied, for a boom that will never follow.

Today, there is no one in Stella's Cove expecting a catalogue store treasure, and, for the aging crew of the Aniak, it is simply a routine provision run. Left in the place of progress, excitement, and prosperity, the sole amusement for the remaining townsfolk is to stand and wait on the Stella's Cove dock, quietly considering the foamy churning of the wake as the boat changes its power and direction, giving a frantic and momentary life to the green water below. A young boy watches, obviously fascinated, off the edge of the dock, exclaiming, "Look, Dad. Look at all the whirlpools." I find myself contemplating the boy, considering how his is probably the youngest resident of Stella's Cove, and not likely to be replaced by a new crop of children. As the boat makes its final docking maneuver, there are large swirling disturbances being spun off by the sizable brass propeller--moving swiftly and then dying quietly as the little whirlpools meander from the dock.

Celeste and I are the only "locals" aboard, but not the only passengers. There are those two matronly women, both from the Vancouver Temperance Society, the same ones who had cast a glance of disapproval at our public kiss three days earlier. I would not know them from any other women of middle age, were it not for the large stick pins on their jackets identifying them officially. They have heard that alcohol consumption is a big problem in Stella's Cove, but it eludes me how they came to know it. I find myself imagining that, in their handbags, they are carrying ball-peen hammers, and they have timed and conserved their only smiles for those moments when the glass and liquor crash against the floor.

Dressed austerely in their dark wool suits, it is apparent that these women have been careful to make themselves look as wholesome as possible, which simply means that no man would look at them with a lustful eye. Except for their pale faces, there is no other skin showing. Their clothes extend from their shoes below to the bases of their double chins; sleeves cover their wrists; and gloves ensure that no one can see their hands. I consider their homely looks for a few moments, and feel happy that their possibilities for reproduction are unlikely at best. I have a feeling that, if ever married, their husbands would have walked with canes, for each of the two women would surely make a man limp. I chuckle briefly to myself; there's a pang of guilt inside me, understanding that my derogatory judgements are both unkind and without a reasonable basis. Celeste is obviously having similar thoughts, and she notes the women's austere presence with a single word of scorn: "Dismal."

Use of the word "wholesome" in describing the Temperance ladies has nothing to do with goodness. In fact, as I look at them, understanding that their intent is to take away the only medications of the Cove's residents, I have a feeling of total disgust. They wear not a hint of lipstick; their bodies would make the average man sick to his stomach; and I can't help but think that their god is nauseated too. And yet I also understand that melancholy and alcohol are the perpetuation of unhappiness, and that a comparatively brief anesthesia is the only positive outcome of the bottle--a disappointing, palliative, and temporary relief from the permanent despair that plagues my childhood town.

Despite their attempts at severe appearances, the taller of the Temperance women is thinking. I can see it on her face, and, for just a moment, I imagine that I am hearing her thoughts, which are surprisingly different than the image she is hoping to project to those around her. (I don't know exactly why I do it, but I've often looked at people as shallow masks of pretense, and it amuses me to ascribe to them the hidden parts that do not show.) "I just hope

I find what I want here," she muses. "That sailor in Bourne River was the best roll in the hay I've ever had. And that shot of whisky allowed me to feel some things I've never before experienced." Her cheeks flush for a moment, looking as if a glow of rouge has been suddenly applied by some unseen hand, and the austere tightness of her lips turns, instantly, into an unbridled smile, temporarily exposing gold on her lower molars. But, then she realizes that the other lady has turned toward her, critically noticing the pleasure on her face, so she immediately suppresses the irresponsible contemplation of her tryst. Her color fades within a fraction of a second, and her chin tucks back into a position of great gravity. "Here on the Lord's duty," she acknowledges with an enthusiastic, pious resolve, "and we're going to save this town." "Amen," adds the other, and they merge back into their prior unity of purpose, understanding that God himself has sent them to Stella's Cove.

For a moment I feel some vague disgust for myself, understanding that both the women may be virtuous and sincere, and I realize that there's a quirky, perverse creativity that sometimes guides my unspoken thoughts and fabricates fiction around the people I observe. Apparently I have some kind of perpetual resentment toward those who advertise their beliefs. When I press myself for the probable source of my little aberration, I have a momentary epiphany, understanding that it relates to the glaring dichotomy of my mother's religious fanaticism, contrasted with her most basic human needs.

"A penny for your thoughts…or, maybe, even a fish scale," offers Celeste. I smile at her, with a surreptitious indication toward the two women, then turn directly toward her, rolling my eyes. I do not tell her what I was thinking, but I also make it clear that I consider such pretentious piety to greatly detract from people. "God must be very dull," I whisper "if that's the way he wants his servants to look." Then, as an afterthought, I smile, "Well, do I get my fish scale?"[1] Celeste, so as not to be heard, answers with only a wink, and the Temperance Society is not mentioned again.

---

[1] A "fish scale" was the predecessor to the Canadian nickel, and was equal to one-twentieth of the Canadian Dollar.

Also among the small assortment of passengers are a couple of sporty-looking men—likely academics--standing near the starboard side of the bow. They watch intently as the ship does its perfect sideways move toward the homemade layered-rope fenders on the dock, which soften the blow when contact is made. I can't help but thinking how durable and effective those bumpers are, absorbing the collision of a one-hundred ton vessel into the creosoted fir pilings, and softening it to the touch of a lover's kiss. Even more impressive is the skill with which the Captain maneuvers, bringing such a large vessel to such a gentle engagement with the dock. The academics are visibly impressed, and I overhear one of them say, "now that was exceptionally well done—no, it was perfect. The Captain is really a maestro." I give no outward response, but my brain nods agreement at the academic's appreciation. I can't help but wondering who else aboard is making the same observation, understanding that some of the other passengers are probably equally impressed, while others may have not even noticed.

There's a short blast from the boat's whistle. Then another, and the hawser lines are now taut around the large cleats that line the edge of the dock, spaced every ten feet or so for its entire length. The two sporty looking gentlemen approach us as we walk toward the gangplank, while a scruffy-haired deck-hand with a long, handlebar mustache, unclasps the rope barricade that prevented its premature use--discreetly picking his nose with the other hand. "Wait just a moment, folks." he warns, for he is the official caretaker of that spot until the steamboat is completely quiet and the engine sputters its final cough.

"How do you do." says the closer of the two academics, holding his briar pipe, cupped in his right hand as he speaks. "I'm Mortimer Williams, and this is Ernest Tane."

"Hello," Celeste and I both respond, and I introduce us to the pair. "I'm Billy Potter, and this is my fiancé, Celeste Murphy." Mortimer shifts his pipe to his left hand, and we all shake hands politely. In a light patter of mostly meaningless words, we engage each other for a few moments, and I can't help but notice that Mortimer does not address Celeste, nor does he turn toward her as he continues his pleasantries. He seems only aware of me, and it is difficult for me to envision any red-blooded man who does not do, at least, a double take when introduced to Celeste. She is that stunning, yet the man's gaze never gets to her.

Mortimer is tall and skinny to the extent of looking unhealthy. Perhaps in his early forties, his neck is long, extending well above his heavy, dark green turtleneck sweater, and his Adam's apple protrudes at least an inch. His face, like the rest of him, is far too thin, and the bony structure of his jaw is as obtrusive as his cheekbones. He takes a few puffs from the briar pipe, and, as he does, I can't help but notice a dark mole just below his left nostril, and there's a large, jagged scar that extends from his left eye to the lobe of his ear.

There is no question, in looking at his clothes, that Mortimer is here to hike or climb, since he's decked-out in the latest European mountaineering look. "Then again, "I silently consider, "It could be the latest in golfing fashion." I dismiss that thought, as there are surely no golf links in Stella's Cove. Below Mortimer's sweater, there's a pair of tartan knickerbockers which are the obvious reason for my thought that golf might be involved. (After all, it was the Scots who invented that game, so they are more-or-less directly responsible for the misery, frustration, and thousands of golf clubs whose shafts are no longer straight, but have the recognizable shape of having been broken against trees during bursts of intense anger.)

Mortimer's tall, gray wool stockings are topped by red garter bands, each with a red maple leaf facing toward the side, and leaving about an inch of bare skin just below his knees. He's wearing a tweed cap, and his graying hair shows obvious signs of good grooming, brushed back against his head and neatly tapered at the neck. It's apparent that Mortimer has shaved this morning, but I can't help but notice there are several whisker stubs that were missed because of their proximity to the mole--prominent enough to obstruct the daily razor,

Noting that I've looked for more than a moment at his scar, Mortimer volunteers, "Yes, I got that scar in a climbing accident about five years ago. The fall could have been fatal, but it seems I'm no worse for the wear." He tacks on an additional comment, and winks as he says it. "I'm much more cautious now."

Ernest is Mortimer's opposite, and a bit younger, maybe in his mid-thirties. He's not thin and he has the look of plump-baby-fat that just never went away with age. His facial features are muted by his generous layer of insulation, and there isn't even the hint of any stubble on his face--just a neatly trimmed blonde mustache that is short of the corners of his mouth, and has a precise lower line that ends a quarter inch above his lips.

I can't help but notice that Ernest seems to suffer from some sort of acne-like eruptions on his face, and, to create a succinct description, I would have to say "...an overgrown, over-aged teen." He's wearing a tweed hat, with a colorful feather set in its band, and he, like Mortimer, is wearing an outfit that would look very much at home in the Alps or on the seventh green of St. Andrew's "Old Course." I can't help but thinking to myself that the pair is really unique. In my life, I have never seen two men so colorful and unorthodox in their dress, even in the liberal environment of the university campus.

Now we are all ready to disembark, and there's a natural queuing of the waiting passengers. Our casual conversation with Ernest and Mortimer is interrupted by the understanding that we will all be departing the boat in just a few moments. I can't help but noticing that there is a confused look on the pair, which seems to impart a question of "What do we do now?" We all shake hands once more, in parting, with what I assume is a combination of genuine cordiality and mutually feigned enthusiasm. I take a quick glance at my pocket watch, noting that Celeste's visit with Mother is going to be even shorter than planned, but we stop with forbearance to hear Mortimer say that they are both geologists from Norberg University in Seattle, and that their sole purpose in being here is to study the Gavins Glacier. In our short conversation, the pair has learned that we are both former residents of the town, so they now pick our brains for some useful information. Celeste and I are anxious to help, since we can both see they're as good as lost.

"We're going to be here for two weeks," squawks Ernest in a high pitched, rather effeminate voice, so we're needing a place to stay. Do you have any recommendation?" For a moment I search my mind for something I've never considered about my home town, and I turn toward Celeste, inquiring if she's aware of accommodations which might be available. But I am distracted from my response to Ernest by the thought, "I'm sure that he's not wearing the right clothes." There is no unkindness in my internal comment--just an understanding that the world contains a vast variety of people and preferences, and that there is something very incongruous about the outer trappings and my perception of the inner person.

Ernest's blonde mustache is his only claim to masculinity, and I noticed, as I shook his hand, that he extended it toward me gracefully and with a soft wrist. Though I consciously struggle to prevent the thought from rooting, an image of lacy underwear darts through my mind, and I can't help but have a fleeting mental image of the relinquishment of chaste behavior that will likely occur at the couple's lodging. It is a taboo subject, but, having been away for the past five years in a much more liberal environment than the one in which I was raised, there are few things in the world that surprise me. Though Rev. Miles Cromwell once gave a sermon about such close relationships between men, and called them "…an abomination against God and nature," and though it was something totally foreign to me, I have since realized that there are people who are born in a non-standard form, and whose intimate preferences are only toward the same sex. And, though Mother would hate my opinion, Mortimer and Ernest's preferences have nothing to do with God. I find myself going, yet, a step further in my contemplation of the pair, "If God created man in his own image, God might also be queer."

Now, to address their question, I choke slightly as I ponder the availability of lodging in Stella's cove. "You're a long way from nowhere, and Stella's Cove doesn't have a hotel." I see a look of dazzling disappointment on their faces, and the tacit recognition that they have not planned their trip very well. Celeste interjects an idea, "What about our old home? It lets out rooms."

"There's the old George Murphy home," I responsively add, as a detached afterthought, because of Celeste's reminder and the realization that Mother had written me, telling me it was now the Point Fay Bed and Breakfast, and was being run by Bart Clemmerton, Sr.

Bart had run the local bakery, which was the only one in Stella's Cove since I was a child, but, like all other businesses in town, it suffered a dramatic downturn in sales and Bart was forced to close it down. Without the Murphy Salmon Company processing plant, all but the most essential businesses have failed, and I am thinking that the Point Fay Bed and Breakfast will be closing its doors as well. At least the bread and rolls must be outstanding, with such a fine baker at the helm, and guests will be able to experience a taste of the better and bygone years that preceded the dismal failure that has descended on the town. The home was the statement of a quiet elegance only seven years before, when George Murphy, owner and sole proprietor of the Murphy Salmon Company, suddenly left Stella's Cove for a quiet retirement in Vancouver.

Mortimer and Ernest thank us for our tip on the accommodations, and begin to collect their gear, moving toward the rail in anticipation of setting foot on solid ground. There's a sallow tint of green on Ernest's face, and I am realizing that the mostly-flat seas have somehow made him sick. After walking down the gangplank, he smiles for a moment, assuring Mortimer, "I'm going to be fine now." I turn away for a moment, watching two men who are loading a small piano to the Aniak's deck. The burlier of the two slips as his feet hit the deck, and the piano takes a bump at its back-right corner. Dissonance erupts from the instrument's soundboard, and I can visualize the bronze brace of vibrating strings, like some giant hand has struck all the keys at the same time. But the piano seems to have sustained no damage and the deckhands secure it safely with a tarp and ropes, against the pilothouse wall.

When I turn back towards the departing geologists, Mortimer is standing by himself with their luggage, and Ernest has made his way to the edge of the dock. Kneeling there, and with his hands firmly planted on the final plank, he drops his head and loses the gruel and coffee he'd been served earlier in the Aniak's little café. I can't help but feel his misery, for I can remember those times when I myself have felt nausea coming on, and been unable to stop its obligatory response.

But it is the mention of the Murphy home that makes it hard for me to think of anything else, and, though I had resolved, only moments before, to break the vicious and unproductive pattern of my thinking, I find my mind stuck, once more, in the fickle history of my town. "Billy," I ask myself, "you just can't do it, can you?"

Remains

As we alight on solid ground, I look back at the Aniak, which is loading an assortment of crates and preparing to resume its scheduled run up the coast after a two-hour lay-by. The old steamboat, with its cloudy contributions to the overcast sky, is connected with many of my childhood memories, for I always possessed a fascination with the sea, spending many hours at the dock and talking with the fishermen who came and left with the tides each day. And it was at that same dock that my own father waved to me as he returned from the sea, and from which he waved goodbye the last time I would ever see him alive.

There are memories, too, of various goods which both arrived and departed from the Stella's Cove dock. Even the steam shovel, used for the first excavations of the Murphy Salmon Company's facilities, was loaded and chained to the Aniak's deck, and the first automobile in town was driven onto this same dock, utilizing a heavy ramp that was constructed for that specific purpose. While the Reo "5" Roadster was a spectacular cargo to behold, none of the residents were able to understand how such a conveyance could be used in a town which, essentially, had no roads at all. It was George Murphy who ordered the automobile, for he often fretted that his old pony cart was too slow a way of getting around.

The Reo "R 5" could seat five adults and its thirty-horsepower "F-Head" engine was considered the most reliable of its day. It was capable of doing over 35 miles per hour on a smooth road--very unlike the gnarly and rutted ones that stretched from Point Fay all the way to the Salmon plant three miles north of Stella's Cove..

I expressed an interest in the operation of the Reo, and George had given me a short course on internal combustion engines, something I easily understood. Not satisfied that I knew everything I needed to know, I asked George, "What does this metal rod do?" Murphy gave me a much abbreviated description of its function, comparing the Reo's transmission with the block and tackle that hung in the blacksmith shop. "When it's in third gear, the wheels are going fast, but the engine is running at a slow and comfortable pace. When the engine is turning at a slow pace, it doesn't create very much power, so, to conquer the inertia of the automobile's resting weight or pull the load of a steep grade, the gears allow the engine to turn faster, delivering the necessary power to the wheels."

George's explanation was a mouthful, delivered in what seemed to be one continuous breath, and, when he finished the explanation, he inhaled deeply. "Billy," he politely inquired, "did you understand what I was saying?" "Yes, sir." was my answer and I continued so he'd know that his explanation was clear. "It's a matter of simple mechanical advantage," I answered, "The gear ratios can either speed up the car, or allow it's small engine to send extra power to the drive wheels." George was noticeably pleased with my response, a brief explanation of a matter of applied physics, and, when our conversation ended, I spent a few more moments contemplating the Reo. Though the gears were cogged wheels, it very much related to the principle of leverage, and I couldn't help but imagining how, if provided with a long enough and strong enough lever, I could, with my own one-hundred thirty pounds of weight, raise the Aniak clean out of the water.

The Reo had amazingly bright acetylene headlights that cast a broad beam across the road and water, much like the reflection of a full moon, falling as a pillar across the gentle sea on one of the few cloudless nights. Those powerful beams of white light created yellow-eyed goblins of the critters that swarmed the seashore and marshes during the evening hours. Short, nighttime rides were a favorite of the Murphys, because, invariably, the bright headlights would expose those same animals which were rarely or never seen during the daytime hours. Deer, fox, raccoons, and skunks appeared to have eyes of fire, and the

Murphy's pony, Oscar, looked like some kind of spooky apparition each time the Reo approached its paddock, returning from an evening excursion.

The people of Stella's Cove were fascinated by the vehicle, and, because Murphy enjoyed Sunday joyrides, there was more than one church service punctuated by the Reo's occasional backfires and the Ah-ooo-gah horn that Murphy loved so much to blow. It was hard to say whether or not the happy hymn of the horn was deliberate. Actually, anyone who knew him was well aware that George had no inclination to step on the beliefs of the other townsfolk. Yet, in obvious horror and disdain over the irreverent interruptions to his sermons, Rev. Cromwell looked heavenward at those moments when the squeezing of that large black rubber bulb marred a momentary sense of god's presence-- preempted by an expression of pure joy and the ruffling of wild hair in the piney breeze outside. "We can be so thankful," he would gloat to his flock, "that we have the light of Jesus in our lives. Sunday is God's day, and we are all blessed by being here in the house of the Lord." While he stopped short of actually condemning those of the community who were not present, there was perfect clarity in his intent.

On one such Sunday I sluffed church and walked out to Point Fay for the Murphy's Sunday ride. When I showed up at the Murphy home, George gently confronted me, "Billy, shouldn't you be in church?" When he'd said it, there was a kind of confused look on his face and he was forced to clarify his words. "You know, Billy, I'm not a religious man, but what I do believe is that Sundays, like all others, should be days of joy. I'm only concerned that your mother will take your absence as a personal affront." "Sir," I answered, dispensing with the usual, casual use of George's name, "I believe I'm old enough to make that decision myself, and Mother will just have to understand that I intend no disrespect." When I'd made that statement, I understood that it was, essentially, a lie, and that my being there was definitely an outgrowth of my youthful rebellion against religion. The fact was, I got some visceral satisfaction out of bashing Mother's beliefs, acting, in a sense, as Father's voice from the grave. As it turned out, the ride was an intense and sheer delight, with the warm breeze of springtime bearing the gentle perfume of wild roses. My neatly parted hair ended-up in a delightful mess, inspiring a smile and spontaneous laugh from both Celeste and

Eva.

I was home before Mother got there. When she came through the door, I cringed at the look of total disgust on her face. As she served the soup for lunch, there was no smile, and she did not speak to me, except once, for the rest of the afternoon. Her only words came later. "Go out and split some kindling, Billy. It's going to be another chilly night." When evening came, it was really cold, and I could not be sure how much of it was caused by the iciness of the wind, which poured every evening from the glacier's face, or from the coldness of anger within my mother's heart.

Because George's home was so far from the town's center, and because the stub railway he would build from his factory to the town did not operate at times other than the changing of the shifts, George believed the automobile would save him hours every week, and it did. Each month a barrel of petrol was shipped to Stella's Cove, and, each month, an empty one replaced the new one being delivered. Covering the distance between town and the Murphy home had taken about six minutes, and the three mile drive from town to the Salmon plant was almost as fast. The pony and the cart would eventually be retired, except for a few short Sunday drives, for the age of motorcars had come to town--at least for one of its families.

George loved the feeling he got from driving that roadster, but, like the Murphy family, it would only remain in Stella's Cove for a few short years, until it was shipped back to Vancouver on the Aniak's deck along with the pony and the cart.

Remembering back, I would have to say that the Reo "R-5" was one of the greatest novelties to descend from the Aniak's deck. But, while the town was thriving, other luxuries, too, arrived by way of the sea. For just a moment, I am remembering the excitement when Mother's leather recliner was unloaded at this same dock only eight years ago, and how, during its first few days in our home, she could not stay away from that chair for more than five minutes. It seemed so obsessive to me, but she was driven passionately to try it, over and over again, to feel the smooth action of its articulated frame and the extension of its soft footrest under her calloused heels.

During evenings, she used the down-cushioned recliner for her reading, and there were many times that the pages of a book slowly relaxed, and a gentle snoring wafted through the room. I am now remembering those times and how I had to nudge her gently to remind her of the lateness of the hour, and how she awakened with a look of soft splendor in her eyes, and a face that read, "I have finally come home." It was the first time, since my father passed away, that I saw my mother looking happy, and I believed that the embracing nature of the recliner reminded her of the comfort, love, and reassurance of my father's arms.

I was sixteen at that time, and it was a window of relative plenty for us. Mother's job at the Murphy Salmon Company eased our financial burdens, and the qualities of enthusiasm and love temporarily seemed to thrive like the response of crocuses to the first springtime thaw. Mother became gentler and less judgmental, and some of her rules, which had always been both arbitrary and extreme, were relaxed during that short period of grace.

The tongue-lashings and endless biblical quotes temporarily waned to an occasional background whisper, and Mother seemed better balanced than in the previous three years since Dad died. Most surprising of all, Mother showed a longing for love and companionship, and even considered the possibility that romance could return to her life. During that summer she went walking, several times a week, with a man from work, and, though it was painful to see her affections directed toward someone who wasn't my father, I was able to appreciate that it was a healthy interest--certainly more healthy than another year of mourning. I made a real effort during that period to accept her need for love, and I actually resolved myself to the possibility that she might even remarry.

I came home from Murphy's, one Saturday, to find Mother sitting in the living room with company. "Hi, dear," she greeted me, "There's someone I'd like you to meet." Ignoring the typical good manners of rising to do such an introduction, Mother remained in the leather recliner, clinging to it as if she feared some usurper would try to steal it if she stood, and I realized, at that moment, I had never sat in it during those times when she was at home. Sitting on the couch, opposite her, was a man I recognized. I had seen him a couple of months before, getting off the Aniak, and I assumed correctly that he came to Stella's Cove for work. Mother leaned forward slightly in the cushy leather, "Billy, this is James Merriman. Jim, this is my son Billy." Mr.

Merriman rose from the couch and shook my hand. "I understand you're one of this town's most capable young men. Do you have plans for continuing your education after you graduate from public school?"

"Yes, Sir." I answered, looking back at Mother's face. "I'm planning on a university education." Mother smiled approvingly, but I detected a distant look in her eyes which seemed to intimate a silent question. "What will I do when Billy's gone?" With the good job, adequate resources, and even a social life, I could not understand the hesitation in her face, for every parent wants whatever is best for their child--don't they? But there was a sudden clarity within me, and I understood that, despite a parent's love and the expectation--that every child will grow up and take its own place in the world--there was both a hint of selfishness and possessiveness within Mother's face and I knew that she dreaded the day I would leave.

I asked Mr. Merriman what kind of work he did, and he answered that he was now the chief financial officer for the Murphy Salmon Company. "I received a degree in accounting from Norberg University," he smiled, "and I've since earned my master's degree in business from Northwestern." Jim was tall and nice looking, dressed like his title at the Company, and was obviously articulate and bright. But even in that short conversation, I couldn't help but wondering why he had moved to a place like Stella's Cove. Except for a few widows, like my mother, it was certainly not a place where a man would likely find romance, and the town's isolation would not be pleasing for most sharp, single, men. Then, as a sort of obligatory afterthought, Mr. Merriman asked, "Billy, do you like fishing?" Before I could answer, he'd added, "I'd like to take you sometime." Inside me, there was a sudden feeling of nausea; it was like someone had grabbed hold of my intestines and given them a hard twist. I hoped that he could not see it on my face, but angry words rose inside me. "How dare you!" I thought, "You could never be my dad, so don't try."

"We're planning a picnic Saturday afternoon, up near the glacier," Mother mentioned, as if in passing, "and you're welcome to join us." I could see muted disappointment on Mr. Merriman's face, and I assumed I was not as welcome to share their picnic as Mother was anticipating. Not wanting to be a nuisance, I mentioned that I would be working at the Murphy home, doing my usual gardening and maintenance chores. "Thanks for the invitation," I said apologetically, "but I won't be finished until about six that evening." Mother looked genuinely disappointed, but I detected relief in Merriman's face.

Saturday came, and I set off, as usual, for the Murphy home. Usually George himself met me near the dock with his pony cart, or, later, the Reo R-5. It saved me a two mile walk each direction, so I was always appreciative to find him or Norwood predictably waiting at our usual rendezvous. I peered down the path that led to Point Fay. I saw no pony cart trotting in my direction, nor was there an automobile in sight, and a quick walk around the center of town failed to disclose the whereabouts of my waiting ride. Understanding that this would cut into my work time, I picked up a strong pace and headed toward the Point.

Upon arrival, Eva Murphy met me at the door, explaining that George's uncle in Vancouver had passed away, and that George hastily sailed on the Bountiful that morning, after asking her to notify the appropriate people. "I'm sorry," said Eva, "but I should have gotten you the message. With all the commotion and haste, I totally forgot. I am so sorry."

"Well, do you know what chores George wanted done?" I inquired, and there was an embarrassed look on her face. Trying my best not to put her on the spot, I suggested, "I can still do a few hours of work, if you know what he had planned for me."

Eva Murphy seemed distracted, but she told me that I could trim the hedge that ran along the western border of their property, adding that she didn't know of anything else that needed attention. I walked to the shed behind the house, feeling disappointed that I would only earn, perhaps, one hour of wages. Most Saturdays, there were plenty of tasks to perform, and I usually ended up with a good four hours of work, or more. The hedge shears were hanging in their usual spot, and I took the time to adjust the blade tension screw and to use the bastard file to remove a few burrs from its cutting edges.

The west hedge served a number of useful functions. Besides its obvious use as a landscape feature, it was an effective impediment to the sometimes-brisk breezes that swept over the rocky point; helped lock down the top soil which had been hauled all the way from the edge of the forest; and, on those days when the waves exploded into an airborne spray, it helped to keep salt off the windows and walls of the Murphy home. I took two, long, pine dowels and used the shorter of two sledgehammers to drive them firmly into the grass at the hedge's ends. I grabbed a ball of cord, paid it out, and tied a taut line to the dowels in order to gauge the proper trim height, then proceeded to clip.

Every eight or ten feet, I did a sighting down the hedge's flat top to make sure I didn't missed a stray. I suppose I could have made the job take much longer in order to earn more money, but there was something of an oxymoron in extending the time it took to do the job in order "earn more." George had given me a great part-time job, and I knew that "spending more time" and the concept of "earning" were not at all the same. When he'd hired me, I'd vowed to never let him down, so, despite the absence of other chores, I worked efficiently and fast, raked the trimmings from the grass, dumped them from the Murphy's wheelbarrow into the burning pit, and put the tools away.

I pulled the Hamilton 940 Pocket Watch from my pocket, and noted the time. It was only two o'clock. The Murphys had given me that watch the previous Christmas, and it was an unexpected and particularly generous surprise. I nearly gasped when George presented it to me, and I knew from Harvey Spoon, the harbormaster, that it was considered the best timepiece then available. It was 14 carat gold-filled, had the railroad-certified 21-jewel movement, which was visible through a secondary glass cover, and I noticed, when I first turned it over to look inside its case, that the back was inscribed, "Time Waits for No Man." The Hamilton served my purposes and the Murphys—though a lesser one would have been more than adequate--making sure that I was available at the appointed times and that there would be an accurate accounting for my work hours.

Disappointed that there were no more chores to be done, I considered simply leaving. But, pressed by my ambition, I knocked on the Murphys' front door, hoping that Mrs. Murphy would come up with some other tasks that needed to be done.

It was Celeste who answered, and, it so surprised me, that I found myself temporarily mute. She stood there with an unmistakable look of innocence, her gingham skirt draping her slim frame, and a smiling pair of eyes which saw through my surprise. The fantasies I'd had, when she was far away, were nowhere to be found, and her presence caused an immediate smile to erupt from my frustrated frame of mind. "Hi, Billy." she spoke. "Mother wasn't feeling her best, so she went upstairs to take a nap."

"Did she mention any other chores for me?" I asked, noting that Celeste was growing prettier by the day, but she had no more information than I. "See you at school," she smiled, and there was a gentle connection as we glanced into each other's eyes. "Yes," I stammered slightly as I spoke it. "I'll see y-yuh at school on Monday."

I walked home a bit more slowly than my outbound pace, checking my pocket watch when I passed the town dock. Just before three o'clock, I arrived at my front door, opened it, and walked inside. Mr. Merriman was sitting in the recliner now, and Mother was kneeling on the floor, facing him. It was clear that no one anticipated my early return, and Mother's head bobbed up and down several times before she realized that I was there. Merriman was gasping as if in pain, and I assumed from his very devout-sounding "Oh, God" that he was at least as religious as my mother. Two distinctly different phenomena came over me at the exact same time. I could feel the rhythmic punctuation of my heartbeat, flushing my face with instant rouge, and, at the same time, I could feel the color of cheer being drained from my whole being.

As I closed the door and walked back toward the dock, I reeled in shock. A bunch of confusing feelings hit me all at once. I loathed Merriman, who was obviously a predatory and opportunistic degenerate; I was intensely jealous and angry over Mother's intimacy; I was thoroughly disgusted over what I'd witnessed; and I felt myself holding my breath, for just a moment, as I thought of the salacious scene that had taken me, oh, so by surprise. All my life Mother had been the flag bearer of piety, and her prudish ranting, particularly about chastity, was a constant theme from my earliest memories.

As I sat down at the water's edge, it occurred to me that Mother's repetitive quotations of scripture and her citations of God's wrathful words may have been rooted in the fears of her own prurient interests. She had told me many times, "The devil is out to get us." And I realized--at about the same time puberty hit me--that it was our own natural inclinations and instincts that often put people at risk. "Who needs a devil to trip us up?" I'd once asked her, and all she could say was, "He's real son. He's real. You need to get down on your knees and acknowledge your savior." And the flip side of the equation was the dubious need of a god to save us from ourselves. I considered that salvation was about dealing with our own physical and emotional needs in a healthy manner that promoted a happy and cooperative existence within our world.

Still, the shock over what I'd just seen was dissipating very slowly. It wasn't that I never heard of such activities. Half the boy-talk at school was about sex, and I knew that there were lots of variations in the ways that men and women pleased each other. I was disturbed for the next several days, and Mother tried to go on like nothing had really happened. But each time I remembered the recliner's delivery to our home from the Aniak's deck and saw it sitting in our living room, there was a momentary flash of an upsetting memory that I could never seem to totally suppress.

Today, the recliner still sits in Mother's small living room, and though it has served for the past few years as a sanctuary of relative security, it has become a symbol of disappointment and failure, rather than the reminder of a brighter time. Since the Salmon processing plant and the electricity are gone, the brilliant electric lights have been replaced by those old oil lamps that were retained for emergencies long after the hydroelectric plant was completed; the perforated, white toilet paper has disappeared from the outhouse walls, replaced by the mail order catalogue pages which served their correct and intended purpose for only one, short window in time; the Scottish single malts have vanished into the oblivion and stupors of an entire community drinking the cheapest whisky; and education, despite Miss Hardwicke's short but dynamic tenure, has returned to the mediocre responsibility of a now-under-funded Methodist congregation. One hopes, in life, that progress will be forever forward, but that has not been true of Stella's Cove.

I can look back at the fearful despair of an entire town. It has haunted our home since that black night, when Mr. Barnhardt ran through the Cove, yelling that the plant was on fire. The entire community instantly erupted into the darkness, in a dreadful unison, lit only by kerosene lanterns, and walked the three miles to the plant site. Like a long funeral procession, the flickering line snaked across the sleeping shore and halted only at the still-flaming burial ground. And, when the people of Stella's Cove stood there, stunned, at the edge of Murphy's vaporized dream— ashes and embers alighting on the mourners from a starless sky--

no one questioned who had struck the match. The bounty of the preceding dozen-or-so good years vanished in that instant, for, when the Murphy Salmon Company processing plant was gone, most of the adult population was left without jobs. Superstition continued, tenaciously, to rule the town, and the people searched the realms between God and the devil to explain the tragedy that so suddenly and summarily destroyed the hopes of Stella's Cove.

When the last smoke vanished into the callous gray of the sky, and the only remaining truss of the Murphy Salmon Company tumbled into the pile of rubble below, only a few of the pious townsfolk were able to admit to themselves that there was a certain poetic justice in the loss of the plant and the ensuing, crushing blow to the local economy. For the others, there was an immediate accusation that the glacier's curse was responsible for the tragedy--one from which the town would likely never recover.

I have always found it a bit strange that the glacier can be seen, by anyone, as the cause of a town's distress. It has been my opinion for many years, that the glacier can do nothing wrong. Unlike my mother and the other fanatic zealots that have dominated Stella's Cove, I understand the glacier is simply the naturally occurring phenomenon of time, energy, and climatic change working together. The glacier does not have a causal relationship with the bad fortune of my town. The reality is that the glacier is not a "cause" of anything. By itself it does nothing, for it, too, is a consequence—not a cause. Despite its slow, grinding progress toward the sea, and an occasional calving of its advancing spires--something that it does, indeed, do with sporadic irregularity--it is moved by the force of natural principles, gravity and nothing else.

The idea that the Gavins Glacier has a black heart is patently ridiculous to me, and falls into the same category as the claims that the sea has swallowed yet another human. Why can't people just say, "He drowned," or "He fell while walking on the glacier's slippery and unpredictable surface?" While the sea has its own kind of movement, and is certainly more "alive" than a glacier, it is only those who challenge its danger--intentionally or accidentally--who are at risk; and to create a monster of nature's gems is, in itself, a sacrilege to any concept of a superior being.

I find it curious--and perhaps inexplicable--how a community of today can possess such a dichotomous set of beliefs. On one hand, the mostly Methodist population of our town has the teachings of Christianity, with its claim that God has power over all things. But there is also a hint of the native religions and the legends of the Tlingits, which acknowledge that the earth has a power of its own, and that its spirit encompasses the sacredness of its rivers and mountains.

Though it was never intended, and probably has never been noticed by anyone else, somewhere in time there has been a merger of beliefs, and the glacier is thought to be endowed with powers beyond all scientific explanations of its creation and existence--a concept contrary to Biblical references. Like the god and devil that continually vie for the control of souls, the glacier is regarded as a force that seeks to destroy the Town.

For me, superstition has died, and religion is merely a lingering, antagonistic challenge to reason. Since ice, elevation, and gravity control the Gavins Glacier--a simple fact established by the meticulous probing of science--then "God" possesses ice, elevation, and gravity and is responsible for it all. Likewise, if the devil possesses power over these physical principles, I guess Satan, instead, is the glacier's real boss.

Despite my firm belief in science, my superstitious and religious childhood has occasionally shown itself--times at which, for just one moment, I've regressed to describe the glacier, like the monstrous mass that she is. "Her mouth has spewed an endless series of curses as she continues her icy tirade, powered by her years of pent-up frustration, and exacerbated by the constant grinding of her body against the rocky canyon that descends the coastal mountains toward the West." One doesn't have to be superstitious to see the truth in that statement, and yet it is almost contradictory for me to take things as scientific as the potential between elevations and use human qualities to describe them. For me the glacier is only a metaphor, but, for many others, it is the reality of evil.

Exploration has shown that the glacier begins over twenty-two miles up the canyon, and that, at its thickest point, the surface exposed to the sky is over eight-hundred feet above the bedrock of the canyon that it has so continuously chiseled and ground. Pressed by the mass behind it, the glacier has used brute force to create its channel to the sea, shearing through rock much older than Adam, and releasing the fossilized creatures of ancient seas. That's what the scientists say, and I believe it, because they can provide evidence supporting their claims. And they can prove that the same forces that have controlled it for centuries are still at work today.

The Glacier's Grip

Whatever disagreement there was on how many birthdays the glacier's bluish glow had celebrated, it certainly blocked, both the possibilities of entry from, or escape to, the East. With the presence of a relentless sea to the west, it was both the glacier and the sometimes-erratic steamboat service that dictated the captivity of the townsfolk. The Gavins Glacier was the most imposing, single factor which both protected and isolated the community, and many of the residents wondered how things might have been if there had been some easy way to reach their town.

While Couple's Ford was only thirty-nine miles from Stella's Cove, and Casey's Bend, a sizable town, was less than sixty, those distances were "as the bird flies" and negotiating the difficult trails could nearly triple the distances. For the people of Stella's Cove those towns might as well have been on the moon. The glacier blocked the gentle valley which rose to the top of the coastal mountains, and surely a road would have been cut through those mountains, were it not for the defiance of the icy glacial mass.

In order for a traveler to skirt the glacier, traveling eastbound meant climbing and hiking the dangerous granite ridges left by the glacier's advance, summiting Garden Pass, which noticeably notched the highest peak, and then descending the tedious and dangerous trails that switch-backed down the eastern side of the mountain. Both Couple's Ford and Casey's Bend lay in fertile valleys on the eastern side, where the Nepachou River meandered through a rich layer of loam. It was some of BC's best farm country, creating the heaven of good soil and a long growing season during its enviable summers, but those places were miserable, sunless iceboxes during the winter months, when Stella's Cove enjoyed the temperate benefit of the sea. Considering the disadvantages, both Couple's Ford and Casey's Bend were blessed with fairly steady economic success, which had persisted over the past hundred years, and there was no question in anyone's mind that it was only the glacier and the sea that retained Stella's Cove's frustrated population.

In the early days, trappers and miners tried to develop a safer way to reach B.C.'s interior. A miner named Ben Gilford envisioned a convenient overland route, and put up the money, with the understanding that the eventual road would be named after him. He was among the original placer miners that quickly followed discovery of gold by the ex-trapper known as Reverend Fox, and Gilford's success made him one of the wealthiest men along the coast. His uncanny luck in finding gold turned out to be much better than his ability to implement the Gilford Road. It was poorly planned, badly engineered, and it attempted to traverse areas that were inherently dangerous and unstable.

Any geologist would have known that the project was doomed, but Gilford, despite numerous initial setbacks, pressed on. After years of blasting and digging, the project ended when an avalanche swept away over a mile of the partially finished roadway. Four workers died when the mountain collapsed from above, and Ben Gilford wisely gave up the fame which would have surely come from the road's successful completion. After consulting with geologists and cartographers, he realized that the project was a miserable mistake, and he withdrew any further financial support. The residents of Stella's Cove considered the dismal failure to be just another example of the glacier's curse, for it was the glacier's undermining influence that brought the project to its end.

The advice of Stella's Cove's residents was all the same: "Look! Don't touch." Stories of the glacier's treachery abounded like sap oozing from summer pines. One was the account of three

Italian climbers from Turin, who had headed up the glacier's icy slope for a two-week climb.

Giuseppe San Giacomo, Rodolpho DiVecchio, and Henri Baccini bragged to the press, the night before they boarded a ship to New York, that the tales of risk relating to the Gavins Glacier were far overstated by the people of British Columbia. "The Canadians have a way of exaggerating everything," San Giacomo told the young reporter in his native Italian. "Frankly, I suspect that their bragging arises from some sort of insecurity, and the understanding that they're a second-rate people in a second-rate land."

"Don't you think such a statement is a bit extreme?" blushed the reporter, and San Giacomo simply rolled his eyes. "There's nothing so special about the Gavins Glacier. Along with my team, I am going to show all the world that, for true experts with the right equipment, it's a cake-walk. It is only the incompetence of the Canadians that has caused so many deaths and left the challenge of traveling the glacier's length for yet another day. We will conquer," boasted San Giacomo, "the full length of her icy flow, and we'll complete the climb in less than two weeks, including the ascent to Garden Pass from the cirque where the glacier begins, and down the rugged ridgeline that runs along the south side of the Glacier and ends up at Stella's Cove."

The colorful trio arrived on the Aniak in 1903, and the scene they saw before them created a stir of excitement. None of them had ever seen such a site, for there stood the mighty glacier they'd come eight-thousand miles to explore and conquer, and each thought the imposing sapphire-blue ice to be the most beautiful thing they had ever seen.

The glaciers in Europe and the ones they'd climbed in the Karakorum and Himalayan ranges of Pakistan, had been a different color, and, because of climatological differences which influenced the calving and the manner in which crevasses developed, the others were much more stable than the one which they now saw, braced against the coastal mountains to the east.

All three were experienced climbers, and were credited with the first ascents of some of Europe's greatest and most challenging peaks. Stella's Cove was full of excitement when the steamboat arrived, because the Italians had been widely heralded by the Provincial Press, and their arrival was preceded by a series of stories on the trio's previous climbing triumphs. Among their ascents were the Jungfrau and the Monch in the Bernese Alps, and they had successfully negotiated the treacherous Aletsch Glacier which was the largest in Europe. Surely, if it was possible to follow the full length of the Gavins Glacier, this team had the experience to do it.

What the newspapers failed to note, and had been purposefully omitted from the publicity, was the fact that the group started out eight years before with six climbers. While attempting a climb of the North Face of the Eiger, which was known to Europeans as the "Mordwand—translated "murderous wall"--a small slide ripped out the pitons that provided safety for the last three climbers. It was only because the lead climbers had just driven a malleable iron piton into a deep crack in the rock above, which saved them from death. The three climbers below the yanked-out aids fell over sixty feet, and though they did not plummet to the valley below and were still roped to the pitons beyond those that had failed, they all struck a lip of rock that extended for about thirty feet across the pitch. None of the three lived.

Giuseppe San Giacomo, Rodolpho DiVecchio, and Henri Baccini were the lead climbers in the team, and, failing to successfully summit, they collected their dead comrades as they descended,, lowering the bodies with their ropes until they reached the forest below. It was a disturbing sight for the people of Grindelwald, as the bloodied bodies were carried into town, and those who saw it understood that such tragedies had occurred before, and that the future of the Eiger would continue to be one of death.

Though, at the time of the Italian's attempt of the conquest of Gavins Glacier, I was only seven years old, Mother and Father shared their accounts of the grand event they'd beheld--standing on the dock when the steamship docked and clapping with the scores of well-wishers who were anticipating that moment. It was probably the largest gathering the town had ever seen, for as many as half of its residents were there on the dock that day, waiting for the celebrities to arrive.

I can vaguely remember being there, but it was mostly my parents' memories of the details that I relied upon. After the Italians walked down the gangway and shook hands with several of the townsfolk, Stella's Cove's Mayor, Damon Sculp conducted a small official ceremony and gave the Italians a symbolic key to the Town. Acting as a spokesman, Signor San Giacomo expressed appreciation for the fine welcome. In a typical, mellifluous Italian delivery, he acknowledged the honors: "Siamo molto onorati dalla vostra accoglienza a Cove di Stella, e apprezziamo la chiava per la vostra citta."

Though they could not understand, both Mother and Father noted that "When Giacomo spoke, it sounded like beautiful poetry. There was something so musical about it." But no one prepared the Mayor for the embarrassing realization that the three climbers spoke only Italian, and there was no one in the community who could translate what was said.

Several Tlingit Indians shook their heads. Despite some rudimentary fluency in Queen Victoria's English, the Tlingits looked at each other with expressions that read, "What?" on their faces, and they wondered about this strange language they had never before heard.

Mayor Sculp, in response to Giacomo's words, turned toward the crowd of people that had gathered, rolled his eyes, and exclaimed, "These bastards don't speak any English." The Mayor's statement was not entirely correct.

Signor Baccini immediately and indignantly responded, "Speak I some English and no like you." A reporter, who'd arrived with them on the Aniak, frantically scribbled some notes on a clipboard, said "Goodbye," and hopped back on the steamboat as it prepared to depart. The reporter definitely had the scoop on a shocking story--one that would confirm outsider's ideas that Stella's Cove was a backward place, full of carryovers from the times when "squaw men" settled the area. In fact, the headlines of the Mayor's words were on the first page of the very next Provincial News. It was a faux pas that all of Canada would remember, and something that cast a derogatory image on the people of our town.

Indignant, the Italians stomped away from the welcoming party, and it was believed that none of them ever spoke a word to the Mayor again. Mother and Father swore that they personally saw Signor San Giacomo hurling the ceremonial key into the harbor, and that he raised his finger toward the Mayor in total outrage.

Because there was no real hotel in Stella's Cove, Bart Clemmerton, Sr. invited the Italians to spend the night at his home. Back then, our town was, more-or-less a dry one, and was not used to such partying, but the Italians, even after the fiasco of their welcome, were savoring their last night with the comforts of a home, and they drank and sang until three in the morning. Clemmerton drank with them until 2:00 a.m., but then he excused himself, trying to convey his reason for leaving his guests. There was some basic recognition of the fact that Clemmerton needed to be at his bakery in just another few hours. No one knew, for sure, just how late the Italians partied, but Clemmerton, in his casual inventory of his home's liquor supply, calculated that each of them had drunk over a bottle of whisky.

There were no early "Buon giorno's" and the hung-over climbers did not wake until noon. They did a final check of their packs and equipment, left a brief thank you note for the Clemmerton's hospitality, and trekked the first two miles, setting up camp at the foot of the glacier before spending their first night in the wilds.

On the morning of day number-two, several of the townsfolk hiked to the glacier to see the Italians' first assault on its face. Just one minute after 10:00 a.m., San Giacomo turned to the enthusiastic onlookers and saluted. The spectators held their breath to see what would happen, but the assent seemed almost disappointing to the small crowd. They were expecting something much more exciting and grand, but what they saw was simply the methodical placement of feet, ropes, ice axes, and pitons.

San Giacomo led the way, carefully hammering pitons into the blue ice, and clipping his carabineers into the eyes as he forged his way slowly up the vertical pitch. Besides their custom-made boots, each climber wore sharpened crampons with multiple points coming from the toes, and their ice axes drove several inches into the ice on each swing. A few of the spectators looked at each other, thinking, "Oh! That's a piece of cake. With that kind of equipment, I could do it too!" For, before they saw it with their own eyes, they were unable to imagine how anyone could climb the vertical towers of the glacier's face. Now they understood.

All three climbers reached the top without any unnerving event, and the people below provided the obligatory applause. When the climbers were no longer in view, the residents stayed for a short time, eventually realizing that there would be nothing more to see, and they went to their homes, relating to their families, in front of their cast iron stoves, the amazing feat they'd witnessed. With pride in their levels of knowledge, the spectators recounted to others the details of the event and the equipment that was used, and each of them suddenly became an expert on the unique custom boots from the factory in Milano, the special ropes that were both braided and twisted with multiple strands, and the razor-sharp points on the steel crampons the trio used. Others, who had not been there, were very impressed with the details, yet the truth was that the eyewitnesses were extremely underwhelmed.

On day, number three, there was no sighting of the climbers. Ed Yeates, climbed about a mile up the south ridgeline, and though he was able to see the glacier's crevassed surface for a dozen miles or so, and was assisted in his search by a large brass telescope, he failed to locate the three Italians. What he saw in its lens was nothing but the glacier's soiled surface in its inching progress toward the sea.

That evening, the cloud cover draped the mountains and the Cove, and it would be six days before anyone saw the sun again. My mother felt concern about the welfare of the climbers, but Father was on a voyage to harvest more fish from the sea. He had not been able to be there to see the questions in the eyes of the Stella's Cove townsfolk, nor could he know that a haunting silence poured over the glacier.

After ten days, and as was largely anticipated by the waiting residents, there was no triumphant parade of the climbers down the town's main lane, and there was no word of the climber's whereabouts. Since there was no communication, and the employment of "runners" was inadvisable, the people of Stella's Cove went about their normal activities, but most were unconsciously holding their breaths. For, the glacier had not been good to anyone they knew, and virtually all close contacts with her ended up in either frustration or tragedy.

On day, number fourteen, several people gathered at the head of Muir Creek. They squinted and peered into the morning sun as it created a halo over Garden Pass, and they watched the south ridge of the glacial valley for any signs of life. After three more days, the people of Stella's Cove ceased their trips to the glacier and no longer held their breaths. It was a foregone conclusion to most. The community simply accepted that the fate of the climbers was the same as so many others--swallowed by the merciless beast that forever ruled their town.

Winter came and the blue was covered by the deep coastal snows that pounded the higher elevations. As Mother sat by the stove, knitting a gray sweater for me, she sighed briefly and declared, "It's official now. The Provincial Press has reported that the Italians are surely dead, and that no rescue party will attempt to find them." I did not need that announcement, for I understood that no one could survive that long, even in the best of weather conditions, and it was patently ridiculous to think that the Italians would ever emerge from what had surely become their icy tomb.

Except for a broad, wool mountaineer's hat found in Muir Creek's spring runoff, the Italians simply disappeared. And there would never be an account of their final moments, for no one could ever know.

––––––––

There was also the story of Amos Johnston and Ivy Klaut, two locals who, with a blanket, a loaf of pumpernickel bread and a bottle of whiskey, had climbed the rocky ridge adjoining the south side of the glacier. It was a fine summer day, and the pair successfully made it out to a flat area behind the glacier's face. A miner found their bodies below, bloody, broken, and dead. It happened when Father was still alive, and he expressed compassion for their untimely deaths, but Mother seemed unable to muster any sadness over the tragedy.

Amos and Ivy were found naked, and it was a reasonable assumption that their relationship was more than friendly. "They got what they deserved." Mother said matter-of-factly, but she did not elaborate on their supposed sin. I had never seen either of the pair in church, so I kind-of assumed, in my early naïveté, that Mother was right. Father was angry at Mother's words, and it was one of the few times I'd seen him raise his voice. "Damn it," he'd shouted with an indignant tone, "They were just kids, and nobody deserves to go like that."

Mother bristled when Father said it, for she was considering the influence of a father on a growing boy, and she feared that he would lead me away to the realms of the unbelievers. From my youngest memories, I was always aware of my parents' marked disparity on the issue of religion, but there was little open friction--just an occasional discussion in which each would make a philosophical argument for their points of view. It was clear that Mother considered religious belief to be an endorsement of a person's goodness, and that she assumed the irreligious had cornered the market on sin. Dad was the ultimate agnostic, seeing no reason to believe, and he viewed religions as a danger in the world. "History," he once remarked, "is full of examples of people who did bad things in the name of "God."

Despite the background religious dissonance that was always there, there were only a few times when unbridled anger shook our home, and the Amos and Ivy incident was one of them. I could still sense that Mother and Father were displeased with each other when we sat down for supper that evening. While most of their discussions were peaceful and reasonable, Mother's avowed commitment--to save me from becoming an unbeliever-- was always a passionate one. What she didn't realize was that it was already too late.

Though, at first, I had truly wanted to believe, largely out of my need to belong, and for the kudos that were showered on young believers by their doting parents and minister, it was something that did not come naturally for me. Though I held to certain ideas out of habit, my conscious moments were not those of a believer, and the arguments of science and reason provided no bridge over which I could return. By the age of thirteen, I had seen religion being used as the yardstick for judging the value of people. I noticed, too, that the worst kids I knew at school seemed to come from the most pious parents.

The Terrible Mrs. Crump

As Celeste and I walk along the dock toward Mother's house, I'm thinking about Old Mrs. Crump. She's been there through the best and worst times of Stella's Cove, and like Rev. Harry Mills and Kimberly Hardwicke before their deaths, she too had been an outcast in the community and certainly not welcome at the Methodist Church. Somewhere, back in time, Anna Crump was a loving wife and a doting mother. But life was not good to her, and her previously bright countenance transformed into a permanent scowl. The sweet girl redeemed by Henry Crump from the whorehouse was now nicknamed the "witch."

Old Mrs. Crump has been our neighbor ever since I can remember, her unkindness as incessant as the bad breath that launched from her mouth in those moments when, confronted by the demands of courtesy, she strained to say "Good Morning." Although it was necessary to pass her house on my way to school, I always skirted it widely, walking over the rocky shoreline of the Cove; the margin which, when added to the expanses of sea, always separated our town from the rest of the world.

Now that shoreline has become the dividing line between Stella's Cove and the world of the living. There are no new residents in Stella's Cove, for there is no opportunity here, and most of the children, believing in themselves and in a future, left when they were old enough to do so.

The thought of Mrs. Crump is disturbing to me, both because her behavior over the years, has been so bad, and because I accidentally discovered that, despite her coarse and calloused exterior, there actually was both a heart and feelings somewhere deep inside her. Of course, I'm not even sure that Mrs. Crump is still alive. She seemed old, even when I was a kid, and it is only the absence of the mention of her death that makes me fairly certain that her spying, foul mouth, and unpleasant stare are still part of the setting of my childhood home.

Mrs. Crump possessed no obvious interest in humanity, or, at least that was my juvenile perception of her pronounced mean streak. Like so many other old folks, she was damaged by the insistence of reality's harshness and the toils and miseries that kill the dreams of youth and steal the aspirations of life.

There was no question that, whatever the misery of her story, Mrs. Crump abandoned any gentleness from the life she'd previously lived. Muir Creek rushed and rumbled just south of her little cottage, and its continuous frothing helped to mute the foul, angry words that somehow spontaneously erupted from her mouth as she hung her laundry each Saturday on the line outside her door. I personally witnessed many of her angry outbursts, which always seemed to be directed toward the darkness of our sky, and her actions imposed in the community, the belief that she was, at least moderately, insane

---

When I was young, the sky, so frequently masked by the dreariness of the coastal layer, reminded me of the inside of the Methodist Church. Like that blanket that persisted so insistently between the earth and the sun, there was always a barrier preventing God from being seen by the people in his church. With its tall steeple, sometimes seeming to pierce the drooping sky, the church was a grand structure. Despite the questions that perpetually pressed against my faith, it was an elegant offering to whatever, or whomever, sat above the clouds. When the organ was played and strains of hosannas rose from the choir, I'd feel a gentle buzz in my heart and mind as the emotions of beauty swept over me. The sensation was real, and I told my mother exactly what I had experienced.

Mother said that what I was feeling was the actual touch of the Holy Spirit. Later I understood that the feeling was replicated--without any modification--each time I saw our Maple Leaf flag; the moments when I saw Father place his hand around Mother's waist and kiss her lips with a reassuring promise of forever; or when I looked into the eyes of a girl I liked. I could have come to one of two conclusions. Either that sensation was the literal touching of the Holy Spirit--something Mother repeatedly assured me--or it was simply a physical phenomenon of an emotion all can experience when the right vision is placed before them.

Behind the choir, and separating the congregation from the bellows and pipes of the organ, was a curtain. It was made of a heavy, velvet fabric, creating a gray barrier that nicely mimicked the sky. From my earliest moments in that church I believed that God himself was behind it, watching us all silently as we worshiped in his house. There were many times I sat there quietly through a worship service, and silently asked the question: "Is He really there?" No matter how many times I considered it, or how many times I prayed that he'd show himself, God never appeared. I blamed myself for not having sufficient faith, and continued my supplications with an even greater fervor. When I asked Mother about it, she was upset. "God doesn't show himself just for the sake of satisfying a child's curiosity. In fact, he has told us, in the scriptures, that it is "a wicked and adulterous generation that seeks after a sign." Billy, I promise you: If you are faithful in following the commandments, you will someday be blessed with a perfect knowledge of Him."

Each Sunday service allowed me yet another frustrated chance to find that God was real, understanding that the mysterious being continued to watch me from his place of hiding. Though unproductive, my preoccupation kept me intrigued and saved me from having to pay attention to Rev. Cromwell's most repetitive and boring sermons.

Well before my father's death, I thought about the sky and about that velvet partition in the Church--how so many people naturally assume that, though unseen, the sun continues to shine above the clouds, and that God, without revealing himself, constantly monitors us from behind that curtain. A few times, I asked Mother why God was always hidden. "It is the faith in things not seen," she'd answer, "that helps our souls to grow."

When I reflect upon Mrs. Crump, I can't help but wonder if her early days of Church attendance were similar to mine. Did she experience the same tingling and gently burning sensations? And if so, why, after such moments of inspiration and faith, had such a permanent gloom swept over her life? Mother told me that Mrs. Crump had been a stalwart believer, but that she lost the two people she loved, many years ago, and had never been to a church service since.

My youth made it difficult for me to understand such a total surrender of hope, but, since my father's death, I have known the anger that the bereaved may direct toward the sky, and that there are conditions in life that can make our hopes an unbearable and questionable blessing. I have been lucky. I lost someone dear but I still find purpose in living, and I grieve for those who are mired in hopelessness and desolation.

The sun rarely had a glimpse of either the glacier or the town, because the prevailing Pacific winds brought an endless procession of dismal weather, and along with it, the continuously-beaten records of the previous year's whisky consumption. Mrs. Crump was almost always drunk and was always the leading contender for the red ribbon. My father and mother drank their share, and it would be fair to say that there were few adult residents of the town who were not at least mildly intoxicated on any given evening. "Seasonal Mood Disorder" was an epidemic in Stella's Cove, and there was no cure, because that same depressing season lasted all year round, except for those short periods in which the sun showed its face with a fleeting wink.

When Miss Hardwicke and Harry Mills were killed in the accident at the foot of the glacier, I was only seventeen, but I took a dollar of my earnings, from my part time job at the Murphy's, and plunked it down on the counter at Young's Mercantile. "A pint for my mother," I ordered, "she's just about out." Mr. Young did not hesitate nor question my purpose. He reached under the counter, producing a bottle of the same whisky I'd found behind the flour tin in our cupboard. If in fact Mother was running out, and would be there the next day buying more, she would appear to Mr. Young to be out of control, something I did not wish on her. Even worse, the consequence of Young's inadvertent revelation to Mother of my visit would likely make it hard to sit down for a week. She hid her quiet addiction carefully, and was not aware that I even knew about her nightly drinking. Only one thing was sure during that evening of shock and grieving: the bottle I bought was not for Mother.

She was furious the next morning, wondering where I'd been and noticing the greenish hue of my skin, which revealed my hangover. "You been with a girl?" she'd demanded, and I'd answered "No." "Well do you have an explanation for me?" Her tone was insistent, and I told her where I'd been, and confided in her the pain that I was suffering and how it demanded temporary relief.

When I revealed my whereabouts and poured out my

sorrow, there was a distant look of mutual understanding in Mother's eyes--one I'd seen only a few times before. But despite whatever empathy she felt in that moment she was not happy that I'd spent the night alone and drunk at the departed Harry Mill's cabin, and even less pleased in her understanding that I worshipped both him and Miss Hardwicke.

While Mother tried to avoid pronouncing a judgment on my two fallen friends, she had never been able to develop any trust in the defrocked minister, and she was verbally at odds with Miss Hardwicke's belief in evolution--an unforgivable affront to God.

I find myself looking back, considering the alcoholic majority of the town, and I feel bad for them, rising from their chairs and staggering to their doors as the Bourne River Temperance Society ladies knock. "We're from the Temperance Society," the two ladies would sing in unison, reeling backward from the powerful breath that enveloped their greeting, "and we're here to help you have a better life." The depressed-but-polite residents would slur their "Hellos," and then run to their back porches to hide their bottles, understanding that the inevitable ball peen hammers were next.

As Celeste and I paused, a few minutes before, at the top of the Aniak's gangplank, the memories began swirling in my head, and I couldn't help but remember Mrs. Crump on one particular day.

It was during the spring of my fourteenth year, well after Father's premature death, and the Saturday morning was an unusually mild one, with the coastal layer dissipating rapidly and the clouds retreating with the upper winds, first climbing the heavily timbered mountain and then rolling down the side we could not see. While the coastal cloud layer still vied for dominance over a determined sun, I noticed Mrs. Crump carrying a laundry basket through her front door. There was a hint of unsteadiness as she approached the clothesline, and I assumed that she'd already started on her quota of whisky for the day. She wore her usual smock and drew from its pocket the wooden clothespins for each damp garment. Occasionally one of the spring clips would pop off when the ears were pressed together, but none were ever left on the ground. For, though Mrs. Crump was the bookkeeper at the Murphy's Salmon Company and was making a substantial wage, she never wasted a thing. There was no question that sometime in her past there were periods of abject poverty, and her resourcefulness was a testimony to the hardships of an earlier time.

I watched her as she hung the garments to dry, and with total predictability one of those little metal clips parted from the clothespin, spinning into the damp morning air. As I witnessed this moment of frustration, it was obvious that either the clip had flipped itself far away or Mrs. Crump's eyesight was not so good. I pressed myself closer to the window, curious how this seemingly petty matter would end, and I believed that one of her angry outbursts would surely follow.

Next thing I knew, she set down her laundry basket and was on all fours searching for the missing part. After five minutes, she was still on her hands and knees. Her distress and frustration were obvious, and those few times, in which I'd been able to perceive a hint of humanity in her, prompted me to help. I watched until I could not bear it any longer, then opened our front door and stepped off the porch.

"Hello, Mrs. Crump, can I help you with that?" She turned from her search and gave me a sour look. "Don't you have anything better to do than watch me work? You need to mind your own business and find something more important to occupy your time." I glanced at the ground and immediately saw the clip. "It's right here, Mrs. Crump. Do you want me to put it together for you?"

"I'm not helpless," she scowled, grabbing the clip from my hand and reassembling the two wooden parts. I walked back to our house, noticing that she had hung only two items and still had two full baskets which needed to be hung.

When I looked once more, the two single clotheslines were completely full, looking like the storm flags that so often flapped over our harbor. Though our sea was usually calm, and the coastal islands provided the Cove a good deal of protection, there were times when the seas churned and fishermen turned quickly toward the harbor. When the wind changed and came blasting out of the East the storm flags flapped themselves into streaming tatters, and the flags had to be replaced at least once a year by Harvey Spoon as part of his Harbormaster responsibilities.

Having accomplished the purpose of her short visit to the yard, Mrs. Crump turned to go inside, letting out a litany of words, dominated by one in particular that preceded each other word of the vomitus series. Because that first word was so explosive, it stood out like the wart on a witch's nose, and I could not help but consider how I'd never before heard that word from someone so old. "Mrs. Crump," I thought to myself, "is a miserable person." Mother told me that miserable people choose to be that way, and that everyone decides, for themselves, the prevailing attitudes that govern their lives. When Mother offered those words of wisdom I couldn't help but reflect on them, for there was always a lingering, self-imposed misery that was an undeniable part of Mother's own life.

Though I greeted Mrs. Crump perfunctorily every time I was forced to cross her path, the strictly enforced manners taught me by my mother were my only reason for civility. I could not understand why we were so unlucky as to have someone so naturally unpleasant for a neighbor. Mother said it was just the luck of the draw, and that our home's previous owners probably died from the toxic cloud that constantly drifted from the Crump home. Father and I laughed when Mother said it, but it occurred to me that unpleasant people steal time and energy from everyone else's lives. After Father's death I was deficient on both accounts. I knew that I didn't have a surplus of either time or energy, so I protected what I had left.

I talked with Mrs. Crump only one more time after the clothespin incident, other than the routine and dutiful greetings I so insincerely proffered. And despite the frustrations and fears that were attendant to my second brief visit, that subsequent contact turned out to be a moment of human connection. The brief exchange revealed a closer look at Mrs. Crump--something very real, and an essential piece of the puzzle I was slowly completing about the scenery and reality of my own life.

It was a time of prolonged sadness for my Mother and I, for we had both been shocked and saddened over my father's untimely death, and I understand now that my sensitivities to the pain of others has grown from my loss. Far from the cluelessness of a child, I found myself projecting my own grief and pain on others, assuming that their suffering was not so different from my own.

My agnosticism was inconsistent with church activity, yet, understanding how important it was to Mother I still tried to please her with a minimal level of stoic, half-hearted participation. There was a church missionary fund drive, and I cringed at the careful instructions given by the youth minister to "not leave one house forgotten." With a town of only six-hundred residents at that time, Stella's Cove was carved up into sections, each of the teenage boys assigned a sector surrounding that kid's own home. Despite my belief, I prayed to God to vaporize the Crump home before I arrived, and I wanted to think that, if he was there, he would hear my prayer. After visiting the other homes on my assigned route, and collecting a surprisingly tidy sum of money, I was disappointed to find that the Crump home was still standing.

When I walked up the two stairs to Mrs. Crump's porch, I was almost overcome by a powerful instinct to run away. There was the gnawing reminder of her rough treatment of me that day beneath her clotheslines, but I held my ground and Mrs. Crump dutifully answered the door. For a moment I declined to look her in the eyes, and I couldn't understand how a strapping young man of my age could be so intimidated by the old lady next door.

"Good Morning, Mrs. Crump." I forced the words out, because the look on her face was not one of welcome, but of a pure and bitter contempt. I noticed an ash falling from the end of her cigarette as she spoke.

"What do you want?" she demanded, in the gruffest voice I'd ever heard. There was no greeting; there was no hint of a smile or a welcome; there was only a snarling anger for my relatively cheerful interruption of her miserable day. In light of her sour words in the past, I should have expected exactly what I was hearing, but I possessed a shakily-founded belief that her meanness was the product her isolation from the community, and that the kindness of a neighbor might, in time, bring her back to a world where there was love.

Transfixed for that moment by the fear I felt, I couldn't help but taking an inventory of the image that stood before me. Her square jaw cascaded in jowls which dragged over the collar of her floral smock, and her nose, which looked as if a bird had pecked at it too many times, hung down in such a manner that a sling might have been useful to keep it in its place. There were little sores that extended from her swollen nostrils all the way to her furrowed eyebrows, and I noticed that there was one single lock of hair that was black--a stark contrast to the gray that surrounded it. As I looked at her with a terror I supposed to be transparent, I could not help but stare at that nose, wondering why there was no wart, for her countenance was certainly that of a witch. Deep lines crisscrossed her cheeks and forehead, and her eyelids hung down it such a way that they mostly covered her deep-set, hazel eyes.

When I first looked into her face, I saw no light in those eyes--no look of hope or tomorrow--and her mouth, which I had never seen without a stogie, held its position firmly, with the corners pointing toward the floor. Now holding the spent remains of that unfiltered cigarette between them, her lips looked like the shrunken husks of rosehips that lost their blooms a century before. I'd heard that smoking changed a person's skin, so I assumed that the canyons of her cheeks and brow were caused by the emptying of the cigarette packs that littered her vestibule and the visible portion of her living room just beyond.

I noticed, too, that her pendulous breasts pressed against her smock, and that, even with the floral pattern of the flannel, her nipples cast their small shadows at the approximate area where her waist should have been. I suddenly understood the slang word, "knockers," and I visualized her gigantic breasts banging against her knees as she walked. That thought brought the faint hint of a smile to my face. This didn't create any greater endearment, and my elevated look seemed to aggravate Mrs. Crump. "What are you looking at?" she snarled.

She loomed over me with an expression that seemed to growl the unspoken words of the venomous mouthful she was just about to speak. "What's the matter?" she demanded, "Cat got your tongue? Or are you another Mongolian Idiot like the Blethers boy? I asked you to tell me what you want!" The unkindness, harsh edge, and, now the insult of her words, made it no easier for me to speak. (She was so unmercifully nasty that, for just a moment, I suspected she could somehow hear the derogatory thoughts that were flooding my brain.)

I stammered as I answered. "I'm collecting donations for the two missionaries the church sent to Uganda." As dutifully as she answered the door, she snarled, "So you can speak! Stay here for a moment, and I'll get something."

Her response actually left me dumbfounded, for I always regarded her as the "witch next door." Though Mrs. Crump's behavior was rude and abrupt, and though I could sense she was burdened with a less-than-winning hand in life, she was now showing some obvious regard for the shepherd's duty of gathering in the distant strays of the flock. Despite my total shock, I was able to squeeze out a few more words. "You will be helping the missionaries. You probably remember them--George Fillmore and Gary Senzee left for Africa two months ago."

"If it's for the missionaries," she grunted, "I'm glad to help out." My mind hung for a moment on the word "glad,". It was an emotion of which I believed her to be incapable. She walked to the back of the house, leaving a blunt order hanging in the doorway. "Stay right here," she barked, "Don't move." After a minute or so, Mrs. Crump reemerged and glumly placed a two-dollar note in my shaking hand.

"Thank you, Mrs. Crump." I said it with all sincerity, for my heart was touched by that momentary revelation of her humanity. Even with my temporary willingness to regard her as a human, I couldn't help but thinking, "Tomorrow she'll be back to normal!" But, as I turned to leave, there was just a single instant when our eyes met. I found myself looking into her sad, deep hazel eyes, not sure exactly what I was seeing, but I was aware of a momentary but powerful connection. I saw something there; it was not the emptiness I anticipated, and I understood in that poignant moment that her eyes were the mirror of my own heart, a heart filled with a sadness that would never really end.

That abrupt but meaningful contact with our lifetime neighbor softened me a bit, for I sensed that she lived with constant pain, suffering from irreparable tragedy in her past, and that the ugly side, which was so apparent, was the only window through which others could see the vague, distorted picture of her grief. It was like a revelation, for I suddenly grasped the concept that anger is simply the amplified voice of suffering.

Shortly after the missionary fund drive, I asked Denton Forsythe, one of our closest neighbors, what had happened to make Mrs. Crump so bitter. "You know," Denton answered, "there was a time when Mrs. Crump was both friendly and happy, but it all ended in one awful year. First she lost her husband in a fishing accident, and, six months later, little Cynthia drowned in Muir Creek. Everyone," Denton continued, "felt sorry for her, but she didn't want any pity, and she was so angry with Rev. Cromwell, she never went back to church." While I tried to imagine what kind of mother and wife Mrs. Crump had been, I couldn't help thinking how inside that exceptionally rough exterior and psychologically damaging snarl there was a human being, defending the only thing she had left: the involuntary continuation of her own existence and the merciless life-sentence of remaining in an overwhelming and constant grief.

———————

Though it was never discussed with my mother with any specificity, it was Mr. Forsythe who provided the terrible details. "Henry Crump died about twelve years before in a fishing accident near Kodiak Island, when a steam windlass chain crushed him between the boat and the Tanarik dock, leaving his wife and five-year-old daughter to a difficult survival in the Cove. Henry was known as a hard worker and was one of the most successful fishermen in Stella's Cove.

"You know," Forsythe continued, "Henry Crump was also practically a celebrity, for he was the only remaining resident from the town's earliest days, and his father, our town's first Methodist minister, had made a good business from the offer of salvation to the men who found success in trapping. Money flowed through the town, just like the water from Muir Creek." "Through" was the right word, for none of the money stayed.

"When the fur boom ended in Stella's Cove," he went on, "other residents left by sea with their families, but Rev. Crump simply told Henry, "Goodbye," leaving him behind when the Sunday donation plate collections dropped to near nothing at all." The story sounded cruel, and it was inconceivable to me how a father could have abandoned his own son. The story was not that simple, and Mr. Forsythe did a fine job of filling in the blanks.

"Henry had already established himself as an able fisherman, and built a reputation for his ambition and hard work. Though only fifteen at the time his father left him, he knew that he would be just fine on his own. His mother had passed away years before from the ague, and there was always a distinct abrasion between him and his father. Henry did not believe that his mother still lived, somewhere above the layered condensation that constantly blanketed the Cove, and he believed, almost without a doubt, that his father's only real interest in dispensing religion was the percentage of the offerings he hid, each Sunday, beneath the mattress of his bed. Though Henry hugged his father and wished him well, it was mostly ambivalence that Henry felt as the Aniak put back to sea.

"The position vacated by Rev. Crump as the Minister at the Methodist Church remained empty until Willis Fox, a placer miner, struck it rich. Through the ensuing mining boom, Henry continued to make a handsome living on his fishing, and, when the boom was over, he never went hungry.

"Henry's 60-foot ketch-rigged trawler was carefully painted with its name, the Cynthia C, and, at least when he wasn't at sea, his waking moments seemed to be consumed by his desire to provide his sweet daughter a good life.

"The Cynthia C was the envy of others who pursued the bounties of the B.C.'s coastal waters and the Alaskan Gulf. It was the largest craft in Stella's Cove, and, because of its range, Henry was able to go to sea for weeks at a time. His hauls of fish were huge, and, after selling a typical load in Eagle City, he still had plenty left for a little fish-monger business in the Cove.

"Before Henry's tragic death," Mr. Forsythe went on, "Mrs. Crump was the consummate loyal fish-wife, running the fish store for several years, and the success of the little business allowed the Crumps to afford a few luxuries, even when Cynthia was still a toddler. In fact, when the Murphy Electric Company initiated service to Stella's Cove in 1905, the Crumps were well enough off to afford a new Fisher electric washing machine. Theirs was the first in the community, but wouldn't be the last, as employment grew and money flowed. But there were problems in the Crump home," Forsythe noted, "and Mrs. Crump was the last to find out. Oh, yes, there were some clues about Henry's infidelity, but Mrs. Crump chose to ignore them or dismissed the gossip as the talk of jealous neighbors.

"Fitted with a small steam engine that ran the windlass and net spool, the relative state-of-the-art capabilities of the Cynthia C allowed Henry to bring back hefty hauls of salmon and to do it with a crew of only three. The trawler carried one additional passenger, a Miss Amanda Courser, who, it seemed, was Henry's mistress. She saw the tragic accident--that moment when steam power became an enemy instead of a friend. For good reason, she did not wish to return to Stella's Cove, but chose, instead, to put ashore at Moose Bay.

"At Henry's funeral, Rev. Miles Cromwell--who took over the ministry after the death of Rev. Willis Fox--gave a sermon on the wages of sin. Even at my, then, tender age, Cromwell's words were surprisingly abrasive, and I found myself angry about his pointing finger of guilt, understanding that it was compassion that should have dominated his words. Not so surprisingly, there were few others in the congregation who found that same offense in Cromwell's words. Only a handful seemed to be aware that his message was unsuitable for such an occasion. Without having actually said it, his funeral message was the equivalent of "It served him right!" A few, like my father, virtually gasped at the insensitivity of Cromwell's sermon, while a few others wondered in silence if such treatment was contrary to Jesus Christ's theme of forgiveness.

"Amanda never returned to Stella's Cove, but hired some workers to remove the furnishings and personal items from her home, load them onto the Aniak, and ship them to her new place in Moose Bay. Her very public departure and her failure to attend the funeral service was assumed to be an act of conscience in saving Mrs. Crump from the embarrassment of her presence and from the intimate last details of her husband's death.

"A plain envelope with no return address was delivered four days later to Henry's widow, containing a hundred-dollar bank note to help with the funeral arrangements and assist the family in its financial crisis, when the primary breadwinner was gone. There was a brief letter," explained Denton, "which accompanied the money. "Dear Anna, I understand there is no way to undo the tragedy of your loss or to erase the betrayal you have experienced. Henry was a good man, and I hope that you will be able to remember him in the kindest possible way. I know you will need this, so please consider it a respectable tribute to his memory."

"There was no signature on the letter, but Mrs. Crump understood that such a generous gift could not have been inspired by anything less than the curse of guilt. Unknown to Mrs. Crump, the Cynthia C had been willed to Miss Courser, who promptly assembled a crew and started her own successful fishing business, eventually building a fine home from the profits--a home Mrs. Crump believed should have been hers.

"Despite the anger she harbored against her dead husband and Miss Courser, Mrs. Crump remained a doting mother, while struggling to provide for her child. When Henry died, money was suddenly in short supply, and she took in washing to make ends meet. Known as a tireless worker, she continued to run the fish shop in town, but the business quickly became unprofitable. Without the catches of her man, and now totally dependent upon Henry's former competitors, the business simply died."

As I ponder the details of Mrs. Crump's tragedy, I know that the mistress's donation was at the same time, both kind and hurtful for Mrs. Crump had not been a fool. She knew that men of the sea could be as flighty as the winds pressing their boats toward the salmon rich seas of the Alaskan Gulf. While Henry searched for salmon and halibut, he obviously found other reasons for his extended voyages. But, as Mr. Forsythe went through his account of the tragedy, I couldn't help but wonder what kind of man would have willed his trawler to someone outside his family, depriving his own daughter of an asset of considerable worth. Despite my commitment to be non-judgmental, I cringed at that act as being Henry's greatest infidelity.

Mr. Forsythe added some more details: "Mrs. Crump, upon receiving the unidentified envelope, reportedly tore the hundred-dollar note into small bits and threw it into the iron stove. For, she was, even with Mr. Crump's death and the prospect of permanent poverty, too proud to take money from someone she considered her worst enemy.

"As if her husband's death was not a great enough tragedy," noted Mr. Forsythe, "while the earth was still settling around Henry's grave, Mrs. Crump was about to find out that the loss of a husband is not the greatest grief a woman can experience. Long before Rev. Cromwell's offensive words would fade, the Crump's daughter Cynthia, while attempting to retrieve a toy boat, was caught in the rushing torrent of Muir Creek. It happened when the spring runoff, paired with the accelerated glacial melt, frothed and boiled into a deadly maelstrom, sweeping her limp body into the quiet waters of the Cove."

Upon hearing of the last tragedy, my mother went over to extend a sympathetic condolence, but she arrived at an awkward time. The Crump's front door was open, and Cynthia was laid out on the dining room table, where Mrs. Crump was dressing her for the burial. Mother's account was ghastly. When she returned, her face was colorless, and she described what she had seen. There was no blood--only the hideous and hopeless bluish skin that seemed to mimic the eerie glacier's hold on the town and which now held Cynthia in the grasp of eternity. "The glacier's doing it again," Mother had exclaimed. "It's pure evil, I tell you." As young as I was at the time, I could not understand why the glacier was being blamed, but I knew that Muir Creek flowed from the Glacier's tongue, and that its raging waters were fully responsible for ending Cynthia's life.

"There was a small funeral," Mr. Forsythe concluded his account, "and all the town's adults paid their respects. The bereaved, widowed and childless Mrs. Crump loathed the idea of another funeral, but, understanding that her sweet daughter was owed that respect, she commenced with the funeral arrangements. Since there was only one minister in the town and there was no one else qualified to address the mourners, Reverend Miles Cromwell, who also doubled as the town's schoolmaster and only teacher, presided over the gathering. Even Ed Pickering, who was a stalwart of the congregation and dutifully sang in the choir each Sunday morning, choked at Cromwell's words, understanding that there was no man of God who could make such an insensitive and offensive statement to the crowd of mourners."

"Our dear little Cynthia," Rev. Cromwell labored "was so young, beautiful, and innocent. Understanding the wisdom of God, we must all consider this to be a great blessing, designed by his omniscient and omnipotent hand. It is through the mercy of our dear Lord that He has taken little Cynthia home to be with her Father in Heaven, and the angels are now rejoicing her return."

"There was no question that his words were eloquent, but, though Rev. Cromwell's words did, in fact, reflect the prevailing beliefs of the town, it was not the right thing to say in the presence of a woman who was already suffering terribly. Mrs. Crump's Henry had been taken from her, and the staggering loss of Cynthia caused her to silently rail against the God she had always believed in. Mrs. Crump understood the principle of "The Lord giveth and he taketh away" and she also fully appreciated that it had been disproportionately applied in her life. She asked herself over and over how God could have exacted such a price from her. Henry's widow actually held to her beliefs, even after his death, but the depiction of her daughter's tragic passing as a "blessing" caused her to explode.

"There was no one at the funeral who could have failed to notice Mrs. Crump's reaction to Cromwell's insensitive words, all the heads in the congregation turning toward her when the minister called Cynthia's death a "blessing." Their anticipation was immediately confirmed. Mrs. Crump's face went bright red, and her fists clenched like a prize-fighter getting ready for that final barrage of punches that would leave the opponent gasping on the mat. In a rage, she jumped up from her pew, the veins in her neck brightly distended. "You fucking bastard," she fumed aloud. "How can you think that this was God's will? ...and a blessing? What the hell were you thinking, you asshole? There's no blessing in being dead." Two of her friends, sitting next to her, immediately rose, held Mrs. Crump's arms, and attempted to sit her back down, but she wrenched herself free and wouldn't be silenced. "You fucking bastard!" she repeated, and Rev. Cromwell, without any hint of emotion in his face, announced. "That will conclude the funeral."

"Mrs. Crump struggled with the death of her husband and the unpleasant details of his last days, but," according to Mr. Forsythe, "she still faithfully attended her church services after Henry's death. Now, the words of the Rev. Cromwell would be the final straw. She would never again step into the Methodist Church."

No matter how justifiable her indignation and how accurate her angry assessment of Cromwell's words, I could appreciate that Mrs. Crump's patent rejection of religion was the beginning of a living death--because the church had been, for all practical purposes, the only contact she had with the town.

I can't help but think it was the social isolation that allowed such a complete festering of her wounded soul. She didn't believe in God any more. She could do without Him, and she could certainly do without the minister who so badly represented Him. But it was the loss of human contact that created the utter destruction of her life. She had lost Henry, lost Cynthia, lost God, lost friends. And she had lost the music of the church--so much a part of her joy in being alive. She had loved the organ and the performances of the church choir. But, the music also resounded with one sour note, because it was at choir practice that Henry Crump had gotten to know the darling and devout Amanda Courser.

No longer worshipping with the little flock at Cromwell's church, Mrs. Crump was regarded, because of her angry words at the funeral, to be a thankless wretch of a woman. George Murphy heard the story of her tragic losses, and despite warnings that she was a nasty old witch, hired her as the Murphy Salmon Company bookkeeper. It was a stopgap financial salvation after she'd been forced to shut down the fish stand, but her job—just like everyone else's--came to an abrupt end when the plant burned, and she had since stretched her government cheques, each month, to cover the slow suicide brought about by the sucking of stogies and the nightly whiskey that would someday do her in.

Collisions

"A dollar for your thoughts." Celeste winks as we walk past the dock's final piling. She's obviously getting more intent on knowing why I'm so quiet and so pensive. "Oh," I smile, noting that the new offer has exceeded the previously offered fish scale, "I see the price has gone up! Coming here is flooding me with memories," I respond. "I was recalling something about Mrs. Crump, our neighbor, and I was thinking about Dad and a big bass I hooked at the end of this same dock. The memories just keep pouring through my head."

"Well, at least they're good memories," she says with a smile, then releases a soto voce[2]"oops." There is no question that the mere mention of the past is a catalyst for reliving nightmares. We look at each other for a moment. It's clear that Celeste and I are thinking the same thought, but somehow we are successful in fighting the gravitational force tugging at our minds. The unshakable bad memories cling to the dark recesses of our consciousness, like a million bats in a Carolina Cave, yet we manage somehow to leave them there, hanging upside down in the blackness. Having conquered our inclination, we share a knowing smile and the subject is summarily dropped.

Suddenly I'm greeted by a friendly voice. "Hey. Aren't you Billy Potter, Delva Potter's son? My, you don't look anything like the little kid I remember." It is old Denton Forsythe. My face erupts instantly into a smile, for he is one of the bright lights of Stella's Cove. I have never heard anything but kindness come from his lips, and, despite his reservations about his neighbors, he has always been cheerful with everyone. He was in attendance at

---

[2] An Italian musical notation which means literally "under the voice."

the funerals of Miss Hardwicke and Harry Mills, and Mother had told me that it was he who crafted their coffins and did so without charge.

"Hello, Mr. Forsythe," I respectfully acknowledge, "You're looking a bit older yourself." Denton frowns when I've said it, and I can tell that he was expecting something much more flattering. I think for a moment and rephrase my reply. "You really don't age at all. You're looking great." Mr. Forsythe is now smiling. It's apparent to me that he prefers fiction to truth, and is very much a fan of imagination. But he is like so many others of the population, for there is more in Stella's Cove to remember than there is to look forward to, and most imaginable fiction is better than the reality of these times.

"Mr. Forsythe," I add, "may I present my fiancé Celeste Murphy?" Denton smiles broadly, turning slightly in order to look at Celeste, "It's nice to see you again." he acknowledges, "I remember you from when your father owned the salmon plant. How's he doing in Vancouver?"

"I'm so pleased to meet you," Celeste smiles, "Dad is quietly retired," she explains, "and he and Mother have been doing some traveling."

"I want to tell you," adds Denton, "George Murphy is a fine man. It is too bad that things happened the way they did. We all wish he hadn't closed everything down and left, but nobody can say he didn't have his reasons." Despite a hint of resentment in his last sentence, it is obvious that Mr. Forsythe is genuinely fond of George.

Five years before, Denton had been there at the dock, among a few well-wishers to send me off to college, but he looks a bit different today than when I left. His blonde hair is moving toward an anemic gray, and an obtrusive hank of the old yellow color circles his left ear. He is wearing the same dungarees I saw him in four years ago. I know they're the same ones; the left leg has an hourglass-shaped patch that looks exactly like Father's old corduroy jacket. After Father's death, Mother gave away all of Father's old clothes, and that little patch of corduroy is like a connection with the past. I give Mr. Forsythe a hug, noticing that the Aniak's crew is busy making preparations for its afternoon sail, and that the two geologists have progressed down the spit toward the Point Fay Bed and Breakfast. As they get further away, I am contemplating that theirs is a mission of great risk and probable pain, for their backpacks are loaded with climbing gear, and the climbing ropes fall in coils off their shoulders. There are crampons strapped to both their packs, clinking together like some badly forged brass bells from Luang Prabang, and each has an ice axe carefully strapped to the right side of this load. There is an ominous thought in my mind, for the men, particularly Mortimer, are no spring chickens, and I can't help but thinking they are biting off more than they can chew. I ponder their shrinking size as they continue towards The Point, and it occurs to me that what I'm looking at is an accident waiting to happen.

I believe I could have saved Mortimer and Ernest a great deal of money, simply betraying the fact that the poverty-stricken people of Stella's Cove would be happy to give them a room and meals for some unmentionably small sum, although I assume, because of the way they look at and brush up against each other, that they are seeking privacy in their accommodations and would not be happy in a somewhat-less-than-private room.

A moment later, the two geologists have completely vanished into a fog that is sweeping over the spit, and I wonder if, like the Italian climbers, I have seen the last of them. The Gavins Glacier has taken other lives, and the two men simply do not look rugged enough for the task of handling something so dangerous.

Over the years, many other scientists and scholars have come to Stella's Cove to study The Gavins Glacier. They've made their statements, how the glacier was born during a great Ice Age, and how it began its ever-sculpting advance to the sea about ten thousand years ago. There were others who said the glacier had been there for at least thirty thousand years, an assertion that cut against the general Christian belief that the world was created in six days and that everything on our planet was less than seven thousand years old.

The mention of such scientific theories always brought anger to my Mother's face, and I can remember, from years ago, her reaction to a newspaper article in the Provincial Press that presented a dateline of both the growth and the now-ongoing deterioration of Stella's Cove's blue crown. "It's a crock of shit," Mother barked, and I recoiled in shock. She was livid. "It's a sure thing--these scientists haven't read their Bibles--and they're going to be sorry in the next life." Use of such language was not Mother's typical practice, but the subject of science versus religion always made her furious, and most of her attitudes were the same as the more fundamentalist people of our town.

My reflections on Mother's anger end, and I now find myself thinking of something totally unrelated--the lingering concern that Mother will not be cordial with Celeste. After all, my leaving and absence were a disappointment to Mother, and the appearance of a fiancé will certainly give her a feeling that whatever was left of the apron strings is about to be cut.

When I left for the university in Seattle, I was aware of Mother's mixed feelings. She was happy to see me on the road toward success, but my education would leave her completely alone, something that seemed to correspond with her growing depression and drinking. I believed that Mother's abbreviated affair with Murphy's CFO was evidence that she hoped to build a fuller life that would persist when I was gone, and I ached inside that Mr. Merriman had not been the promise of a less lonely life for her. It was right for Mother to seek another human to spend time with, since a son can never be the man in a woman's life, and it was sad that Merriman turned out to be merely a fraud.

Mother's romance with Mr. Merriman ground to a stop almost immediately after the time I'd found the two together, at the leather recliner, in such a compromising position, but it was not because of my intrusion. Mother, like me, was able to put two and two together. The question of why a nice looking, middle-aged man would move to a place as obscure and isolated as Stella's Cove, was quickly answered, and any hope for a lasting relationship between Merriman and Mother died at the moment Mother confronted him. "You have a lot of nerve," she'd barked. "I will not see you again." And then she'd added, indignantly, "Married!"

Mother has told me many times that she is praying for a return of my religious beliefs, and I have told her, in the kindest way, that is not going to happen. Celeste is strongly agnostic, and she has come to seek her own answers from science, rather than from what she has referred to as "the fairy tales that hold mankind in ignorance." Despite her own non-belief, Celeste does have some friends who are devoutly religious, and she does not actively promote the abandonment of their beliefs. "I know that some people don't function well without the notion of a life that continues after death," she once noted to me during a quiet and philosophical moment between us, "but I can't allow the fear associated with dying to extort a belief in a God."

The infrequent but predictable flow of articles about the glacier always sent Mother into a maelstrom of vigilante words, particularly before I showed that I could not be intimidated into seeing things her way. But it was my own statement of belief--that the scientists are correct--that sent her completely over the top. "Lad," she'd once spewed, looking disturbed and indignant, like one who'd just been accused of her own illegitimacy, "you watch your mouth. Son. It isn't possible. Why, God created heaven and earth in six days, and even speaking in thousand-year-days, the earth hasn't reached Sunday yet." Mother's words were so impassioned, and her face such a pumped-up red, that I was alarmed about the threat to her health. I worried that her skin would be inadequate to contain the explosive powers that threatened to distribute her wrath over the ceilings and walls of our home.

"Settle down, Mother," I'd been able to say. As I'd gotten older, I understood that such an explosive anger could actually precipitate a heart attack or stroke, and my words were not intended as chiding but as my real concern over her life.

The occasional coarseness of her language still bothers me a bit today, but I understand how someone, uneducated, is likely to have unreasonable opinions, and she never even finished her high school education. It is one of those little peeves I've just had to accept, because the growing body of scientific knowledge only crystallized her naïve defenses, and she seemed to be getting even more inflexible with time.

There was something incongruous about Mother's attitudes. I am the first to admit that I don't know everything, and that, while scientists are learning more each day, they, too, find that some of the answers are elusive. When I was confronted with Mother's sometimes frenzied defenses, and I realized that I was also fighting my way through life, I had no trouble understanding why Mother clung so tenaciously to her Bible. For her, it was like the mariner's chart, guiding her through the rocks and reefs of an otherwise complicated life.

While her delusion seemed so complete to me, I'd have to agree that life has been mostly simple for her. She held all the answers in her hand, encased in a leather binding, and embossed with gold-leaf lettering. I realize that, from a strictly emotional standpoint, she may have been far ahead of me, but I would never have given up the chance to be wrong and to find, at some distant juncture, the knowledge that I sought for so long. Metaphorically, my attitude has always remained, that I would rather die upon the rocks than sacrifice truth for the illusion of safe passage.

Transitions

When I first heard her speak, I knew that Miss Hardwicke and I shared a similar sense of values, and that she had exposed herself to great risk when she took the teaching position in our town. Truth was something she was passionately committed to, and she refused to be intimidated by the fear of saying what she believed. For there was little question in anyone's mind, especially after her first few weeks in town, that her presence in Stella's Cove was creating an immediate crisis, and that a majority of the community's residents wished to force her termination at any cost.

Even the Town Council understood, deep down, that the minds of the youth would no longer be controlled by an old, demented preacher who was so unfit to teach. Stella's Cove had been desperate to replace him. The Council was forced to make a quick decision--partly because of the understanding that Rev. Cromwell was no longer capable of handling the students.

Cromwell's obvious dementia had progressed at what seemed like an accelerated pace, and his corporal punishment of those children he loathed most was far out of hand. Jerry Epps sustained damage to his right cornea when Cromwell's hardwood pointer missed its mark and caught him across the face, and I would likely have pain for the rest of my life when manipulating tools or pencils with my right hand. There were several others, mostly in the older grades, who had scars to show caused by the Reverend's hand. Cromwell's violent actions had, despite the obvious impropriety, been very effective, and Jerry would never again talk to the girl whose desk was next to his.

Everyone understood how the crisis had developed, and the Town Council understood the need for compromise in the recruitment of Cromwell's replacement. The selection of Miss Hardwicke reflected that there simply was no time to extend the selection process in an effort to find a "better-suited" candidate.

Mother regarded Miss Hardwicke as one of the Devil's workers, an evil force in a community of God-fearing folks, a view shared by most others in Stella's Cove. When Miss Hardwicke was dead and buried, Mother would be very simple in her opinion. I would recoil at her statement, which crystallized the conflict between the two women I most loved. "Whatever you're thinking, Son, it served her right. This town's a hell of a lot better off without her." Mother seemed to have no sense that a young life was taken and that there was no way to give it back.

Despite Mother's ranting, exacerbated by the unorthodox views of Miss Hardwicke, I knew that the change of teachers was the best of moves, and I thought about what drudgery school had previously been. Rev. Cromwell, shepherd of the local congregation, was the only other teacher I'd known before Miss Hardwicke's pert appearance. At the time she arrived, my first five grades of public school had labeled me a low-achiever. Once, in Cromwell's absence, I surreptitiously viewed my own school file, and noticed, after a cursory examination, the words, underlined in Cromwell's hand, "not too bright."

That all changed when the Stella's Cove Council announced that Rev. Cromwell, because of age and health issues, was to be replaced. I'm sure the other kids all thought the same thing I did. "I guess they'll find another starched collar to fill his space." That was not to be so. In fact, there could not have been a more stunning opposite found.

I have since considered, many times, how much Miss Hardwicke influenced the lives of her students, and I am thinking, as Celeste and I walk past the general store, how my life would have been today if she had not been there to broaden my view of the world and help me develop the self-assurance and ambition that has led me to higher education and a promising future. I also can't help thinking of the shock effect she had on the adults of our community and how her ability to think in unorthodox ways completed the perfection of her exterior. And I understand that she has marked Stella's Cove indelibly.

I chuckle to myself, thinking of my mother's harsh

criticism of the new teacher, and I muse upon Miss Hardwicke's image in my mind. She may have been the Devil's messenger, as Rev. Cromwell asserted, but she certainly understood how to make learning an adventure, and how to pique, without any intent, the tender yearnings of a teenage boy's heart.

Both Celeste and I consciously turn away as we pass the old coal bin that had been used to display Miss Hardwicke and Harry Mills, on ice, for those three weeks after their deaths. Yet the memories are there, and we're both feeling the horror of the spectacle that occurred on this very spot.

Continuing our short walk toward Mother's place, I find myself, once more, smiling about Miss Hardwicke and the young infatuation that possessed me when she first came to Stella's Cove. Mrs. Gerbens, my friend Joe's mother, passes us as we turn onto the lane toward my childhood home, and her words note that she has seen the joy of Miss Hardwicke's memory on my face. "Good morning," she chirps, "You look awfully happy about something!"

"Good morning, Mrs. Gerbens." I respond with appreciation that she has actually looked at me and noticed my mood. "Yes," I add, "I was just remembering something wonderful. ...and, by the way, this is my fiancé, Celeste Murphy." As she passes us, I notice the gentle fragrance of some floral perfume, and I am pleased that there is at least one person in my town who exceeds the local standard of mere survival. It seems that, since the tragedy, there is little pride in Stella's Cove, and that the survivors are merely moving creatures. That is not the worst of it, for it is guilt that haunts them all, collectively. Each person surely understands that even those "God-fearing" people who were not directly involved in the horrible display that followed Mills' and Hardwicke's deaths still bore some responsibility for the un-Christian attitudes that flooded their conversations and thoughts, and that allowed them to do what God forbade. "Judge not that ye be not judged." That was applauded as one of the Bible's most important lines, but, except for the few kind-hearted folks, the residents of Stella's Cove all judged.

That thought has changed my mood back to one of sad reflection, and I feel the darkness of Miss Hardwicke's terrible fate. I feel weighted down by the gravity of loss, and my smile fades as my mood is darkened by the feelings of grief that come from losing a person I will always love.

———————

Celeste pauses at the bottom of Mother's front steps, obviously expecting me to go first. Taking a moment to pull my sleeve across my cheeks, I make my ascent, counting the three steps to the top. The porch is crowned with a small shed roof, creating a pleasing dissymmetry from the rectangular regularity of the rest of the bungalow. Mother's rosebushes seem to be thriving in the flowerbed next to the house, and the fragrance floats in the air. For a moment I am motionless on the porch before knocking, and I notice that the paint on the window shutters--hung back when Mother still worked for the Murphy Salmon Company--is beginning to peel. The house is like everything else in Stella's Cove--a mere reminder of the vibrant surge when life was so much better.

I can't help realizing that my good memories of the Cove all center on the time when Mother, Father, and I were all together, but that the rest of my memories are sad. I feel temporarily mired in the same sort of depression that dominates the remaining population. The only consolation is that I was not an active participant in the horrifying events. But even I have felt some continuing guilt, for I believe, without any reason or validation, that even a mere boy could have screamed loudly enough to wake the sleeping conscience of the town.

During our walk from the dock, I have noticed that, after only five years away, there's a deterioration in the faces of the townsfolk. Like the buildings and houses that are falling into a state of disrepair, the town, itself, seems to be enveloped in the blue of the glacier's spell. The feeling is so unhappy that I am not sure now if I ever want to return again. This may well be the last time for me, depending on how long Mother lives. For, those people, like my mother, who remain, Stella's Cove is merely a temporary storage yard for life, as the creeping necrosis advances across the remaining years.

The door opens and Mother greets me with a warm hug. "Billy. Billy." She repeats it several times and I am surprised at her level of emotion. It is a hug that I have only felt a few times before. "Welcome home, Son. I'm so proud of you." There's an embarrassing expression of whisky on her breath, and I am hoping Celeste will not notice it. Despite my concern, I am suddenly feeling the warmth I knew from her as a child--something that seemed to wane and die by time I became a teen. It's the same hug that she'd given me when I regained consciousness after the fall, when I was nine, down the scree at the glacier's tongue, and it is an expression of feeling as strong as the comforting arms she'd provided at Father's funeral, when I broke down, sobbing uncontrollably, and understood my own need for her sympathy and care.

Mother," I announce, "may I present to you Celeste. Celeste, this is my mother." The introduction seems just a bit too formal, for there's a chill that accompanies it. For a moment I'm worried that I have unnecessarily created distance between them, largely because of what I believe will be a cold welcome. I am relieved and happy when Mother gives Celeste a well-reciprocated hug too and tells her "I've heard so much about you, and I'm sorry you're not able to spend more time here before going on to Eagle City." It is obvious from Celeste's pleased look that she is relieved by Mother's unexpected warmth, but she takes a moment to look at her wristwatch, noting with a sad tone, "The Aniak leaves in an hour and a half. I'm sorry there's not more time to visit, but we'll just have to make the best of our time together." If Celeste has noticed the whisky on Mother's breath, she certainly has not betrayed it.

As we walk into the living room, I am studying Mother's motion, and, fortunately, I'm able to detect that the alcohol has not impaired the lightness of her walk. Mother offers Celeste a chair in front of the iron stove, announcing, "I'll go into the kitchen and make us a light lunch." But Celeste declines the courtesy, "I'll come and help you, "she offers. "It will give us some extra time to talk."

A gentle mist has already replaced the balmy weather that dominated, only one hour ago as the Aniak docked, and there's a noticeable darkening of the sky as Mother and Celeste disappear into the kitchen. "Looks like we just lost our sun," Mother notes, and the shadows on the living room floor instantly disappear. It may be only psychological, but there's a chill running through me.

I push one of Mother's chairs--not her treasured leather recliner--close to the iron stove, toss my shoes off, and sit down, to bask in the warmth of its radiant heat. I remember back when I was young, how Mother and Father took turns reading me stories in front of this same stove, and the feeling of contentment and love that felt much like the infrared now warming my feet. It is a feeling that I sorely miss but that has mostly eluded me ever since my father's death.

As I reminisce, Mother and Celeste seem to be having a happy conversation in the kitchen. There's a flurry of laughter, and I'm able to pick up just a few words--something about "...Billy running down the lane naked..." so I know that Mother's telling embarrassing stories about my childhood. I feel a wave of hopefulness enveloping my heart, for Celeste is getting the you're-part-of-the-family treatment. It reminds me of the good times, and I'm feeling what it was like to be the young boy in a happy home with two loving parents.

Ruby and the Bear

Though both my parents read to me, it was only Father who actually told me stories of his own making. As I bask in the warmth of the iron stove, I remember him there creating a special story for me, and for a moment it is as if he'd never left.

"Ruby was scared," Father started, "because there was something banging on the front door, and there was no one else at home. Her father and mother were in town shopping for some provisions and food, and Ruby was carefully warned as they left. "Don't open the door for anyone."

"But the banging continued, getting louder and more insistent with each knock, and Ruby, being a very inquisitive little girl, was both afraid and curious. She had heard of little girls being carried off by strangers and held for ransom, and she'd also heard vivid stories about the wild creatures of the forest that saw children as an easy meal, simply placing them between two oversized slices of bread, adding some lettuce, tomato, mayonnaise and mustard, and sitting down for a lovely meal. Ruby imagined herself between two slices of bread, and the idea of being a bear's lunch was very, very scary. There had been a newspaper report of those exact details, when a bear made a sandwich out of a little girl named Doris, near Guffins Mountain-- not far from Ruby's house--eaten it in one gulp, and burped loudly as he ran off into the woods."

Almost like the sound of severe flatulence, Father did one of the greatest burps I'd ever heard, patted his tummy, and pretended to be loping, on all fours, through the woods. I could vividly see the bear, its huge, hairy mass moving like fluid across the meadow.

"Being such a curious girl," continued Father "the first knock was difficult to ignore. It was followed by one slightly louder, and the third knock was louder still." Father tried to sound like the knocker. "Bang! Bang! Bang....Bang......BANG!" He escalated the volume as he got to the fifth knock.

"Well," Father noted, as though it were some fact out of the newspaper, "there were reports of a marauding bear in the forest where Ruby's family lived, and signs had been posted in all the surrounding communities warning that children should be very cautious and that adults might also be in danger. It was that fact that had inspired the warning that Ruby should not open the door for anyone.

But, after the "Bang! BANG!" seventh knock, Ruby could not take the suspense any longer. She was scared because the insistent knocking was almost deafening, and whoever, or whatever, it was could not be ignored. Ruby walked quietly to the front door, and spread the curtain just enough to take a peek outside. She closed her left eye and looked with her right. But all she could see was the porch and the little lane that led to the house. She spread the curtains, just a wee bit wider, and looked with both eyes. But she saw nothing outside, and she wondered, "Could it have been Mrs. Carmen, who lives just the other side of the lake? She doesn't hear very well. Maybe she didn't realize what a racket she was making...and, even worse, what if she'd hurt herself and needed some help?"

The story was a fresh one I'd never heard it before. I was always amazed that Father could create fiction on the spur of the moment, and that it sounded so much like a story being read from a book. I was loving the feel of the fire and the drama that was so dramatically spoken by Father's vocal intonations. When Ruby spoke, it was the voice of a little girl, and when Ruby's parents warned her of danger, Father sounded just like Ruby's mother and father. He continued the story as I felt the penetrating warmth of the stove and the closeness of his love.

"Because Ruby had looked carefully and determined that nobody was there, she unlatched the door and walked outside. She saw no one, and she was worried that someone, needing help, had walked away, believing there was nobody at home. "Hello." shouted Ruby. "Is anybody there? Hello. Helloooooooo...." The sound echoed gently off Harper's Hill, just across the lake, and there was a fragile veil of mist hanging over the water." Father's echo imitations were so real. It made the story come to life inside my mind. I could see Ruby. I could see the lake and the large hill reflected in its quiet waters. And I could feel the perplexity of a child, unsure of what to do next.

"Hearing no reply," Father continued, "Ruby ran down to the end of the little lane outside her front door. She looked right and then she looked left. Then she looked right and left once more, seeing no one and feeling some concern over her decision to come outside. "After all, " thought Ruby, "Mother and Father told me not to go outside and not to answer the door for anyone." She suddenly felt guilty because she understood that she was ignoring her parents' strict instructions. Walking back to the cottage, she carefully wiped her shoes on the rug outside the door, went inside, locked the door and went back to the paper dolls she'd been playing with.

"Grrr." Father's voice was so convincing and the growling was so much of a surprise that I nearly jumped out of my chair. "Grrr." Father smiled when he saw my startled reaction, but then his face went absolutely serious once more.

""Grrr." Ruby did not see it when she came back into the house, but there was a large brown bear sitting on the couch. It was holding one of her father's favorite cigars between its lips and striking a match to light it. There was no alarm in the face of the bear, and he was absolutely charmed by the interior of the cottage. "Nice place you have here," the bear gently growled, "but you won't be needing it anymore, because I'M GOING TO EAT YOU."" Father sounded just like a hungry bear, drawing an enthusiastic breath as he sank down into the couch making a grunting noise, while placing a pencil in his mouth and pretending to light it up.

""Oh, please, kind Bear," Ruby pleaded." "Father squeaked like a terrified little girl. ""Please don't eat me. You look like a nice bear, and not the kind that would want to bring such a terrible sorrow to my parents. I'm the love of their lives," she implored, and they would be heartbroken."

The bear had a puzzled look as it considered the sorrow of parents losing their child. It took the cigar from its mouth, blew one smoke ring towards the ceiling, and stroked its furry chin with the empty paw. "I've eaten a lot of kids," said the bear, and not one of them pleaded for their lives with the claim that it would hurt their parents so terribly."" Father stroked his chin as if in deep thought and pretended to blow a smoke ring into the air.

""Tell you what." growled the bear, seeming a bit friendlier now, and Ruby felt a sigh of possible relief coming over her heart. "If you can find me something good to eat, I may be willing to make a deal." proposed the bear, and Ruby immediately went about the task of finding something the bear would surely like.

Well….Ruby rummaged through the cupboards and she could immediately confirm why her parents had gone into town. The cupboards were almost completely bare, and Ruby felt a lot like Old Mother Hubbard, who had failed in the task of "fetching her poor doggy a bone." "Oh, dear,"" Father squeaked in the most discouraging way. "I don't know if there's anything here that you'd like."

"After hearing the apologetic excuse, the bear growled. "GRRR!" The growl was so powerful that it rattled the windows and door, and a large piece of plaster fell from the cottage's ceiling. "Well, if that's the case," chided the bear, "I'm going to eat you after all." He took another puff on the cigar, and wiped the drool from his mouth, for he was already savoring the magnificent dinner ahead and it was causing his mouth to water.

Because the bear had wiped his mouth with his furry arm, leaving a smear of drool all over it, he politely asked Ruby for a handkerchief. "You know," he spoke, "my own mother would be appalled if she had seen me do that. Please excuse my rudeness." Ruby obligingly found the bear her mother's lace handkerchief. The bear dabbed the wetness from his furry arm and then blew his nose so hard it sounded like the foghorn at the mouth of the harbor. "Thanks for the use of the handkerchief."" Father sounded just like the bear when he said it.

Father grabbed a glass of water from the kitchen, and savored it as the sparkling water of Muir Creek streamed down his tiring vocal chords. He sat back down and gave me a hug with his left arm. "Do you want me to continue?" he asked in a playful way, and I begged him to finish the story. I desperately needed to know what happened to poor Ruby, and I wasn't going to sleep that night until I'd found out. I climbed up and sat on Father's lap, and stroked the dark hair that covered his arm.

"Would you like some oatmeal mush?" asked Ruby.

"Actually," answered the bear, "I love oatmeal mush, and my family doctor says it's very healthy for me. But I don't like it unless it's topped with a generous layer of brown sugar or honey." Ruby searched the pantry and she could not find any brown sugar or honey." "I'm really embarrassed," admitted Ruby to the bear, "It seems we're all out of honey and brown sugar."

"Grrr." mumbled the bear with great frustration. Ruby was so scared her knees were knocking together, but she composed herself and asked, "Do you like chicken soup?" The bear took a moment in thought. "Well," he said, "I like chicken soup as long as it contains the feathers, claws, and beaks!" It made Ruby sick inside to think of such unpleasant ingredients, but she knew that bears possessed totally different taste preferences than humans. When Ruby searched the pantry, she found six cans of chicken soup. Five of them were plain, but the last one had noodles in it. The labels all had a large square in the middle of the ingredients list. "NOTICE: THIS PRODUCT CONTAINS NO BEAKS, FEATHERS, OR CLAWS." Ruby was alarmed, but she said nothing about the notices to the bear. "How about Chicken Noodle Soup?" asked Ruby, thinking that it would surely please the bear.

"Grrr." growled the bear. "I won't eat it unless it has the feathers, claws, and beaks. Does it have feathers, claws, and the beak?" Ruby was feeling frantic, and she understood that a hungry bear is not so easy to negotiate with. "How would you like a slab of salt pork?" she inquired, and she felt so much better when the bear answered. "I love salt pork. In fact, there's absolutely nothing I like better. That would definitely cure my hunger."

"Ruby went to the larder and opened its heavy door. There was no salt pork, and Ruby remembered it had all been used up when Grandfather visited the week before. "I'm really embarrassed." admitted Ruby. "It seems that the salt pork is all gone. Mother served it when Grandfather was here for dinner last week."

"Grrr." raged the bear, and he added one really big "GRRR." to express his anger. "Looks like I'm going to eat you after all." he threatened, and poor little Ruby's knees knocked together even harder than before. She did not know what to do about the bear's angry disappointment.

Understanding that she was running out of excuses, Ruby ran once more to the pantry. "Do you like cookies?" she asked the bear. We have a cookie jar that's always plum full of yummy treats!" The bear's countenance changed. "Mmm," he purred, just like a kitten anticipating a bowl of warm milk, "That would make me, oh, so happy, and, if they're as good as you say, I won't be eating you today."" Father purred like a kitten, and licked his lips, back and forth, grinning ear-to-ear.

"Ruby dragged a chair across the kitchen floor, positioned it right in front of the pantry cupboard, and removed the cookie jar lid. Because it was sitting high on the shelf, she could not see what was in the jar, so she reached over the top and stuck her hand inside. She could not feel any cookies, so she got up on her tiptoes so that she could reach deeper into the jar. Ruby still felt nothing, so she made one final effort. Standing on her very tip-tip-tippy-toes, she plunged her hand to the bottom of the jar. "Hey, watch it!" came a squeaky voice from the bottom of the jar, "Can't you see I'm trying to take a nap?"

Father was sounding just like the squeaky mouse and the complaint was done with absolute indignation. "Very carefully, Ruby lifted the heavy jar from the shelf, placed it on the kitchen counter and looked inside. There were no cookies in the cookie jar--not even one. Just one very fat mouse wearing blue jeans, a white T-shirt, and a red bandanna. "I'm really sorry about the cookies," squeaked the mouse, "but your mother put the lid on while I was eating a cookie, and I've been stuck in here for weeks." Ruby was ready to cry, but she thought to herself, "I refuse to be a bear's dinner."

Then Ruby had an idea.

She turned toward the bear, who was busy searching the refrigerator for the mayonnaise, mustard, lettuce, and tomatoes he would need for his tasty meal. "Uh-oh.!" exclaimed Ruby. "Uh-oh!"

"What…what is it? Why are you saying, "Uh-oh!"?" the bear asked with a tentative voice." Father took an unusually long time repeating what Ruby had said, and he intoned a convincing sound of dread in his voice. "Uh-oh!" repeated Ruby, this time putting heavy emphasis on the "Uh-" and placing a lengthy extension on the "oh!" The bear looked upset. Why, why" he frantically asked, "are you saying that?"

"Ruby knew that what she was about to say had to be spoken with authority, and that how she said it could make the difference between having supper with her parents or being eaten by a hungry bear. "UH-OH! I JUST HEARD MY GRANDPA

WHISTLING AS HE ALWAYS DOES WHEN HE ARRIVES ON OUR FRONT PORCH....YES, HE'S THE SAME ONE WHO ATE THE SALT PORK LAST WEEK, BUT HIS VERY FAVORITE FOOD IS BEAR--AND HE HAS A REALLY BIG SHOTGUN. ...QUICK! IF YOU DON'T GO OUT THE BACK DOOR NOW, HE WILL SURELY SHOOT YOU!"

Ruby pointed to the back door and opened it for the bear. There was a look of fear on the bear's face. He did not stand there and think about it. He didn't even thank Ruby for the great effort she'd made in trying to find him a tasty treat, nor did he stop to empty the ash tray that held the remains of her father's cigar. He bolted out the back door in an absolute beeline, his feet smoking from the speed as he ran, and...."

"He never came back. When Ruby's parents returned from town, they put their arms around her and gave her a big squeeze. "We love you." they beamed. "You're a wonderful, obedient girl, and we don't know how we could ever live without you."

"Neither," thought Ruby, "do I."

That was the end of Father's story, and my eyelids were heavy as he finished. Smiling, he'd picked me up and carried me to my bed, and the story, though others might consider it silly, is one of my fondest memories.

As Mother and Celeste prepare lunch in the kitchen, the stove's warmth is still something magical, but since Father's death, except for the memory it creates, it has never felt quite the same.

Waves of Fortune

Over the years, Stella's Cove had remained pretty stable. It wasn't that things were always the same—just that all the changes fit within a fairly narrow norm. At least, from the standpoint of a young school boy and from the shallow perspective of a few short years, things in our town seemed mostly changeless to me.

The routines of the Town's existence were certainly predictable, not because nothing actually changed, but because the changes themselves were part of the repetitive scenery of our lives. Transitions from summer to autumn, and the warming of winter into spring, occurred like clockwork. The tides faithfully lapped at the rocky shore by the dock, and left a sea of mussels and barnacles each time the ebb fell toward the West; hermit crabs always scurried across the seabed during the times the bottom was exposed. The pelicans, too, were constant, soaring fifteen or twenty feet over the water and turning into big darts as they dove for the smelts dotting the gentle waves. I often watched them as a child, amazed at their accuracy. While pelicans sometimes bobbed to the surface without a catch, it seemed to me that the prospect of a smelt escaping was extremely unlikely. In the success of their hunting, the pelicans reminded me, too, that the predatory nature of animals and man must include both a hungry diner and a meal. While it excited me to see such successful fishermen, I cringed to see the smelts, flapping frantically in their mouths. I knew that, while adult pelicans died like every other creature, new ones hatched and took their places, providing new actors for a never-ending scene that played out just beyond where the ruffled waters fell upon the sand.

Also a part of the sameness, Stella's Cove's weather came, almost invariably, from the Northwest, and the faithful jetty's seamless presence ensured that the harbor was well protected.

While the natural protection of Point Fay and the channel islands made the jetty's service largely unnecessary, there were times when I saw the sea so angry that spray from the distant barrier actually showered the shore, drenching Father and me and sending us both hurrying for home. The narrow band of forest that began where the sea ended, was also, mostly, unchanging. On any given day, deer appeared and disappeared; chipmunks and squirrels constantly frustrated the hounds that Mr. Heckly allowed to run free; and the skunks left a periodic smell that became locked-in by the foggy layer that was so often there. Each Sunday the same church bells rang, with their enthusiastic, grating dissonance, and most of the town flocked to hear a sermon that seemed very much the same as the one delivered the Sunday before.

Rev. Miles Cromwell was another of the predictable, stagnant, staples of Stella's Cove, and, despite the accelerated deterioration that plagued his aging mind, it was his narrow, harsh attitudes that so effectively suffocated the community. If it were possible for one man to choke others into agreement, the minister largely succeeded, for his voice was stronger than the public conscience. Cromwell ignored anything that was not specifically about religion, and he seemed to actually believe that there are no words of significance in the world, except those found in the Bible. "The words of men," he'd preached in more than one sermon, "are plentiful and common, like the grains of sand that press at the shores of our town, but it is the Bible that holds, for us, the pearls of wisdom by which to govern our lives--those wonderful treasures that can only come from the voice of the living God." Each time I'd heard him repeat that statement, I'd reviewed, in my contrary mind, the fact that pearls are simply the oysters' reactions to irritation and injury--not gems that they graciously offer to mankind.

I knew that words of value were not the Bible's exclusive domain, but I could also appreciate that the Bible did contain some enduring truth. For, just as the much-revered book stated, it was undeniable that "the rain falls upon the just and the unjust." It was that Biblical passage that forced me to consider the random acts of nature and luck. I knew Father had been a virtuous and good man, so there was certainly no justice in his death. I sometimes thought how much more fair it would have been for God to have taken the disagreeable minister and spared the man I loved, but as I'd walked away from Cromwell's Sunday services, there was always an additional reminder of the randomness of life: the church steeple, reaching into the persistent grayness of our sky, was streaked with the same seagull droppings that left the offshore channel markers a dull and chalky white.

The harbor was small, with a single dock that extended about two hundred feet into the Cove, and there were dozens of buoys, which secured the fishing fleet through the gentle evening hours and the occasionally violent gales, sporting their mossy green skirts as they rose and fell in the swells. The harbor was protected by a long jetty, which extended from its north side, and it took a long turn toward the south about 300 feet from the dock, extending that direction for several hundred feet more. The jetty had been built during the town's first fur trading boom, and it was that jetty that allowed the faithful docking of the Aniak, which for many years was the only steamship to serve the B.C. coast.

Like the other constants in the life of our town, there were always a few boats, coming and going from the sea, ranging from the little dories which always stayed within sight of the land, to the handful of larger craft that ventured days into the Gulf. After the failure of the fur and gold industries--events which occurred before my memories began--the professional fishermen headed to larger towns, following the sea to places where their profits could be sustained. The remaining population barely survived, floundering clumsily in its attempts at fishing and taking an occasional fur from the shrunken forest. During prosperous years, the town's fishing fleet numbered forty-one boats, and there were always fishermen tending to their jobs ashore, cleaning the fish, mending the nets and splicing new eyes into the mooring lines. On virtually any day, with the exception of Sundays, the scene was exactly the same.

At low tide, Mother, Father, and I often dug the exposed mud flats with our toes, collecting the clams that failed to burrow down with enough haste, and, after the tough job of shucking them, Mother cooked up the best chowder along the coast. I found a simple joy in digging for those clams, and I understood that it was one of the high points of my childhood—one of those moments when the camaraderie of kin is so complete.

Looking at the history of Stella's Cove, there were only a few memorable events which stood out from the town's mundane and constant life. Consistent with the common notion of a stable existence, no mariner, nor a mere young man in a seaside town, ever suspected that the tide might go out and never return. I had whimsically contemplated such a time, wondering what would happen if the accepted repetitions of our world were to be suddenly disrupted. "What if," I'd asked myself, "after millions of years rising and falling, the sun set and never rose again? What if, the pelicans whose satchel beaks always contained a smelt or two, suddenly failed to make their daily quotas of food? What if, after centuries of similar Sundays, the church bells never tolled again and the pulpit stood empty throughout the day? What if, after Mr. Heckly's hounds intimidated and treed the pesky squirrels, those squirrels united in one decisive offensive and left the dogs dead, stewing in their own juices under an unusually hot sun? And what if my parents and I walked down to the sea when the tide was low, only to face an aggressive clan of clams, tearing at our toes in an effort to ensure that their futures would not be relegated to the tasty chowder on our dinner table?"

One becomes used to the familiar routines of life in a place, never stopping to think that some things may change forever. For, some things in Stella's Cove had, indeed, changed-- matters that would mark the map with the footprint of man, and leave an imprint of his failures.

In 1853, two intrepid trappers, Henry Gavins and Edwin Muir, rowed their dory northward from Bourne River, along a forbidding and jagged coastline. As they'd rounded a bend, they'd first spotted the glacier. "Oh, my God." Gavins exclaimed to his equally stunned companion, "Have you ever seen anything more beautiful than that?" It required no discussion or even an agreement on what to do. Working their way up the narrow inlet, they beached their boat in the obscure isolation of the unnamed cove. As an experiment, and having no idea what to expect, they'd each set up a trap-line along the base of the mountains, just inland from where the denseness of the forest dissolved into the tidal marshes. Then they pitched a tent and waited.

After two days Gavins and Muir returned to their trap-lines, and there was death along the entire length. They rejoiced in finding there were no empty traps, for, in every one was a dead or writhing animal, and, except for two skunks, all were foxes or mink. What they saw made their decision easy, and setting up a more permanent camp along Muir Creek, they spent a productive winter, trapping the furry creatures that filled the forest, and salting and rolling the pelts every afternoon.

On a mild May morning, Gavins turned to Muir. "Well, we've got lots of pelts," old buddy, "but they're not doing us any good here, eh? Gotta get 'em sold." Muir leaned over the fire, lifted the coffee pot from its rock shelf, and poured himself another cup. "It's a long way to Vancouver," he lamented, "but we're not likely to get a good price in Bourne River; Goodman Fur doesn't pay shit. If we're gonna get what they're worth, we need to get 'em to the Hudson Bay folks."

"I've been marking the dates," mentioned Gavins, "and that coastal steamer seems to be headed north, around the beginning of each month--usually heads south about a week later. Our best chance to sell our pelts is to flag 'er down."

So, on the first day of June, the pair waited offshore in their dory, believing that the Steamship Aniak was scheduled to make its monthly run along the coast. On the first day, they saw no steamer, and an early afternoon squall sent the wave crests flying, causing them to fear for their lives. Unsure of the steamer's schedule, they repeated their morning forays, sitting silently in the channel between the mainland and the offshore islands. The weather cooperated, for the following days were dominated by a gentle sea.

After six more days, Muir noticed smoke on the southern horizon, and, an hour later, they flagged the Aniak down. "Ahoy there." shouted the two, and the captain responded, "Ahoy, there. You can pull up on the port side." Gavins felt immediate discomfort when a dozen or so curious passengers flocked to the port rail, in obvious amusement, gawking over them and commenting, somewhat indiscreetly, on the rough looks of the pair. He caught a few words of a conversation between an elderly couple. "I don't think the captain should have stopped," whispered the woman, "They could be pirates." Muir heard it too, and unlike his shy partner, he turned toward the lady who'd said it, flashing a broad smile and making sure she could see his gold tooth. "A good day to you, Madam." And he'd bowed deeply as he spoke.

While Stella's Cove did have a natural harbor, it was barely deep enough for a boat of the Aniak's size, and only a few larger boats with very shallow drafts could make it within rock-throwing distance of the beach. In windy weather, no larger craft could even approach the town, and there would be many times, over the years, that various craft would be forced to continue along the coast rather than risk the danger of a landing in the Stella's Cove harbor.

Unfamiliar with the shallow inlet, the Aniak's Captain carefully made his way within two-hundred feet of the cove, but required the two trappers to ferry their furs to the ship's side, so that the furs could be hauled aboard. The pelts were counted and registered as they were loaded, and the total was an astounding twelve-hundred and fifty-five furs. The first mate, acting as the Purser, handed Gavins a receipt. "Dorrance Shipping will take a five-percent fee," he noted, somewhat apologetically, "for acting as your agent, and we should have your payment on our next run. Typically--though it depends on the weather--we're abeam of this place on the fifth of each month. But," he added, "with the sea, you never know."

The Aniak sailed again as soon as the pelts were stowed, and an agent of the Hudson Bay Company would meet it when it returned to Vancouver. Mink and fox were being worn by every lady of means across Canada and the U.S., and the prices were being driven by the demand. Forty-six ounces of gold were shipped to Gavins and Muir in early July, and less than a year later, they each built large cabins at the edge of the inlet. Understanding that this was to become a regular stop, the Captain of the Aniak asked Gavins and Muir, "We'll be stopping here once a month, as long as you have pelts to sell. We'll go ahead and list it as a scheduled port of call. Oh, by the way, what do you want us to call this place--you know, it doesn't have a name." The two trappers consulted for a few moments, and then turned to the Captain, answering in virtual unison, "Stella's Cove." Gavins face was momentarily transformed to one of pain, and he added, in explanation, "That was my mother's name; she died two summers ago."

With their success now a matter of public knowledge, Gavins and Muir soon found themselves with dozens of neighbors. The initial sale of the twelve-hundred and fifty-five pelts to the Hudson Bay Company's agent in Vancouver created instant fame for Stella's Cove, and, by 1855, the settlement had grown into a real town, complete with log cabins on nicely laid-out lanes, and a fine fir dock that extended into the sea.

And, for a while, the hauls of fur kept coming, bringing

women and families, saloons and brothels, lumber mills and mercantile to Stella's Cove. Suddenly the potential fortunes of the Cove were widely known, and there were even a few who came just for the lore of the glacier and for the challenge of the rugged, menacing coastal mountains that kept the town so safe from the rest of the world.

Along with its rapidly growing population, Stella's Cove was suddenly flooded by a tide of goods that reflected an abundance of money. The women wore bonnets and fine linen dresses to Sunday services, the men enjoyed cigars shipped all the way from Cuba, fine single malts replaced the local rot-gut, the passage of the donation plate, each Sunday, stank with the message, "Look at me," and the people of Stella's Cove believed that the town's future was secure

While the other townsfolk gloated in their new found success, some of the original residents, particularly Gavins and Muir, became concerned when the number of pelts being taken began to drop sharply. "I talked with Bill Lordsley today," Gavins mentioned one morning as the pair set out to check their traps, "and he's seeing what we're seeing. The foxes and mink are quickly disappearing, and pretty soon it won't even be a living." Muir looked at Gavins with an unmistakable resolve and a hint of sadness. "Looks like the writing's on the wall…just going to have to call a spade a spade. It's time," Muir added with a wistful sort of tone, "to be moving on." Just like they'd arrived there, the two founders of what was now a real town, silently made their way to their boat, without fanfare or goodbyes—hoping to avoid the panic they believed would follow. Heading north, they knew that, though it might never be another Stella's Cove, they would find another inlet and another bounty in foxes and mink.

By 1858, the number of pelts taken in Stella's Cove, for the year, fell to a fraction of the earlier harvests, and everyone was painfully aware of the town's impending economic collapse. It had been less than six years since Gavins and Muir spent their first winter in that pristine spot, and now there was no way to make a living in Stella's Cove. Everyone wanted to leave, but it wasn't that simple. The matter of transportation posed a substantial problem for those who desperately needed to move on. The population could not exit by land, as the treacherous trails in all directions were virtually impassable for all but the toughest packers, and even some of the most experienced ones had also died, either from the hazards of the terrain or from the assaults of weather that could rise up at any time. When times were good, those packers made big money for crossing the coastal range, but, when commerce abruptly ended, there was no longer any reason to take such a risk. Everyone knew that Stella's Cove was dying, and the cash that had been so plentiful was gone. When there were no longer any foxes or mink to be taken, the town took one, last, gurgling breath and died.

Dorrance Shipping, owner of the Aniak, which contracted regular pickups of the pelts for market, suddenly failed to make the steamboat's scheduled stops, and people became frantic to pull their roots and move before it was too late. Without the monthly steamboat, there were over two hundred residents who were desperate to leave, but they were blocked by the sea, to the West, and by the Gavins Glacier and the formidable mountains to the East.

When the winter of 1861 pounced with ferocity upon the B.C. coastal towns and left icy goblins in place of the Muir Creek fir trees, there were prayers, tears, and nightmares that descended upon Stella's Cove. A wave of fear swept over the remaining residents, and there was a sense of earnest futility that dominated the previously perfunctory evening prayers. In the best of situations, good choices are hard to make, but the hopelessness that swept over the townsfolk was a bad state of mind in which to make life-defining decisions.

Escape

The day started out as a typical one, with the beams of morning piercing the coastal mist and lighting up the ripples of the harbor with dazzling ricochets of light. But, by mid-morning, an ill wind stirred up waves that were breaking violently against the jetty, and there was salt spray whitening the windows of those homes closest to the water's edge.

Before heading home to the warmth of their stoves, the Stella's Cove fishermen rushed to their boats for one last confirmation that the hatches were safely battened down and that the painters were securely tied to the mooring buoys. Under the solid slate afternoon sky, Harvey Spoon sat in his little office at the end of the dock, watching the barometer. The mercury column was plummeting like a duck full of buckshot. Though anxious to retreat to the security of his own home, he still took the time to fulfill his responsibilities, grabbing the storm flags and running them up the pole, noting that he would probably have to replace their tattered remnants when the storm had finally passed.

Well protected from the brutal onslaught outside, Margaret Ste. Claire was reading a Grimm's Fairy Tale to her children. Between the words of wonderful fantasy, there were occasional pauses, when the kids looked at their mother with concern and her enthusiastic smile thinned into the drawn look of fear. For the wind outside was tearing at the shutters and whistling across the chimney top, and a chill ran across the floor as the bitter gusts slammed against the door. During the most violent surges of wind, the family held their breath as if waiting to see whether their log house would blow away, and the strain was accompanied by a groaning and creaking of a magnitude they'd never heard before.

The Maple Leaf Flag had whipped over the harbor earlier that day, so the townsfolk knew the storm was coming. But nobody knew just how bad it would get. The most violent gusts caused the Ste. Claire cabin to shudder and rock under the strain, and a driving sleet plastered the wavy windows on the north side of the living room with an icy white film. Margaret finished the story and shared a bedtime prayer with the children, asking god's protection for everyone, but, especially for Jeremy, who had set out to check his trap line four hours before. As she said "Amen," there was an ear-splitting sound like a rifle shot, and the whole family ran to the front door just in time to see the tall fir in front of the Granby's home crash to the ground. As long as they'd lived in the Cove, they'd never seen a tree come down, and there was a concerted sigh of relief that it hadn't fallen on the Ste. Claire home.

Minutes later, the cabin door opened, and in came Jeremy. Margaret couldn't help but laugh when she saw him standing there, for his beard and mustache were coated with a thick crust of ice and there was an inch of snow on his shoulders and sheepskin hat. "Better get out of those clothes and come sit by the fire," she coaxed, "You look like a giant snowman." But then Margaret's smile turned to concern. "How did you do with your traps?" she asked Jeremy, fearing that his answer would be the reliable echo from the past four months. "Not so good," he replied, and a depressing pall fell over the room.

Understanding that the future was not getting brighter, and facing an inescapable poverty, Jeremy Ste. Claire and his family struggled through the winter of 1861, barely surviving on their dwindling supply of canned goods and an occasional fish caught off the Stella's Cove dock.

After waiting all winter for the Aniak, which never did make any of its scheduled stops, the Ste.Claires viewed the situation as hopeless. While the steamship Aniak had been spotted on its regular monthly coastal runs during the previous fall, it did not put into the town's harbor. That was the result of a simple "business" decision by the board of directors at Dorrance Shipping, who suddenly understood that the people of Stella's Cove no longer possessed furs nor cash. Captain Nordstok, a compassionate man, pleaded with Dorrance's general manager,

"We need to make some stops there, just for humanitarian reasons. Those people are stranded and we can't just let them die."

"I'll take it up with the owners," the manager reassured Nordstok, "but they're not like you and me, Hans. The only thing they understand is money." The owners considered the request, and, mostly out of their concern for bad publicity, they finally relented. John Dorrance personally made the announcement. "As a matter of good will and our Christian duty to our fellow men, I am approving one more stop in Stella's Cove for humanitarian reasons. Tell Nordstok he can put in there during his northward run in June, and to make sure that there are plenty of staple items aboard." The announcement was welcomed by Nordstok and his crew, but the townsfolk of Stella's Cove had no way of knowing that help would be on its way.

———————

At the peak of Stella's Cove's fur boom, Jeremy Ste. Claire was one of the area's most successful trappers, but this winter's harvest of pelts had fallen to near zero. On a cold March evening, after their children nodded off to sleep, Jeremy turned toward Margaret with a demoralized look. "Margaret, dear," Jeremy started, with an obvious reluctance to finish the sentence, "I'm not sure just how to say it, but I find myself worrying, everyday about how we're going to make it. The pelts I took this winter aren't even enough to buy the supplies and food we need to survive another season, and I'm seeing no signs that it's likely to improve. Sure, I know you've grown fond of this beautiful place, but the beauty can't pay the bills. It's not a choice; we have to leave."

"I've been thinking about it too." lamented Margaret, "Isn't there anything else we can do?" But Jeremy responded, exhaling as if he'd been holding his breath, "I don't see any alternative but to get out of here as soon as we can. Even that is going to be a problem. Bill Gibbens was telling me that the Aniak ain't coming back, 'cause its owner has finally seen the "writing on the wall." Without the Aniak this place is dead, and everyone's pretty much in the same predicament."

Jeremy had trapped in other places, where the supply of fur grew and waned much like the cycle of the tides, and there was, up until this year, the expectation that the population of fur animals would recover. Like everyone else in Stella's Cove, the Ste.Claires wanted to believe that the town's economic collapse would be temporary and that the trapping would improve. Lulled by the dream of a better day, the Ste.Claires waited too long, and, as the fur animals became frighteningly scarce, it became apparent that immediate action was mandatory. Their supply of cash was exhausted when the outgoing expenses exceeded the family's income, and their last money was spent on canned goods and supplies the previous fall, when the Aniak had made its last stop in Stella's Cove.

Though others tried and failed, and though a few remaining friends warned him not to attempt it, Jeremy Ste. Claire believed that he and his family could successfully cross the coastal range. His knowledge of trapping could be used along the way to gather food, and he felt that he was unusually well equipped physically to endure the rigors of such a journey. Because the family made it a regular activity to go for hikes to the glacier, and having watched his girls scamper effortlessly up the steep canyon, Jeremy believed that, pacing themselves carefully, they could easily make the journey.

So, in a final surge of effort to find new resources, Jeremy, his wife, and two young daughters packed provisions enough for a ten-day trek to Couple's Ford, a mining and lumber town which sat along the Nepachou River, on the leeward side of the coastal range. There were credible reports that Couple's Ford had jobs available, and there was simply nothing left to keep the Ste.Claires in Stella's Cove. Margaret secretly dreaded their departure, while Jeremy carefully watched the snow line, inching its way up the mountain, as the arrival of spring boosted the temperature of the air.

While confident of his own capabilities, Jeremy was particularly concerned about his children. The Ste.Claires' two girls, Dora, age 9, and Abby, 11, despite his assessment that they were great little hikers, both were recently plagued by a disabling fatigue. Little bluish, red spots dotted their normally unblemished skin, and they were complaining that their legs were aching, enough that it was hard for them to sleep at night. Margaret exhibited some similar symptoms, along with an uncharacteristic coarsening and drying of her previously luxurious, silken blonde hair. She noticed when she brushed it, that the flaxen tresses were brittle and that the brush was actually breaking the hairs as she did her customary fifty strokes each morning. When she was young, her own mother had stressed a regimen of "one-hundred strokes per day." But it was becoming obvious that, even halving that number, her hair was being depleted even more quickly than it grew.

With the suspicious skin blemishes and diminishing energy, Jeremy was convinced that, if they didn't leave, they would all die during the following winter. James Kindred, Jeremy's best friend, remarked on the sickly appearance of Jeremy's wife and daughters. "I'm no doctor," he'd offered, "but I've heard about scurvy, and I suspect it has to do with the fact the Aniak didn't come to town all winter and hasn't shown up this spring. Heaven knows, we can't be healthy without our lemon juice. We've always had a few barrels of it unloaded on the Stella's Cove dock each month, but winter, this year, has gone by without any re-provision, and no one in Stella's Cove has found any lemons washing up on the beach." James smiled as he said it, but gravely added, "Scurvy's a real threat."

The snow on the eastward ridge was typically gone by the beginning of June each year, as the days grew longer and the mild, temperate breezes blew in from the Pacific. This year Jeremy watched extra carefully to see when the last white specks disappeared, and, on May 18th he'd gathered the family together. "I've been watching the snowline," he enthusiastically announced, "and we're going to head out tomorrow." He and Margaret had spent a few hours of their spare time during the past month, systematically packing what they'd need for the journey, and those preparations were now done. Though completely anticipated, the abruptness of the departure schedule was still a shock to Margaret and the girls.

In the back of Margaret's mind was the unlikely hope that the Aniak would once more put into port and that arrangements could, somehow, be made to transport the family to a new life. As Jeremy watched the expressions on the faces of Margaret and the girls, he noticed that their usual enthusiasm for a hike was startlingly absent. Margaret, in fact, experienced a moment of intense fear, but she dared not share it with Jeremy. She'd always had a sort of superstition that just the mention of possible failures could help create them, and she did not want to be a prophet of doom. Turning to Margaret, Jeremy reassured her, "Honey, it's all going to be fine."

Except for Jeremy's experience as a trapper, the Ste. Claire family was inexperienced in long distance trekking and climbing—other than their short weekend hikes, those two miles to the glacier. But they were determined to find a new home in a place where there were possibilities for financial success. One thing was for sure. Though Ste. Claire had been one of the Cove's most successful trappers, the past two years of failure were no kinder to him than the others. They were totally broke.

During moments of troubling introspection, Jeremy reviewed the bounty of the past five years, and he secretly wished he'd spent less money on booze and women during those wildly prosperous times. Now it was obvious that his indulgences had helped exhaust the family's resources and he understood that the end could have, at least, been forestalled, had he always put the welfare of his family first. Margaret never questioned his loyalty as a husband, and, while she understood that he wasted some of the family's resources at the town's saloon, she had no idea that there were women involved in Jeremy's predictable, evening forays--all to the detriment of their financial situation. When times were good, those cash expenditures seemed negligible, but Jeremy now wished the money was still in his pocket, and he couldn't help but thinking what a waste the women had been.

The family's declining health, particularly the girls, was a major concern. There had simply been no fresh produce during the long winter, and, in an effort to supplement the meager supply of food for his family, Jeremy borrowed a boat on a fairly regular basis from a fisherman he knew. But his attempts at fishing were mostly unproductive, and he knew that children needed a balanced diet. For a while he'd traded household items for food and other necessities, but the Ste. Claire family was now sleeping on the bare floor of the their cabin, which was nestled in the canyon next to Muir Creek. It was the final coup de grace when Jeremy sold his traps for a few bars of soap and a few weeks of lamp oil and food. There was simply no turning back.

Jeremy was now thinking about how robust and healthy his family had been in the past, but how his girls were beginning to look like the skeletons of the Sweiger party. When he looked at them, he was disturbed about just how skinny they'd become over such a short period of time. Everyone in Stella's Cove was well aware of the Sweiger Party's fate, when all the men and mules died in a freak blizzard, years before, while headed west on the overland trail. The storm totally arrested their travel, and that one was followed by an unrelenting series of storms, equally as devastating. Blocked by ten feet of snow, the party hunkered down, waiting for the relief that would never come. When all the mules were eaten, the men simply starved, and it was only the notation in Papa Sweiger's journal that sadly chronicled the party's final days.

Jeremy wished he owned a mule, understanding that having to carry the family's provisions was certainly going to take its toll, and a beast of burden would have been ideal. But, as he thought about it, he couldn't help but wondering how provisions could have been made, on a mountain of virtually solid rock, to provide adequate feed and water for the animal. The last mule in Stella's Cove had died that previous winter, when its owner, in resolute desperation, butchered it for food.

Stella's Cove was experiencing a frightening poverty, and even those who were hunters or fishermen found themselves without the essentials needed to continue. While the sea seemed to be the natural answer, low catches made the most accessible areas of the west coast an unreliable source of fish. The hunters, though successful in previous years, were unable to find game, for the number of deer and elk had declined each year with the excessive taking of kills. Everyone in Stella's Cove was scared.

Ste. Claire was told that it was only thirty-nine miles to Couple's Ford, which was true. Another trapper he'd worked with during the profitable years provided him a map. But, unlike the line that was drawn in pencil across the crude chart, there was no way to get to Couple's Ford by following a straight line. Despite Ste. Claire's visual guide, the representation of Couple's Ford's distance would not have been correct, and every one of his calculations would turn out to be wrong.

The first two days of the Ste.Claires' trek was mostly uneventful. While the going was difficult, Jeremy felt encouraged by the family's steady pace and the irrepressible cheer that seemed to accompany their quest. The girls sometimes sang as they walked, and Margaret was all smiles each time they stopped, talking about how good things would be in their new life, with regular wages, a comfortable home, and a bevy of kids for theirs to play with.

On the third day of their journey, Jeremy surveyed the scene behind them, where the dazzling view of the sea to the west now sparkled on one of the area's few clear days. His heart sank, for the pass to the East seemed to be getting no closer. Margaret turned to him after the girls were asleep, "How are we doing?" she asked.

"We've only gone about eighteen miles," he admitted to Margaret, "but, after we summit the pass, it should be easy from there." As he said it, he was acutely aware that he was simply dispensing encouragement. Privately Ste. Claire determined that they had only made, at best, thirteen miles of progress, and that his words to Margaret had been deceptively encouraging. He understood that the family's supply of food would be inadequate for anything over the ten days he'd planned on, so he quietly told his family, on the fourth night, that they would have to cut everyone's rations by half, something the children bitterly protested. Jeremy quietly lamented their suffering. He scouted the terrain each day for the possibility that some lone deer or elk might have wandered onto the mountain, but the inhospitable terrain was not easily negotiated by anything in the deer family. The only signs of life were the golden marmots, which scampered between the rocks with amazing speed.

The slowness of the family's progress was demoralizing, but what happened next was the dread of every parent. Jeremy had warned his two daughters to be very careful with each step. He'd instructed them to feel the stability of each rock before applying all their weight to the leading foot. It wasn't as if she failed to be careful; Dora was following closely behind her father, and was trying to match his footing on the rocky ridge. Although she was cautious, her next step was indecisive, and the rock upon which she placed her weight, suddenly teetered to one side. As she fell, her other foot became lodged in a crevice between the rocks, and she was pitched forward with an accelerated force, hitting her forehead and face on the sharp edge of a granite spine.

"Dora, darling," Jeremy cried out, running toward her "are you OK?" Dora wasn't moving and Jeremy leaned over her to check her injuries. After just a few moments, the family was relieved to hear a whimper. Dora opened her eyes and even managed the hint of a smile, so the Ste. Claire's felt an assurance that the injuries were not serious. Jeremy did his best in administering first aid, dressing the jagged cuts with carbolated jelly, and wrapping them with clean linen strips. Then, lifting Dora to his shoulders, the family resumed its trek, but Jeremy's heavy load sorely slowed their progress. "Dora," Jeremy joked, "How did you get so big? You're like a ton of deadweight." "I'm sorry, Daddy," she'd weakly responded, "I can try walking for a while." "Maybe we should give it a try," lamented Jeremy. "I'm really having a difficult time." Then he lifted little Dora up over his head, carefully seating her on a flat rock and giving her a drink from Margaret's canteen. When she attempted to stand, she wobbled a bit, so Jeremy lifted her back onto his shoulders.

Dora's condition first seemed to improve, but, by the next day, it became obvious she was not doing well. She complained of dizziness, and her forehead was warm to her mother's touch. On the evening of the sixth day Dora became listless and pale. With the whole family gathered around her, she was barely able to say the words, "Mama, can we go home?" Jeremy and Margaret glanced at each other, swallowed, and gently reassured her, "Dora, everything's going to be all right."

On the sixth day, Dora, who'd developed a high fever, died. One moment she was asking for a drink of water, but those were her final words. Margaret held the limp child in her arms, while the rest of the family bawled in painful grief. Creating a stone cross against the face of a large boulder, the Ste.Claires were forced to leave little Dora at the side of the trail. "I wish we could bury her right," Jeremy whispered in exhaustion, "but I'm having trouble now, even carrying my own weight. I just can't do any more." Next to her body the family lay a small stuffed dolly, the only personal possession that she had been allowed to bring along, and each of them kissed her still cheeks before resuming their trek.

The prospect of leaving little Dora, silent and exposed on that ridge, caused the family great pain, for none of them even once envisioned the possibility of such an event. Margaret, who was always so strong and resolute, threw her head rearward as they left, launching a long, frantic scream at an unresponsive sky. Then, turning to Jeremy, she shrieked, "This is all your fault. We should have never listened to you. This would have never happened if you hadn't been so sure of yourself." Her sound was one of anger, but her look was one of pain, and Jeremy, though reeling from Margaret's verbal assault, instinctively placed an arm around her. She immediately ducked and twisted away from him, adding "You might as well have killed her yourself." Even Abby was horrified by her mother's words, and hugged her father sympathetically. Then there was silence. Everyone stood there, stunned by their grief. "Dora," Jeremy finally spoke as they turned to resume the journey, "was such a sweet daughter and sister, and I know she has gone straight to heaven."

It had always been Jeremy's plan to supplement the food supply, if necessary, with animals caught in a trap he'd brought along. But he'd slipped and fallen on the morning of the third day, and the trap, along with his canteen and matches, had disappeared over a rocky ledge and bounced to the glacier below. Since then, the food supply had been shrinking rapidly and, even with one less mouth to feed, the rations were entirely gone by the morning of the tenth day.

Ste. Claire carried a rifle, but the pickings along the ridge were limited to, mostly, small critters, and his own exhaustion took its toll on his aim. He was surprised at his consistently bad shots, and the speed with which the critters disappeared back into the rocks. On the twelfth day, Jeremy got lucky, cleanly shooting the head off a large Golden Marmot, and the family was forced to feast on the raw, fatty meat, as no firewood could be found. Eleven-year-old Abby vomited while trying to get the meat down, and both Margaret and Jeremy gagged. The six canteens of water they'd started out with were empty, and their water supply was limited to the little accumulations of snow that survived the late spring sun, and still stood at the base of some of the larger boulders. Now, high above the tree-line, the nights were bitter cold, and Jeremy even considered the possibility that returning to Stella's Cove was the family's best chance for survival.

Day thirteen began with one-half slice of bread for each of the three, but Garden Pass was only a couple hours ahead, and Jeremy knew that they would find large game in the forested slope on the leeward side. While the tragedy of a dead child stole any joy that could have surfaced, there was, nevertheless, a certain optimism that showed in the trio's faces. When compared with the rugged, uphill trek, Jeremy considered the ease of the descent along the soft, forest trails, calculating that the family could make Couple's Ford in as little as two days. With their spirits lifted just a bit, the family pressed on.

Announcing that he was going to scout the trail ahead, Jeremy left his exhausted wife and Abby sitting on a rock. After making his way over a small ridge, he noticed a curious slab of granite, which looked unlike all the others. Its outward-facing side was perfectly flat--just like someone had sliced through it with a crosscut saw. In fact, to Jeremy, it looked like the work of some skilled stone-carver who did it intentionally. But, what fascinated him even more, was the perfectly straight white line--about an inch wide--that crossed the slab about half way up. In it he saw the outline of a fish, and the undeniable existence of a backbone, ribs, and jaw.

Ste. Claire turned for a moment, looking down across the glacier's flow toward the sea, noticing how far the Pacific was from his current location. The discovery of the fish baffled him, and he wondered for a moment if some trapper of long ago had consumed a meal at this very point, and that the fish in the rock was the remains of somebody's dinner. But his perplexed look transformed, in an instant, to one of concern, for he found himself face to face with a grizzly cub. With hunger gnawing at the Ste. Claire family, Jeremy's first instinct was to level his Henry and take the cub for food, but he stopped, instantly perplexed that his mind was not working as it should, and realizing that exhaustion and starvation were taking their toll on his normally good judgment. It took only a moment to settle his mind. Ste. Claire knew about bear cubs. It wasn't the first bear cub he'd seen in his life, and he understood that, no matter how cute cubs appeared, there was always a mother close by.

"There is nothing worse than a mad grizzly mother," he'd thought to himself, and he cocked the hammer of his .44 Henry Rifle. But, before he could react or plan his careful withdrawal, there was a growl, and five inches of razor claws removed Jeremy's scalp and forehead. As the blood ran down his face, he closed his eyes for a moment, but then realized that his eyelids were also gone. The second swipe of the sow's claws tore through his flannel shirt, and Ste. Claire knew, as his intestines spilled out over the rocks, that he would not survive. With his last thoughts for the welfare of his family, he mustered enough strength to raise the Henry, fired it without the benefit of eyesight to guide his hand, and fell with a sickening thud to a boulder ten feet below him. He never moved again. The bullet, in fact, neither hit nor killed the bear, and the sow and cub left Jeremy's remains only when their appetites were satiated.

Margaret and Abby were alarmed when, after two hours,

Jeremy failed to return, and they discovered his half-eaten body on the trail ahead. Somehow the pair made it back down to Stella's Cove, wandering in at dusk on the seventeenth day, looking like withered skeletons with oozing sores from the sunburns on their faces. After hearing what had happened, no one in Stella's Cove dared to try the overland route again, and more than two hundred desperate residents faced the prospect of spending another winter there. Though no one knew or even expected it, the Aniak would make a stop in Stella's Cove only a couple of days later, allowing sixty townsfolk to board, and providing an adequate supply of lemon juice and fresh produce to help those who would remain. The bodies of little Dora Ste. Claire and her father were never retrieved, and there was no one who dared to try.

When the remaining people in Stella's Cove heard the gruesome tale of Jeremy Ste. Claire's last days, the hope of escaping by land was dismissed as an unnecessary risk of life. But there was one more option, for the sun set each evening over the horizon, laying down a long red shaft across the waves, reminding those incarcerated there of the freedom lapping invitingly at the shore. Those who had experience with the sea dreamed of redemption from their present peril, and a few began to form a plan.

The sea was, indeed, the only other escape from Stella's Cove, but most of the boats had left with the fishermen, in search of a stronger market. Except for one or two, the discards were unseaworthy. During the same week that Jeremy Ste. Claire failed in his overland attempt for a new life, and even before Margaret and Abby returned to Stella's Cove barely alive, Noah Parker also determined to leave. His wife Geraldine balked at his proposal. "I don't want to go," she protested. "It's too dangerous, and I know the steamboat will come before winter."

"We've been waiting for the Aniak, now, for almost eight months," Parker reminded her, "so there's no way of knowing if and when she'll ever come back." In the next few minutes Parker described the plan--how they would go by boat to Bourne River; that they would never be far enough from shore to be in danger; and that the Tlingit villages, which dotted much of the coast, could be used for safe haven if they encountered bad weather conditions.

When he explained it to Geraldine, she'd been relieved, for Parker's plan, along with its contingent safety measures, made perfect sense. In his effort to gain Geraldine's support Parker reviewed, over and over, the fail-safe nature of the venture. She felt both relief and encouragement when her husband pointed out how the extremely predictable winds would assist them in their short voyage. "Besides," noted Parker, "the seas between Stella's Cove and Bourne River are usually gentle, and dories are designed to be exceptionally seaworthy and stable." Noah, Jr. was fourteen at the time, and he, like his father, believed that the family needed to get out of the Cove. Sensing that it would not only be salvation, but a great adventure as well, Junior heartily rallied for his father's plan. After all, the winter would arrive before anyone was ready, and both Noahs understood that one more season in Stella's Cove might well see them all die of starvation or scurvy.

On a gentle May evening, Parker excitedly told Geraldine and Noah, "We can easily make it to Bourne River. It's only thirty-eight miles to the south, and most likely we'll be able to complete the sail in less than one day. I don't know why we didn't do it sooner, but it will surely end our financial woes."

Though Bourne River never enjoyed the times of wild success experienced by its neighbor to the north, it had actually been infinitely more fortunate. Bourne River's industries were not flashes in the pan, and its economic successes were steadily growing from the very beginning. The area around it was a dependable source of pelts, and its residents were blessed with steady jobs in its three anchor industries. There was a large wood pulp mill there that employed hundreds, which was now enjoying its nineteenth year in business; the Bourne River Textiles factory, which shipped fabric to every part of North America, advertised job openings on a fairly regular basis; and the Bourne Salmon Processing Plant, though constantly struggling, was in its twentieth year.

In addition to the bold but safely hedged plan to depart by sea, Parker held another favorable card in his hand. He was friends with a Mr. Bertrand Storm, a longtime resident of Bourne River, who held one of its most respected positions. Bertrand was the general manager at the mill, and his status in the community was one of unquestioned respect. Storm and his wife had been in Bourne River for years, and the Parkers and Storms were close friends from when their families were neighbors in Kokeemah

Bay. "They'll help us get started." Parker assured Geraldine. "I know they'll put us up for a while and Bertrand will help me get a job."

The problem was that Parker made too many assumptions, and that the success of the exodus depended on matters beyond his control. Unknown to him, his friend Bertram had died in an avalanche the previous winter, and Bertrand's wife had moved back to Kokeemah Bay, where her parents were still living. There would be no friend waiting for the Parkers in Bourne River, no free board while they got settled, and no assistance in securing a job.

Parker was familiar enough with the coastline that there would be no problem finding protected areas to wait-out threatening weather, and the question now was simply "When?" On the evening of June 3rd, Parker looked at the horizon, watching the red sun as it sank into the sea. "Red sky in morning, sailors take warning..." he recited to himself, and then finished the couplet, "Red sky at night, is sailor's delight." That night's sunset left a pile of glowing coals on the horizon, and Parker knew that the time had come. Turning toward Geraldine, he gave her a warm hug and kissed her gently on the lips, "Can't ask for better weather than this, sweetheart. We'll be shoving off at dawn." The days were getting longer, and the possibility of reaching Bourne River before the next sunset was looking extremely promising. Parker turned once more to address his wife and son. "Let's get to bed early so we're on the water at six."

Taking the precaution of provisioning the dory with a week's rations; salt pork and smoked venison, two large pottery water jugs, three heavy blankets, and a covered chamber pot, the Parker family was well prepared for the short voyage. He had done the calculations, and he believed that the northwesterly winds would do most of the work and that the family would arrive in Bourne River in as little as eight hours. As planned, they set out at first light.

While not the nicest looking of the boats in Stella's Cove, the dory was the best of the abandoned craft that littered the beach next to the dock. It featured a particularly wide beam, and the bow and stern were unusually high. Instead of the old thole pins--the two wooden dowels that acted as fulcrums against the pull and push of the oars--this dory included the newest version of "U" shaped swivel oarlocks which were both more secure, in terms of ensuring oars were not lost in rough seas, and efficient. On each of the oars there was a cushioned leather collar which snugly held the oar in its lock and assisted in keeping the oars' blades perpendicular to the surface of the water. And, as an added protection, each oar had a four-inch leather "button" just above the leather collar, which prevented the oars, once they were in the oarlocks, from sliding through into the sea. In preparation for their journey and in order to test the integrity of its hull, Parker and Junior rowed the boat as far as the Point Fay Lighthouse each day for a week, finding that they could make almost four miles per hour--even without a following wind--while pacing themselves carefully for the preservation of energy.

At six a.m. sharp, Parker lifted Geraldine over the dory's transom, and she made her way to the bow. Under her wide white bonnet she smiled tentatively, and sat down facing the rear of the boat. Parker and Junior pushed the dory into the gently lapping waves and climbed in. Junior sat down at the stern facing forward so that he could give his father corrections on their heading, and Parker, having carefully pressed the oars into their locks, took his seat and began to row. He first gave the oars four or five hard strokes to break the inertia, and then settled into a comfortable and steady pace.

Geraldine sported a happy expression. "I can't believe how fast we're going. This is amazing." Besides her surprise at the boat's speed, she did an excited series of "ooh's and ah's" as the mighty glacier came into view over the town. "I've never seen it from this vantage point," she remarked, "It's so spectacular." In only minutes, the sunlit crest of the glacier disappeared into the typical morning mist and there was a common understanding that they were now completely on their own. Passing Point Fay, Parker noticed that the wind intensified, and it was coming from the Northwest exactly as predicted. The breeze tickled and tweaked the surface of the water, and, by 8:00 a.m., there were whitecaps on the sea.

Even Geraldine was not alarmed. The coastline was only a hundred yards off the port side, and she knew that all three of the family, in the event of an emergency, were capable of swimming that distance. Parker continued to pull, and, by 3:00 p.m., he cheerfully announced, "I can see it. There's Bourne River." And, sure enough, the powerful northwesterly breeze pushed the boat forward, augmenting the power of the oars and making a

remarkable five nautical miles per hour. There were smiles of
relief, for they were now in sight of their destination. Junior
relieved his dad at the oars, and the progress continued at an even
faster pace.

The little squall, that seemed to have come from nowhere,
made Parker nervous for a moment, but then the wind died to
almost a whisper, and young Noah continued pulling toward the
town. Yet, at 8:00 p.m., the dory appeared no closer to Bourne
River than it had been hours before, and the Parkers, for the first
time that day, felt a rush of adrenaline and a twinge of fear. Not
wanting to create alarm, Parker slowly and deliberately picked up
a spare oar from the bottom of the boat and stood near the bow on
the starboard side, adding some thrust to the seemingly motionless
dory. As the sun began to set, they could still see the town, but it
seemed that they were further away now than they were before.

Parker looked at Junior, and Geraldine looked at both of
them. The usual color of her cheeks suddenly blanched, and there
was a foreboding that swept over her previously buoyant mind.
"It'll be O.K." assured Parker, "We'll just head for the beach and
spend the night there." There was a look of relief on all their
faces, for, just as he'd promised, Parker had been careful to make
sure the boat stayed close to the shore.

"Let's head straight in," Noah directed his son. "There's a
sandy beach just off to the left." But the wind suddenly changed.
In only moments whitecaps churned up once more, and the wind
became so violent that the crests were being blown like harvest
chaff into the air. "Pull, son," Parker commanded, and he could
proudly see that his boy was now as strong as he, for the power of
Junior's oar strokes was exceptional, and the dory seemed to leap
as Junior leaned his back and pulled toward the beach.

Ten minutes later Parker knew that the weather had tricked
them, and he tried to remember where the next Tlingit town was
to the North. The Dory was now several hundred yards from the
shore, and the waves were no longer rolling out of the West.
There was a stiff breeze coming directly from the Northeast, and
the two men frantically pulled with all their strength. A larger
wave smacked the port bow, temporarily halting the dory's
progress, and Noah, who was standing and paddling with a single
oar, was pitched into the sea. There was no bow line on the boat,
and unlike some dories that had a metal rail just above the
waterline, there was nothing to help Noah climb back in. Middle-

aged and a good forty pounds overweight, he struggled to get into the dory, but even after wrapping his legs around the dangling oar shaft, he was unsuccessful.

Finally Geraldine and Junior grabbed fistfuls of Parker's shirt, and succeeded in raising him high enough that he could get his hands on the gunwale, and pull himself, exhausted and cold, back inside the boat. As the sun set, Noah was chilled. He complained that he was nauseous and was suffering a sharp pain in his chest. Geraldine poured him a cup of fresh water from one of the jugs, and he seemed to immediately rally, "Thank you, Dear. I'm feeling a lot better now." On the morning of the second day, realizing that they'd all slept through the night, Geraldine collected herself and cheerfully announced, "Time to get up." But her buoyancy was immediately squelched by what she saw. She looked toward the portside; she looked toward the starboard; she peered intently over the bow and the stern but saw nothing, for a thick fog enveloped the dory. Cupping her hands to her ears, she listened for sounds of surf, but she could hear none. There was only the lull of an unusually placid sea.

Junior stretched and yawned, remarking how he couldn't believe they'd all fallen asleep, and Mother poured him a cup of water, then handed him a strip of smoked venison. "Is this the deer Dad and I got last spring?" he asked, and Mother acknowledged that it was. Only one person in the dory did not speak; Noah still lay peacefully, with his feet toward the stern and his head propped against the bow. "Wake up, Dear." Geraldine raised her volume repeatedly, but Parker did not move.

Junior and Geraldine couldn't believe what they saw, for when the diffuse, reddish dawn faded to a muted white glow in the sky, there was no longer the illusion of color in Parker's cheeks. Junior bent over him and poked him a few times, barking "Wake up! Wake up, Dad." And then he frantically slapped his father's cheek. Junior was shocked to find that it was ice cold, and he understood that his father had probably died not long after he'd declared, the night before, that he was feeling better.

"It can't be," Geraldine exclaimed with a tone that echoed both incredulity and despair, but Junior and Geraldine could not even stop to cry. They could not see the coastline, they could not see Bourne River, and there were no Tlingit villages that stood, as security, within their view. A devout Methodist, she prayed, and she asked Junior to pray too. Neither knew where they were, for the eerie fog draped the sea and obscured even the sun from their view.

Just a short time after they'd discovered Parker's death, the winds whipped up once more, and a powerful blast pushed the boat toward its port side. Junior sat back down to man the oars and immediately got the dory turned into the wind, rowing gently to hold the boat's heading. A moment later, he abruptly ended his effort, concentrating on a faint sound that seemed to come from behind him. "Listen, Mother," he exclaimed, and then Geraldine heard it too. "Thank you, lord." She uttered it out loud, and Junior waved his father's unneeded jacket back and forth across the mottled sky. Feeling both relief and momentary elation, the pair, almost in unison, exclaimed, "We're saved." As she rallied, Geraldine thought for a single moment on how she'd survive as a widow, but the immediate providence of salvation from the sea overwhelmed both her concerns for their future and her intense grief.

The Aniak emerged from the depths of the fog and was heading north, making better than eleven knots.

. Geraldine looked up at the fog bank above, and uttered another prayer of thanks. "Oh, Jesus," she prayed. "Thank you, Lord."

The sound of the steam engine grew louder, and a few moments later the Aniak made it to the lost and floundering dory. But the Aniak did not stop, and the only notice of the Dory's existence was the remark of the First Mate to the Captain. "I think we just hit something, Sir." he said, with a disturbed look on his face. And Captain Nordstok answered, "We'll take a look when we get to Stella's Cove. After the Captain's usual, meticulous approach into the harbor, and the boat made its controlled and almost silent contact with the large white rope fenders, the hawsers were lashed tight to the cleats, and the steamboat was securely docked. From the appearance of the crowd, the entire town was happily gathered at the dock. There would be provisions aboard, including the much-needed barrels of lemon juice, and there were audible utterances from the town's many faces. "Thank you, God." "Thank you, Lord Jesus." for they had not seen the ship for over eight months, and they knew that their prayers were answered.

As provisions were unloaded and dozens of people clamored to arrange their getaway from Stella's Cove, the First

Mate barked, "Let's get a diver to check for damage." It was the same pelican deckhand with the blonde hair and protruding lower jaw who donned the diving helmet and was now being hooked to an air-line that ran from the small air compressor that was an accessory on the Aniak's steam engine. Once the hoses were attached and the deckhand could hear the rush of air through the helmet fitting, he lowered himself to the water and sank beneath the boat.

The water was icy cold, and the young deckhand felt a momentary, frantic claustrophobia under the large brass and glass diving helmet, but he did what duty called for. Starting at the bow and surveying every inch of the keel and hull, he checked the large brass propeller last. Had he not been thorough, he might have missed it altogether, but his meticulous inspection revealed that two of the propeller's four blades showed slight curls on their leading edges. The young deckhand thought to himself, "We must have hit a heavy piece of driftwood."

Climbing from the water, he talked with the Captain, who was waiting at the top of the rope ladder. "It's not severe," said the deckhand, "but the propeller definitely hit something, and it needs to be changed out. There's just enough damage to two of its blades, I believe that replacement is necessary to prevent vibration and possible failure of the shaft seals." The Captain conferred for a moment with the First Mate. In less than five minutes, the spare propeller was brought from below, and lowered over the stern with a light piece of sisal rope. The diver submerged one more time, returning with the damaged propeller and announcing, "Good as new!"

Captain Nordstok directed the deckhands to dry and clean the propeller, then set it down on a deck bench so that he could assess the damage. He was troubled by what he saw. Two of the blades did show some light damage, and the only obvious explanation was driftwood. But there was also a faint hint of white paint on one of the damaged blades, and the Captain was immediately worried that they had actually hit a small fishing boat. "But, then," he thought silently, "what fisherman would be out on such a foggy morning, and so far away from a town." Considering all likely possibilities, Captain Nordstok decided that the faint hint of white paint was surely caused by a piece of debris surfacing from one of the many wrecks submerged along the coastline.

The Aniak loaded up its usual fuel and supplies and boarded those stranded refugees who had been successful in either scraping enough cash together or bartering for their passage. Left behind in their Stella's Cove homes were the reminders of a better time, when the community prospered and when they believed that the prosperity would go on forever.

When it was time to depart, the whistle blew three times as the Aniak made its way cautiously to the main channel and churned out of sight.

Three weeks after the Aniak's collision with the driftwood, an old lobsterman reported two bodies washed up on the shore between Bourne River and Stella's Cove. The RCMP was summoned, and it was assumed that the bodies were of two missing fishermen who battled a freak spring storm and lost. Their boat was found, unmanned and casting about in the heavy seas, just a few days before, and because the area was rocky and the surf posed a danger for the landing of any boat, the lobsterman, who saw the two from his boat, far offshore, did not attempt to reach the beach where the dead lay. Because there was no known passable route that traversed the rocky coastline, the corpses were left for the animals and seabirds that would feast until there was nothing left but a few of the larger bones.

Faced with a series of punishing storms, the RCMP made the same necessary decision--to allow the bodies to remain where they lay. Craggy and forbidding, the beach would be the final resting place for Parker and Junior, for the sea, which had stowed them there in that forlorn place, blocked the possibility of a safe retrieval. Geraldine's body was simply swallowed by the sea, for there were no reports of any woman ever being found. The assessment of the old lobsterman and the RCMC would be spot on, for the bodies were, indeed, quickly devoured by the feasting raptors and bears, and the crabs that tore voraciously at anything meaty.

It would be many years later that one of the Parker's neighbors in Stella's Cove would ask the question, "I wonder how Noah, Geraldine, and Junior are doing in Bourne River."

The Fine Imposter

Over the next year, all the remaining residents who wished to leave were successful. Only two were left behind, and that was a matter of their own choosing. Remaining in the town would become their fortunes, for the glacier, though viewed as an evil presence for years, had a gift to share. With its slow, grinding movement over the canyon it had been carving for centuries, the glacier was releasing a special bonus into Muir Creek

Gold was discovered in 1865, when a left-over trapper, known only as "The Fox" asked the question, "What can I do here to make a living? The foxes and mink have disappeared," he spoke to himself as if in a conversation with a friend. "My friends have all left, I'm feeling lonely as hell, and my only real neighbors are an eighteen year old boy and an abandoned Methodist Church." Though not considered, at that time, to be a religious man, Fox did have some fundamental belief in God, and every time he uttered that prayer, he held hope that it would be answered.

With the town deserted except for one other human being, Fox considered everything there to be, essentially, his. He "borrowed" the kettle from the deserted, original Muir cabin, and carried the wooden dining table out of the vacant Waldford's house. It took a large wheelbarrow to move the Superior cast iron stove from the empty Bentley home to his own, and Fox's gas lamps, with their beautifully etched chimneys, were a "gift" from the Clarkes, who acquired them during the town's first period of prosperity. He now wore the clothes that were abandoned on the dock by the fleeing townsfolk, when Captain Nordstok announced that the Aniak could carry no extras, and Fox had quickly used up the few cans of food that remained on pantry shelves. Making regular forays into the band of forest, he'd hunted for game and there was a regular supply of food hanging from his log cache rafters.

Like most other things in the deserted town, Fox considered the church to be his as well, and several times each week he stuck his head inside the building, uttering the simplest of prayers. "Give me a reason, Lord, to stay here," he implored. "This town is almost dead, and I'm about the only thing standing in its way." He was anticipating the demise of the town, which was so close to being terminal, and wishing that he could find some way to keep it alive. His only real prayer was for the resurrection of Stella's Cove, and he looked for a way to save it. There were times that Fox imagined the town was actually gasping for its last breath and clutching at its heart, a specter that haunted him each evening, when the only two remaining oil lamps were snuffed out.

Henry Crump was the son of Rev. Sinclair Crump, and it was his lamp, along with Fox's, that threw a dim light, every night, over the deserted lanes of Stella's Cove. His father had left him in Stella's Cove when the dwindling Sunday donations had all but petered out, and Rev. Crump's savings, gleaned each week from the offering plate during times of plenty, had become a small fortune. Only seventeen when his father uttered a terse goodbye and left him on the dock, Henry had not even stayed to see the Aniak depart. There was no wistful watching as the steamer disappeared into the mist, and he felt no hunger for his father's empty sermons or sour countenance. At the time he became essentially orphaned, Henry had barely been able to grow a beard, and, even now, there were still the vestiges of pimples on his face.

Despite his age, Henry Crump was an able fisherman and never lacked for food. Because there was no schooling available in Stella's Cove during its fur trading glory, Henry was apprenticed, at age thirteen, by Ahab Rowen, a fisherman who'd made a fortune supplying the town with his reliable catches. When the mass exodus emptied the town, Rowen understood that, if he wanted to continue making money, he'd have to leave Stella's Cove. "You're welcome to join us," Rowen suggested to young Henry, "I can always use a good worker like you, and, knowing folks the way I do, I can tell that someday you'll have your own boat and be making it big. I like you, son, and you'll always have work if you need it." As Rowen's trawler pulled out of Stella's Cove, Henry wondered if the offer had been recklessly declined. There was no assurance that there could ever be money in Stella's Cove again, and he mulled over the prospect of an empty and solitary life. Rowen and his crew went on to Eagle City, and his business success continued there. Little did Rowen suspect that there would, once more, be a market for fish in Stella's Cove, and that, had he stayed, a second wave of fortune would have surely followed.

Henry Crump's problems were that he lacked a capable craft and crew, and, even more important, that if he'd had them, there would still be no one in Stella's Cove to buy his catch. Waiting out the days, as if some vision had given him an expectation of economic change, the boy spent a year in relative solitude, interrupted only by Fox's short but frequent visits. Each time there was a knock at his door, Henry had to consider, briefly, what his response should be. Raised by a father who stressed the value of manners, but eviscerated the meaning of goodness, the rules of proper etiquette had been drummed into Henry's head, so each knock required the mandatory response expected of a man of God. For every knock, he made the simple utterance, "Hello. Who's there?" Under the circumstances of the town's two living residents, "Who's there?" seemed a bit out of place, and so the formalities and courtesies were quickly dispensed with. The standard response to a knock at either door became, "Come on in," and a camaraderie quickly developed between Fox and Henry, out of the basic need for contact with others.

With little else to do, Fox took frequent hikes to the glacier. While drinking from its milky effluent, early one morning, he noticed a flake of gold lodged in an eddy where the current, at the edge of the stream, turned back on itself. Never whispering a word to the wind or to Henry, he went back with a shallow pan the next day. By the following evening, he reckoned he had close to an ounce of gold, and he stashed it under the floorboards in his cabin. The next day, the same routine was repeated, and he knew that he must keep his secret secure

Understanding that his success could become a double edged sword, Fox kept the rich find to himself, and when he went to Bourne River in one of the abandoned dories, he took only a small quantity of flakes, something he exchanged for a small stash of cash—just in case there would ever be a use for it. Fox knew that staking a claim could bring the world to Stella's Cove, and, as much as he wanted to see the town revived, he loathed the idea of a boom-town--something he'd seen once before--that would first explode in growth and eventually die for a second time. That predicament kept Fox constantly thinking, but it was simply chance that stole the choice from him.

Henry Crump had been the one exception to Fox's commitment to privacy, for he saw the lad's courage, in remaining, as a mark of indomitable spirit. "Henry," Fox looked into the kid's eyes as he said it, "there's something I've been wanting to talk with you about. I think there's a fortune of color running down Muir Creek. That glacier's been grinding away at the mother lode, and there's plenty of gold for both of us." Fox was gob-smacked at the boy's response. "I don't want your gold," Henry almost mechanically asserted. "I'm a fisherman, and my living will be the sea." Though Fox had difficulty understanding such a dismissal of the wild prosperity that would likely follow, he also understood that any boom would richly reward young Crump, and he vowed, in his heart, that, when the time came, he would finance a wonderful trawler and help Crump in seeking his own fortune, any way he chose.

Fox had never seen it before, and he felt a rush of fear as an unfamiliar trapper and his two mules worked their way down the south wall of the canyon. Fox immediately stood up, concealing the gold pan against a large boulder and pretended to be merely viewing the scenery. But the trapper had stopped by the creek, only a few yards away, and watered his mules.

"Howdy. Looks like you're a-pannin' fer gold," the stranger drawled. "You prob'ly won't find none here. 'Bout twenty years ago thar was some, but I think my ol' friend Marvin Chance goddit all. …it paid out a bit, but then it plumb died." Fox knew the short history of Stella's Cove, and he'd never heard the name "Chance" before. But there was an unmistakable authority in the stranger's voice, and Fox realized, for the first time, that Gavins and Muir had not been the first white men in Stella's Cove. "Fergotta tell ya," noted the stranger, "the name's "Bud Weatherly."

Disturbed as he was by the sudden appearance of Bud, Fox got real chatty, and he went right along with what the man was saying. "You're sure right about that," he answered, "nothing but a few tiny specks…not even worth the effort to pick them up." The conversation ended abruptly, as it had started, and Fox watched the trapper head down the trail with the two mules tugging at their leads while trying to reach the tufts of grass that grew at both sides where the trail fell off into the drainage. "Git up!" Bud barked, and the mules followed without argument.

When Fox got back to town that evening, he'd noticed Weatherly down by the dock, and he engaged the man in another friendly conversation. "How was your day?" Fox asked. "Pret' borin'. This is jest a ghos' town," the stranger observed. "Where in the hell did everyone go?" Fox told him that the fur animals had been depleted by too many trappers, noting that it was in utter desperation that the townsfolk had fled the town. "You should have seen it," related Fox, "a whole town lined up at the dock trying to escape this place." Weatherly turned directly toward him. "Dat so? Giss id ain't da place f' me!"

Fox walked outside the next morning and prepared for his day, planning to pan for most of it, and figuring he'd jerk some venison he'd shot several days before. Taking the usual hike to the glacier, he'd worked the gravel that was barely visible beneath the towers of ice, and, by the end of the morning, he'd found close to another ounce of gold flakes and a large nugget that weighed, likely, another half-ounce. Squinting in the noon sun, he inspected his treasure more closely, and it was then that he saw Weatherly again, standing on the ridge above him. The trapper called out, "Howdy." but this time Fox ignored him, left in a hurry, took his dory, and headed to Bourne River.

When he returned home, Fox had accomplished what he'd set out to do, and the placer claim at the head of Muir Creek was his and his alone. But the stranger had, subsequently, also staked a claim, and one month later Weatherly returned to Stella's Cove, this time with parts for a sluice, which he hastily constructed just below Fox's claim.

The Aniak, once more, began making regular stops at Stella's Cove, and anxious miners hired fishing boats in Bourne River to make up for the times when the Aniak was somewhere else on its ports of call. There was no way to keep the news from spreading, and the old cabins in the town were immediately occupied by the men who sought the treasures of Muir Creek. Because of Canada's abandonment laws, the houses were mostly up for grabs, but there were not enough of them to go around. Hearing of the gold and the imminent requirements for housing, Pacific Lumber set up shop in town, and sawyers went out each day to harvest lumber from the strip of forest running between the town and the coastal mountains.

The rampant growth caused concern to a few, for a community simply could not function properly and peacefully without some rules. A newcomer named Garrett Daily appointed himself the mayor, and chose four of his friends for the Town Council. No one objected, and Daily took it upon himself to bring some order to the matters of zoning, construction, and law enforcement. Setting up his office in the abandoned Gentry home, there was soon a steady flow of residents, making applications for building permits, and reporting the various infractions of their neighbors.

Right behind the lumber company sprouted Young's Mercantile General Store, and a man named Bart Clemmerton rushed to set up a little bakery on the Main Street. Within a few months of Fox staking his claim, there were no less than eleven businesses in Stella's Cove, and the number of miners, spread over the two miles of Muir Creek, swelled to nearly five hundred. Henry Crump, the old preacher's son, took his dory to sea each morning, bringing back surprisingly large catches each afternoon. Enterprising and hard-working, Henry sold the fish from a small monger shack near the dock, and he, too, was stacking the pouches of gold as fast as it came in. Everyone was making money.

Next to arrive were the twenty-six women brought in from Vancouver by the enterprising Mayor, and Daily hastily re-zoned a parcel of land on Main Street, constructing the town's only two-story structure--a large log building with a bar, a tinny piano, and lots of bedrooms. Miners came--not to be making a pun--and left, each leaving a contribution that made Daily richer, and, despite the soiled dove labels that haunted the women from their time as working girls, there were more than a handful of men who bought out the contracts from Daily, and married the girls. Henry Crump was one of them. His first visit to the whorehouse left him hopelessly in love, and he immediately approached Daily about his intent.

"I'm just a businessman," asserted Daily, "so everything's for sale at the right price. Anna Wright is a real doll, but give me thirty ounces of gold and she's yours. Otherwise I'll need to work her until she's given me a proper return on my investment. There's a signed contract." And so, Henry Crump rescued a girl his age from sin and made her an honest woman. In most of the world, the thirty ounces of gold would have been a fortune, but with the money pouring in, it took Henry only two weeks to come up with the purchase price, and he saw it as the best investment of his life. Fox had been the best man, as the Mayor spoke the words, "You may now kiss the bride." Immediately after the ceremony, Fox announced, "I got you a little wedding gift. Leading the blushing couple to the harbor, Fox pointed toward a 60-foot, ketch rigged trawler, moored just beyond the dock, adding, without any fanfare, "It's yours." Henry was speechless, and it was the first time that Fox had seen the kid emotional. Henry threw his arms around Fox's neck, voicing a simple "Thank you."

Because so many of the wives ended up sharing a common history, there was not much gossip or criticism in Stella's Cove. Like Anna Crump, the soiled doves transitioned to legitimacy, and people who had previously been nobodies became the respected elders of the town. And through those years of wild prosperity, while gold practically leapt from Muir Creek's placer claims, there was a general harmony in Stella's Cove, born of the realization that there was plenty for all.

There was one more thing that the gold brought to Stella's Cove. Since the town's first minister, Rev. Crump, had left for the richer climes of heaped-up donation plates, organized religion had totally died. While the whiteness of the chapel stood there in all its glory as a contrast to the often dreary heavens, there had been no one to serve as the shepherd of the growing-but-orphaned flock. As necessity is so often the mother of invention, it was the preacher-less void that had created a vacuum, and the town would find a capable preacher in the man they came to know as Rev. Fox.

Fox's transformation, from a trapper and miner to the town's minister, was even more miraculous than the runaway growth of the town. He had become tired of mining, for the spaces under his cabin floor bulged with years of placer flakes, and he knew that he'd had enough. Besides his disenchantment with his work, the glacier had become recalcitrant in its steady excavation of the gold, and Fox's placer claim had become almost as worthless as it was in the early days of trapping. Since his claim was closest to the source of the gold, it was he who first noticed the diminishing supply. Just like the stranger had said, someone had worked it before, but the gold had petered out. Fox knew it was just a matter of time before the other claims would also become first less productive and then totally worthless. He also understood that until the glacier finally disappeared it was likely that new releases of gold would be a predictable but sporadic event in the never-ending flow emerging from the glacier's tongue. Somewhere under the glacier's massive body was a rich vein, and the glacier itself was digging it, slowly, in her grinding push toward the sea.

In the dead of night, Fox lifted the bulging floorboards of his cabin, packed up the gold, and headed for his dory down at the dock. It took him six trips to get it to the boat, and he worried constantly that some late-night drunk would detect his activity, compromising the security of his stash. Yet no one saw him with his saddle bags, feed bag, three burlap sacks, two leather valises, and a pair of denim pants tied off at the ankles with leather curb straps from a horse's headstall. When he lifted the makeshift containers into the dory, he'd figured that they totaled well over nine-hundred pounds.

Rowing through the night under the benefit of a full moon, and assisted by a light, following breeze, he sighted Bourne River in the early morning mist, put into the harbor, and tied the dory to the dock. At about 9:00 a.m., a man drove up with a pony cart for hire, and Fox paid him for the mile drive to the Bourne River Branch of the Vancouver Commercial Bank. The pony whinnied as it plodded along, greeting other ponies beginning their day's labors of delivering people and goods, the early steam of morning snorting from their nostrils.

The cart's driver, a slight man with graying hair, whose facial capillaries betrayed a life of heavy drinking, made no small talk, pointed out no sights along the way, and upon arrival at the bank took his fare and tip with a look of quiet appreciation. Then, seeing an opportunity for another tip, he offered to help Fox carry the motley array of packages inside, and Fox obliged him, giving him yet another tip as the bags were placed against the vice-president's desk. There was silence in the bank. Upon seeing the feedbag, valises, saddlebags, burlap sacks, and tied-off denims, the tellers abruptly ended their morning conversations.

"I'd like to make a deposit," announced Fox to the vice president, opening one of the valises to reveal its contents, and the vice president's face showed an immediate look of alarm. Before him stood a scruffy, ordinary looking miner with a pile of gold almost as tall as he. "Oh, my God!" exclaimed the vice president. "Miss Dougherty," he shouted at one of the tellers, "run for the Mounties!" For a moment, Fox was alarmed, and he supposed that someone was accusing him of theft. "What are you doing?" he inquired of the vice president, and the lady teller in the nearest cage piped up, "That's a hell of a lot of money, Mister. We're going to need some additional guards."

Two Mounties arrived and tied their horses outside, each drawing their service pistols and looking warily down the lane that bordered the bank. "Mister, you're crazy!" barked the first Mountie incredulously, and the second Mountie added, "That's more gold than anyone's ever brought into this bank." And the vice president noted with concern, "I don't think the bank can handle it. It's simply too much."

The doors on the bank were promptly locked, and a teller hung a sign on the door. "Closed for repairs until tomorrow." It took the tellers six hours to carefully weigh and inventory the stash, and by closing time that night, the gold had been carried into the bank's vault. "Not a word of this to anyone." whispered the vice president. "If anyone knew it was here, we'd all be dead."

The Bank decided that the gold could not be permanently deposited in such a small branch, and the vice-president immediately made arrangements to have the gold transferred to its main office in Vancouver. Not trusting its security, Fox purchased a small revolver and personally traveled with the gold aboard the Aniak to help ensure its safe passage. The Aniak hired four armed security guards for the trip, and the Bank itself sent a contingent of four more armed men to ensure the treasure's safe arrival.

After arriving at the Vancouver dock, Fox and the guards immediately escorted the gold to the largest bank in town. It was quite the sight, with nine men, all heavily armed, walking alongside the horse cart, looking down each lane and byway for any possible threat to the gold's security. The president of the Vancouver Commercial Bank greeted Fox like an old friend and turned to him, shielding his mouth with his hand. "You know," he confided, "you're the richest man in British Columbia." Fox understood that he was truly rich, but had not understood that, after his years of privacy and resourceful living, he had opened his life to one of an instant celebrity.

Somehow, everyone knew. Though he was dressed much like he did back in Stella's Cove, it was as if someone had placed a conspicuous sign on his back announcing, "I'm filthy rich." During his stay in Vancouver, his reputation as a "soft touch" and "easy score" had spread like the flames in a pile of tumbleweeds. Saloon owners, clothiers, and dance-hall girls made bets on how much money they could take from him in a single evening, and with nearly a half-ton of gold in the bank, his word was as good as his wallet.

For a month or so, Fox stayed at Vancouver's finest hotel, dined every night on menu items which he did not recognize and which required both pronunciation and a description from the waiters, drinking bottles of watered-down imported "single-malt" Scotch, specially prepared by the posh establishments for the deception of gullible, rich travelers. He spent a few days at clothiers who, in no time at all, had him decked out in a gentleman's garb, and he found some satisfaction in leaving his old clothes at the Salvation Army.

After a month of what would have been considered by most to be the "good life," Fox traveled to Seattle, and his experience there was virtually the same. On one of his last nights there, he found himself in an expensive suite at the Imperial Hotel. The girl who had been with him vanished without a word of farewell, simply taking a handful of money from the nightstand. Fox emptied the contents of an overpriced bottle of champagne and promptly passed out.

Reflecting on the events of his last couple of months, Fox noted that there was lots of excitement and a sense of power that came from his wealth, but he was also developing a distinct loathing for his new life, and he was forced to consider how money did not really bring respectability. It was all about to change.

―――――――

Rummaging through a thrift store in a seedy part of Seattle, Willis Fox stumbled upon some discarded ministerial garb. He purchased the shirt and the cleric's collar, changed in his hotel room, and signed for his bill when he left. The desk clerk dipped his head in reverence as Fox left. "The Lord bless you, and a good day to you." Not so surprisingly, the advances of curvaceous women immediately stopped, something that did not especially please him, though his disappointment was offset by the bar owners, who offered him free drinks because, after all, he was a man of the cloth.

Before leaving Seattle, Fox shaved off the bushy red beard that had been with him since he first grew whiskers, and cultivated a neatly trimmed mustache. He paid for a proper haircut during the last day of his extended "vacation", and, when the barber held up the oval mirror, and asked, "How does it look?" Fox was visibly shaken at what he saw. The face in the mirror looked nothing like Willis Fox. His appearance had always been a bit rough and unkempt until now, and, except for a few ladies of the night, he had felt little motivation to impress anyone. Understanding that his transformation was so stunningly complete, he actually felt like he was no longer the same man and believed that others would not recognize him in his new form-- even those who had known him well.

Fox's new look was a fortuitous accident; it had not been his intention to fool anyone. Yet Fox also understood that the change could help him escape the grand notoriety of his mining success and the target he had become for a growing rush of extended, open hands. He had lost thousands of dollars during his weeks in Seattle and Vancouver, simply because his reputation preceded him, and everyone recognized him as a man of great wealth. Having a special love for the beauty of Stella's Cove, he decided to return to live out his days, and his trip aboard the Aniak had been mostly uneventful. The seas were calm, and except for two Orcas which followed the boat for several miles, rising and falling gently a few yards off the port side, there was nothing that disturbed the placid surface, which continually mirrored the coastal range as the steamship puffed north.

As it had always done, the Aniak proceeded carefully up the channel past Point Fay, and the Captain performed his usual gentle landing against the bumpers on the Stella's Cove dock. There was no fanfare from a brass band, no newspaper article heralding the return of "the town's favorite son," and no applause from those who were gathered as Fox stepped down the gangplank. The predictable array of townsfolk dotted the dock, and Mayor Daily was there, conducting a very short ceremony--

presenting the traditional key to the town to Roderick Edwards, a noted Toronto author. Fox stood there for a moment as the key was presented, curious if anyone would recognize him. When there was no hello or familiar banter, Fox was emboldened in his disguise. The mayor, whom Fox knew well, and with whom he'd shared many pints at Bud's Saloon, did not even note Fox's presence. As a sort of test, Fox said "Hello. How are you?" as the mayor finished the key ceremony, and, except for a brief pause and a slightly quizzical expression, there was no hint of recognition in the mayor's face. Fox suspected that Mayor Daily sensed a certain familiarity, but a subsequent conversation proved that Fox's masquerade was complete.

In Stella's Cove the hustle and bustle had reached no greater level since its first establishment as a fur trading post. Miners, downstream from Fox's claim, were still enjoying success, and, because of the rapid growth, Fox realized that virtually all the people he saw were the recent transplants of the last few years. As he walked from the dock, people were friendly--smiling, and greeting him as some important member of the community. For a moment Fox thought he was being recognized, but the recognition was only of the Bible he carried, and the neatly starched cleric's collar he wore.

Fox considered no specific plan and had wished for only an innocuous melding with the townsfolk and a life of peace, but when he ducked inside the white Methodist chapel that dominated the town's buildings, a lady with too much lipstick and rouge addressed him. "It looks like we have a new preacher." she said tentatively, more as a question. The friend who was with her, a sluice miner that Fox had seen before, added, "It's about time we got some religion in this town."

After exchanging some small talk, the lady inquired, "What time is the Sunday service?" It was only for one, single moment that speech eluded him, while the new "Rev. Fox" was temporarily transfixed by a vision of his future identity. He didn't know why; he tried to stop it, but there was a sudden, involuntary rush of air and sound emerging from his mouth. "It will start exactly at 10:00." Willis Fox stood there, perplexed, with the realization that he would have no graceful way to retract the "harmless" deception. But the new Rev. Fox let no one down. The word quickly spread that the Methodist Church was no longer abandoned by God, and that a shepherd had been sent to watch after the flock in Stella's Cove.

Though it was never his intent to enter the clergy, Rev. Fox quickly established himself as everyone's favorite minister. His short but leisurely retirement came to an abrupt end, and his Sunday sermons were among the best the congregation of Stella's Cove had ever heard. While his first sermons took him days to research and write, his dedication brought him instant success as the only shepherd in Stella's Cove. Raised with the standard religious upbringing, he was not unfamiliar with the Bible, but it had still been no small task for him to decide on and complete the sermons for the coming weeks.

After years of lying low so as to not attract attention, Rev. Fox became the town's most visible leader, and he found substantial satisfaction in his new "calling." Fully expecting that he'd be hearing from the regional Methodist Council, he simply did his best by filling the vacancy left by Rev. Sinclair Crump. He understood that his days were numbered, and that one official letter could bring his ministry to its end. There had been one particular theme that was almost always mentioned in his sermons, for they invariably included the golden rule and the admonition to refrain from judging others. His simple presentations of the principles of true Christianity touched the hearts of Stella's Cove, and, after each sermon, there had been a re-dedication of the townsfolk to treat their brethren well.

Rev. Fox's treatment of religion as a simple recipe for living became the faith of Stella's Cove, and the community sensed that the Lord was right there, in every one of the church meetings. Baptisms and weddings were performed without flaw, and Holy Communion was offered weekly to all those who expressed belief. Though he'd never attended a seminary, nobody ever knew, and with his bright mind, those sacraments had been performed perfectly every time.

While Rev. Fox had his own lingering doubt about churches in general, he noticed some significant changes in people, which seemed to come from an increased awareness of their own frailties and faults. His congregation worshipped him, for he presented himself as one of them and was humble about his own imperfections. Rev. Fox also understood that the congregation could throw him out at any time because of certain weaknesses of the flesh. He exhorted the faithful to follow the Ten Commandments, knowing they were an ample key to the smooth workings of a community. But, as much as religion had become the center of his activities, he loved to drink, and women were his favored confection.

Stella's Cove actually enjoyed the best preacher it would ever have. Sure, Rev. Fox may have done a bit too much imbibing, and, yes, he was known to rock a bed or too, but it was the forgiving and Christ-like attitude of the man that expanded the little church to the biggest single congregation in all of B.C. Rev. Fox's wisdom was extraordinary, and his counseling of sinners was both reparative and therapeutic. Women with problems came to him for spiritual guidance, and the underlying prurient nature of Rev. Fox helped to cure their physical ailments too.

One of them was Angela Maroni, whose husband Joe was a placer miner. Working hard for meager takings, Joe faced the disappointment of having chosen the poorest claim along Muir Creek. The claim was just a few feet from where the creek met the harbor, and Joe's harvest of "heavy material" was a mere gleaning of what those miners, further upstream, had missed. Consistent with his disappointment, he sought his bravado in the local saloon, spinning yarns and boasting of the success which had so sorely eluded him, and believing the drunken words of the girls who made their livings by stroking the egos of men.

One Sunday morning, after the others of Rev. Fox's flock had walked out of the chapel, complimenting his sermon as they left, one person remained behind, and the gentle pastor saw the troubled face of Mrs. Maroni. The church had a small office next to the entry, and Fox invited her to sit down and talk with him about whatever it was that afflicted her soul. "Sister Maroni," he asked. "What seems to be troubling you?" She did not answer, but her eyes immediately filled with tears, and Rev. Fox instinctively gave her a compassionate hug. "Whatever it is," said Fox, "I am here for the people of this church, and there is no problem too great for God to fix."

In subsequent counseling sessions, Rev. Fox was able to glean the sketchy details of the Maroni's troubles, and it was largely his deep compassion that allowed him exposure to the substantial risk. For it was the compassion that drove him to help, and it was compassion that led him to drop his guard. During the weeks ahead, Rev. Fox prayed, more than once, for strength to overcome the weaknesses of the flesh. But, after their first meeting, Rev. Fox noticed, each Sunday, as he handed out communion, the shape of Mrs. Maroni's lips as they curled around the bread, and how they pursed as she drank the wine from the cup. Mrs. Maroni also noticed things about the preacher--mostly the gentleness of his eyes and the kindness of his look. Each experienced fantasies that followed them out the door of their counseling sessions, and both imagined themselves in the arms of the other. Rev. Fox was determined not to submit to his instincts, for he understood that his position of responsibility did not allow any physical dalliance with his charges.

During his fifth counseling session with Mrs. Maroni, Rev. Fox asked, "Do you think it would be helpful to get Joe in here? My belief is that the problems of your lives can be fixed, but it is going to take both of you to work on the solution." Mrs. Maroni's expression turned to a momentary blank stare. "I don't think," she answered sadly, "that he'd come in, and his behavior with the women and booze has made it clear that he has no interest in salvaging the good feelings of the past." Rev. Fox pondered her words for a few moments, and seeing only a sad desolation in her mood, he gave her one more compassionate hug.

Mrs. Maroni had drawn Rev. Fox into the middle of her life, and he had already become uncomfortable about the impropriety of having counseled a married woman in the privacy of his office. Perhaps Mrs. Maroni was a great actress, or, perhaps her motives were mostly sincere. But, even as a "man of God" the Reverend was blind-sided by both the feelings he experienced and the overt romantic move of the unfulfilled wife. There was an immediate transition from the compassionate hug into a lingering kiss, and Rev. Fox felt a sincere sadness at the obvious loneliness Mrs. Maroni had endured.

Compassion, though considered a strength for most men, was actually the softest and most vulnerable chink in Rev. Fox's armor. He noticed the pressure of her body against his, and wondered how her breasts were suddenly bare and how they now pressed against his chest. He did not know how it happened, and he was as bewildered as he was aroused. The cleric's collar and Sister Maroni's clothes had ended up on the floor, and the two made love on the counseling room settee, well into the night.

On a Sunday evening, about one month after his intimate slip, there was a knock at Rev. Fox's door. "Yes...who's there?" But no one answered and Rev. Fox approached the door, carrying his Bible, for the interruption had come as he'd been working on the next week's Sunday's sermon. When he opened the door an angry miner stood there, pointing a pistol at Fox's chest. Though he'd not introduced himself, there was no question on the man's identity. "Howdy, Reverend," the caller mocked with a drunken slur, "I hear you've been doing some wonderful things for my wife." Understanding that his own actions had created an enemy, Rev. Fox knew that a humble apology was in order, but Joe Maroni said no more, simply smiling at Fox and pulling the trigger. Rev. Fox instinctively drew his arm across his chest as it happened. Joe fired once more at Fox as he fell, but the bullet somehow hit the Bentleys' old Superior cast iron stove, ricocheted from its firebox and pierced the miner's neck, killing him instantly. There was no other noise--just a ringing sound that continued from the iron stove for several moments, and a faint gurgling as Brother Maroni took his last breath.

Rev. Fox fully believed in forgiveness, and he was weighed down in his understanding that his sins were grievous in the sight of God. With no other way to make amends, he generously officiated at Maroni's funeral, and the man who had sought to murder him was given a marked burial in the little cemetery north of town. The man's widow had graciously asked Rev. Fox, "I know he tried to kill you, but would you find it in your heart to deliver a sermon on his behalf?" As obliging as always, and with an understanding of his own guilt in having created the crisis, he delivered one of the best sermons of his life, along with a touching eulogy that avoided Maroni's faults and praised the efforts of a "hard-working man." And, in the months ahead, the appreciative and grieving widow continued to receive counseling.

With most of his rascality left behind, Rev. Fox dedicated the rest of his life to helping others, and the heavy Bible, complete with the bullet it had stopped, stood on Fox's mantle until he died of cancer five years later. He never did run out of either human compassion or money, and he left a legacy, when he died, that would build the seventy-four foot steeple on B.C.'s largest Methodist Church and cause his name to be remembered as the best preacher the town had ever known.

As a sharp contrast to Fox's kind and compassionate leadership, the Rev. Miles Cromwell, though seminary-trained and fully empowered by the Methodist Council, would take the helm of the Methodist Church four years later, eviscerating community conscience and cementing the future of our town. When Rev. Cromwell stood there behind that ornately carved pulpit, detailing the miracle of Jesus feeding 5,000 with only five loaves of bread and two fish, my mind had wandered, instead, to the visible inhumanity that was so pervasive in our community. If that story was a parable of what Christianity had to offer, and fish were a symbol of the spiritual nourishment that flowed from the Good Book, something had gone terribly wrong. Maybe the food for life had really been there, but it was grimly obvious to me that there had been a failure of fish to nourish the souls of our town.

A Rising Phoenix

If there ever was such a thing as out-of-control growth, Stella's Cove had become the example of what happens when individual interests and greed dictate the evolution of a town. There were few rules or zoning ordinances, and illicit businesses popped up everywhere. During the same year that Joe Maroni was buried, the success of virtually all the miners had gradually ended, and the town shrunk to a small group of stubborn holdovers.

The Aniak stayed busy that year, ferrying frustrated miners to towns that offered jobs. It was apparent to everyone: The town's short history seemed to be following a pattern of boom-and-bust, and its remaining residents wondered if the good times would ever come again. For the town had literally risen from its ashes when Fox found those specks of gold in 1865, and, by 1875--only ten years later--the thriving community had died once more, leaving more homes, a handful of commercial buildings, one empty whorehouse, and abandoned mining equipment for the full length of Muir Creek.

While not quite as colorful as the town's first two explosions of growth and its subsequent economic implosions, one of the town's most memorable events would be the abrupt transition that followed Rev. Miles Cromwell's removal as the town's school teacher--when education suddenly put on a happier but controversial face.

Though, in itself, the replacement of Cromwell as the town's teacher did not make or destroy our town, it set the stage for a disaster greater than Stella's Cove had ever before experienced. The short burst of educational enlightenment that followed led to the moral failure of an entire town and, unlike the ancient Phoenix, it would likely never rise again. The angry sapphire-blue glacier would have few subjects left to torment, and would have to find satisfaction in those she had already consumed.

When only a small core of its population was left, the town would have what was the equivalent of the stink of dying, and no one remaining in Stella's Cove would believe that good times could come again.

During that year, when education in Stella's Cove took its giant leap out of the dark ages, life changed for me. Before the school got its new teacher, I consistently failed to bring home my books. I failed to get my assignments done, and Mother's admonitions to "Buckle down," which were reliably voiced after each semi-annual parent-teacher conference, fell on both deaf ears and an unwilling mind.

"You're a smart boy, Billy," Mother chided "and you shouldn't be happy with the grades you're getting. Rev. Cromwell says you're just not applying yourself." Then she paused for a moment, and I noticed a sad and empty look in her eyes. "I know that some of this is about losing your father," she sympathized, "but you can't let his death determine what your life will be." I knew she was right, but there was something inside me that was constantly beating me down, and I struggled to identify its source and to understand the force that seemed to render me powerless over the inertia that was dominating my life.

After Father's death, I had always looked for ways to get out of going to school. There were times I'd even feigned illness in order to stay home, and summer vacations were always too short. The arrival of Miss Hardwicke changed it all. I no longer looked forward to holidays and the annual summer break, and I put my best efforts into homework and assignments. Something had come into my life that I had never before known from education, and I knew exactly what it was--real inspiration, and it came from a combination of factors.

The boredom of Rev. Cromwell standing before the class for all those years, from kindergarten to the tenth grade, had been a colorless experience. He always dressed in the same dark clothes, imposing an incessant, un-articulated statement that he was not just our teacher, but God's servant. Like the blackboard upon which he squeaked his chalk, there was simply no engagement with his students. In fact, I sometimes thought that he was much like the striped wallpaper in our outhouse--something that was just "there" and always had been. I sat in that outhouse enough times, considering the spider webs that reappeared daily, despite cleaning, and wondering how any creature could have such determination--to repair or rebuild its home so many times in such a smelly place. Though I stared daily at that wallpaper, I never read the quotations from famous writers and statesmen that were integrated into its pattern. It did not matter that those words were important. What did matter was that the words, though there, were never spoken in a way that commanded my attention, and the necessity of sitting there had been my only compelling activity.

Rev. Cromwell's greatest failing as a teacher was that he only spoke words, rather than inspiring our fertile young minds, and his delivery was as tiresome as the fifteen minutes of Bible reading my mother insisted upon every evening before supper. Except for the speeches about hell, and his rousing words of exhortation against sin, Cromwell's delivery was in a predictably monotone voice. And the introductory language, in so many Bible verses, "and it came to pass," was so branded on my mind that I expected, for certain, those would be the last words of my old age. After all, I would surely "come to pass."

When Cromwell was suddenly terminated from his schoolmaster job, it was the first unscheduled delivery of dreams to the children of Stella's Cove, and while Miss Kimberly Hardwicke was there, each day would demonstrate that there is no such thing as a mere word. I would have to describe it as buoyancy, and I was lifted, in a sense, to a new level of life, and the ordinary and mediocre would never appeal to me again.

Rev. Cromwell had never been a favorite with the young people of Stella's Cove. While he'd seemed to have some healthy warmth toward the kids in the younger grades, teenagers in the Cove believed that Cromwell actually hated them. He spoke to them in snarls, and was remarkably artistic in his application of corporal punishment. His severity was a tragic impediment to the cultivation of young minds, and no child would ever say "I like him." or "He's a great teacher." Of course, it is respect, not popularity, that endorses a teacher's worth, and even the parents understood that he had, largely, failed at both. His presence created fear, and not much else.

Such a unanimous awareness of Rev. Cromwell's disagreeable nature should have ended his teaching career years before, but the Town Fathers all dreaded the possibility that a replacement would be too liberal for such a strongly religious community. The graceful application of his pointer stick to our knuckles left me with a painful joint injury, and though many parents complained of Cromwell's impatience and unsuitability as a teacher, the alternative was daunting. They did not want outsiders to be mentoring their children.

It was a fear of a greater evil that had allowed Rev. Cromwell to remain the town's teacher for all those years, and the parents and Town Fathers had perpetuated his reign by reprimanding their children and always taking the minister's side. Had a child ever complained, the parents simply assumed the minister's position, constantly calling their children to repentance while the authority of a cleric's collar ruled the people of the town. Reason, on the other hand, had been entirely neglected.

Mother looked at my cracked knuckle as justice for my headstrong ways. "Well, Billy," she'd chided "you wouldn't have this problem if you hadn't made Rev. Cromwell mad. I'm on his side, you know, the same side as our Lord Jesus Christ." When she said it, I noticed a hint of faltering faith in her voice, and I instinctively understood that she was hiding some of her feelings, anticipating that the power of the minister would someday fail. It made me happy to know that, while she sided with Cromwell, she was, nevertheless, aware of his failures.

There was no question about it. The whole town had surely understood that Rev. Cromwell was out of line. Every time I picked up a pen, my cracked knuckle hurt—a rather extreme consequence for questioning his assertion that the world was created in six days.

It had occurred to me that Rev. Cromwell was actually insane. There had been more than a handful of times when he literally frothed at the mouth during one of his out-of-control tongue-lashings of a student's incompetence or insolence. I will always remember having to wipe the frothy spatter from my face and shirt with my handkerchief after one such episode. Later that day I tried to recall my first years at the Stella's Cove School, and it seemed to me that the cleric's behavior had become much worse over time.

Looking back on it, I believe that those prone to mental problems are easily sucked in by religious fervor, and that it is the promotion of belief in the unseen and imaginary that is so insidiously destructive to an objective view of our world.

Religion seemed to play a part in my own mother's emotional imbalance. Likewise, the minister's ideas were based on a surprisingly fragile delusion, and it seemed too obvious to me that he possessed a morbid fear of colliding with reality. I noticed, also, that that same fear was the reason why religious people are so easily placed under the yoke of submission, but I also understood that the simplicity of a life without individual responsibility was an enviable position. I could empathize with the nature of the devout, for theirs was simply a surrender to the will and rules of a group—making it totally unnecessary for any personal, moral and ethical decisions.

———————

In the end, Cromwell's deteriorating health and his growing impatience with his students necessitated a replacement. And the community leaders were forced to take action.

Regrettable Decision

In the minds of the Town Fathers, there had been a constant and agonizing review of just what went wrong in the matter of finding a new teacher for Stella's Cove. The Council members thought back to that evening, when the ball had started rolling and then accelerated out of control, at the monthly Town Council meeting in April of 1912.

At exactly 7:00 p.m. Mayor James Burroughs stood up.

"The meeting will come to order." Burroughs officiously shouted, and the room became immediately quiet. "As the most important matter for consideration at this monthly Council meeting, we have the matter of replacing our school teacher." The room buzzed with a half-dozen personal conversations that all seemed to sprout from the business on the agenda. "Order!" steamed Burroughs, and the room became immediately quiet again.

Willis Stanley addressed the group, emphasizing the urgency in making the necessary change. "As you all know," Willis began, "Rev. Cromwell, though a very educated and God-fearing man, is getting up in his years. When he came to Stella's Cove in 1874, he was only forty years old, and he has become a favored member of our community--a voice of wisdom and righteousness at a time when the morals of mankind are failing. Though not everyone has liked his personality, his goodness has seemed irreproachable, and he has been a leader in our Church, our lives, and the lives and education of our children. As you're aware, he has been both our ecclesiastical and educational leader, and it gives me no pleasure to announce that he will not be our teacher when school resumes this coming fall." Again, the buzz of council members resumed and the room was, once more, called to order.

George Murphy was a relative newcomer to the town, but he was on the Council because he employed more than fifty percent of Stella's Cove and had a net worth that exceeded the collective total of the Town's other residents. He owned the Murphy Salmon Company processing plant, the only deep-water dock in the area, and he owned the only hydroelectric generating plant north of Vancouver.

"Well," asserted George "that doesn't give us a great deal of time, so my first recommendation to the Council is that it must immediately advertise for the school teacher opening, in order to find some suitable applicants. Since the Town's resources are limited, applicants should be immediately screened, according to criteria set forth at this meeting, and the best three applicants should be interviewed, using the most economical and expedient protocol. I believe it would also be appropriate, at this time," Murphy continued, "to set a salary for a two year contract period, and address the matter of lodging for the successful applicant." There was a perplexed look on the faces of the other eleven members of the Council. Most had not considered that replacing Cromwell was going to be, not only an educational concern, but a financial drain on the community as well.

Gordon Wilson expressed nervousness over the matter. "As we all know," he asserted, "Rev. Cromwell has taken no salary during his years of teaching and he has considered his duties as schoolmaster to be included in his responsibility as the shepherd of our flock. There's not going to be a free teacher anymore."

Jeffrey Farnes made a suggestion. "Maybe it's time to retire Cromwell." There was a look of sudden clarity in his face. "Cromwell is old enough to go on his pension, and we can simply get a new preacher who is willing to serve as the teacher for our school. We're already doing our duty in passing the plate each Sunday, so why should we have to pay someone more than that to handle the teaching position?"

There were immediate nods from two Council members, but Sam Harper reminded them, "Public education is not to be parochial--that's a matter of our Constitution, and has been enacted as law by our Parliament." He was obviously offended by Farnes' suggestion. "Though it has been handled loosely in the past" Harper barked, "I don't think it's appropriate to continue the merger of Church and State--that's essentially what we've been doing--so our course of action must adhere to our commitment as Canadians. It is simply a matter of the law and the rules on public education."

"Has anyone contacted the Board," asked the Mayor, "to see if a teacher is already available for the position? It must have contacts and applicants that would be available on short notice." Mayor Burroughs seemed to be confident that one would be available, and asked Mr. Wilson to make haste in the appropriate inquiries. "Well," mentioned Wilson, "since the Board has only recently been mandated and organized, it is pretty improbable, and, besides that, attracting a teacher to the isolation of our town is, in itself, going to be a difficult undertaking." There were nods from the other Council members. Mayor Burroughs reminded the group that there was business to conduct. "Let's not get sidetracked on the perpetual problems of our town. A vote, please, on the initiation of advertising."

"Here, here!" Eldon Sather seconded the earlier recommendation, and he was given the task of arranging newspaper ads in Vancouver and Seattle. "How much budget can I allocate for the advertising?" he added, and there was an instant pall of discouragement that descended on the meeting, for the Town had borne few expenditures in the past, and Council members were unsure of the available cash resources.

"Treasurer," addressed Mayor Burroughs, "read the accounts." Bill Morley was a college degree in accounting, and had kept the Town's books for almost twenty years. He was still dressed in his work garb and had a green visor sticking out of his forehead, just above his eyebrows. Where the headband pressed against his red hair, a bristly bunch of wild quills seemed to reach for the ceiling, looking much like the grasses that grew on the coastal dunes, but the wrong color. His thick round lenses accentuated the size of his eyes, which resembled those of a raccoon, sitting on a front porch and startled by the appearance of someone at the door. He was wearing a pressed blue shirt, and his tweed trousers broke slightly where the tops of his shoes began.

Because, for a long time, there had been shortfalls in the budget, it had been Morley who insisted, eleven years before, that a small municipal tax be imposed on all commercial transactions. The fishermen moaned that they couldn't afford it; the idea of more taxes was greatly opposed; but, in the end it had been a boost to the needs of Stella's Cove. While the local fishermen and merchants had proven fairly successful at avoiding the taxes, and most far understated their profits, the bulk of the treasury funds had been generated by the Murphy Salmon Company and Murphy Hydroelectric.

Harvey Moyle had a daughter who taught school in Kokeemah Bay, and he mentioned that she was receiving a salary of $65 per month in addition to room and board. The matter was then voted on, and there was a unanimous "Yea" predicated on the availability of the funds.

Because of Bill Morley's foresight, there was money in the general account, and it had grown substantially over a run of a dozen very prosperous years. "$4,923.40," Morely proudly announced, and the members of the Council were all smiling at each other, understanding that was a healthy sum, and plenty to accomplish the recruitment and two-year salary for a qualified school teacher for Stella's Cove.

Morley could then answer the question of the advertising budget. "My recommendation is that, because of the pressing time element, we blitz the Vancouver, Seattle, and Provincial papers, and I believe $50 would accomplish a very good advertising effort."

"Here, here." Sather added, "I second Morley's recommendation."

Mayor Burroughs stood and asked, "Do we have suggestions from the members of the Council regarding the qualifications criteria for the new teacher?" Everyone was quiet, and, for just a few moments, there was no sound in the room at all. The matter of qualifications brought consternation. Each Council member heard only his gentle rush of air during inhalation, a purposeful statement in the audible exhaust of carbon dioxide, and each Council member found that the thumpa-thumpa of his own heartbeat was louder than the frantic gyrations of brains at a time when each man felt the gravity of the matter, pressing on his existence as a human being.

Gerrod MacBean had never felt anything quite like it. He was considering the security of his only daughter, Gertrude, and the undeniable influence a teacher could have for good or for bad.

He listened to the pounding of his heart and asked himself why he was feeling so queasy but, he understood, it was the ominous realization that the business then at hand was the most serious decision in the life of the town. It was only the authoritative voice of George Murphy that ended what seemed like an interminable silence.

"I don't believe that this should be a problem." Murphy interrupted the spellbound Council. "I think it is fairly obvious what the minimum standards for our school teacher should be..." Turning toward the Mayor, Murphy asked, "Is it recognized by the Council that I should continue, or do you wish someone else to present a proposed list of the required qualifications?" Understanding that Stella's Cove had never quite grown to love him, Murphy was willing to defer to the group, but Mayor Burroughs was actually enthusiastic that someone has expressed the interest and willingness to tackle what suddenly seemed like a mammoth task. "Please, go ahead." directed Mayor Burroughs, and Murphy started.

"Let's do this by the numbers," noted Murphy, "so that we can all address each specific item. Number One: We need to make sure that the applicant possesses a teaching degree from an accredited university and has basic teaching skills in reading, writing, general sciences, and arithmetic."

"Here, here," shouted the group with great enthusiasm, as if being roused by a charlatan giving his sales pitch on a bottle of "Kickapoo Joy Juice." Since no one else was choosing to tackle the subject, there was an immediate deference to Murphy's suggestion.

"Number Two: The applicant must be of good character and refrain from public drunkenness." The Council was vocally unanimous, and there were no members dissenting.

"Number Three:" Murphy continued, "The applicant must have five personal references attesting to their honesty and integrity." It all seemed very simple, and the Council members were feeling that Murphy's suggestions were well taken and should be used as the minimum standard.

But Gerrod MacBean was still feeling uncomfortable, because he understood, from his own personal experiences in the Province's public schools, that teachers can be an even greater influence, in the lives of the young, than the parents. "Gentlemen," he spoke with a pronounced air of piety, "we must make sure that, whomever it is that teaches my little Gertrude and the other children of our community, is a good and God-fearing human being who reads the Bible and attends Sunday services at the Church." There was a second wind in the tired Council, though the hour was late, and the business had to be finished before they left. Each of the Councilmen had now seen the writing on the wall--the inevitable truth that, like the hand that rocks the cradle, the teacher at Stella's Cove's school would be either a good or evil influence.

Suddenly there was whining from the Council, and Sam Harper was bristling with annoyance over MacBean's suggestion. "For God's sake," Harper moaned with obvious frustration, "there's a reason why Rev. Cromwell isn't on this Council. It's improper to mix religion with politics and education, just as it's improper for us to have the Methodist Church occupy a place in our local government." Everyone heard what he said, but only two of the men were actually embracing his words.

"I realize," said George Murphy, "that I am, in a sense, an outsider, and though I have sought to improve the lives of people in this community, I fully understand that the Church is an unquestionable power in Stella's Cove. But, like the honorable Mr. Harper, I must agree, on the basis of law, that religion cannot be a factor appropriately considered in the teacher qualifications." There was a general agreement, in principle, with what George Murphy had just said, but Morely and Sather were thinking about the rumors they'd heard, how Mrs. George Murphy was a dance-hall girl and prostitute before she and George were married. No one had ever confirmed it, but the gossip had been so juicy as to not be merely dismissed. Those who actually tried to verify that accusation miserably failed, and the brightest of the townsfolk all understood that such allegations were an outgrowth of the jealousy they felt for the Murphy family. But, then again, who would start such a vicious rumor if there hadn't been some truth in the story?

"Oh, just one more thing," George reminded the Council, "There's the matter of lodging for whomever is hired." Bart Clemmerton, Sr., who had been very successful as the Town's baker, said that he'd be happy to provide a room and board for the new teacher, and he asked for a $20 per month stipend to be approved by the Council. That was unanimously approved, and the board and room would be included in the final contract. Bart

Clemmerton, Sr. was in his sixties, and though he had four children, his two older daughters had chosen to move away when they were old enough to do so. Only his eleven year old daughter Sarah and his adult son, Bart, Jr.—known to everyone as "Junior"--still lived in the home with him, and the large stone house, sitting at the top of Main Street, had plenty of space for whomever the new teacher would be. Bart, Sr.'s wife had died of the flue three years before, and the home had been feeling too large for only the three of them.

―――――――――

A vote was taken. George Murphy's three criteria for the new teacher were adopted by the Council, and the meeting was adjourned with the usual shot of single malt whisky for each of its members. There was a flurry of conversation as the members left, and the educational needs of the town flooded each man's brain. It had occurred to them all that finding a successful and suitable applicant might be harder than it appeared, for there were few outsiders likely willing to deal with the total isolation of Stella's Cove and the homogenous nature of its population.

Outside the old house the Council used for its monthly meetings, the group dispersed, each member filled with a sense of both the gravity and excited urgency of securing Cromwell's replacement. Murphy's pony cart sat outside, and he greeted "Oscar" with an apple he'd been saving in his pocket. Oscar stood about twelve hands tall, and, unlike most ponies--which tend to be troll-ish in their proportions--he had the conformation of a fine, adult horse, and an unusual chocolate-palomino coloring. "There you go, boy." Murphy talked to Oscar while running his fingers under the head stall and giving the pony's poll a little massage, As George drove the two miles home, he savored the beauty of Stella's Cove. A pale moon was peering between the sheets of coastal fog, and there was a noticeable scent of salt and seaweed because the tide was at its ebb. "This," considered George, "is why I love this place."

When George arrived at his mansion on Point Fay, he unhitched Oscar, gave the pony a handful of rolled oats, and turned him lose in a large grassy paddock that bordered the south side of the garden. Oscar immediately rolled, and George asked "Why do you always roll in the one muddy spot?" Not surprisingly, Oscar didn't answer, and, as George walked to the home's side entry, he noticed that all four of Oscar's white-socked feet were still in the air.

Inside there was excitement as Murphy smiled sweetly at his wife, Eva, hugging her gently as she rose to take his hat. "There's some big news this evening," he announced, to her and his 15-year-old Celeste. "The Town's going to get a new teacher."

Eva Murphy had never understood just how miserable her daughter Celeste had been in Rev. Cromwell's classes, because, despite Celeste's beauty and the expectation that such a pretty, willowy, well-dressed young lady was likely spoiled by her family's wealth, she never once complained about Cromwell, and had stoically avoided, in general, the condemnation of anyone. But her Father's news gave Celeste the opportunity to colorfully vent her disdain. "God," she responded "I can't wait to see him replaced. He has the personality of a stick, and I've never once seen him smile." There were similar words being spoken by children in the living rooms of other Council members. It really was unanimous. Their children's response made all the adults feel better about the coming change, for it had been the first time that most of them considered just how unpleasant a teacher Rev. Cromwell had been.

Judgment

The matters of gossip and judgment always haunted Stella's Cove. And there were other problems that went hand in hand. For it was gossip that provided accounts of questionable origins, and it was upon the missing merit of such questionable information, that people were judged, ridiculed, and ostracized.

Harry Mills, a defrocked minister from Eagle City, became one of the town's favorite victims. The essential ingredients of the gossip and judgment largely cemented his fate. It all seemed so simple. Mom often reviewed Harry's story as a lesson on how God uses such evils as the glacier to bring justice to the wicked. Her account was that a green-eyed, redheaded woman of his congregation brought lust into Harry's life, and that, in a moment of sexual frenzy, he had taken her by force. His congregation's righteous wrath and embarrassment spawned threats of lynching, and he was banished from the community of Eagle City. The offended lambs of Harry's flock beat him brutally, then mercifully laid him in the bed of a wagon of a party transiting the area. "God's punishment!" Mom would declare.

All but a few of the religious folks in Stella's Cove accepted the account of the rape, and only a few asked Harry if he was guilty of his crime. Later I would know that the story was not true, and understand that it had been Harry's own kindness toward others, and his belief in the value of every soul, that had led him to the end of his ministry. It was, in fact, his goodness and guileless nature that had made him so vulnerable. Even at my age, the story I'd been told about the Rev. Harry Mills did not seem to ring true. If he'd raped a girl, wouldn't he have been arrested, tried, and sentenced? Crimes like that were so serious. It made no sense to me, how the RCMP had apparently ignored the matter.

But the public removal of Harry Mills' cleric's collar and the broken jaw, inflicted by his beating, that never healed properly and left him with a mush-mouthed speech impediment, were only the beginning of what Mother described as God's wrath. The cruelest punishment was his chance relocation to our town, where a community of God-fearing died-in-the-wool Methodists regarded him no higher than the occasional skunks that left their disagreeable stink hanging over Stella's Cove. In all the years that the town had been there, its people had never seen such a perfect opportunity to match good against evil, and the pious population had determined that they would help deliver the wages of sin that Harry so obviously deserved.

In September 1911, Harry Mills had arrived aboard the Aniak on its southbound run down the coast. The day was a typical one, with a shroud of mist defying the frustrated persistence of the sun, and with an offshore wind that penetrated even the best woolen coats. Beaten, cold, and ill, Harry had begged for a place to spend those first chilly nights--at least until he could erect some type of temporary shelter.

With almost six-hundred people in Stella's Cove--brought by the lure of good paying jobs at the Murphy Salmon Company processing plant--one would anticipate that at least someone would have helped Harry. Upon his arrival, he spoke to several of those gathered on the dock, inquiring if there was any inexpensive lodging available. When he was told there were no inns in the town, he inquired if there might be someone who'd let a room for the night. The people at the dock had been surprisingly unfriendly, and one had barked, "So you're that rapist. You'd better stay away from our wives and daughters, or you'll find your throat cut." and, as an afterthought the man had added, "We don't want you in our town, and you're not going to find a room here."

Disappointed by the harsh welcome, and understanding that the rumors rolled in even faster than the steamship, Harry walked around the town, knocking on virtually every house that was lit. Many of the knocks went unanswered, and one woman actually threw trash on him from a second story window as he stood there humble and in need. He knew that he probably hadn't been to every door, but his aching body made him anxious to lie down. He reflected on how terrible he must have looked, for there was still blood oozing from the worst of his wounds. After about an hour of knocking, and hearing an endless stream of rejections--some of them truly vile--Harry had simply given up.

For it was certainly true that Harry's infamy had preceded his arrival, and the townsfolk would not show mercy, particularly to someone who was guilty of such a vicious act. I was just fourteen years old at the time, but I felt compassion for him. Like everyone else, the story of his vile nature was gossiped to me, and I couldn't help but thinking how quickly unseemly news spreads. When Harry Mills knocked on our door, my Mother told him in a remarkably civil way, "Don't you come near this house." I felt sad and embarrassed as the fallen-minister-sex-maniac dropped his head, turned and walked away, and I wondered, for a moment, if my Mother was any kind of Christian at all. But I also understood that no mother would want to expose her family to the risk of having Harry Mills stay, even if it was in the woodshed, out back.

The cold breeze from the northeast had intensified, and, with no immediate prospects for lodging, Harry looked for a protected spot to lie down. He'd noticed the Methodist Church, so tall that its steeple seemed to impale the moon that rose above the coastal mountains. The steeple was taller, in fact, than any Harry had seen before, and he wondered how such an imposing edifice had come to be built in such an isolated spot.

Feeling very much at home in a church, Harry thought to himself, "Surely no one would take objection to me sleeping just inside its vestibule." and he anticipated that he'd be gone long before any people came. It was a Sunday night, so the church would likely sit idle until the end of the week. The hour was late, and he accepted that no one would bother him there. Limping to the church, he opened its impressively carved door, and walked inside. Two of the overhead lamps were lit, but trimmed, and the gentle glow of whale oil filled the church. Even with the small amount of light they shed, the scene before him was awe-inspiring.

Though the Murphy Hydroelectric Company had brought electric power to the community years before, the minister of the church had chosen to keep the building's original oil lamps, for he considered it a matter of purism to have flames that were real, instead of filaments that never burned, and he regarded the new inventions of science to be like the Sirens who lured sailors to their deaths--something very appealing but lacking in honest substance.

Once inside, Harry leaned his head back, noticing a pain as he lifted his eyes upward. The ceiling was at least thirty feet high, and was covered with pressed cellulose paneling--obviously custom made in some larger town. While many businesses used such material to cover the unsightly rafters, Harry had never seen it in a church. The panels were pressed with a pattern of an empty-cross motif, and he was dumbstruck, trying to comprehend the exorbitant cost of such custom-made materials. A choir loft stood about ten feet higher than the pulpit, and had beautifully carved, curved staircases, rising to it from each side.

The pulpit itself appeared to be made from clear-heart fir, but its mantle, made of what looked like Koa Wood, had deep, contrasting striations such as Harry had seen only once before at a Polynesian exhibit at the provincial museum. It too was ornately carved, and the same wood was inlaid into the pulpit's face in the stylized shape of a cross.

Massive beams formed trusses supporting the elegant roof above, and Harry noticed that they were not the typical, rough-hewn logs cut by run-of-the-mill sawyers along the coast. He could not tell what kind of wood they were, but each beam was hand-carved with a shepherd capital rising from its center, and with flocks of sheep streaming toward Christ from each side. The carvings extended the beams' full lengths, and Harry understood that there were no finer buildings in this part of the world. As assistant minister in Princeville and as the most successful cleric in Eagle City, Harry had never seen anything like it, nor had he even imagined that such a building existed along the west coast of B.C.

The brass oil lamps that hung from its ceiling looked like something from the Tiffany's branch store in Seattle. (Mother had taken me to Tiffany's, once, as a child, and I could still remember the elegance that filled its shelves.) The pews were obviously not of native pine and fir, but appeared to be solid mahogany with a Koa Wood top rail that continued from the left aisle to the right. Harry walked the length of the pews, detecting that there were no seams in the rail, that each one was a continuous piece, and that each one had a mural carved into its back depicting a different Bible scene.

Harry's head ached as he walked back to the cloakroom, rolled his blanket into a pillow, and fell soundly asleep.

Wakened by a door opening, Harry gasped in pain. His

whole body literally came off the floor in response to the toe of a shoe being buried in his side. "Get up, you bastard…and get out. We don't want your kind around here." It was Harry's second introduction to Stella's Cove's minister, and he remembered the unpleasant encounter that had occurred, only hours earlier, at the Cromwell house.

Rev. Miles Cromwell was one of those who'd summarily turned Harry down that first, terrible evening in the Cove. It had been Cromwell's wife who came to the door, finding Harry beaten and cold, asking for a place to spend the night. She had begun to say it, "We're a good Christian fold, and, of course, you're welcome to stay…." But as quickly as she spoke, she was silenced by her husband's hand, which was suddenly placed on her shoulder, sharply squeezing it with the force of a vise, and eliciting her muffled gasp. "You can find another place to rest," interrupted Rev. Cromwell, "because we, simply, don't want your type here in Stella's Cove."

The minister's wife had been drawn by the opportunity for kindness, but her husband callously dug-in against the needs of the assumed sinner standing at their door. "I'm no Samaritan," he barked to his wife, as she held her bruised collar bone in a silent expression of pain, "and I'm not about to extend a Christian hand to every immoral bastard that seeks refuge here." Mrs. Cromwell tried to keep the door open, but Rev. Cromwell's hand slammed it shut. Harry understood that there was no value in pushing the matter, but simply turned and made his way to the next home on the street.

What Rev. Cromwell did not appreciate or understand was that he, himself, was neither a favorite of the townsfolk nor of the God he so fervently preached. (I feel safe to say that, if there is a god, God certainly disapproved of the minister's behavior, and had withdrawn his spirit from the town because of the misguided and often vicious piety of the community.)

By now, the reverend had worked himself into a frenzy, standing over Harry and hissing like a snake. Harry was clutching at his ribs as he rose from the vestibule floor. "We know all about you," Cromwell snarled, "and you'd better be getting out of our town." This violent second meeting did not require a response, and Harry, in utter silence, took one more look at the back of the last pew, where there was a carving of Jesus forgiving the sinners. He pulled his pocket watch from his pants, and noticed that it was

2:20 a.m.

As Harry walked out the church's front door into a chilly fog, now drifting over the town, he noticed a large silver plaque on a stone base. There was enough moonlight to make out the words: "This church was funded by the generosity of Rev. Willis Fox, a man who shared his bounteous fortune, kindness, and spiritual wealth with the community of Stella's Cove."

Stunned by the shameful behavior of a man who was ordained to be God's servant, Harry walked down the lane from the church, and, finding a sheltered spot behind the Clemmerton Bakery, he rolled himself into the old blanket he carried, and fell asleep again.

The night hours were far too short, and the battered minister arose to a sun-less morning. Bart Clemmerton, Sr., who owned the bakery, noticed Harry as he threw some rancid grease into a receptacle behind the store. "Mornin'" Clemmerton chirped, and Harry could not immediately tell whether the man's voice was friendly or curt. "Hello," answered Harry, "it's sure cold around here." Clemmerton seemed to warm a bit, and he acknowledged that the weather was typical for the town. "Well, the sun'll come out later," he noted, "'cause it usually does."

Harry bought a roll from the bakery, and Clemmerton thanked him for his business. "I hope your day's a good one," spoke Clemmerton, and Harry sensed a genuine kindness in his voice. "Could it be," thought Harry as he headed toward the dock, "that he hasn't yet heard about me?"

Just like every other place along the coast, it was the water itself that was the Cove's most charming attraction. The sounds of the seabirds became almost a steady cry as Harry walked toward the water's edge, still finishing his roll. The morning was one of relative calm, and it looked to him as if only a few fishing boats had put out to sea. There were just a few buoys that sat vacant upon the gentle swells, for all the others held boats, tied fast by their mooring lines, perfectly facing into the breeze and nodding together in perfect unison. Harry thought about the boats, thought about the townsfolk's virtually-orchestrated prejudice against him, and realized that the people of Stella's Cove were not much different than those buoys and boats, for they too were simply being played by the powerful forces that engulfed them. Like the boats, the townsfolk faced the same direction and bobbed in unison over each little swell.

Two young boys, braving the morning chill, had walked out onto the exposed land that slithered from the sea as the tide went out, and they were using small trowels to expose the clams that burrowed beneath the mud. "Good morning," called Harry, "What a beautiful day." But the boys did not answer, looked at each other for a moment with a strange hint of both recognition and fear, climbed the rocks to the east, and ran down the lane toward their homes. It occurred to Harry that these, too, were evidence of the misdirected and un-Christian unity of the town. "Boys..." he thought, and then he changed the spelling in his mind. "No," he silently added, understanding that the boys were simply moved by the currents of the community. "They're buoys."

At the opposite end of the dock there were two fisherman casting out over the bay. They already had two nice fish in a bucket, and Harry noted their success. "Those are mighty nice fish," said Harry. The men ignored him, although Harry noticed that the two exchanged glances and that their response was in silent agreement. For a moment Harry thought of the "Big Fisherman," and how so few fish and loaves it had taken to feed the multitudes that came to hear Christ speak. "If everyone," mused Harry "provided even the tiniest amount of nourishment to others, the world would find itself satiated with love."

When found himself in Stella's Cove it was early fall, and he'd felt immediate concern because of the erratic steamboat service and impassible overland routes blocking both access to and exit from the town. The blatant rudeness of its people was now echoing through his brain, and though he soon found a handful of people who were willing to engage him in the standard banter and show some rudimentary courtesies, Harry wanted to leave. As he looked toward the west, he'd noticed a fine home that sat at the end of a point miles away and looked out over the throbbing sea.

He walked back to Clemmerton's Bakery, just as Rev. Cromwell exited, making a muted grunt and an exaggerated scowl that stank of disgust. Clemmerton was there, rolling some dough on a table just inside the door, and he didn't look happy. "Yeah," Clemmerton volunteered, "He just told me who you are. I don't want any trouble, and I don't want you hanging around."

Harry looked at him with forgiving but questioning eyes, and Clemmerton, for a moment, looked exposed, like a boy sitting in an outhouse when someone else opens the door. He gathered himself together with obvious difficulty, and said, "I'm sorry, but Rev. Cromwell said some terrible things about you." Harry appreciated the softness of Clemmerton's heart, and he tried to undo the harm that the vicious preacher had caused. "It's not what you think," Harry asserted. "I did nothing wrong." Clemmerton had a surprised expression on his face, and was considering the possibility that the defrocked cleric was not guilty. "Well," finished Clemmerton, "I hope that's true."

As an afterthought, and pleased that someone was actually considering the unfairness of the callous treatment others so readily and enthusiastically dispensed, Harry asked. "By the way, what's that big house out on the point? It's huge."

Clemmerton answered that it belonged to George and Eva Murphy. "They're transplants in the Cove," he volunteered, "and they're not very well liked. I think they had a small fortune when they came here, but now it's for sure--they're the richest folks around. I guess you've heard of the Murphy Salmon Company?" "Can't say that I have," Harry answered." Well, Clemmerton continued, "George owns it—it's the biggest business in the province, I think. He owns the hydroelectric plant too, and this town's way ahead of most others. We've had electricity for years." He said it with an obvious pride, and it was clear that he understood how his own good fortune in the bakery business was linked to Murphy's successes. "The town," noted Clemmerton, "was pretty much dead when he came here, and we all owe him a debt of gratitude."

In the darkness of the previous night, Harry had not seen the mansion, and, even if he had, his sore, tired body would not have cooperated in such a long walk. Besides, he considered it to be almost fact that the rich were usually the worst, and that, while showing off their money, they were typically miserly. He'd watched the plate being passed in his Eagle City congregation, and had noticed, over the years, that the richest ones gave the least. Catching himself thinking about the seemingly typical parsimony of the wealthy, Harry felt the need to chide himself, biting the thought as if it were his tongue, and reminding himself, "No one can judge, and generalizations are particularly dangerous." For he understood that there were no hard, fast rules about people, and he thought, for a moment, of Bart Clemmerton's transparent epiphany. Clemmerton was obviously very successful, but when informed that the malicious gossip might not be true, he'd been willing, at least, to listen.

"Rich" was not necessarily Godless, and Harry remembered the generosity of some rich folks named Perelli, whom he'd met while attending Divinity School. They had extended themselves and given Harry a home away from home. He was always welcome to spend time with them on weekends, and they had taken him out on the town for some fine meals. Mario Perelli immigrated to the U.S. in the 1870's, worked for years in the Allegheny Coal Company Mine, and then left his mining job to start a furniture business in Pittsburgh. It made him a fortune. After his retirement from the furniture business, Mario took his family to Vancouver. The air in Pittsburgh had been too dirty, and his asthma had become more severe with age. They built a lovely home looking out over the Vancouver waterfront, and their daughter Andrea was admitted to the University.

So Harry knew that, for every generalization a person made about others, there were always exceptions, and that the practice of judging others, no matter how difficult to control, was responsible for many unnecessary bad feelings. As he walked away from the bakery, he was eating another roll he'd just purchased, and he thought back to the Perelli family and Andrea, who had become his wife.

While Harry was discouraged by the apparent absence of Christian charity in Stella's Cove, he really wasn't looking for handouts. He had adequate cash, and a reasonable account in an Eagle City bank. If he could find, at least, some temporary housing arrangements, he understood that he would be able to manage just fine. The Murphy mansion intrigued him, believing that no family could totally utilize such a large residence, and that there might be a possibility of securing a room. As he looked down the spit and over the timidly retreating sunset, the home seemed to have a red halo around it, a fiery, encircling shroud that radiated outward through a rapidly forming layer of fog. The solitary setting appealed to Harry, and he determined that he would walk there the following day.

Harry slept again in the protected spot behind the bakery, and the second night was not as cold as the first. His sleep was interrupted at about 5:00 a.m., when Clemmerton came through the bakery's back door and threw some more used fat into the barrel outside. "Mornin', Harry," he smiled, "...looks like another overcast day."

"Do you mind if I stash my bag and blanket 'til later?" Harry asked, and Clemmerton had given him a spot just inside the back door. "Just don't be too late," Bart warned. "We close exactly at 6:00. I hope your day goes well."

Harry, now unburdened, walked toward the mansion. It took the better part of an hour to get there, and he estimated that the walk was well over two miles. As he entered the mansion's magnificent gardens and savored the view of the sea, he could easily see the islands that formed the protective chain to the west, and he could make out a ship, miles offshore, leaving a long, straight trail of black smoke compressed between the layers of mist.

The Murphy home, standing there all by itself, showed no signs of life. Harry knocked on the door twice, but nobody came. He looked at the windows to see if anyone was suspiciously looking at him, and then, realizing that the owners were simply not there, he started the long walk back to town.

The mansion and garden had a gentle look, for the typical severity of formality had been largely ignored. The shrubs and flowers were a statement of their wild natures, and the trees had been allowed to grow, without apparent pruning, to their potential. Harry liked that, for he believed there was a metaphor in it— perhaps something for one of his future Sunday sermons--if he ever got another congregation. "People aren't so different from those trees," thought Harry, "and no one should be held back from exploring his own potential. It is too much pruning that stifles individuality and the creative nature of the soul." As Harry hung for a moment on that thought, he couldn't help but ask himself if his present predicament could have been averted by a stricter application of the rules. "Maybe," he thought, "I could have used a little bit of pruning," and he considered how kindness, though much applauded as an essential human trait, could be a weakness as well. As he walked eastward, seabirds combed the ebb-tide mud for mollusks, and there was a salty stagnant odor which spoke of organisms decaying beneath the tidal flats.

Though Clemmerton had mentioned that the Murphy's were not well-liked, Harry had no idea why. In time, he would find that the town's benefactor was also its greatest critic, and that the Murphys did not generally align themselves with the attitudes of the community. Their home was on the end of Point Fay for a reason--as far from the town as they could practically arrange-- and, while they were friendly with the townsfolk and employed much of the community, there were only a few people that the Murphys actually liked and respected. It wasn't that the Murphys didn't like people. They simply did not, for the most part, like the people of Stella's Cove.

In fact, there was to be a serious conflict between the Murphys and the town. While their mansion stood securely against the sometimes angry seas that pounded the shore only a few yards away, its owners were braced against the harsh prejudices and conduct of the community. It was partly for the mere variety--and partly because the Murphys had considered the slowly growing schism that marginalized them from the rest of Stella's Cove--that prompted George to build a second home in Vancouver. Harry's walk to the end of the spit was ill timed, for the Murphys had sailed the previous day for Vancouver. They would not return until early October when school was back in session.

On his return to Stella's Cove, Harry asked Clemmerton about more permanent lodging. "Is there a room," asked Harry, "that I could rent for a while?" Bart's face changed from his normal, friendly look, and there was only embarrassment in his eyes. "I can't really do that," he apologized. "It would hurt my business. It's one thing to allow you to sleep behind the bakery, but giving you a room would be the end to my success." Harry had to face the reality, that a tight hand gripped the town and that people feared to cross Rev. Cromwell. Finding even Clemmerton so unwilling to help, Harry reviewed his options. The townsfolk had made it clear that they would give him no chance. (Actually, the Murphys, who were out of town, would have been the exceptions, gladly inviting him to spend time, and making their own determinations of his character.) Stella's Cove wanted nothing to do with the fallen preacher.

Harry spent several more nights shivering beneath his blanket behind the bakery. On the fifth day, Walter Young, the owner of Young's General Mercantile, offered to sell him a tent and oil heater, for a price well above their accepted values. That was the beginning of a productive and cooperative relationship, for Young made it clear that he was simply a businessman, and would help Harry in any way possible--for the right price.

When faced with the town's callous treatment, Harry had considered leaving Stella's Cove. But the opportunities for departure were grim. The trail over the mountains was both treacherous and long, and the supply boat, which had been there only a few days before, came only once a month--if the weather was good.

Because of my age, the matters of the community had not drawn me in, and, though I was disappointed in my Mother's un-Christian response to Rev. Mills, I understood that hers was based on the constraints of group psychology, and that any individual evaluation of moral implications was greatly frowned upon in Stella's Cove. There was one church, one leader, and one set of prevailing attitudes, so there really was no need for anyone to develop any views of their own.

———————

Harry's decision to stay in Stella's Cove was simple: He had arrived tired, beaten, and despondent, and there was no quick way to leave. Being marooned in such a place was an unpleasant prospect, but besides the inconvenience and hazards of leaving Stella's Cove, it was his captivation with the beauty of our town that inspired him to stay and explore. Looking westward was the ever-changing landscape of the sea, where the throbbing heart of the deep could raise wild whitecaps with its pulse, or, on a whim, bring gentle swells to bend the rays of evening as the sun sank into the sea.

But, even more intriguing to Harry Mills was the silver tongue of the glacier, majestically reflecting the moon's smile as it emerged from the canyon's mouth. Though it stopped almost two miles to the East, its scale created the effect that it was virtually lapping at the edge of the town, and Harry, having been forsaken and black-listed by most of the town's residents, pitched his new tent just down from the glacier's tongue.

Any suppositions on Harry's thoughts and actions are simply conjectures created by my rather naïve point of view. I was there when he came to the Cove, and I knew, only through the gossip that my mother heard and spread, the supposedly true but mostly imagined tales that surrounded his time in our community.

I don't believe that, except for rumors, the circumstances of Harry's fall from favor were ever verified by anyone, including the town of Eagle City, which had turned on him and sent him packing to our community--all because of accusations which could never be proven. It was only the convincing drama of his alleged victim that had stirred the angry mob mentality, and, though there were no signs of trauma on the girl, Rev. Mills had been presumed guilty.

There was a pervasive and persistent pattern which merely continued with Rev. Mills' arrival in Stella's Cove, for it was a town that had proven its inclination to judge, its enthusiasm to gossip, and its willingness to condemn so many times in the past. Mills was certainly not the only victim of the town's perverse need for spiritual superiority, for virtually all those who chose not to worship at the Methodist Church were the predictable targets of Rev. Cromwell's devious stories.

And, although Harry Mills would never be able to return to the life he had chosen, attending to the spiritual needs of a community, there would be a time in the future when Harry's story would be heard from his own lips. But it would be only George Murphy, me, and the dead who knew it--the real account of the green-eyed, red-headed accuser who had changed Harry's life forever.

Like the lust that an entire community assumed had destroyed Harry's soul, it took little time for him to be seduced by the glacier's noisy voracity--the thunder as the advance party of her icy taste buds tore away in a frantic frenzy to taste and to consume. Harry spent many of his first, autumn evenings in visual ecstasy. Unlike the superstitious town folk, he viewed the glacier as a treasure of Stella's Cove—not as an evil force. He looked up at the pale moon as it profiled the gnarled trees that formed its lips, and he felt her frigid winds as they ricocheted off the grandness of its breast.

Each evening, when the campfire faded to a crimson bed of embers, Harry fell asleep to the glacier's eerie singing as it pierced the inadequacy of the small tent's canvas walls. Though it was not easy, and Harry had wanted desperately at times to abandon his spot along Muir Creek, he survived through that first winter, through the cold gales of a heartless and cruel community, and when the bold crocuses erupted from the spring snow, he believed that he could remain in his little canyon heaven forever, away from the townsfolk and the duplicity that plagued the town.

Harry's curiosity brought him dangerously close to the glacier, and the town folk came to regard his level of sensibility to be a personal weakness almost as low as his morals. No one in their right mind was fearless of the glacier, and Mills seemed to have disregard for the risks that were always there. My curiosity over the strange newcomer was piqued by the rumors I heard, for there was a part of me that was born-sleuth and I wanted to know the truth. Mother was disturbed by my willingness to allow the facts to speak for themselves. But that need was a necessary part of my transition from youth. It was an expression of my autonomous mind and what I saw as an imperative of my being. My unwillingness to simply fall into line behind Cromwell caused Mother great consternation, and it gnawed at the harmony of our home.

Early in life I had felt both compelled and inclined to agree with my mother and the powerful prejudices of the community. While I have since felt remorse that I initially bought into the plentiful and stubbornly-clinging lies, I can't help but feeling that my failure was rooted in the most basic principles of the parent-child relationship. Nature has a way of protecting the young until they're able to fend for themselves, and it is the young's instinctive belief in parents that serves that purpose. Bear cubs don't argue with the sow about the dangers of predators, and young birds rely on their parent's judgment as to whether or not they are ready to attempt flight.

But as I grew older--and, perhaps, cultivated by the death of my father, whose attitudes had been far different from Mother's--I no longer had the blind faith in either her or a god. There was also a slight suspicion in the back of my mind that my divergence from Mother's attitudes was, at least in part, a way of honoring my father's memory.

————————

The arrival of Rev. Harry Mills was to have a stunning effect on an already unhealthy population, creating an instantaneous, hostile polarization which was unequaled in the town's history. It was, in part, the onset of manhood that made me more resistant to the judgments of Stella's Cove. By the age of fourteen, I had already dug in my heels against the prevailing popular attitudes. I had lost the one man I loved and trusted, and I began to understand that I was the only one who could choose my course in life. My father had been cautious about running with the flock, and I believed that he would have been proud to see that I had hadn't fallen into the moral failure of allowing a group to dictate my values and bury my conscience.

I talked with Harry Mills several times after school, as I walked from home to my chores at the Murphy home, and I found an immediate liking for him. His greatly exaggerated left eye— magnified to twice its size by a mostly ineffective monocle--was tragically comical, and his mush-mouth speech impediment seemed to frame the events that had led to his relocation in our town. The less than comely features were initially disconcerting, and, at our first introduction, I almost turned to walk away. But his smile was disarming, coupled with the words I would hear him repeat dozens of times in our short friendship, "Isn't it a wonderful day to be here on God's earth?" When he said it, there was a part of me that wanted to say, "There is no god," but his sincerity preempted my distrust. Having been forewarned by my mother, and actually forbidden to talk with him, I instead, felt pride in having violated her rule. The meeting had been an uplifting moment and an expression of my right to choose for myself. Harry's authenticity was a compelling attraction, and, though he mentioned God often in his conversations, it never carried the typical judgments I had always associated with religion.

Here was a man who was not at all bonnie to look at, yet his kindness and genuine regard had found him another ally. It was an awakening for me, for there could not have been a better illustration of the adage, "You can't tell a book by its cover."

Suddenly I had found one of those precious pearls of wisdom that Rev. Cromwell had so carelessly spoken of, and I understood that the real nature of people could be an elusive and confusing charade. Though I had made a commitment to myself that I would never allow myself to become a cynic, what happened in my community was a harbinger of things to come, and, over my lifetime, I would find the reality of an endless supply of shallow veneers.

Unlike the sourly pious Rev. Cromwell, Harry Mills could tell a joke or two, and seemed to love the smiles and laughter of people. And I wasn't totally alone in my growing affection for Harry. Walter Young also took a strong liking to him, and he vocally challenged the veracity of Harry's moral failure. He didn't know how to describe the source of his certainty, but he was absolutely confident that the gentle, defrocked minister would not have been guilty of those acts that had resulted in his summary condemnation. Young was courageous enough to mention his kind suspicions to others, in an effort to create acceptance for Mills, but they adamantly insisted that Mills was a very evil person, and one warned Young, "Don't let him suck you in."

Young, in time, came to feel the deepest compassion for Harry's suffering, for his displacement from his previous congregation, and the injuries he'd sustained from the actions of a vicious mob. Almost overnight, Young's attitude was transformed from the original strategy of overcharging Harry for everything he bought, to one of "Go ahead and take it. If it helps you out, I'm happy to give it to you." So there was a Christian ideal in Stella's Cove, and it did not center on the town's minister. The town was philosophically and morally upside down.

Rudderless

During the many slack economic years before George Murphy resurrected the town, most of the remaining Stella's Cove locals had been fishermen, toiling faithfully to satisfy a meager market for their catches. A few worked for the provincial government's welfare department, and there were more than a few who depended on the dole during those difficult times.

My Dad was a salmon fisherman through the fickle years of the town's economy, and I was raised on tales of the sea. And, though I never actually rowed past the outer limits of the Stella's Cove harbor, I always understood that the deep expanse of water was wider than any child could imagine. My father and mother had tried to describe it to me at an early age. In an effort to state the sea's dimensions in a manner that could be understood by a mere child, they made wide gestures of their outstretched hands and told me how many million pine trees it would take, placed end to end, to span its broad expanse. Still, the size of the ocean was unfathomable to my young mind. I had seen for myself, over and over, the phenomenon of my father's trawler disappearing slowly into the mist beyond the jetty, and he had told me that the sailors' sight of land was also similarly, summarily, lost in the boil and roll of the sea and the layers of moisture which drifted from its surface.

Enchanting as they were, Father's stories sometimes had a sadness about them, remembering the souls who had been lost and how mothers and children cried when the crews returned short a man or two. As impressive as the sea was to my young mind, my dreams of being there with my father were never realized, for, when I was thirteen, he was dragged overboard in a loop of rope, and drowned before the crew could free him. Even three years later, I still wept when I thought of him.

The feeling and mood of our home changed abruptly when Father died, and I was lost in a rudderless gloom. Activities I previously loved disappeared when he did, and I found a general disinterest in life. It was hard for me, in fact, to do anything at all. My commitment to school had always been marginal, for I fully expected that I would be joining Father as his apprentice, and never considered the possibility of a continuing education. But after Father's death, Mother had a hard time just trying to get me to go. Each morning I lay in bed, looking at the clock, with a powerful inertia riveting me to the mattress, and when it was time for me to leave, Mother often found me with the blanket pulled up over my head.

I noticed that Mother, too, was suffering from the sudden vacuum in our lives, and, as the wise have said so many times, there "is no one who can take his place." Our mourning left a haunting vision of my father's pale face as he lay in his coffin, and that constantly cursed those moments when my eyelids could no longer resist their weight. Though my last post mortem view of him was sad, it seemed that the memory of his cheerful morning greetings was even sadder, for my visions of the good times that had been lost clouded the joy of my days. There were times the world seemed so hopeless that I envisioned myself walking into the sea and not returning. It wasn't that I would have actually committed suicide. The pain was simply so great that I wished to no longer exist. Sad days turned into months, and the tears were often near the surface. My interminable mourning was neither happy nor healthy, and I finally came to understand and appreciate that the bogged-down weight of my heart could not be allowed a permanent residence there.

"You're going to have to start getting up by yourself," Mother announced one day. "I got a job at Murphy's." She didn't have to say the name of the business. I knew she was talking about the Salmon Processing Plant, which paid good wages and was the essential key to the revival of our local economy. She looked at me with a kaleidoscopic mirroring of several conflicting and contrasting emotions, but, deciding not to battle with me that morning, she noted "Things have to change, Billy. You can't go on this way. If you're going to have a successful life, you need to kick yourself out of bed and start taking school seriously." For a moment I saw that lonely look in her eyes--the one that appears when, for a moment, the lost are momentarily found, only to be consumed by the reality of the instant, when they fade again, back into the realms of our dreams.

After the gentle but direct admonition regarding my schooling, Mother took her purse, and walked out the door. The new job would be good. I knew that Mother had struggled to make ends meet since Father's accident, doing a few part-time tasks for those who could still afford help, and, like our neighbor, old Mrs. Crump, she'd taken in some laundry and ironing. Murphy Salmon Company had a good reputation as an employer, and I had seen the lives of several friends enriched by the new fortune in their families' lives. There would be no question about it, for Mother's earnings, working for Murphy's, would end our financial woes.

When the fears of poverty had finally been allayed, I saw other changes in Mother's attitudes and personality that could not have been anticipated at such a fortunate time of plenty. At first there was that obvious relief from her previous worries about finances, but it did not persist for long. The happy lightheartedness she experienced during her brief courtship with Mr. Merriman transformed into an extended, miserable mood. I could not figure out what was going on, for those things I always took for granted were suddenly in question. The Murphy's Salmon Company job did not lighten Mother's spirit as much as I'd expected, and her life seemed, suddenly, strangely out of balance. Saturday cleanings, washing, and ironing, were sometimes done partially or not at all, and our home was looking untidy most of the time.

But, worse than the household evidence of her obvious illness, I noticed that her interest in religion, though always strong, escalated into an outright fanaticism. There were few evenings when she did not rant about God and the devil, and she kept telling me, "You've gotta repent, Billy, or you'll be burnin' in hell." Each time she exhorted me to repentance, I felt angry inside, wondering why she did not appreciate the goodness in me.

The truth was, I was a kind young man, and I did not believe myself bad in any way, despite my fascination with women's bodies and the compelling feelings that accompanied my entry into manhood. There was never a time that I failed to greet others in a friendly manner, and I had a sense of fairness and honesty that I knew was irreproachable. Why Mother constantly did her repentance routine was an insistent question.

"What have I done, Mother?" I'd pleaded for an answer over and over, and then, with more intensity, I'd insisted, "Are you hearing me? I asked you, what have I done?" Without any further explanation, she repeated it, looking like she was having a revelation, "You have to repent, Billy, or the Devil will get your soul. You have to repent, Billy."

Despite her occasionally mute but often loud accusations of bad behavior, I felt a great deal of empathy for Mother. I understood how personal and unique a person's feelings are, and I had no way of experiencing what she felt. And yet I was able to comprehend the emotional stresses that she faced, and though she was never able or willing to articulate her distress, I could commiserate in the general darkness of her moods. For she and I had both lost my father, and the physical and emotional changes of a teenage boy spoke to her--the inevitable understanding, that I would grow up, and that I was not likely to remain in Stella's Cove. All she could look forward to was the unavoidable loneliness when I too would be gone. The job at Murphy's had provided money, but it had no way of repairing the sadness of the future.

It wasn't long after Father's death that I realized the buffering influence he'd had on my Mother's eccentricities. He'd always been a more sensible person, and, essentially, not a believer in any church. With him gone, Mother became unbearably pious, and her formerly mostly-warm nature seemed to have disappeared with the drowning of her man. Through it all, I felt a nagging guilt within me, because I knew, that if I had the chance, I would not remain in Stella's Cove.

Kindness and Contrasts

My first real contact with George Murphy was shortly after Father's death. I noticed him, multiple times, riding to and from town in his pony cart, and I'd heard the buzz about his wealth. I saw him, one afternoon, talking with Young in front of the Mercantile. "Excuse me for just a moment," he'd politely said to Young, and, then, turning toward me he voiced a sincere greeting, and I could hear in his voice, and see in his eyes, that his motive was compassion.

"Good Morning," he smiled, "You're Billy Potter, Delva Potter's son, aren't you?" I acknowledged it, and he continued. "I was sorry to hear about your father, Billy. I lost my own dad when I was only ten, and I have never totally gotten over it. Even now," George continued, "I miss Dad dearly." There was emotion in his voice as he said it, and I choked a bit. Yet there was something so comforting in the way George spoke. His words actually gave me some feeling of assurance that I was not alone, and sparked an understanding that, like him, I would be able to deal with my pain and that I too could become a success.

"If you're interested in making some money, I have some chores that you could do, and I'll pay you twenty-five cents an hour. Would you be interested?" he asked, and he raised his eyebrows, opened his eyes widely, and nodded as he said it, as if he was answering his own question. I could not say "no." Twenty-five cents an hour was great pay for a part-time job, but I was concerned with the four-mile round trip I would have to make each time I worked.

"I won't be able to do it every day," I told him with some hesitation. "I have some chores at home, too, and I have studies as well…and I'm not sure I can get there fast enough after school to have much time for work." I was afraid Mr. Murphy would see my logistical concerns as negativity, but he immediately acknowledged that my worries were valid and that he'd find a way to address my transportation to Point Fay.

"We'll set a schedule," George assured, "and either I or Jim Norwood, my secretary--you've met him, I think--will pick you up with the cart or the Reo and take you back to the Cove when your work is done." It sounded great to me. "Sure, Mr. Murphy. I'll do it, and…thank you so much."

I thought for a moment about Norwood. Anyone, having met him, would surely remember him. I talked with him twice down by the dock when the Aniak was there, and assumed he'd been there for business, as he wore a neat tweed jacket over a pressed shirt and a smart silk tie pulled into a precisely tied double Windsor. Less than five feet tall, Norwood walked with a limp, and had a pronounced speech impediment. His looks were striking, with slightly bigger than normal blue eyes, the color of the glacier, and crowned by heavy dark eyebrows and a well-groomed head of equally black hair. His smile was warm and genuine, not like someone who is putting on a show, and his upper lip was covered by a large but well-trimmed mustache.

My first meeting had been initiated by Norwood's friendly "Hello," and he asked me my name. "Billy Potter, Sir." I replied. "Oh," he acknowledged, "yours is that white house with the green shutters." and he motioned in that direction. "Yes," I said, "That's correct." Though I often displayed a natural shyness with adults, I felt inclined to spend a minute chatting. "So, what kind of work do you do, Mr. Norwood?" I anticipated that he might think it bold or improper for me to be asking, but there wasn't any hesitation. "I work for Mr. Murphy. I'm his executive secretary—sort of an accountant, business manager, and boy-Friday. If there's no one else assigned to do something, I'm the one who gets it done."

When Norwood talked with me in casual conversation, I noticed that there was a pronounced lisp and some obvious difficulty in speaking certain words. I watched Norwood's lips as he spoke, and could not help but noticing a thin area in his mustache where there appeared to be a large scar.

Norwood noticed my gaze, fixed for just a moment on that mostly-hidden harelip, and, rather than showing any embarrassment, he volunteered, "I was born with a cleft palate— you've probably heard it called a "harelip." It was so ugly and interfered so much with my speech that my school teachers believed me to be mentally retarded. Everyone looked at me as a freak, and I was always referred to in the most disrespectful ways.

"Because of my speech impediment, people called me a moron, retard, or idiot. The endless insults and teasing were more than I could take, so I dropped out of public school by time I was thirteen. When I approached possible employers for apprenticeship positions, it never took more than two sentences out of me. "Sorry, kid, we don't hire the mentally defective."

"No one would give me a chance--except, that is, Mr. Murphy. I met him years ago on the dock at Vancouver, where I was working part-time unloading ships. He was the first person who'd talked with me as if I was just another human being, and I couldn't help but wondering when his kindness would end. I tried to enunciate as clearly as I could, but Murphy, like everyone else, noticed my deformity."

I watched Norwood in apprehension as an uncomfortable expression washed over his face, and he stammered awkwardly for just a moment. "Instead of judgments about my intelligence or rude comments on what my parents must have done to deserve such a deformed child—comments which would have been sadly familiar to me—Mr. Murphy voiced a resolute understanding. "Oh," he had practically whispered with an unmistakable kindness in his tone, "I know a surgeon who can fix that problem. He's done dozens of them."

"I told Mr. Murphy that I could not afford surgery," Norwood continued, "and he answered that he would pay the bill if I would come and work for him for two years. "I'll start you at $60 per month," Murphy confidently asserted, "and that will be in addition to your board and room." Norwood's voice cracked as he said it, "It's changed my life. I've had the best job in the world for the past fourteen years, for it is a blessing to work for such a man. I can tell you, he's a wonderful human being." Norwood dabbed his eyes with his sleeve. "I'm sorry," he admitted, "It makes me very emotional."

I was so excited about my new opportunity. When I arrived at our front door later that afternoon, I wanted to tell Mother, but I knew she would not likely be pleased. Understanding her probable reaction, I practiced a few times before I actually spoke. During dinner I tried to say it matter-of-factly, in passing, as a way of sidestepping any confrontation. "George Murphy gave me a part-time job, so I'm going to be working for him after school and on Saturdays."

Though I'd anticipated that Mother would be less than enthusiastic, her words took me totally off guard. "You might as well just sell your soul to the devil. George Murphy and that harlot Eva will be your spiritual death. It's just another step on the road to hell. You can't play with fire and not get burned!"

"But Mother," I started to talk…

Mother was screaming now at the top of her lungs, and I was embarrassed that one of our neighbors might hear her fury and assume that I had committed some unpardonable offense. "I can't believe you'd do that without even asking my permission. I'm responsible for your well-being," she shrieked, "and I don't see you running around looking like an under-fed orphan. I'm doing a good job of supporting this family." There was a slight pause, and Mother seemed to regain control. "We don't need the Murphys' charity and I'm not going to allow it. You need to get down on your knees and repent, Billy, if a few shekels of silver is going to be your god."

I spent a few moments trying to collect myself, finding it an uneasy chore to choose the words. "This is an opportunity for me, Mother, and I'm not going to give it up because of you. I know you work hard and that we have all the necessities. But I have my own ambitions, and they're going to take money." Then, half-way believing that I was about to be hit with Dad's old leather belt, I finished. "I'm going to start tomorrow."

Mother didn't speak to me the rest of the evening, and I saw her, later in her room, poring over the Bible, her hands shaking with what I believed to be her intense anger.

———————

It was George himself who picked me up at school and drove me in his pony cart to the home on Point Fay. He was not a verbose man, and much of the two mile ride was occupied by each of us merely taking in the beauty of the changing landscape, passing the tidal marshes on the north side of the spit and watching sea birds rising from the dune grass into the offshore breeze, floating effortlessly, and diving for their unsuspecting prey.

I silently thought to myself how the growing intensity of the sea breeze failed to drive the seagulls and pelicans backwards, for the birds merely changed the angles of their wings to increase their lift, first rising to greater heights and then increasing their downward speed to compensate for the wind. Though no philosopher, I couldn't help but consider that there was some lesson in their strategies. For everyone, in life, would face headwinds that threatened their forward progress. I had experienced such a wind when my father died, suffering inertia and even being driven backward for a time. In the birds, I found inspiration.

George turned to me only once during that drive. "I know I'll be pleased with your work, Billy. Just make sure that, if there's anything you don't understand about my instructions, you take the time to ask. I would much rather explain something twice, than end up with the job done incorrectly. There are too many people who are overly concerned that they'll be viewed as stupid if they don't understand something the first time."

"Yes, Sir," I answered. "I won't let you down." And I never did.

George Murphy had a well-planned but very natural-looking garden surrounding his house, and he found me capable in trimming the hedges and keeping the grounds free of weeds. On a property so large, there were always odd jobs—a little repair here, a cleanup project there, washing the outside windows, repainting a weathered piece of door trim. One time, after a savage gale blew through the night, I cleaned up the scattered debris, spending hours with an axe to reduce the large fallen branches to a more manageable size. And, just as George Murphy expected, there were no misunderstandings, and each task was performed according to his instructions.

The offer of a job was fortuitous, and I was able to work about eight hours each week, four on Saturdays, so my monthly income launched from zero to over six dollars a month. It was growing into a tidy sum, and by Christmas of that year I'd saved enough for a nice present for Mother, and one for the Murphys. I was also able to start a small account in the Stella's Cove Savings and Loan, which was open for only three hours on Mondays, Wednesdays, and Fridays. Every weekend, I'd pull the little passbook out of my dresser drawer, admiring the growing total, and dreaming of how I'd spend it when the time finally came. Even at 1 1/2 percent, I loved to see the interest posted, for it was an extra bonus.

The biggest impediment to my work at the Murphy home was the distraction imposed by its views of the sea and the offshore islands, which were not typically visible from the town. And there were the regular sightings of ships, always creating a wonderment in my mind of where they were going, who was aboard, and how they would look as they encountered the roughness of the seas in less protected areas. I'd heard about waves one hundred feet high in the Bering Sea, and I could only imagine the fear of captains and crews when such weather marred an otherwise peaceful sail.

The loss of my father seemed to create some sort of responsibility in Mr. Murphy to see that I was properly befriended. There were many times he joined me in the garden and talked with me as a father would have done. "How's your mother doing?" he inquired one afternoon. "I know she works at the processing plant, but I am not personally acquainted with her. I guess I should make more effort to know all my employees." Murphy said it with a look of both concern and guilt on his face. While I thought it a reasonable expectation to know all one's employees, I also understood that the size of his business made such a task difficult, if not impossible. "Oh, she's doing OK," I'd answered, "and she really likes her job--she's said so many times." Murphy looked pleased; he was obviously a man who cared about people, and it would have troubled him greatly to find that anyone in his employment was unhappy with either the job or the working conditions at the plant.

Half the town worked for George, and virtually everyone in Stella's Cove was blessed by his remarkable vision in creating the Murphy Salmon Company and the hydroelectric generator that had been feeding the town's lights and motors for almost twelve years. While much of B.C. still lacked electricity, the miracle of Murphy's dreams launched the Cove into a new age. There was prosperity, and the Sears catalogues found a place in something other than the outhouses. Toilet paper came to town, and the catalogues became the source of merchandise that had been a mere dream in previous years.

As is often the case in situations of great disparity, the people of Stella's Cove secretly resented their benefactor. It did not matter that George Murphy had brought commerce back to their long-dead town. He literally breathed new life into what was a veritable corpse, but except for the money and the residents' improved lifestyles, it made no difference to them. They resented him because he was so smart and successful, but even more because he was guilty of a level of kindness which few of them possessed and which stood in stark contrast to the collective behavior of the town. The insolence was so well defined, they might as well have voiced their opinion, "It just isn't right--acting like a Christian when he doesn't even believe in God."

George's attitudes were certainly not those of the churchgoers, who were a majority and openly railed against the few who did not attend the Methodist Church. While the weekly choruses of hymns moved upon the misty landscape like a gentle blanket of love, there was an epidemic of disease infesting the town with its general disregard for humanity and the golden rule. The townsfolk were guilty, and the goodness of George Murphy was just another reminder to them of how far they strayed from Christianity's lofty ideals.

Murphy always held a firm resolve that he should judge no man, and the unfolding events of the town would show that, if he judged at all, his judgments were confined to the matter of the Town's callous and ill-founded prejudices--something he vocally criticized in a few of his less-controlled moments.

The townsfolk took predictable verbal pokes at the Murphy family and created a variety of stories to tear at their reputation. The most commonly heard was one claiming that Eva was once a "soiled dove" before her marriage to George. Like all of the vicious gossip that circulated the Cove, each accusation could be traced, like a genealogy, back to its source. A few of the town's maverick residents made an informal game of discovering the source of bad rumors, and Richard Twiddle, our neighbor to the north, was a man interested in the truth.

The bold, scandalous Eva Murphy story was relatively easy to trace. Twiddle, as the chief rumor-sleuth of Stella's Cove, heard it from his wife, "Derry Aire" Twiddle. (Despite his success in researching the sources of various community lies, Richard, out of desperate curiosity, had futilely tried to determine how his orphaned wife came by that name.) She had certainly been of little use to his investigation, intentionally side-stepping his questions. Derry Aire told Richard that she had heard it from Letha Gorrs, who was a co-worker at the Murphy Salmon Company and ran the adjoining fish dryer. Letha Gorrs, though mostly a harmless sort, had been talking with Amos Dowdle, as he mended nets next to the dock, and it had been Amos's darling Minnie who'd heard it, while standing outside the church.

On the family tree of hurtful accusations and baseless indictments, it was Rev. Cromwell who was the father of so many bastard tales. It was he who started that vicious rumor about Eva Murphy, mentioning it to a handful of worshipers one Sunday when services were over.

"Of course you can never repeat this," Cromwell had confided, "because of possible retaliation by the Murphy family, but Eva Murphy's father was a convicted felon—sent away for armed robbery. The victim was so badly beaten that he could never walk again, and the trauma to his head left him a hopeless idiot. Poor little Eva…" (Cromwell threw in sympathy in order to make his story more believable) "She became a working girl, starting at a very young age. I've heard from a reliable source that she worked in a Seattle saloon and brothel up until she found George. You've all seen," Cromwell added, "the open displays of affection that are so disgustingly contrary to the actions of decent folks."

Twiddle was successful in determining that the story bore no resemblance to the truth. With surprisingly little research, he discovered that Eva's father was a respected architect, well known for his revolutionary building designs, particularly for the magnificent Seattle Public Library. Eva's father was certainly never charged or found guilty of any crime, and Eva worked as a governess for the family of the Vancouver, Washington Mayor while pursuing her University degree. Indeed, there was never a hint of any impropriety in Eva's family, which was, in fact, one of Seattle's most respected. But Cromwell understood that when lies are planted in irresponsible ears, they become truth; and irresponsible ears are virtually always attached to irresponsible lips. When he'd repeated that same lie multiple times, Rev. Cromwell, who rarely smiled, did, in fact, smile at the satisfaction of having hurt the Murphys' reputation.

I couldn't help musing about the alleged "public displays" of affection. They were never the least bit offensive in my opinion. I had seen Eva and George holding hands and personally witnessed a few gentle kisses, and I saw the three Murphys in a family hug after the Easter Services they annually attended. The kisses were neither prolonged nor passionate, and spoke only of the depth of their love and commitment. I know I was not so different from the other kids in Stella's Cove, who longed to see such sweetness displayed by their own parents. Those moments in time, when a gentle hug or kiss drew my parents close, were the lingering highlights of my sometimes disappointing childhood, and I often wished that Mother and Father had provided me more of those same recollections.

There were other stories too, and at least two of Stella's Cove's supposedly reputable citizens alleged that Eva Murphy flirted with them and made suggestive and seductive innuendos reflecting an unholy prurience. Whatever events were part of Eva Murphy's past--and it did occur to me that some of the stories were at least plausible--I saw nothing but goodness in her during the family's residence in our town. I appreciated how very lucky Celeste had been in having such a responsible mother, and Celeste reflected the essence of good parenting and a home that was filled with love. While she was by far the richest of all the Cove's school children, she never showed even a hint of being spoiled. Obedient and respectful, she lifted others with her kindness, and she spent time after school, every day, tutoring a couple of slower classmates on their math.

Just like her parents, Celeste's goodness made her a target too. Despite the pronouncements of her own agnosticism, Celeste was, paradoxically, the essence of good Christian values. Rev. Cromwell, once, in a rude display of disrespect, mocked her agnosticism in front of our class. "Celeste Murphy," he declared, "You're a fallen angel without any hope of salvation." A few in the class cringed when he said it, but Edgar Cromwell gloated delightedly, savoring his father's words.

The endless supply of unsubstantiated gossip flowed through the lanes of Stella's Cove like the effluent of leaky septic tanks. There was a real stink that enveloped our town, and it seemed entirely futile to arrest its insidious progress. Among the nastiest of rumors, spread by those who resented George's success and financial power, was that George, besides being godless, was also a buggerer and that Norwood was more than a personal secretary. Richard Twiddle made careful inquiries into that accusation. Not only was it untrue, but it was found to have originated from the same mouth that started the Eva Murphy stories. Shortly after carefully leaking the story to a shocked couple, Rev. Cromwell gave a sermon on buggery. He concluded with the words, "God has no place in His kingdom for those who engage in such abominations, and he has told us that we must purge such monsters from our midst. The Bible has declared that such deviations are of the devil, for they are a sin against God and nature." And, there was no one in the congregation who doubted which man in their community would be guilty of such aberrations.

The sad reality was that these stories were always submerged in polite secrecy to ensure that the accused would have no hope for redemption from the pall that would always remain. The pattern was totally predictable. Rev. Cromwell would first verify which people had no interest in the Methodist Church, and then create whatever fabrications were necessary to illustrate their ungodly natures. And the very evil that Cromwell preached against every Sunday morning was actually the man standing there behind the pulpit.

One Saturday afternoon in the spring of 1912, my friend Junior, the baker's son, and I hiked to the glacier's tongue, responding to Harry Mills' invitation to join him for supper. When we arrived, he was kneeling at the streambed, washing some clothes in the milky glacial flow. His quarters, at the time, were the crowded wall tent that he'd purchased at Young's Hardware, and there was a small campfire, where a few spruce logs were being reduced to coals. "Good afternoon," he greeted us as we approached, "Isn't this the most beautiful spot in God's world?" and there was that typical infectious smile on his face. Both Junior and I felt uncomfortable, because our parents had forbidden us to talk with him. Junior's father had warned him, "Personally, I doubt the stories about him, but associating with that man could hurt our business." Mother, too, practically drowned me in her endless flow of "loving" admonitions, warning me of both the dangers of the glacier and the hazards of associating with the "devil's helpers."

But now we were there, talking to the man who throughout the Cove was referred to as a monster. Though Rev. Harry Mill's friendliness had won over a handful of people in Stella's Cove, he was still regarded, by most, as an anathema. Our initial apprehension quickly died, and the three of us pattered away in light conversation. Harry took a moment to wring out his wash and hang it on a makeshift clothesline next to the tent. "Pull up a chair." invited Harry as he ducked inside, "It's crab for dinner."

Junior and I sat down at the table, a seamless fir slab with bark-shrouded, sapling sized legs. There were four rustic chairs, obviously home-made, and there was a solitary, steaming, untouched cup of tea, a small sugar bowl at its side, and a neatly folded napkin.

A light breeze cascaded over the glacier, giving the air a crisp chill, and I noticed the faint fragrance of wild roses. I was happy that there was just enough radiance from the fire nearby to warm us. As I looked up Muir Creek at the massive blue behemoth, I couldn't help but think, "There really couldn't be a more beautiful place to live." Though I loved the wide vista our home enjoyed of the sea, I might gladly have traded it for the wind tousled trees and the elegance of the blue ice at the glacier's tongue.

The open flames of the fire quickly disappeared, leaving a deep bed of coals. Harry filled a large pot from the stream and brought it to a boil. Without calling undue attention to an unpleasant task, he quickly dropped the six Dungeness into the water. "I hate that part of it," said Harry, with a hint of sadness, "We need to be thankful for what we have, and understand that something that's alive is being sacrificed for our sustenance and pleasure. Lord, thank you for your bounteous gifts, Amen."

I noticed that there was now little steam rising from the tea. "Harry, your tea's getting cold." After I said it I knew I'd made a mistake, for there was an instant, powerful silence that arrested our conversation. Even the creek seemed to momentarily stop its babbling, and the sweet sound of songbirds, which had been a chorus only moments before, was muted in a dark oblivion. Junior and I looked at each other, then at Harry. His face streamed tears, and he turned away.

"Andrea," he finally broke the silence, "loved her cup of tea, and I used to take pleasure in bringing it to her every afternoon, as my schedule allowed." Harry's voice faltered, just a bit, as he spoke, and he wiped his eyes with a sleeve of his shirt.

Should we just gently say goodbye and leave? The thought did cross my mind, that this was a moment belonging only to Harry, and that we were somehow stealing the tender grief he needed to feel. I worried that our visit was now in ruin. It may have been a minute or more, but then Harry lifted his face toward us and there was the unmistakable hint of a smile. "I loved her so much." As he said it his face reminded me of the first, warm days of spring, and the sun, which had been mostly shrouded in clouds that day, peaked through a little gap in the sky, creating an immediate and pervasive warmth.

"I know," Harry continued, "not everyone is a believer. But I have faith that Andrea and I will be together again. Life is but the blinking of an eye, and we will have our joyous reunion soon. I don't know how I could even live, were it not for that faith."

No matter how I felt about the existence of a God, I was very touched by Harry's love. I grieved, inside, at the thought of a man losing his most precious gift, and my thoughts turned to my own father and that instant in time that had taken him from me. I felt just as I had at Father's funeral, and my own grief merged with Harry's.

"Every afternoon," Harry reflected, "I still get Andrea her cup of tea. It's almost like I expect to see her at this table, and the tea bears the message that she is loved, welcome, and sorely missed. It might seem silly to you boys—to still be doing this so many years after her death—but I'll be doing it until I'm gone." Harry had a far-away look in his eyes, one that spoke of the moments they had shared. I looked at Junior. His eyes were wet, and mine were too. Only moments later, it was over, Junior and I taking in that warm ray of sunlight, and Harry attending to the cooking.

Though the sea was forever with us, and seafood was a staple for all the coastal folks, the crab tasted unusually savory. I wasn't sure why, but it may have been the simple pleasure of eating crab in such a beautiful spot. As I chewed the Dungeness, I thought of what my mother would say if she knew I ignored her instructions to stay away from this man, and I dreaded the understanding that she would surely find out. Despite my fear of her tirades, the contrary Billy Potter would surely reveal where he'd been for dinner. When I thought about it, I wasn't exactly sure of why she needed to know. I suspected that it concerned my own sense of honesty, but there was also an adverse side of me that took some kind of pleasure in disclosing what I knew Mother dreaded to hear.

After sharing the crab, the conversation evolved into a discussion of education, and Harry told us, "I have a lot of books. You're always welcome to borrow them, as long as you faithfully return them after you've read them." We both told him we'd take him up on his offer, but, feeling uneasy about the lateness of the hour and understanding that we were in defiance of our parents' warnings, Junior and I experienced a mutual recognition that it was time to go. "Thank you, Rev. Mills, It was so good," we chimed in unison, and we both added that we hoped to visit again. Our use of Harry's title felt a bit strange. He had told us, before, that he preferred being called by his first name, but we had inexplicably slipped back into an old formality. We stood there, taking one more moment to feel the beauty of the scene, and then we left Harry to his solitude

If anyone in our town had seriously presented the question of where Harry would be in another one or two years, there would have been a likely consensus.   Stella's Cove anticipated Harry's demise. He explored the Glacier and walked it with impunity, and the community assumed that it was just a matter of time until the glacier's evil claimed another--this time, one who truly deserved to die. But Harry discovered no evil in the glacier--only the realities of her being. When pushed far and hard enough, the glacier would speak--first, by groaning, and then with a deafening thunder as her foremost spires fell, littering the stream bed with their icy blue shards.

The following spring, Harry noticed a few sparkling yellow flakes, masked by the milky effluent of the glacier, for the Glacier was releasing the gold she'd collected in her travels from the peaks toward the sea. He filed a claim with the Province-- about ten feet of streambed at the head of Muir Creek--and noticed, when he filed it, that it had been claimed by someone else during Stella's Cove's big gold rush. Now, officially abandoned by its deceased claimant, Harry inspected the old claim certificate, and was able to make out the name. "Willis Fox."

Now, it would have seemed surprising for someone to

have discovered gold again in Muir Creek, for everyone knew that the creek, like Sarah in the Bible, was barren with age. The area had experienced a gold boom already, but the richness that had exploded the town's growth and brought big businesses to the Cove died after a few wildly prosperous years. That same vein made the man known as the Rev. Willis Fox the richest man in all of B.C., and it was that same vein that roofed the homes, painted the siding, brought expensive single-malts to replace the local rot-gut, elegantly finished the church's interior with exotic woods from around the world, and raised a seventy-four foot steeple that became a symbol for the town. The brothels and hotels had all gone belly-up, and the builders and sawyers left with everybody else. Depletion of the gold was responsible for the town's second decisive failure, and the idea of finding more gold, after so many confirmed that it was gone, would have been considered totally ludicrous.

What the earlier miners failed to realize was that, underneath the glacier was a vein, richer than all others. It was the "mother lode," but, without the glacier's assistance, it could not be reached. Even if people knew its approximate location, any attempt to reach it would have been suicidal. The glacier's instability, combined with its constant forward movement would have quickly created a glazed mausoleum for whomever tried. It was the glacier's slow grinding against the bedrock of the canyon that was now releasing gold again into the waters of the creek, and Harry was the only one who knew. Despite his excitement over his find, he launched no ecstatic cries of "Eureka." In fact, he was just as careful to "share" news of his discovery as the town had been to "share" their resources with him during his hours of greatest need. It was his secret. It really was not the lust for money that committed the matter to secrecy. Instead, it was the defense of his privacy, for solitude was now a matter of his worship.

Purchasing a one-dollar gold pan from Young's store, Harry was practically reproached by Young: "It's a waste of your time, Harry," Young asserted, "You won't find any more gold. It's been gone for years." Harry simply smiled, "Well, it doesn't hurt to give it a try." In the next few months, Harry made friends with a young crewman on the Aniak, and the man kept Harry's secret as he transported the gold to the bank in Bourne River, returning on each subsequent run with a proper deposit receipt.

Soon Harry had scraped together enough money to fund a

respectable log cabin at his original campsite. The cabin was large but simple. It consisted of one large room that served for a kitchen and living area, one generous bedroom, and a slightly smaller one. That second bedroom became the town's best library, for Harry loved great literature and the wisdom of the ages. As the glacier groaned outside, and with his oil lamp illuminating the tireless wisdom of the ages, Harry opened the windows of the world to himself and the few brave friends who ventured there--people who obviously didn't believe the grand legends of his evil.

For two years, Harry alternated between exploring the glacier, panning for the rich color that flowed from her mouth, and seeing the world through his books. The crew of the Aniak knew of Harry's passion, and they bought up used books at all the steamboat's stops, understanding that they could sell them to Harry on their next landing in Stella's Cove. The secret of the rich gold strike was easily kept, since there were few in the town of Stella's Cove who dared venture into Rev. Mills' domain; and Muir Creek, despite its rich past, had long faded from the town's curiosity into just another element in the town's changeless landscape. In fact, it was largely the town's loathing of the defrocked minister that silenced the knowledge of his find. Rev. Cromwell inadvertently helped provide that protection, noting in one of his sermons, "The ever-reaching clutches of the devil are attendant to those who have chosen him as their god, and the best way to avoid Satan's power is to stay as far away as we can. We must not suppose that we can outsmart the devil, so avoidance is our only protection."

Over time, Harry's presence was gradually simply accepted, but there were still only a few in Stella's Cove who would say a perfunctory "Good Day" when they saw him in town. Junior and I were two of those exceptions, and we made more than a few trips to the glacier's tongue, where the Rev. Mills talked with us of life, and shared his precious collection of books. It took a while to get used to his thick monocle and the mushy impediment that cursed his mouth, yet he quickly assumed the position of hero in our lives. He knew so much about the glacier, the world, its people and inventions, and we could honestly say that there was a reward for each of our visits.

Now, there were times when the glacier's groaning and creaking combined with the breeze to create a gentle singing--not a song of icy judgment from God's frigid mouth, but a loving entreatment to... Well, in Harry's early days at the foot of the glacier, he swore to Junior that, listening closely to her song, he'd heard the unmistakable words, "Come unto me." Junior had been only twenty-two at the time, but he regarded Harry's words as a little bit "touched" and believed that Harry's beating in Eagle City was responsible for an infirmity far deeper than his damaged jaw.

———————

Junior's life was comfortable enough. He lacked for nothing, since his work at the bakery was rewarded with his board and room, and Clemmerton Sr. always gave him a generous allowance as well. But Junior's story was a sad one. He dropped out of school at 16, to work in his Dad's bakery. It was simply something his father expected him to do, for, like the farmers that tilled the ground on the leeward side of the mountains, extra boys in a family were essentially free labor as long as they chose to live at home. Junior was interested in continuing his education, but his father's need for a reliable employee bound him to Stella's Cove and to the dead-end lane that lay just around the corner. Unknown to his father, his seven years of allowance was faithfully saved, and it was earmarked for one purpose alone.

After years of mixing and rolling dough at the shop, the growing friendship with Harry Mills inspired Junior to continue learning, and Junior once confided in me, "When I get enough money saved, I'm getting out of here. I've put it off for years for Father's sake, but I am going to get a college degree." I was joyous at his announcement, and, though I understood what friction it would cause between him and his father, I vocally applauded his plan and it became our little secret.

Harry appreciated quality in literature, and he made regular recommendations of books that would help Junior in his ambitions for college. Delighted with Harry's suggestions for reading, Junior continued with his own, independent education. Everyone in town knew about the library at the end of the trail, but the pious people conjectured and speculated on the dangers of Harry's influence. "He probably has books on witchcraft," one said, and another accused, "And I'm sure he has some very dirty ones too."

There was something else that helped create a bond of friendship between Harry and Junior. Junior felt a sort of brotherhood with the shamed cleric--comforted in his own guilt by the understanding that even the holy can err--assuming that, while Harry was likely not a rapist, there must have been some sort of moral turpitude that led to his expulsion from Eagle City. Junior kept a secret that he shared with no one else, and it involved a certain young woman who resided in Stella's Cove. He had remained a virgin until shortly after his twenty-fourth birthday, largely because Stella's Cove suffered from a dearth of eligible young ladies his age, and partly because his staunch Methodist upbringing made him afraid of the eternal consequences. As the floodgates of love opened to him, so did his understanding that the hunger for closeness and affection was a compelling need and nothing to be ashamed of.

Yet, during most of Junior's waking moments--at those moments when dreams collided with the stark imperatives of his existence--he regarded his endless work at the bakery to be his loveless lot in life. He sometimes felt that his ambitions for a university education and new opportunities would never materialize, and he lamented the possibility that he would live and die in Stella's Cove. His new exposure to romance was the taste of another dream, but it was also the intensification of his fears. For, though he knew his love was reciprocated, he was disturbed that the girl was unwilling to marry, and that she often spoke of dreams, dreams that would likely take her away from Stella's Cove.

When Junior shared his guilt with Harry, the defrocked minister did not rebuke him. "Love is a wonderful thing, and there are many worse sins than fornication," Harry asserted, "but," he continued, "she and you need to make it right--with a proper marriage--or find some way to gracefully end it." Because he was unable to do either, Junior's guilt continued. During his visits to Harry's cabin, they often polished off a bottle and joined the glacier in her lonely song, filling the chilly air with resounding choruses of "Rock of Ages" and "Amazing Grace." And Harry always offered Junior the same reassurance, "My dear friend, Christ's blood has washed you clean."

Miss Kimberly Hardwicke

It was by chance that, only two years after Harry Mills was defrocked in Eagle City and relocated to our town, the problem of replacing Stella's Cove's old teacher became an urgent matter for the Town Council. And it was only two weeks later that one Kimberly Hardwicke noticed an advertisement in the Vancouver newspaper. "Stella's Cove, B.C., seeks public school teacher, grades 1 through 12. Two-year contract. Reply box 12 of this paper." Though she wasn't sure about the place, the pay was reasonably good. The clincher was that board and room were generously provided by the local baker, a Mr. Bart Clemmerton, Sr., who hoped a good education could give the town's children the best prospects for successful lives.

Kimberly viewed the two years in Stella's Cove as an opportunity to save her wages, and as the providential opportunity to pay back her Uncle Devlin MacWrae, who had graciously advanced her college tuition and paid her expenses along the way. She also saw the detour to Stella's Cove as her chance to grow a little older and wiser before being pressed into the business of marriage and babies. She simply wasn't ready for that, and believed that Stella's Cove could provide a welcome deferment of matters she was not ready to face.

Collectively, the roughly thousand residents of Stella's Cove were apprehensive about hiring Miss Kimberly Hardwicke. While her references and scholastic record were flawless, she had minored in Anthropology, and the Cove's residents were quickly informed by Rev. Cromwell, that there was an essential disagreement between religion and anthropology on the development of mankind.

Though the resolution of the town council specified that

the job would be awarded to "the best of the three top applicants," it found no one else who wished to relocate there, so availability became the more pressing requirement. Only days before the meeting of the town council, Miss Hardwicke had graduated from Arnold University with a Bachelor of Science Degree and was awarded a Teaching Certificate. She was also recognized as the "Dellwood Scholar," a title and cash award reserved for the graduating class's top student, and it was she who delivered the valedictory address.

Also sitting at the podium as she spoke, her long-time beau, Edward Stevens, felt a mixture of emotions running through his mind. He was a very competitive young man, and he was experiencing a quiet, troubling anger toward his Kimberly. "She's so damned smart," he'd found himself thinking, "and I'm so damned mad that it's she who was first in the class." Edward would give a speech at commencement too, but the top honor was not his. As Kimberly spoke, Edward was confronted with his own immaturity, realizing that jealousy was a wasted emotion and that he should be showing the greatest pride in the girl who had been his steady for the past two years.

Only the night before, Kimberly interrupted a warm moment on his dormitory cot. "Edward, dear," she'd softly whispered, "there's something I need to tell you. Please don't get upset. It's not forever, and it doesn't have to be over for us, but it will be a change. It's only fair to tell you that I've taken a teaching job north of Bourne River--in a town called Stella's Cove. I probably should have said something sooner, but it was only yesterday that I received the letter announcing the town's decision. It's a two-year contract, and I'll be able to save enough money to pay back my Uncle Devlin."

Now, running through Edward's mind, there was a fear that, after Kimberly's two years in the obscure and isolated community of Stella's Cove, their romance was likely to cool. He'd never even heard of Stella's Cove, and Kimberly's announcement came as an abrupt shock. Edward always believed that the two of them were of like mind—marriage and babies; perhaps another couple of years for graduate studies; a little house with a white picket fence; and a life of never-ending bliss. When he thought about it, the script was, in truth, written only by him, and it wasn't being followed.

The Stella's Cove School was a model of efficiency, and educators from other parts of the Province had studied it as an example of how a small town could adequately handle the needs of all the age groups. With multiple students in every grade, it presented a very substantial challenge, but the teacher was credited with an amazing job. Education was faithfully provided, for almost four decades, by Rev. Miles Cromwell, and the Stella's Cove School was considered far above average.

Cromwell could brag about it, and he did, stressing the assertion "I've left no child behind, and the proficiency levels for each grade have been confirmed by the nationwide, newly-instituted Standardized Student Assessment Program. As important as the core academic studies, I've also made sure that the Devil has found no admirers among the young souls of Stella's Cove. Our Holy Bible has been read each day and has protected our children against the sins of the world." he added, and then, in review, "and everyone in our community should be proud that our school scored in the ninety-seventh percentile on the three "R's."

There was a general acceptance in Stella's Cove that its school teacher considered religion to be one of his most essential teaching responsibilities, and Rev. Cromwell tried to ensure that the heresies of the outside world would not touch the town's young. While his view was largely shared by the other adults of the community, some visiting educators were concerned by what they considered an overstepping of the local religion in the educational process. The townsfolk were in accord with their preacher, for they were more concerned that a strictly secular education would create attrition of church participation. So, when it became clear that Cromwell was no longer fit to teach, the hiring committee searched for a teacher with an appropriate degree in divinity, but one could not be found. Fragmented in its resolve, and with no other applicants available on such short notice, the committee gave the almost-angelic Miss Hardwicke a two-year contract. She insisted on a clause making herself the sole determinant of curriculum, although the contract also specifically required that the Provincial study guidelines would be met.

Those who heartily supported the appointment of the innocent looking Kimberly, and were encouraged by the tiny gold cross gracing her pale neck—a gift from Edward—quickly became disenchanted. Over the period of only a few months, a clean and decent town was suddenly deluged with children's voices talking of Neanderthal Men and glaciers well over forty-thousand years of age. Righteous rage came over the town like a chameleon changing its color from green to red.

Throughout my childhood, I couldn't help but feel a pang of penitent remorse when my good, Christian upbringing collided with science. The growing schism between Mother and I became outright hostile when Miss Kimberly Hardwicke took over the public education of our community. While Miss Hardwicke's tenure as Stella's Cove's schoolmistress was a short one, she impacted the way her students saw and understood the world. She also made, because of her liberal views of scientific discovery and her unabashed agnosticism, a fair number of enemies.

When Miss Hardwicke appeared, I had been enduring Cromwell for ten years and was thoroughly accustomed to the fact that there had never once been a hint of joy or laughter on his face. I am sure he regarded laughter and levity to be against God's purpose in having all mankind trembling with fear about the consequences of sin, and I believed that he considered any student's revelation of happiness to be an abject disregard for the serious nature of life.

It was surprising to me that anyone would have ever married him, but Rev. Cromwell was married, and I could understand why I had never seen his wife, Bertha, looking anything better than austere. She was a very pretty woman, much younger than her stick-in-the-mud husband, and I found myself feeling sorry for her and imagining how happy she'd be to have a young lover. I was disgusted with myself for thinking it, but Bertha looked like she had a romantic streak, and the minister was definitely not the one to cultivate any romantic interests. I had stood in the outhouse and abused myself, all the time thinking of her arms around me and being entwined in her naked body. Each time I felt guilt, but the perpetuation of the activity made it impossible to seriously embrace repentance or remorse. I understood that repentance was worthless unless a person was actually willing to stop whatever annoyed God, and it felt so good, I knew I wasn't about to stop. Perhaps even more important, I also believed that, if there was a god, it was he who had created the desires of men and their need for fulfillment.

Several times at church, I looked upon Bertha Cromwell with lust, and I noticed how her breasts rose and fell, almost imperceptibly, during her husband's sermons. Maybe she wasn't thinking, at all, about Christ's death on the cross, and, just maybe, she was playing the part of Bathsheba, seducing an innocent David. I didn't even know why I went to church, except for Mother's prodding and her assurance that it would someday be clear to me. I did not believe it, and there were few services I left without a hard-on, because the women, in their Sunday dresses, looked so appealing to me.

The Cromwell's son Edgar was a schoolmate, two years ahead of me in age, and he was the mirror of his father, both in looks and demeanor. He had pimples underneath his nostrils; his cheeks were always pocked; and his skin looked like it had never been touched by the sun. His pale skin accentuated his festering blemishes, and there wasn't a hint that his facial follicles could grow whiskers. The pomade he used on his hair gave it the appearance of being coated with axle grease, and there was never even one hair out of place in the part that ran down the left side of his head. He was weak, never even attempted to play soccer during the P.E. hour, and he was a frequent target of derision for other more manly boys who looked at him as a sissy.

There was no question about it. Edgar was pale, anemic, and frail, and he spoke in the same colorless tone that plagued the Methodist congregation each Sunday. Despite the things I found so objectionable about him, I believed without question, that Edgar would someday marry a girl--one who would also never smile, and who would bear him a kid just like himself.

Edith Cromwell was my age. She had been sickly through the years, and there were many times her chair sat empty during the school day. It seemed that she was out on "home excuse" for much of her childhood. No one ever elaborated on just what was wrong with her, but, out of a natural sympathy, she escaped the disrespect the class had shown for Edgar. When she talked, she squeaked like a mouse, and she had a very awkward gait. And though Edith was skinny, knock-kneed, and pimple-faced like her brother, I never saw any of my classmates being mean to her. The whole family--except for Bertha--qualified for the wallpaper in our outhouse, with the sad color of blue dominating their lives and no one finding any power in their words.

I remember the day when Rev. Cromwell asked Eddie

Sant, a classmate of my own age, to read a paragraph aloud in front of the class. "Silence, children." Cromwell barked, and the proverbial pin-drop could have easily been heard by all. Eddie began, "Half a league, half a league, half a league onward, into the valley of death rode the six hundred." There was a brief hesitation before the next line, and Eddie's expression transitioned into a look of fear. For a moment I believed he was simply adding dramatic impact to Tennyson's lines, but then, with his face showing all the symptoms of resolute terror, Eddie let off the ripest expression of gas anyone had ever heard in the Province, and the class roared with laughter. It wasn't that the children of Stella's Cove were rude or intended to embarrass the poor kid. There was simply no way to suppress the spontaneous eruption of delight that followed--any more than there had been any way for Eddie to avoid the noisy release. Even Edith Cromwell was unable to suppress her giggle. Only two people in that classroom had not smiled for even a moment. Rev. Cromwell and his son Edgar were obviously well above such a reaction, and their faces spoke a firm disapproval to the response of the class. While only one of them wore it, both Edgar and his father suffered from the same case of rigor-mortis-starched collars, and I mused on the belief that they would both die from gangrene, their circulation impaired by the dour and changeless positions their lips always assumed.

And so, it was the contrast between the boring and stiff old teacher and the spring-fresh appearance and countenance of Miss Hardwicke that gave the children of the Cove what amounted to a fresh start in life. Though learning and the stimulation of my mind had become the greatest factor in my new enthusiasm, I cannot say that they were the only reasons why my performance in school suddenly soared. Yes, the new teacher was refreshing and steered away from the pious views of the church folks. Yes, she was more interested in what scientists were saying, and showed enthusiasm over the accelerating pace of discovery which was flooding the academic world. But there was one other reason for my rise to academic excellence, and I had never known anything quite like it. I believed I was in love.

As I understand now, it is very difficult for a teenage boy to know what is the sudden clap of the door knocker by thousands of little hormonal messengers, or what constitutes real love. All I knew was that it was hopeless to dismiss the emotional and physical hungers suddenly flooding my life. I had a secret that I could tell no one--an infatuation that swept over my mind whenever I failed to concentrate on my studies--and I used my new, academic diligence partly in sublimation of the powerful currents running inside me.

I can still remember the first day of school that fall, when the bell rang and our class sat down. Like something out of a magical fairy tale, a new ingredient had been added to our classroom. In her first few minutes as our new mentor, she both smiled and laughed while presenting a brief autobiography.

"Good morning," she'd sweetly spoken. "I'm Kimberly Hardwicke, and I am your new teacher. I know that you've been in the capable hands of Rev. Cromwell ever since you've been at this school, and I promise you that I will continue in his high standard of education." (There had been a brief sigh of disappointment from most of my classmates, for no one wanted Cromwell's "high standard" to continue.) "I love teaching," Miss Hardwicke continued, "and my hope is to inspire all of you to seek knowledge and to be the best people you can be." On Edgar Cromwell's face there was a look of resentment that his father had been supplanted, but I saw Edith Cromwell responding with a smile to Miss Hardwicke's introduction.

I remember thinking that Miss Hardwicke's verbal applause of the Reverend's excellence was definitely overkill. For, frankly, I could not have endured one more year of the miserable boredom I'd suffered since I'd started school. For the incoming teacher to give credit to the previous one was a requirement of propriety and etiquette, and though I hated to hear Rev. Cromwell being praised, I understood that Miss Hardwicke was doing what was appropriate.

Secretly the class all loathed the drudgery of school, and it was mostly because Rev. Cromwell so thoroughly gutted the purpose of education. He stifled all curiosity for knowledge—a curiosity with which many of his students were naturally imbued-- and caused all his students to recoil at the approach of his lectures.

When Kimberly Hardwicke replaced Rev. Cromwell as my teacher, I suddenly grasped just how lack-luster my own existence had been, for, without a cleric's collar, and with the unmistakable kindness that exuded from her warm smile, I saw the vision of a softer world. It was the second time, since the sadness of my father's death had saturated my life, that I understood life was really a series of losses and recoveries, and that I was on a new path leading in a more positive direction.

After her first day in class, I lugged all my books home, did the required reading for all subjects, and faithfully completed the homework that Miss Hardwicke had assigned. I was surprised how much work there was, and it had been necessary for Mother to call me into dinner--something that had never happened before. For I had always been like a runner at the starting blocks, when it came to the word "food."

"What have you been doing?" There was a kind of demand in Mother's voice, and I couldn't help thinking that I had finally done something right, and was about to get scolded for it.

"I've been doing my reading and homework." I replied, and there was a sudden look of puzzlement in Mother's eyes. She had already served the food and she could not recall any time in the past when I had not been there anxiously awaiting it. "Well," she stammered a bit as she tried to say it, "I was worried that this day would never come." She walked over to where I was standing, put her arms around me, and broke down, sobbing gently, pressing her face against mine. She did not say what I was anticipating, and there were no more accolades. "I love you, Billy." Her emotions were flooding. "...and I miss your father so much."

Mother's stoicism had been so complete. Except for her tears at the funeral, I had not seen the grief she held inside her, and had secretly been angry that she did not seem to miss my father the way I did. While my life had been torn apart and my wounds were still open, her job at the Murphy Salmon Company processing plant seemed a therapy for her sorrow, and the commitment of love to a fallen man had been replaced by the need to continue as the family's provider in his absence.

Mother and I struggled to eat supper that night, because we were both overcome by the pain inside us and the sadness that flooded our hearts.

I wanted Miss Hardwicke to think I was smart, for there was an immediate, special link between Miss Hardwicke and the brighter kids in our class. She used their assignments as examples to the other students, and took delight in posting their "A's." At the same time, she made an obvious attempt to help the poorer students improve, and she was always available to those who needed tutoring after school. During her first four months in

Stella's Cove, I went from a "low achiever" to becoming one of her pets. There was no question. The academic strategy had worked surprisingly well, and Miss Hardwicke had definitely noticed me.

Despite my secret love, I sometimes looked at Miss Hardwicke with a guarded suspicion, considering my Mother's allegations of the teacher's godless nature. During those moments of question, I understood: though I no longer believed in religion, some of its notions were not easily shaken. While Mother and a few other adults did seem to appreciate the new educational vigor which appeared in the young people, virtually none of the parents in Stella's Cove trusted our teacher. Surely, they could easily see the difference in their children's enthusiasm for school, but the consensus was that Miss Hardwicke was a dangerous emissary from the outside world, and that her recognition of science, over a God in heaven, was both blasphemous and evil.

I was old enough to understand that whatever my mother was saying about Miss Hardwicke was simply an echo, originating from the thin lips of the minister, and drifting through most other homes in the community. The people of Stella's Cove were proud of their common values, but, in a sense, they were the uncreative mirrors of pathetic narrowness that incessantly dominated our town. There were few who ever thought an independent idea, and Rev. Cromwell had been nothing but a curse to progress and enlightenment.

For the first few months of school that year, education went on as usual. But, in early February, Miss Hardwicke introduced the subject of who, exactly, man is, and where he came from. "I realize that you have been satisfied, at least up until now," she acknowledged, "that God created man--that He first sculpted Adam from the clay of the earth, and later made Eve from one of Adam's ribs." There was a short pause that seemed interminable, She didn't even have to say more; I could see where she was headed, and I secretly wished that she had stuck to our old curriculum, understanding that she was likely creating an immense gulf between herself and the parents of our town.

"I know you've been told that the Bible should be your source of trusted knowledge, and I am in agreement that the Bible contains many words of wisdom that seem to simplify and protect our lives. The parables of Jesus," she continued, "are full of useful lessons for living, but the notion that all wisdom comes from the

Bible is not a realistic point of view."

I glanced around the room; there were troubled looks on the faces of virtually all the students, and Edgar Cromwell's expression bore a silent message: "Just wait 'til my father hears about this!" In sharp contrast to her brother's smirk, Edith's face was one of enthusiastic curiosity Though there were a few kids who seemed willing to listen, I think the class emitted a unanimous gasp at the words that followed: "Charles Darwin was a scientist who studied a variety of animal species, and it is his work that gave us another theory on the origin of mankind. He noticed how creatures evolved—changed—according to their habitats, and how the ones that were best able to adapt to their surroundings were the ones that survived. This led him to the conclusion that man was likely descended from the ape family, changed over a period of millions of years into what we are today." Edgar, who was straining to remain seated, blurted out, "The world's not a million years old. That's pure heresy."

Miss Harwicke didn't look angry, nor did she chide Edgar for his comment. "I know that's a hard concept to grasp," she almost whispered, "but science has proven the earth is very, very old. And, yes, scientists have evidence that it has existed for millions of years."

What she was saying made sense to me; she gave examples of animals that had changed over time, with reproduction largely limited to those that had the traits necessary for survival. Still, the thought of me being descended from monkeys was shocking, and there was a part of me that ran and hid under the cloak of my religious education. As Miss Hardwicke spent more time on the subject of evolution, the ideas became less foreign, and by April, my belief in the legends of the Bible had been displaced by scientific learning.

There was certainly no way to keep Miss Hardwicke's views from the parents. Kids talked, especially about the concept of evolution, and parents immediately realized that an entire generation was now in spiritual peril. I chose not to confront Mother with my growing agnosticism, yet I was acutely aware; she knew exactly what was happening at the Stella's Cove School.

While the furor over the schoolteacher spread throughout the community's adults, my view retained a singular simplicity. I could only think of the way Miss Hardwicke's dress gently cascaded over the curves of her body, and imagine how she would look if the clothes had been lightly shed on my bedroom floor. Such thoughts plagued my mind, and, when school was over and there was no one around, Miss Hardwicke had replaced Bertha Cromwell in my most private fantasies. I found myself, while Mother was still at work, pretending that my pillow was Miss Hardwicke in my arms. The visions of her soft, pale skin and pink nipples were so vivid during those moments, and my body responded with the typical spontaneity of an adolescent boy. My trips to the outhouse also became more frequent, and mother noticed that my stays had gotten longer. "Billy," she had inquired on a Sunday afternoon, "are you having a problem with constipation?"

"Mother!" I'd exclaimed with both embarrassment and indignation, and she admitted that I was likely too old to be lectured on regularity. "Just in case,"--she simply couldn't let the subject go--"there's some castor oil on the medicine cabinet shelf." It was then that I decided I would limit my self-abuse to those times Mother was not there.

Aside from my powerful attraction to Miss Hardwicke, there were times, too, when the winter sun poured through the classroom's rippled glass, casting its gleam on the whites of Miss Hardwicke's words---times I suspected her of being an angel, and her sentences, treasures of wisdom far brighter than my mother's pious belief in the blackness that surrounded anything not included in the Good Book.

When I considered the significance of Miss Hardwicke's arrival, it was surprising to me that she had been hired by the town. Stella's Cove had always been dominated by the interests of narrow minds, and it eluded me how she had been able to secure a contract.

Within six months of her arrival, the Town Fathers knew that they'd made a mistake. Their own children were asking questions--ones like "Dad, do you think men came from apes?" "Mother, how old do you think the world is?" "If the Gavins Glacier is somewhere between ten million and forty million years old, when did God create the earth?" "Was Mary really a virgin?"--that had been one of the most upsetting--and "If God created us, who created God?" Parents were both irate and insecure about the very adult questions their children were suddenly asking. They worried about the safety of their children in a world where all was not black and white, and, even for the smarter of the town's parents, there was a brutal discomfort accompanying their children's highly unorthodox queries.

A town of pious and God-fearing people suddenly found themselves emotional and ideological orphans. There was horror in their minds, for an element of doubt was suddenly being raised from the "mouths of babes," and there was a panic over how to fix the situation and please an angry God. When adults tried to answer their children's questions, they felt concern that their answers weren't making sense, and there was a horrifying recognition in some of the children, "See, you're not really sure either."

Stella's Cove had approved Miss Hardwicke, the Town Council had signed her two-year contract, and now the shrinking numbers of youth in the community were being 'led astray'. By all but a few mavericks, who actually possessed curious brains, Miss Hardwicke was considered to be a threat to the morality of the community. How could they ever have entrusted their children's minds to someone who had no fear of hell and who did not read daily from the Holy Bible? Most of Stella's Cove shook their heads and understood that a serious and pressing crisis had developed--one that would have to be dealt with quickly and decisively.

The boredom and pat answers fed to the students at the Stella's Cove School for so long by the narrow-minded, backward-thinking Rev. Cromwell, were interrupted for that one period in time. The children of Stella's Cove finally had an excellent teacher, though it would probably be safe to say that only a few adults were happy she was there. My mother was not one of the exceptions, but Celeste's parents were openly supportive of the displacement of Rev. Cromwell as the teacher, and delighted in Celeste's reports that Miss Hardwicke's lessons would be considered heretical by most of the community.

The war between religion and science became stridently vocal virtually overnight, and the polarization of the townsfolk was almost complete, with only a few holdouts who believed that truth was the most important value. Several angry parents approached Miss Hardwicke that spring, asking her to refrain from teaching anything that didn't follow the Bible. An envelope was handed to her by a stranger as she walked toward her lodging at the Bart Clemmerton home. The stranger seemed to vanish after placing the note in her hand, and Miss Hardwicke stopped for a moment to look down at the envelope, then looked every direction to see the man who'd delivered it.

On the fog-shrouded lanes, running all four directions, she saw no one, wondering to herself, "Where did he go?" Feeling uncomfortable, she slipped the note from the envelope and read its terse message. "God doesn't like you," it stated with an exclamation point, "and you'd better not teach our kids any more of that Darwin shit if you expect to live."

Under the written portion of the note was a small, poorly sketched, picture of a naked woman, hanging from a disproportionately large gallows noose. The breasts were exaggerated in size and extended with udders the size of a cow's, and there was what appeared to be a stick, emerging from the triangle of pubic hair where the figure's legs joined together.

Horrified, Miss Hardwicke felt a frantic instinct to run. The crude illustration of death and the portrayal of feminine characteristics in such a lewd context, sent a chill through her. The color drained from her rosy cheeks, and fear flooded her mind, questioning the wisdom of having come to such an isolated place--one in which the people were totally opposed to the intrusion of outsiders, and feared the influence of new ideas.

Even Bart Clemmerton, at whose home she received lodging, invited her into his study that evening for a "heart to heart talk." While not as militant as most of the other parents, he asked her, as she entered, "Please, sit down."

Kimberly Hardwicke had anticipated his words. In the kindest tone, he articulated how much the Clemmerton family liked her, and then approached his real concern. "While I was working at the bakery," he spoke with consternation, "this came through the side bedroom window of our home." He held up a fist-sized rock in his hand, embellished by a small wrap of pink yarn, which was tied around a piece of paper and terminated in a neat bow. "I'm concerned with my family's safety, and I never dreamed, when you came here, that you would be the focus of such hate."

"I'm sorry," lamented Kimberly, "but I am just trying to be a good teacher."

Clemmerton then handed the rock to Miss Hardwicke, exhorting her to back-off a bit from her, essentially, heretical teachings and try to stick closer to the teachings of the Bible. "I don't have a strong belief that the world was created in seven days," he noted, "but you'll have to appreciate the traditions of this town if you're going to be here for very long." Kimberly pulled a loose end of the bow, and the note fell to her lap. It looked almost identical to the one she had received from the stranger on the lane, earlier that day.

For a while, Stella's Cove tried to overlook what was happening, but the problem was not going away. One morning in late April, Kimberly was greeted on the steps of the school by the same committee that hired her. They had already talked with Rev. Cromwell, and he had agreed to resume the duties of schooling until a God-fearing replacement for Miss Hardwicke could be found. Having that assurance, the committee asked for her resignation. It was no surprise. She certainly knew, mostly from conversations with her students, that the parents of Stella's Cove were both angry and unhappy with her teaching. She also saw first-hand the wall that was being placed between the children and a good education, for the Good Book alone was not her idea of a suitable textbook, and she had taken the initiative to order new ones—ones that the Town Fathers saw as offensive and blasphemous.

I had actually begun to figure it out years before, when the growing availability of scientific articles about the earth's age was irrepressible, and the insulation of the young minds became the townsfolk's greatest concern. Rev. Cromwell held a special meeting for all the residents with school-aged children, ranting and raving about "intellectual purity" and how it was the Bible that could keep evil ideas from rooting in young minds. "It's our sacred responsibility," Cromwell spoke, trembling with emotion, "to protect our children from the heresies which are now infecting our academies of higher learning. They're turning out graduates that have sold their souls to Satan, and as the soldiers in God's army, we are going to defeat the foe in Stella's Cove." A backlash of paranoia spread among the parents, like a pebble released from a slingshot into a deep pool, and the avowed protection of the town's youth became a rallying cry.

One day before school, as the matter of "intellectual purity" intensified, Mother called to me as I was leaving. "Billy, Rev. Cromwell's asked all the parents to line up on the side of God. Satan may have deceived one-third of the heavenly hosts, but I'm going to make damn sure you don't become one of them. Whatever your plans were after school, you need to make sure you're home half an hour early. We've got some scripture reading to do." My first thought was to fight it, for I knew that reading the Bible was not the key to enlightenment. In a remarkably concerted assault, the parents of Stella's Cove doubled the scripture reading and added an extra family prayer--insisting on one just before school for special protection--as well as the evening prayer which was our routine for so many years. Any attempts at scientific objectivity were overridden by fear, and it was, at least on the surface, about preserving the ideals of the youth.

"Our children need to believe in something," an impassioned Gordon Foulger exclaimed, "or they'll end up getting into all kinds of trouble. If this doesn't come to an end soon, we'll have a crop of pregnant teenagers and after-school poker games destroying our children's lives." His sentiments accurately mirrored those of the community's majority, and those words had been taken, virtually verbatim, from one of Rev. Cromwell's recent Sunday sermons.

Looking back on it, I cannot understand how Miss Hardwicke lasted as long as she did. I heard it from my mother, who talked with me at the dinner table on May 1st. (I remember that date, because there was a short "May Day" festivity arranged in the town square.). "Cromwell's upset," she volunteered, "and the Town Council agrees with what he's saying. Kimberly Hardwicke will be the damnation of you and all our children if we can't get her out of here fast." The insular nature of the Cove allowed ignorance to prevail, and the domination of its religious core was essentially ensuring that real education was a veritable impossibility.

Miss Hardwicke was totally dedicated to the fulfillment of her responsibilities, and, when accosted on the school steps by the hiring committee, she had simply ignored the men, stepping forward and reaching for the handle on the door. "Excuse me, gentlemen," she glared, in a tone that was somewhere between controlled civility and obvious contempt. Jeffrey Farnes immediately stepped in front of her, his feet set stubbornly apart, and his arms outstretched in an effort to block her.

"Don't you dare," she snarled, and Farnes stepped aside, allowing her to pass. Miss Hardwicke walked into the classroom just like no one else was there. She proceeded to the blackboard, grabbed a short piece of chalk and wrote in giant capital letters, "I HAVE A CONTRACT."

Then Miss Hardwicke turned away from the blackboard, and, as sweetly as nothing had happened, said "Good Morning," and walked over to her desk, adding, "Mr. Farnes, You know I have a contract, and I have no intention of leaving." School went on as normal that day, but when Miss Hardwicke arrived the next day, the doors of the School were all locked. Mr. Farnes stood there with a smug look on his face, and he mocked her. "What! You don't have your lock-picking tools with you?"

Kimberly exercised amazing self-control. Her first instinct, on hearing Farnes's insulting words, was to slap his face. Instead she became quiet, sitting down on the school steps and reflecting on her sadness. A few remaining children tried to comfort her. "It's going to be all right," said one, and another half-whispered, "We love you, Miss Hardwicke, and they're not going to be able to find anyone else that's willing to come to Stella's Cove. See you soon." The children turned and walked sadly away.

A moment later there was the familiar sound of the Reo's squeaky brakes, followed by a sputter, a cough, and then silence. George Murphy got out of the "R-5" and walked toward Miss Hardwicke, nodding slightly as he greeted her. "Hello. Do you know who I am?" he asked.

"Yes," she answered, "You're Mr. Murphy, Celeste's father. I've seen you about the town." Miss Hardwicke extended her hand and the two spoke almost in unison, "It's so good to finally meet you. How do you do?"

Murphy wasted no words. "I realized, when you came to Stella's Cove, that it might turn out to be an ambush. These people aren't like you and me. They don't care about science and truth, and they reject anything that isn't written in the Bible. I've heard from Celeste that you're a fine teacher—she really loves you--and you've definitely piqued her curiosity about our world. From what I just witnessed, it looks like the problem has gotten out of hand, and I want to offer my help."

"Mr. Murphy," lamented Miss Hardwicke, "that's so kind of you, but I'm worried about your involvement, and how it's going to affect your relationships in this town."

"My interest isn't one of kindness, Miss Hardwicke, and I'm not one to act out of cowardice. It's my civic duty as a member of this community. I want you to understand that I'm doing it for the good of Celeste and all the other kids. They deserve a real education, and you're the best thing that's happened to our town in a long time."

George had a gentle, understanding look in his eyes. "I realize that affording legal counsel on a teacher's salary is impossible, so I will retain an attorney for the purpose of enforcing your contract. I believe the circuit judge will grant summary judgment on the matter, and it should be fast. After all, there's no question about it. You have a legally binding document."

———

Most of the children heard from their parents that there would be a short "vacation from school," No one told me-- probably the result of a very inefficient system for disseminating news. When I got to school the following morning, a few other kids were pacing and waiting for someone to come and unlock the door. We'd all showed up promptly at 7:55 a.m., but by 8:15 there was no Miss Hardwicke. The educational crisis had obviously developed well past the stage of parental dissatisfaction, and education in Stella's Cove seemed to be suffering a sudden death. As I walked toward home, I felt a futile sense of discouragement. I loved my newly-energized education, and I dreaded the possible outcome. If Miss Hardwicke were to leave, I would terribly miss her, and I hoped that the town would come to its senses and agree to keep her on. That seemed unlikely.

For three weeks the school hours were reduced to part-time, with Cromwell filling in for the embattled Miss Hardwicke, who petitioned the Circuit Court Judge to enforce her contract. On May 22nd, the town council received a letter from the Judge. It simply read, "Please be advised that Miss Kimberly Hardwicke's contract with the Town of Stella's Cove is an enforceable agreement, and Miss Hardwicke's legal footing is not in question. You have no choice but to reinstate her and compensate her as the contract requires, including any back wages withheld from her during this interim period. Signed, Hon. Wilfred Whiting."

By the time the teaching crisis came to a head, George Murphy had already lost his seat on the Council, largely because the other members felt that George's influence was responsible for the installation of the irreligious Miss Hardwicke as Cromwell's replacement. Understanding that George was not likely to agree with the concerns of the town and would not approve of any attempt to fire Miss Hardwicke, the Council took an impromptu vote. "All in favor of removing George Murphy from the Stella's Cove Council," barked Gerrod MacBean, "say "Aye.",

Thus, George's voice of authority on the issue of education was summarily silenced, and Edgar Phelps, a flaming supporter of Cromwell, was given Murphy's seat on the Council.

There was only one man in Stella's Cove who'd received some legal training. Jeffrey Farnes spent more than a year in law school before his dwindling funds forced him to quit. Nevertheless, he was regarded as a resource when the town had faced legal issues in the past, and now the town council turned to him for guidance. While the town held its breath, Farnes read and re-read both the contract and the Judge's decision. He pored through the small print, and looked for possible interpretive issues and ambiguities.

After a day, Farnes announced that he was unable to find any loopholes. Not willing to give up, the town council discussed its shrunken options but believed that there must be an alternative course of action to rid the town of Miss Hardwicke's curse. Farnes also pointed out to the council, "We need to understand that an appeal of the Judge's decision could take as long as a year or more, meaning that Miss Hardwicke's teaching position would likely be protected and sustained through the final year-and-a-half of her contract. Furthermore," added Farnes, "it is likely that the appeal would be decided in Miss Hardwicke's favor, and that the town would, almost surely, be charged with any legal fees she incurs, something that would likely empty Stella's Cove's coffers and force the bankruptcy of our town." To the other members of the Council, Farnes's words sounded like a coup de grace.

But Farnes wasn't finished. Spurred on by a few last, futile "Can't you do something?" pleas, he looked at the contract once more and made a startling discovery. It was so simple, but everyone had missed one very important matter. As the town conceded its misguided attempts to force Miss Hardwicke out, and the Council prepared to reopen the school, Farnes called a special meeting. "The contract," noted Farnes, "is very strong and any attempts to circumvent it or interfere with its provisions would surely be both a legal failure and a financial drain on the town." The heads of the Council members all faced the precisely same spot, where the cuffs of their trousers broke over the toes of their shoes.

"But," continued Farnes "we have one bonus." and everyone's heads immediately rose. "While it was to have been included in Hardwicke's contract," smirked Farnes, "the final signed contract inadvertently omitted the provision for Miss Hardwicke's board and room, so that's not an expense we'll have to deal with." There was a buzz of excitement as the trapped council saw an escape strategy. After a brief discussion, the committee made its decision: The town will simply pay Miss Hardwicke's salary for the entire contract period, and send her packing. "Money," added Farnes, "is the key, and, as long as Miss Hardwicke receives her full two-years' compensation, there will be no legal grounds under which she can fight her dismissal.

Now, one might think that, even in 1912, the roughly $1,235 that was still owing on Miss Hardwicke's contract was a paltry sum, particularly when compared with the value of sixty-seven young and impressionable souls. Yet, despite the incessant pressure of the Town Fathers, the eighty-eight working families of Stella's Cove were either unwilling or unable to scrounge up the required amount. The town had already exhausted most of the funds in its treasury on a sharp legal team from Bourne River, and the expectation was that the hefty legal fees would be balanced by the termination of all obligations to Miss Hardwicke. Instead the money in the town treasury was all spent, and the problem of Miss Hardwicke was still unsolved. Without donations from the townsfolk themselves, there was simply no way to satisfy the contract and be rid of what the residents mostly considered a scandalous and godless curse on their town.

Of the over $4,900 that constituted the town's account only months before, there was less than $400 remaining. The Town Council was alarmed, and its members shook their heads at the size of the legal bills, understanding that, even if Miss Hardwicke was sent packing, the town would have to hire another teacher, and it wouldn't be for free. A frantic panic fell across the Council's faces, and, as a last resort, a penitent petition was delivered to George Murphy, pleading for his help on the matter. While he could have easily bought the entire town, George responded angrily, "Why? Why would I do that? You know how I feel about the previous quality of education in this town, and Miss Hardwicke has certainly raised the standard to its highest level in forty years. Ask your children, for god's sake. They'll tell you.

There's finally a reason for our children to start loving education, and you're trying to destroy it."

What Murphy had spent on saving Miss Hardwicke's job was far greater than Stella's Cove's legal costs. His personal interest was for the good of the town's youth, and, in particular he couldn't stand the thought of his own child's education returning to the dark ages.

The people of the community had never accepted George Murphy after he decided, on a lark, to move his family there, but it was the charm of the glacier and the home site on Point Fay that convinced him. "The Cove," he declared to an old friend, "is the most beautiful place on earth!"

The Murphys' arrival was so much more than just a new family in Stella's Cove. With them came George's remarkable vision--that there were opportunities to revive the town, while increasing the size of his personal fortune. Some warmed up to George and Eva over the years, but the Murphys were still regarded as pariah in Stella's Cove and were tolerated only because George had, in effect, created and provided the most valuable resources of the town. As it turned out, there was no one in the community who did not owe their prosperity to him.

While the fishermen of the town continued to seine the sea for salmon, cod, and other seafood, almost all the other jobs in Stella's Cove were either working directly for George Murphy, or immediately connected to the immense success of his growing empire. Typical of the failures of human nature, the town's dependence on the Murphy family was not a source of endearment toward the new father of Stella's Cove, and there was always a general resentment of George and Eva, despite their generous and kind dispositions and their various endowments to the town.

Though most of the alienation came from the understanding that Murphy controlled the future of the town, it was also no small issue that George, in particular, held a very negative view of Rev. Cromwell's influence, both on the community's attitudes and on its educational system.

The tight group of overzealous Methodists, all poked and prodded by their shepherd's crook, showed no patience for anyone who didn't believe in the Good Book and God. The Murphys, after the perfunctory greeting of the town, immediately advanced to the head of the list. While piety ran firmly against the town's few agnostics, the smug superiority actually went beyond that. Even avowed Christians who did not believe exactly the same way, were shunned. Cromwell's flock of sheep were equally prejudiced toward the Alvin Morten family, who, though proclaimed believers in Christ, did not subscribe to any formal religion. The Mortens read the Bible and prayed in their home, and though I was no more drawn to their faith than toward the Methodist majority, I knew both the parents and the kids, and believed them to be a wonderful family.

Brian Morten, their oldest boy, was my age, and the Mortens, concerned by their son's virtual marginalization by other classmates, asked me to dinner one night in an effort to encourage our schoolyard friendship. Mother demanded that I decline their offer, giving no reason for her concern except the brief explanation, "They're not like us, Son. They may be good people, but they have been led astray." The prejudice was predictable. If you didn't worship at the Methodist Church, you were of little value as a human being. Politely ignoring Mother's concerns, I spent the evening with the Mortens and found their home to be filled with cooperation and love. Mother remained sore with me for over a week, but finally seemed to grasp the concept that it was not a good idea to interfere with my personal decisions. The Mortens were excluded from the town's social circles, and the children of Stella's Cove were told to stay away from their children. The Mortens were on the black list, just like Miss Hardwicke, the Murphys, and the defrocked minister, Rev. Harry Mills.

The parents of Stella's Cove considered it a moral issue to protect the impressionable teenage minds--particularly to keep the boys away from Celeste Murphy. All the mothers of boys my age spoke as if with one voice: "You can't look at Celeste Murphy, Son. She'll never be a marriage prospect for any God-fearing man, and she will lead you into sin if you let her into your life."

The mothers were obviously unaware that they were creating an even greater hazard, because the boys who were close to Celeste's age were intrigued and excited by the tacit accusation that she was a "naughty" girl. The idea of being "led into sin" sounded downright appealing to their adolescent minds. David

Jardine's mother issued a warning about Celeste, and he immediately asked Celeste if he could walk her home from school the very next day. She'd said, "Yes," but she'd immediately felt concern that she was suddenly receiving so much attention from her male schoolmates, for there were multiple social contacts with boys with whom she'd never before spoken.

Believing that Celeste would be easy, David tried to kiss her about half way between the town and her home, and, when she'd made it clear that she wasn't interested, he'd groped her breasts. "Don't touch me!" she frantically warned, and David immediately stopped, but his thorough parental indoctrination was all too clear, "You really want it," he taunted, "but you're just a stuck-up little bitch." Celeste ran the remaining distance to her home, and David turned, with a sour grunt, and walked the opposite direction.

Rather than answering the anxious questions of his classmates honestly, David concocted a story about that walk to Celeste's house. "Oh, yes," he tantalizingly described, "She kissed me, all right, and she knew a few little tricks that I'd never even heard of." The fantasies of Celeste Murphy swirled through the young male population of Stella's Cove, and, despite the warnings from concerned parents, they all became obsessed with the naughty little girl at the end of the spit. The parents' preoccupation with un-Godly influences merely increased their sons' times in the outhouse, and doubled the use of toilet paper.

Celeste had been afraid when David grabbed her, for she'd never dreamed that such a thing could happen in such a small community, nor was the thought ever there, that there were risks in being pretty. After reviewing the incident on the walk home, she'd decided that she would not mention it to her parents, for she was well aware of the friction between them and the townsfolk, and she feared that her story would surely deepen the bad will between the other residents of Stella's Cove and the Murphy family. Predictably, Celeste's years of solitude after school were interrupted by other boys asking to walk her home, but there was, luckily, never a repeat of the David Jardine incident.

The same mothers who had warned their sons that Celeste would lead them into sin also noticed her sudden rise in popularity, realizing that they themselves were largely responsible. Contrary to any wild expectations the boys may have held, Celeste possessed a natural balance in life that, at least for the time being, foreclosed the possibility of even a kiss.

––––––––––––

George Murphy's reputation as a godless man started shortly after he moved his family to Stella's Cove. He vocally opposed attempts of the church to convert the local indigenous population, publicly decried campaigns of the town's leaders to make Stella's Cove a dry town, and voiced the speculative audacity that the glacier, indeed, might be tens--even hundreds of thousands of years old.

Despite his differences with the town folk, George certainly cared about his neighbors, and consistently demonstrated his unflagging dedication to improving the lives of those who shared Stella's Cove. He believed that the smugness and fanaticism were largely rooted in the pervasive insecurities of the townsfolk, and that the attitudes would surely improve as the people felt a new joy in their success and a new faith in the promise of a future. The previous year, George funded and built the Town's only public park, and he had recently unveiled plans to build a library. And, in an effort to restore the former beauty of Muir Creek, he assigned me the job of cleaning up the mess that had been left by the departing miners.

He picked me up at home, one Saturday, announcing, "I have another job for you, Billy—something that will be a departure from the routine chores at my house, and that's likely to take the better part of six months." My curiosity at this point was driving me mad; I didn't have a clue what he was talking about. "Do you think you can learn to drive the Reo?" he asked.

I'm sure George detected the delight in my face as I contemplated the joy of it, but he stopped me abruptly from my grand anticipation. "Billy," he warned, "it won't be all fun and games. You'll need the Reo to drag some of the heavier equipment away from the creek, but joyriding is something I expressly prohibit." George's words were a bit of a let-down, but I was still loving the idea that I could learn to operate the Reo. After three afternoons of driving it, I felt total confidence I could do the job. George purchased a twenty-foot length of chain from Young's Mercantile, showed me how to secure it to the discarded pieces of equipment, and how to use the lowest gear, along with some skillful clutch operation, to accomplish the job. He was right; I started cleaning the canyon in late May, and I moved the last remnant of a sluice just before the first snow fell. For much of that time, George allowed me to keep the Reo at our house, for convenience, and there were times I was tempted to take it out for a pleasure ride. I never did.

―――――――

The townsfolk despised George Murphy despite his philanthropic activities, and, were he not the provider of the church's new slate roof, pipe organ, and lightning rod, Rev. Cromwell would have let him know, in no uncertain terms, that he was not even welcome to worship there. "I don't even like them coming to church on Christmas and Easter," Cromwell lamented to one of the most staunch brethren. "Every time I see them in the house of the Lord, it feels like an act of sacrilege being shoved in my face."

The reality was that George did not worship at all--certainly not in the conventional sense of the word. He, Eva, and Celeste attended church only on religious holidays, but George made it clear that they were there for the music and social interaction--not because they were believers.

The Murphys came to Stella's Cove in 1895, bringing a small financial stake and a new, creative vision for the town. For more than twenty years after the gold rush ended, the town had been beset by a lingering poverty, but, in the next five years, George would become one of the richest men in the province and bring prosperity to the entire community.

At first the Murphys found the community to be rather strange. It was not at all like the liberal community of Vancouver, with its broad acceptance of a diverse and cosmopolitan composition. But the Murphys also realized that there are many places around the globe where there are distinctly different beliefs, and so it was not surprising that the people of Stella's Cove were so homogeneous, considering the total isolation and encapsulation of the town. When the Murphy's yacht Bountiful first pulled into their harbor, the community had seen the family as a well-to-do addition to their congregation--and to the weekly donation plate--and, as it turned out, the Murphys' wealth benefited both the church and the town. The Bountiful was aptly named, for it brought prosperity to Stella's Cove.

Methodists who initially rushed to fellowship the Murphys

almost immediately withdrew their efforts upon finding that the family did not even believe in God. When that became common knowledge, the Murphys were both ignored and ostracized. Rev. Cromwell even mentioned them in one of his sermons. "There are those in our community whom we must avoid—those who openly confess to belief in a godless universe. I realize that some of you may be asking if this is Christ's way, but the risk of allowing their pernicious philosophies into our own lives gives us good reason not to befriend them. Some of you may ask if it is our right to judge, and I say "Yes." God has already judged them. He did so when they rejected His holy word, and we are not required, as Christians, to spend time in the company of the unholy. Amen."

Hope Springs Eternal

"Billy. Billy." I hear Celeste calling to me, gently trying to get my attention. "Would you like some cheese in your soup?" "Yes" I answer, adding "It sounds yummy."

My attention drifts away again, as I review, for a moment, the colloquial use of the word "old" in my description of the Point Fay Bed and Breakfast to the two academics, and I can't help but thinking how words, in context, sometimes contradict their own meanings. When I told our fellow travelers, Mortimer and Ernest, about lodging at the "old" Murphy home, I simply meant that the Murphys no longer lived there. The word "old" was just a figure of speech that was often applied to anything familiar or to that which faithfully fulfilled its purpose. Compared with the rest of the community, much of which dated back to the early settlers of more than fifty years before, and which boasted only a few really nice residences, the Murphy home would have qualified as "new." Stella's Cove was dotted with mostly primitive and humble dwellings at best, so describing the Murphy home as "old" was a misnomer. It wasn't old at all--built only twenty-one years before--and it was constructed of the finest materials and workmanship that money could buy.

The loss of the Murphy Salmon Company as the community's only large employer has greatly impacted the values of the residential properties in Stella's Cove. In fact, the local real estate market is entirely hopeless, and, despite the home's quality of construction and its fairy tale setting, there have been no buyers to be found for the Murphy home. When the Bountiful sailed away and the Murphys relocated to their other home in Vancouver, it was the end of prosperity for Stella's Cove. With Murphy's permission, three locals--with Bart Clemmerton, Sr. at the helm--were allowed to turn the home into the town's only transient lodging.

The three men who run the Point Fay Bed and Breakfast are among a handful of people in Stella's Cove who were friendly or had, at least, done some kindness for the Murphy family or their friends. There were not many who treated the Murphys well, despite the fact that George had taken a dead town, deserted by the trappers and miners who gave it its start, and revived it so completely that a new period of great prosperity ensued. Without the probability of him ever selling the home, and feeling, after what had gone on, a lingering apprehension at returning, George wrote up a simple contract. This stipulated that proper maintenance and upkeep were the trio's responsibility, and that, after normal expenses, any revenues would be shared, with George taking only twenty-five percent of the net profit. It was like almost everything George ever did, for his "deals" predictably favored the other person, and he could honestly say that he'd never taken advantage of another human being.

My benefactor and soon-to-be father-in-law, George Murphy, footed the bill for my university education and gave me a glowing letter of recommendation in my search for a job. Along with letters from my professors and the Dean, it is George's stunning letter, as a man of unquestionable status and fame, who made me the successful applicant in Eagle City. He has always remembered those people who, though surrounded by bigots, showed some human decency. Conversely, he has also maintained a very harsh view of those who preach the Bible yet are dominated by anything-but-Christian ideals.

While Murphy has always been a man of careful opinions, and was loathe to make judgments of any other human being, Stella's Cove left indelible assessments of a community's bad behavior on his mind--so deep, in fact, that he could never erase them. His disgust for the townsfolk's attitudes and actions, particularly in the ghastly display of the bodies, left him so angry that he simply closed off his heart, and when he withdrew his heart and money from the town, he would never be able to bring them back.

Transformation

The townsfolk had only laughed when George Murphy mentioned building a salmon processing plant at Stella's Cove. The old boardwalk wandering from the harbor through the town was suddenly full of rude exclamations, like "What's he smoking in his pipe?" "He's as much a dreamer as a sinner, and God'll answer his stupidity." "The man's a lunatic," and "he's probably the offspring of incest." Even the few who loved him saw evidence which might have supported the idea that Murphy was merely an optimistic nut case, for history and the facts did not seem to support his enthusiasm.

After the failure of the fur and gold economies, the isolation of Stella's Cove was viewed by all its residents except Murphy as a fatal impediment to the creation of profitable businesses, and though the Aniak more-or-less faithfully served as a link to the rest of the world, Stella's Cove could not accommodate the larger vessels that would be necessary for the success of any sizeable operation. Even the Aniak, with its shallow draft and relatively flat bottom, was grounded several times at low tide, so the idea of landing any large ships was simply out of the question. The shallow inlet that served for years as the town's harbor was inadequate, and George himself, though not acknowledging it to any of his detractors, was troubled.

Reviewing all the options in a sort of internal question and answer session, George asked himself if the harbor could be adequately deepened by dredging; whether or not the dock could be extended far enough into the sea for the larger ships to approach; whether the composition of the channel bottom would allow the success of a dredging operation; and if the harbor could be widened enough for the big ships to have adequate maneuvering room. Though pricey, he knew that extending the dock and expanding the size of the harbor were likely feasible, but he also understood that the harbor's limitations might be the project's death knell. Knowing that the composition of the channel bottom was going to be the biggest limiting factor, he employed divers from Vancouver to inspect the inlet. After spending two days doing core samples, there was no encouragement. "There's no way." the divers disappointedly asserted "There's a layer of mud about a foot deep, but under it there's nothing but bloody rock, extending far into the sea." When George heard the divers' reports, he was temporarily engulfed in depression, but he was not a man to give up.

For a while he even reconsidered the possibility that a practical overland route might still be possible, but after reviewing the tragedy of the Gilford Road the idea was quickly dismissed. While there were land routes that were occasionally used, they were dangerous and were abandoned after being strewn with the frightful reminders of suffering and death. Those trails were impassible in the winter and spring, and even in the best of weather dozens of travelers met their fates at the hostility of the weather and the land. One was the Dillworth party, who lost their lives in the fickle conditions of Garden Pass. Despite its name, one derived from the heavy forest and colorful wild flowers that crowned her slopes in summer, the Pass was no garden. Mom and Pop Dillworth were beckoned to Stella's Cove by the discovery of gold in 1865, but died in a blizzard only twenty-two miles from our town. Only two of their six children survived the final trek to the Cove, and relatives did not claim the two orphaned children until the following summer.

George was familiar with all those tragic stories and knew that no one could trust the stability of the mountain or the weather. A summer storm could dump five feet of snow near the summit, and, until recently, carcasses of the Sweiger party's mules littered the Trapper's Trail, which was considered by most packers to be the shortest but most dangerous route. Overland routes were simply not a practical alternative, and George quickly realized that, even if it were possible, overland transportation would make the processed fish far too expensive, and that it was only the much larger world markets that could make his salmon processing plant a financial success. There was no question about it, and he concluded that the sea was his only hope.

With such isolation and the now proven limitations of Stella's Cove's shallow, rocky harbor, people believed that Murphy's madness would be abandoned, and talk about town centered around the townsfolks' satisfaction that George would be proven wrong. During one of his frequent visits to Clemmerton's Bakery, the Rev. Miles Cromwell noted to Bart Sr., "Well, I guess Murphy's seen the writing on the wall. He's found out that the harbor's solid rock, so his pipedream of a salmon factory won't be happening. What incredible gall he had! If God hasn't blessed the faithful of this town, why in hell would he ever grant success to an atheist?" Cromwell's words were a pattern for the conversations in Stella's Cove. Though the entire town secretly wished there could be some hope for economic resurrection, the people wallowed in the decisive failures of the fur and gold booms, and seemed to get some kind of sick satisfaction from rehearsing the woes of their economic hopelessness.

On a spring morning in 1899, George asked Eva to pack him a lunch, explaining, "I'm going to head north out of town and see what's up there. It's a sure thing--there's no place in Stella's Cove big enough for the plant and its harbor will never be sufficient. Maybe this whole thing isn't going to work out." Eva was surprised by his candor, for he'd never before expressed any doubt about the completion of his dream. At 9:00 a.m. George set out on his cart for town, first giving Oscar a carrot from the Murphy garden, and scratching the pony's head. "Giddy up," he clicked, and the pony leaned against its collar.

He turned north at the town, following the little lane, which soon fizzled into a narrow, rugged path. The pony struggled against the rocks and branches that lay on the vanishing trail. George got off the cart at one point and moved a few of the larger branches, but the easy part was over when the pony stopped at a small, glacial scree field which poured down from a rocky slope above. "I guess this is as far as you can go," he commiserated with Oscar. George removed the lead rope from the cart, clipped it to the halter, and tied the other end to a small tree. Noticing that the browse was scarce in this particular spot, he gathered up a few handfuls of grass from a clearing they'd just passed, placed it in the feedbag, and ran the strap behind Oscar's ears.

The scree field was almost impassable, but George successfully negotiated the first half of it, where the rocks averaged a couple feet in diameter, with angular chiseled faces on several sides. But the far side of the scree field was unstable, and, when George jumped from one rock to the next, one teetered for a moment and then tipped, sending him crashing into the rocks below. Dazed for a moment, he did not immediately get up, but lay there in an awkward position, with his feet high above him and his head stuck between two large boulders. As he looked up at a blue sky, the sun lay warm against his face, and, for a moment, he actually savored being on his back.

George struggled to get up, not because he had suffered any serious injury, but because of the awkwardness of his position. Except for a small cut on his left arm, he sensed no other damage, but, lying there between the rocks, he found it difficult to find an advantageous position for his hands. He fumbled and slipped several times, but was finally able to rise back to his feet. His clothes showed abrasions from the fall, and he took a moment to brush his jacket and pants with his hands.

He assumed that he was at the end of the trail, but, surprisingly, it continued north from the far edge of the scree, and he resumed his exploration, negotiating more slides and finding himself at a stand of small willows, so thick that it was necessary to place his hands in front of him, forming a "V," in order to move through the brush-like trees. Just north of the willows, a knife-edged granite ridge jutted out into the sea, providing a jetty-like barrier that stood in the way of the prevailing northwesterly winds. There was a sizable stream amid the willows, and George followed it eastward, breaking out of the trees after about two hundred yards.

Where he emerged, the sunlight, mixed with frothing water, leaped from the rocks above. George estimated the waterfall to be over sixty feet in height, and its flow was impressive. Climbing up a rocky outcropping, he was able to get above the narrow gap at the top of the falls. Above the falls was a flat area, several hundred yards across, and, just beyond, a large moraine that held back a sizable lake. It was from that lake that the considerable stream plunged toward the sea.

George stood there, virtually dumbfounded, with a silly grin on his face; he was tickled pink. Until that moment, he had no idea the lake existed. "Surely," he thought, "if others knew of it, someone would have mentioned it to me. Wouldn't they have? With all the early trapping and mining, how could it have been overlooked?" The fact was, just a few people in town were aware of its existence, and those, who were, regarded it only as a place of great natural beauty, not as a potential resource in bringing jobs and money to Stella's Cove. For George, it was the discovery of the missing link to the chain. He was elated, and he knew that his dreams were within his reach. He lifted his journal out of his coat pocket and entered a notation: "I found a large lake above the waterfall, and since it's not shown on maps of the area, I have appropriately named it Lake Celeste." Tiny Celeste was only an infant at the time, but already honored with the lake that bore her name.

As George emerged from the western side of the willow grove, he noticed that, unlike the muddy shallows that cursed the Stella's Cove harbor, a secondary, smaller waterfall fell steeply into the sea, where a fjord-like channel of deep water extended from the canyon above it. When he first saw it, he noted in his journal, "The drop of the stream into the bay is abrupt, and I can see nothing in the clear water that looks like a hazard. It is naturally protected and calm as the town's harbor, but it looks like it could accommodate ships of much deeper draft." He returned home, excited and anxious to return to the spot. Eva met him at the door, taking his hat and helping him off with his coat. "My," she exclaimed, "what happened to you?" George had no idea what she meant, for he'd not noticed his coat tore when he fell. "Oh," he acknowledged, I took a little fall—nothing serious." He kissed Eva and sat down to supper.

On his second visit to what he was envisioning now as the plant's future site, George looked for a spot where he knew he could easily enter the water, and, more importantly, climb back out. There was a large fault in the granite, extending from the sea almost to the willows at the canyon's mouth, and George, without hesitation, shed his clothes down to his skivvies, and launched himself from a little outcropping that sat about fifteen feet above the water.

There was a shock of both impact and cold as his bare feet cut through the surface. He did not try to check his descent and figured he'd go as deep as he could. His feet were locked tightly together, and his hands pressed tightly to his sides. Within moments he sank as deep as his velocity and buoyancy would allow, then floated back to the surface of the cold, green pool, gasping from the cold. He realized his feet had not touched the bottom, and, though he had looked carefully before jumping, he was both surprised and disturbed by his own relative absence of caution. Even though he'd seen no rocks or driftwood lurking beneath the surface, he also understood that he could have emerged from the sea, bleeding and broken, and that the jump could have cost him his life.

Yet that jump provided grand enlightenment, for George estimated that his feet submerged fifteen feet or more below the surface, despite the fact that the tide was at its low ebb. If that was true, there would be no question that larger ships from the U.S., Japan, and Australia could actually make it almost to the shore, and he thought about how a cantilevered dock, anchored to the natural jetty-like rock face, could accommodate even the largest freighters.

A few days later, George hired an unemployed fisherman, with a small boat and crew, and they used an anchor hanging from twenty-five feet of chain to systematically drag the bay. For days they crisscrossed the bay and channel, searching for shallow areas, but the anchor never dragged bottom. When the Aniak docked at Stella's Cove one month later, George felt pretty sure about his find. He paid the ship's captain fifty dollars to remain an extra day, and a small boat was dispatched to do additional soundings at what George was now referring to as Murphy's Bay.

By the following evening, the crew of the small boat determined that there were no obstacles between where the creek cascaded into the briny depths and the main channel to the west. The depth of the natural harbor exceeded twenty-five feet, everywhere. Murphy's Bay, though overlooked by the original settlers of Stella's Cove and unnoticed by the mining population that followed was far superior to the town's harbor which barely accommodated the Aniak, and which could never be expected to handle anything larger.

George carefully descended the outcropping, making his way back through the willows and returning to a contented Oscar and his transportation home.

As he left Murphy's Bay that afternoon on his pony cart, George was whistling a song his mother sang to him as a child, and, as he passed the center of Stella's Cove, little Oscar joined in with a friendly whinny to Bart Clemmerton's mare. She was a tall, lean, bay thoroughbred-hackney mix with four white socks and a star between her eyes, and, whatever she lacked in breeding was well compensated by a truly classy look. Though not considered a particularly good mixture of breeds, she was a fine horse, with a smooth gait and elegant leg action, and it was apparent that she had had several years of professional training before coming to the Cove.

In Stella's Cove, there were only two horses--Oscar, who was too short to qualify as a real horse, and Sally, the Clemmerton's bay mare. There were a few others in the town's earliest days, but they were eaten during the long winter and endless blizzards of 1861, when the trappers failed in sustaining their trade and found both money and food in a disastrous short supply. A few other horses and mules, brought in during the gold rush, met similar fates, when the placer claims became unproductive and the miners failed to find transportation to places of greater opportunity.

Stella's Cove extended less than a half mile from the north to the south; there was only a one-mile band of woodland between the base of the foothills and the edge of the sea; and, because the rocky and unstable land to the east was too dangerous to ride, horses were of little use and were considered a great luxury in such a place. Besides the matter of questionable utility, horses were extremely pricey in this part of the world, for they could only be shipped in by sea and were expensive to keep in an area providing so little natural feed.

Only two years earlier, Bart Clemmerton, Sr. had noticed a growing restlessness in his oldest daughter, Dorothy, and he feared that she would leave--though this was the simple inevitability for any young person of promise. After losing his wife, he'd felt a growing fear that his whole family would soon be gone. Dorothy was helpful with chores, and was the only one of the Clemmertons who could cook a decent meal. That was not Bart Sr.'s main concern. It was his sense of loss and the likely prospect of his eventual abandonment that cast an ominous gloom over his life. Dorothy was both smart and pretty, and in an effort to encourage her to stay, Bart purchased Sally in Bourne River and had her shipped in on the Aniak.

For a while, Dorothy lived and dreamed horses. She rode Sally up and down every one of the little lanes in the cove. When the tide was low, she galloped on her energetic mare over the salty flats that were exposed along the shore. At first, Clemmerton believed the horse to be a great idea. Dorothy was unable to think of anything else and once even played hooky from school in order to spend more time with Sally.

Clemmerton actually became concerned that Dorothy was spending too much time with the animal, regularly cantering up the trail to the glacier, and working her around some barrels placed in the Clemmerton yard-- sometimes for hours each day. He actually decided that he would have to place a restriction on Dorothy's riding, but her interest fizzled abruptly and it became obvious that she was experiencing a growing sense of frustration. In Stella's Cove there was a shortage of the kind of gentle land that is suitable for horses, and the confines of the mountains and the sea greatly limited the places where Dorothy could ride. In fact, though her father specifically bought the horse to keep Dorothy at home for a while longer, it was largely Dorothy's rides that contributed to her growing realization of just how small a community Stella's Cove really was.

After hundreds of rides up the short canyon to the headwaters of Muir Creek, where the glacier created a steady flow of milky water and a gentle waterfall fell from a crack on the north side of the glacial channel, Dorothy became bored by the limits of her travel. Wishing for a life where there was more to explore, it was boredom that caused her to dismount from her horse permanently.

Dorothy saw, in that horse, the gloomy metaphor for what her life might become. She felt much like the mare, locked up in a small paddock, where the views were always the same. There was a pervasive feeling of loneliness that rolled over her like the foggy coastal layer that was so predictable, and her darkening mood was accentuated by the absence of other creatures with which she could find a connection. After graduation from public school, Dorothy explored her options--particularly the choices of eligible men within the community. While her exploration provided one prospective mate, it did not turn out well. In the end, she faced the sea, took a deep breath, and walked up the Aniak's gangplank, never to return. There was no one who wished to take on the horse, so Sally spent the next two years pacing the paddock that had become her permanent prison.

Oscar's whinny was inspired by the presence of another horse, and it came from a sense of kinship. Dorothy was able to "whinny" for a while, when she experienced a short romance with Egbert Ralph, whose wife had died two winters before. Faced with the clear contrast of their ages, and understanding that she did not wish to raise someone else's children, she knew it would be a bad decision. Besides her own concerns about Egbert as a marriage match, the community was immediately abuzz over what appeared to be a torrid affair, and Dorothy's reputation suffered accordingly. Barely eighteen, she was ostracized from her own community.

At the center of the commotion was the Methodist Church. Rev. Cromwell, without any specific references to the couple, gave a Sunday sermon decrying sexual immorality and preaching a searing tirade on how the unmarried were still required to remain pure and how such behavior would be punished on judgment day. While not actually mentioning their names, the transparency of his sermon left no question of whom he spoke. Some in the congregation remarked to each other, after the service, "Why, that dirty old man." and one of the devout ladies of the congregation declared, in a voice that everyone heard, "We don't need girls like her in Stella's Cove. She's a hussy, and you could always tell."

Cromwell's declaration created a public furor, making the relationship known to the entire town, and Egbert pulled up his stakes and moved his little family to Princeville. There was really no other choice, for the town was too small to contain such sentiments, and there was no chance that its residents could simply live and let live. Like the single choice Oscar and Sally had for a social life, there were simply no other eligible men in Stella's Cove to keep Dorothy there--or, at least, not one that found her fancy. With her father tenderly hugging her at the dock, still wishing that there could be some reason for her to stay, she left, one year after her graduation, abandoning her motherless family and leaving Sally to die of old age.

Sally continued to pace the confines of her paddock until that day when Oscar nickered his friendly greeting. Understanding that the horse was no longer being ridden, George Murphy compassionately asked Bart if the horse was for sale. "I think," he said, "Sally's lonely and Oscar could use some company too. Would you sell her?"

"I'll give you an answer tomorrow," Bart replied, "because I'm not really sure about it." Bart Sr. labored that night over the prospect of selling the animal that every day reminded him of his sweet daughter and the joy she experienced when she first saw the gift. By morning, there was no longer a question, because Bart knew that Sally, like people, needed company, and that it would be a terrible disservice to keep the mare alone for the rest of her life. When George came for an answer, Bart could only look down at the ground.

"Take her," he sadly whispered. ""It's for the best."

George tied Sally's lead rope to his cart and headed back to Point Fay. As they trotted along, he was thinking about much more than his pony and its new equine friend. For no matter what skepticism plagued the town, and despite his own fears over the many impediments that lay in his way, the Murphy Salmon Company was going to be a reality, and the town of Stella's Cove, despite its previous, multiple setbacks, would have a prosperous future. The bequest of another dying glacier, Murphy's Bay was endowed a fjord-like channel that provided sanctuary from the open sea. Protected on one side by the natural jetty extending from the long ridge above it, and on the other by the coastline itself, the harbor was deep and secure. No one seemed to have ever thought about it before, yet it was the ideal, pristine and embryonic harbor that could save the town from extinction.

There were plenty of skeptics, and, though people, at first, winked and rolled their eyes at George's grand scheme, they were now understanding that he was not a man to be mocked, and that his hopes were actually being strengthened by the absence of outside support.

George Murphy returned home from his impromptu swim in Murphy's Bay overwhelmed by the excitement of the moment. Greeting Eva with an enthusiastic hug, he excitedly announced "There isn't a question now. The salmon processing plant is definitely going to happen. With the deep water channel, the largest trawlers and freighters can land, and with the huge glacial lake, there'll be enough water to ensure the continuous generation of power to supply both the needs of the plant and the town."

"That's wonderful," said Eva, trying to show her enthusiasm, though not totally understanding it all. She was keenly aware that romance, which was such an important part of their life, all but died after Celeste's birth, and was now being totally displaced by George's passion for his new project. Though she was excited about his discovery, she wished that he would simply notice her, for a change. During dinner, George could talk of nothing else. Every other word was "hydroelectric" or "potential energy," "pilings," "depths," or some other word related to the new dreams of the man she'd married, and she asked herself, with just a hint of anger, "What happened to his other dream?"

When dinner was over, George wound down a bit, and Eva swallowed her pride, understanding that if something was going to happen, it would require a woman's resolve. After tucking Celeste under the covers, she poured George a drink of one of his finest single malts. He sipped it for a moment, then emptied the glass in one swallow. She poured him another and disappeared into the bedroom, first freshening up and then reapplying the lipstick that had slowly paled during the evening meal. The dress she'd been wearing slipped to the bedroom floor and was replaced by a sheer nightgown. Eva picked up a crystal decanter from the nightstand, filling a glass with sherry, and drinking it in one continuous flow. As she headed back to the living room, she stopped, picking up a tiny, oriental porcelain atomizer, spraying just a hint on her other hand and touching it to her neck.

Eva's use of alcohol was not typical, but neither was George's neglect of their romance, and both understood that, no matter what the Temperance Society was saying, there were times when only medication could relax them, and this was one of those times. Eva walked up behind George, who was sipping his Scotch, placed her hands gently between his shoulders and chest, and leaned over to press her cheek to his. "I love you, George." she purred

Celeste never stirred until the dawn lit the east windows of the mansion, and her gentle cry disturbed the peaceful scene on the master bed, bathed in the afterglow of the night before. Understanding that the gravity of parenthood beckoned, Eva rolled on top of George, and she kissed him once more. "I love you…and that was wonderful," she swooned. "Let's do it again tonight." George would always remember that night, for it called his attention to a potential weakness in their marriage. His salmon processing plans were a consuming interest, and he recognized how his plans were distracting him from even more important dreams. He would never again fail to respond to the romantic and affectionate needs of his angel.

Even after the discovery of the deep-water access to Murphy's Bay, there were still many potential problems to be addressed.

The local fishing catch was small—certainly not sufficient to supply the needs of a large processing plant--so one of the first questions about Murphy's plans for the processing plant was simply. "Where'll he get the fish?" The local hauls of fish were, more or less, merely subsistence catches, and Stella's Cove ate most of what was caught. It would take a lot of fish to keep a plant of any size operating, so there was no one else in town, other than Murphy, who could visualize a successful processing plant.

The second question was, "Where will he ship it to?" Locals rolled their eyes as they voiced the question, often suggesting that George was both delusional and crazy. Yet George believed he had an answer for that question as well, for he envisioned a world-class facility and customers across the globe.

Everyone thought that the financial feasibility of Murphy's project would be doomed by the existence of the large processing plant only thirty-eight miles to the south. The Bourne River Salmon Industries plant had been operating there for years, and that plant struggled just to keep its doors open, yet Murphy was talking about yet another. People shook their heads in disbelief, and they pooh-poohed the possibility that Murphy's idea might have merit. There was no question that the bigger cities possessed an enormous advantage when it came to processing fish, and the isolation of Stella's Cove made it an unlikely center of trade.

There was a fourth question, but that one was already answered. With the diminishing band of forest between the coastal mountains and the town, it was becoming quite obvious to the townsfolk that the absence of cheap fuel would doom the project. Whether canning, smoking, or salt curing, all salmon processing required a plentiful supply of fuel. The residents of Stella's Cove admitted to each other, in their moments of total clarity, a fear of how they would get along during the future winters without logs. Everyone in town understood that the narrow belt of forest, separating the coastal mountains from the harbor, was depleted to the point where a different fuel would have to be found.

Every year the fires that heated the houses in Stella's Cove became smaller, and every year people relied on more bedding to keep them warm during the evening hours. People went out to cut firewood, and ended up with a pile of the willow sprigs that grew along the stream bed. The crisis was one of futile awareness, and no one seemed to know the answer to the predicament they were in. There was, of course, the abundance of coal, which could have replaced the diminishing supply of split wood, but coal would require shipment from distant ports. It wasn't free, particularly after the cost of shipping, and, after the economic failures of the trapping and mining booms, there was no money in the town. So, the residents of Stella's Cove settled for what they already possessed: more blankets.

The word "hydroelectric" put that concern to bed, for Murphy believed he could provide endless power to the processing plant, while granting the townsfolk the dream of household electricity.

There was another problem that seemed equally perplexing to the townsfolk. Even if Murphy could get his plant started, it would take lots of workers to keep it running, and Stella's Cove suffered the specter of a shrinking population. The size of the work force had been pared down dramatically by the loss of jobs. While there was no shortage of retirees who were either too old or too senile to work, there was a shrinking supply of children in the Cove, and each year the attendance was dropping at its school. The aging population was simply not reproducing, and the most capable and motivated children were leaving after graduation from public school.

Where could such a town find workers for a processing plant? Only Murphy claimed to have the answer, and Bart Clemmerton, Sr. asked the question point-blank. "You know our population is dying," he'd remarked to Murphy, "so how can Stella's Cove ever have enough people to run a large plant?" There was no delay in Murphy's response. "You're forgetting," he reminded Bart, "that new opportunities will inspire others to take up residence in the Cove, and the population will grow according the number of jobs available." It was the first time that the old baker had seen the light, and he understood that maybe Murphy's far-fetched ideas weren't so stupid after all. He considered how, along with the salmon processing plant's success, his own business would also grow, and there might well be a new era of good fortune for the entire community.

As Murphy's plan gained momentum, and most of the pressing questions were answered, he took an inventory of the dozens of vacant houses--ones left by the miners when the gold ran out--and he saw them as a vacuum. "When I get the plant running," he noted to Eva, "those houses will fill up overnight." In anticipation, Murphy bought the houses for a song and knew that he could sell them when the plant was up and running. Those who had already left the Cove and thought George's idea to be a remarkable fantasy gladly sold their abandoned homes to George for pennies on the dollar, with the belief that the town was dead and that no recovery was possible. They were the ones who saw no future, and they'd left as quickly as they could arrange passage on the Aniak. There was no reason for any rational man to believe that the houses would have any value at all, for, despite George Murphy's prophetic dream, the rest of the population embraced no illusions of hope.

While George Murphy was unhappy to see people leaving, he understood that what he needed most was a core of people who believed in Stella's Cove's future. He worried about the labor force, but he also believed that those who left would be replaced by others who possessed faith in his plan.

As Murphy studied the feasibility of the salmon processing plant, the same questions kept popping up. The catches of the local fishing fleet were just enough for consumption by the local population, so where would the fish come from? People asked that question, and it was certainly a legitimate concern. Murphy, like so many dreamers, found the answers in his hopes. Big answers. He knew that hundreds of fishing boats, up and down the coast, went after salmon, cod, and halibut, and that the large ones would go wherever there was sufficient capacity to buy and process their catch. The fish available for processing would not be dependent on the local Stella's Cove fleet, but on all the hundreds of larger trawlers that plied the B.C. and Alaskan seas.

With his dreams crystallized by the negativity of the community, George began to draw up the plans for B.C.'s largest salmon processing plant. He did rough drawings of how the plant would look, listing on the pictures what materials he would need for its construction. Sketches of the hydroelectric facility followed, and he consulted with a Seattle engineering firm that had approached him on the project, creating the basic plans for the generating equipment.

Though George was not educated in engineering, he had read some books on load-bearing structures. His basic knowledge of materials and stress enabled him to create a concept for a cantilevered deep-water dock which would be mounted directly to the bedrock wall that extended into the sea. Using balsa wood, he built a model of the structure in the Murphy mansion's guest bedroom, and called Eva in to take a look. She knew that George was working on something late each night, but she was not prepared for the balsa dock mounted on the bedroom's wall. "What do you think, dear?" he asked her, and all she could say was "It certainly looks like it will work." Up until that moment, Eva carefully hid her own doubts about the project, but here it was, the visible, wooden manifestation of her husband's dreams, the first vision of how things were actually going to happen. Smiling, she threw her arms around George's neck and kissed him. "How could I have expected anything less," she whispered. "You're my man."

Everyone mocked and laughed again when George asked them to invest their money, with his, to build the cantilevered deep-water dock that could accept the largest fishing vessels and freighters. It was only out of kindness that George invited them to invest. He knew, by then, that he would have no problem raising the money himself, but he hoped that at least some of the community would share in the direct profits of a successful venture, and he also appreciated the fact that workers who possessed an ownership interest would perform at a higher level of efficiency.

Everyone scoffed at George's plans for the plant; They lampooned his notion that hydroelectric power could be used to run it; and they rolled their eyes, one last time, when an impressionable and progressive banking group in Vancouver loaned George over one-hundred-fifty-thousand dollars to do it.

A newsman for the Provincial Times arrived on the Aniak for the express purpose of interviewing Murphy. The article was printed as a front page write-up on the capitalization of the effort. The headline read, "Stella's Cove Businessman Receives Funding: Will George Murphy Be the Town's Savior?" Most offended by the headline was none but Rev. Cromwell. When he saw it, his temper flared to such a level of violence that Bertha felt it prudent to run out of their front door to a neighbor's. She and the neighbor stood listening, just inside, as pots and pans, a bucket, and a two-pound clothes iron rattled the timbers of the

Cromwell home. "Savior! My God. Savior! That fucker will be no savior if I have my way."

Even Bart Clemmerton, Sr. remarked, "Those bankers are as stupid as George," but, inside, Clemmerton's feelings were not well-matched to his words. He actually thought, to himself as he said it, "George might just be able to pull it off. Then it will be all the rest of us that are proven stupid." For a moment Bart questioned why he and everyone else in the town always chimed in agreement on most matters, and why he could never seem to find the courage to have an opinion of his own. He could vividly recall times when he'd been acutely aware that his own feelings did not exactly match those of the majority, but then again, everyone in Stella's Cove shared an un-written commitment to agree, and he was not going to damage his bakery business by bucking the current prejudices of the group.

It seemed to happen overnight. George employed Fritz Freisen, a German structural engineer, to refine the rough plans for the new dock, which would allow large ships to get within yards of the plant. Unlike other docks, built where steam powered pile drivers could easily pound redwood hearts deep into the muddy seabed, the abysmal, fiord-like cleft in the bottom of Murphy's Bay was far too deep for such conventional methods. Freisen expanded on George's prototype guest bedroom model, employing an improved diagonal bracing system which would originate in the solid rock just above the sea. The dock would be four-hundred-thirty feet long, and would be constructed of wood and concrete, using steel reinforcement. In a few weeks, the materials were already ordered, and the execution of plans for the Murphy's Bay dock was launched by the power of Murphy's dreams.

Hundreds of skilled workers, used on the construction of Seattle's new dock only two years before, were hired to build the cantilevered, deep-water dock below the willow grove. To accommodate the transportation of workers and the loads of materials that were arriving every day, George built a three-mile rail line from Stella's Cove's dock to the new site, using an old engine that he'd found rusting in a Vancouver junkyard. He'd first seen it while rummaging the wrecking yards for suitable materials for his project, and the sight was a welcome relief. Understanding that finding a used locomotive would be unlikely, he originally resolved himself to a small, simple locomotive of his own design. Dreading the amount of work, the ordering of specialized parts, and the allocation time it would take to build such a locomotive, he was thrilled to find that this discard from the Seattle dockyards was perfect for his rail spur. It would easily accommodate the need for transportation between Stella's Cove and Murphy's Bay--not just for the workers, but for all the supplies that would be needed for completion of the project.

The old steam engine was considered obsolete. It was built in 1847 by the Hector Locomotive Company, destined to become a dinosaur in a world where technology was improving at an astounding pace. On the left side of its cab was a wooden plaque, torch-carved with the name "Tuggy," and the leather engineer's cushion was totally rotten from the wetness of the Seattle climate. When it arrived by barge in Stella's Cove, the residents smiled at the rusty old machine, but there was a sudden sense of pride after the engine was painted and the boiler fired up for the first time in years.

When George first saw it, the steam locomotive was sitting in the scrap yard behind some massive steel sheets, and he was unaware it was there until he walked past them. His mouth opened in surprise on finding such an unlikely treasure. The salvage company believed that the obsolete locomotive was only valuable for scrap, but George bought it for $1,000 and sent it north on a barge fitted with a set of narrow gauge rails. When it rolled off the barge at Stella's Cove, no one could believe it, and less than six months later, the locomotive would be pulling a set of two freight cars and an old caboose--utilized as a passenger car--the three miles from the town to Murphy's Bay.

The salvage yard had been stacked with the discards from hundreds of other projects, and George was elated to find three miles of narrow gauge rails sitting there in the same wrecking yard, covered with rust. Used rails, like the locomotive, were also in short supply, but it was a matter of luck that one of Seattle's trolleys had been recently re-routed to circumvent new development in the downtown area. Now George was looking for the ties and was tickled to find the yard also contained a generous supply of them. But, when he inspected those stacks of used ties, he decided that they were all too denatured and dry. George did not see his rail spur as a short-term project; he believed that the Murphy Salmon Company processing plant would be operational for many decades. He refused to use substandard materials, so it was necessary to order new ties from a lumber company in Bourne River.

They say that rolling stones gather no moss, and Murphy certainly "rolled.". In two days, he had found the locomotive, the rails, ordered new ties, and arranged to have the materials shipped to Stella's Cove by barge. And, in less than two weeks, there were twenty-five-foot stacks of materials sitting on the Stella's Cove dock. When the dock creaked and threatened to fail, George ordered the rails moved to the solid ground on the shore. Frankly, no one could imagine how much three miles of narrow gauge weighed, and it actually took the barge four trips to get the rails delivered, each delivery costing as much as one of the better homes in the town.

A small temporary office at the land's end of the dock seemed to build itself overnight, and it sported a simple sign over its door. "Help Wanted. Top Wages Paid." Until the project was finished, Norwood manned the desk each day from 9:00 to noon, signing up every qualified worker in town. After a long dearth of money, Stella's Cove became, for the third time, a boomtown, where money flowed and people smiled, ending the notion that the town's second death was to be permanent. Workers flocked to the dock, anxious for the high pay that George so generously offered. In the next two months, the three miles of trail going north to Murphy's Bay were leveled and ballasted in anticipation of the new ties which were already being shipped from the mill, and the multiple scree fields were blasted so thoroughly that the large granite rocks were now the size of medium gravel.

George arranged for Bourne River Lumber, LTD. to furnish the new railroad ties, and ordered them soaked in creosote before delivery to the Cove. While untreated ones would have lasted faithfully for many years, the creosote was a statement of George's commitment to, perhaps, a century of prosperity for the Murphy Salmon Company and the community. The town of Stella's Cove was abuzz, because the arrival of construction supplies was understood to be the evidence of a dream that was already in motion. People were no longer laughing at Murphy's visionary imagination, and there was an optimism that seemed to envelop the town, forcing even the greatest doubters to relinquish the depressing sense of futility that had persisted ever since the end of the gold rush. Those same people who believed Murphy to be a nut were there, carrying rails with enthusiasm, and loving the $1.00 per hour that was an unheard of wage in its day.

There had been an explosive release of steam as the relief valve opened at maximum pressure, and the refurbished locomotive chugged back and forth between the factory site and the town four times that first day, as a sort of introduction to the new era of prosperity that was about to be so generously granted to the townsfolk. A brass plaque quickly replaced the locomotive's old wooden sign, and it read, "Stella's Cove." There was only one person in town who didn't ride the rails that day with a sense of pride. Bertha, Edith, and Edgar Cromwell were among the happy riders, but the Reverend was nowhere to be found.

For two years, the "Stella's Cove" engine would perform reliably, but, after the plant's completion and the initiation of hydroelectric power, it would be replaced with a newer electric trolley, which would be used primarily for transporting the plant's workers to and from their jobs at the Murphy Salmon Company plant.

Just as the dock and rail line had been designed and built at a dizzying pace, the hydroelectric plant, too, became an overnight marvel. Murphy was well-read on the hydroelectric plants that now dotted North America, and he hired a Seattle firm to design the project. It was a simple dynamo, much like the ones that powered the City of Niagara Falls, New York, and which were now supplying almost twenty percent of Canada's power. When completed, the generator would provide the town virtually unlimited electricity as well as powering the ovens, dryers, and canning equipment for the Murphy Salmon Company. Years later, engineers would study the installation and declare the Murphy's Hydroelectric Plant to be the most efficient power generator along Canada's western coast.

The generator's main shaft was machined by the Marvel Ship Works, as were the six large carrier bearings, and Seattle Electric's journeymen spent weeks hand-winding the field coils and creating the large terminals. The Livingston Iron Works cast the eighteen-ton turbine housing, while mining specialists designed an anchoring system to attach the generator to the stone face above the willow grove falls. There were weeks of blasting, using over one thousand pounds of dynamite, to prepare the solid granite to receive the generator's unique base.

When everything was in place and the water-gate on the diversion weir was opened, there was a gentle whirring noise as the generator reached its governed speed. And it was three-year-old Celeste Murphy who threw the switch, heralding the beginning of a new, industrial era and dispelling the darkness that plagued the Cove, every evening when the sun sank below the horizon. Within weeks, a power line was strung from the hydroelectric plant to the town, and the people of Stella's Cove pulled their light chains and saw for the first time the miracle of electric power.

The plant was constructed in record time, and the whole town stood at Murphy's deep water dock as a large American trawler pulled slowly in and gently bumped the fenders. When that first load of salmon was delivered for processing, Murphy's detractors secretly hated the remarkable progress. Murphy's success, though providing plentiful jobs, became an embarrassment to those who previously forecast his failure. Nevertheless, even those who secretly resented Murphy's triumph were unable to sustain their rude criticism, and the entire town was caught in the ensuing wave of fortune.

The following year--no matter what their views had previously been--the residents of Stella's Cove could no longer laugh at the absurd dream of a major industry in their town, for, virtually overnight, George Murphy's salmon processing plant was now British Columbia's biggest fish processor. Trawlers from all over the Alaskan Gulf and the Pacific shore were bringing their huge catches to the Murphy Salmon Company; shipping created profitable links to all of North America; and contracts with Russia, Japan, and even Australia made Murphy rich beyond all dreams. His success was a boom for Stella's Cove's residents, in the form of good jobs, and a huge boost to the local fishing industry.

During the spring of the third year of the plant's operation, Murphy conducted a short ceremony on the Stella's Cove dock, marking the day on which the last dollar of the $150,000 loan was repaid. British Columbia's Lieutenant Governor was there for the memorable event and delivered a rousing address, centered on the remarkable success of Murphy's vision. "Who could have known that Stella's Cove would become a center of commerce and industry?" he remarked. "This town and the great Province of British Columbia owe a great debt of gratitude to George

Goodwin Murphy, who, despite a history of crippling setbacks for this community, closed his ears to the naysayers and resurrected this town. For his vision and implementation of a new life for Stella's Cove, I take pleasure in conveying Canada's greatest appreciation to George for his contribution to our great nation."

Regardless of George Murphy's remarkable success, much of the town sought satisfaction in the form of criticizing him. "He's a man whose only God is money," they'd sanctimoniously exclaim, noting that his attendance at church was, at best, semi-annual. Then they'd smile and add how thankful they were for the much more humble rewards of the meek, hardly considering how much George's triumph improved their own lives. It wasn't the first time in history that a dog bit the hand that fed it, and it was, in fact, not so atypical of the unkindness that often develops in the heart of the beneficiary toward its benefactor.

Despite the allegations that George only worshiped money, what he worshiped most was his wife, Eva, and the day they'd met at Roundley College. He'd lavished her with the best of everything, and his worship was returned. Heads shook and the sanctimonious whispered those unpleasant rumors about Eva's past, and the "flagrant" displays of hand-holding, cuddling, and an occasional kiss in broad daylight, were considered, by their jealous neighbors, to be evidence of her soiled life.

Maybe it was the hindsight of not having invested in the processing plant, when Murphy offered it that perpetuated the vicious malignancies of the gossip. Maybe it was the resentment that George was so successful while they would be resigned to only modest circumstances. Whatever drove it, the town folk proved themselves capable of creating any kind of story in order to maintain their own pious superiority, and any story about George or his family was considered fair game.

Mother, as a loyal subject to community interests, was certainly not innocent in the matter of spreading the vicious gossip that plagued our town, and it was obvious that she applied no critical standard in attempting to determine what was fact. After hearing some of the stories she so willingly spread, I asked Mother where she'd found the information. She was incensed, telling me that the only important thing was that the stories were true. I didn't believe any of it. My part time job and personal relationship with the Murphys revealed that they were fine people and I found it distressing that they were always at the center of some unkind gossip. When I'd worked for them on the weekends, Mrs. Murphy always brought me a lovely lunch, and I found, in George Murphy, a little bit of the father I so dearly missed. He told me that they were building a second home down in Vancouver, and that he'd be happy to have me do some odd jobs there while I pursued an education at the University--something I considered only after Miss Hardwicke became my teacher.

The contrived stories that portrayed Mrs. Murphy as a woman of low repute, were detestable, but it seemed that there was always an endless supply of lies. How could the parents of Stella's Cove have known that their vicious preoccupation with Eva Murphy would make her the inevitable fantasy for their sons' self-abuse...or that the repetitive patter about the rewards of the meek would lead to a younger generation that worshiped George Murphy's dapper manner and the sins of his lifestyle? Mothers all warned their boys that the "bratty" Celeste would turn out just like her Mother---something that her devoted father heartily hoped for.

Failure and Renewal

Despite the next dozen years of wild prosperity, no one in Stella's Cove could make the statement, "All is well," for trouble beset the town. As the furor over schoolteacher Kimberly Hardwicke grew, and the Council was unsuccessful in removing her, Bart Clemmerton, Sr. was faced with intense pressure over her presence in his home. Despite the pleas of Junior, who was very fond of Kimberly, and eleven-year-old Elizabeth, Kimberly returned from school one day to find an addition to Clemmerton's back porch. Her carpet valise sat there as an announcement that her welcome was retracted. She walked over to the bakery. "Junior's not here." his dad said coldly. "He's making some deliveries."

"I understand your position," Kimberly begged, "but can't you at least allow me to stay until the Aniak returns?" Clemmerton was unable to look her in the eyes, but mumbled, "I'm sorry that things have gotten so bad for you, but I too need to survive. As much as I've wanted to help you out, I simply can't buck Cromwell's power. Please forgive me." Next, Kimberly protested to Mayor Burroughs, but he brushed her off. "There's really nothing I can do about it," said Burroughs. "The Council has made up its mind."

The God-fearing citizens of the Cove implemented a plan: After reviewing the teacher's contract numerous times, the Council was sure that Miss Hardwicke's board and room, though agreed on, were not actually a part of the written document. Though the moral implications were all too obvious, no one on the Council complained that, while not actually spelled out in black and white, Miss Hardwicke was nevertheless entitled to her board and room. It was anticipated that, with no place to stay, she would be forced to leave, although the matter of her unpaid salary still loomed. Upon finding herself temporarily homeless, she was distraught. She'd talked with the parents of some of her favorite students, finding that none of them were willing to take her in. She asked Walter Young if he would be willing to allow her to use his back shed for a temporary residence, but he admitted, weakly, "The town's made up its mind," he explained, "and while I feel compassion for your situation, giving you a place to stay would only put off the inevitable. I don't want to encourage you in any false hopes, but I wish you well." She did not consider the Murphy home, although she would have been welcome there, because she was still hoping that her teaching would resume, and believed their home was too far from the school.

Whatever faith she generally possessed in people, Miss Hardwicke was now reflecting on the injustice of agreements not honored, and thinking about her students, whom she'd grown to love during her time in the Cove. She was concerned that the children of Stella's Cove would be relegated to an education of religiously drawn boundaries, rather than the open windows of scientific learning which were shedding light on a dark world.

Deprived of her room at the Clemmerton home at least temporarily, Kimberly left her valise and took a soul-searching hike, and, when evening came, the fading light found her sobbing near the glacier's tongue, where the sounds of her hopelessness joined in a trio with the glacier and the coyotes. Only a few hundred yards away, there was a warm fire and the arms of two who would have welcomed her, yet in her state of depression and despair she preferred to be alone.

Bart Clemmerton, Sr. lied to his son, concocting a story of how Kimberly suddenly left Stella's Cove earlier that day. "Son," he soberly declared, "Kimberly came over to the shop at about 2:00 in the afternoon and told me she was leaving. She said she felt bad that she wasn't able to tell you personally, but that circumstances demanded she go. Apparently there was a government launch down at the dock and its captain agreed to drop her in Bourne River." That announcement was no great surprise, for Junior was well aware of Kimberly's embattled status with the town fathers, and he had fully understood that she would probably not be the Stella's Cove schoolmistress for much longer. What he could not understand was how she could have left him without even a parting kiss, and he was worried what would happen to their child. Bart Sr. immediately loathed his own words, understanding that a revelation of the truth would surely come and that there could be no excuse for his fabrication.

Junior left the bakery heartbroken that evening, finding solace with the only other person he believed really cared, and the most maligned man in the community, the Rev. Harry Mills. Neither man knew that Bart Sr.'s story was false--that Kimberly was sent unwillingly from the Clemmerton home, and that she was still, somewhere, in Stella's Cove.

As the last glow of sunset merged with the blackness of the East and a few bright stars ruled the onset of evening, Junior sat inside Harry Mill's cabin, shaken by the events of the day. He'd told Harry about Kimberly's sudden departure, lamenting "She never even said goodbye."

When the sadness of the current crisis was exhausted, Junior asked Harry, point blank, what had happened in Eagle City. Harry, instead, poured out the story of his life, from his earliest memories to his being defrocked, and his chance relocation to Stella's Cove.

Harry was in his late fifties. Except for his thick monocle, scarred lip, and mostly muted speech impediment, he was a robust man. Junior was shocked to learn that the reverend had enjoyed an early career as a prize fighter. That career ended when a left hook partially detached his right retina. The thick monocle he now wore created an almost comical magnification of his bad eye.

Successful in his early fights, Harry became the champion of Grand County and won the regional championship as well. A Chicago promoter, who saw one of his fights, assured him of his shot at greatness. Approaching Harry directly after the fight, he'd introduced himself. "Hello," he smiled "that was some fight! I'm Bull McBride and my business is boxing." After the typical pleasantries of their conversation, Bull made a proposal. "Harry, you come and work with us and I'll get you the best trainer money can buy. You're a great fighter and I believe, with a little coaching, you can become the middleweight champion of the world."

Harry was sent to Chicago, all expenses paid, and trained for one year under the legendary John Mackay. During his first professional fight, Harry suffered a small cut on his right eyebrow, which bled profusely and obliterated his view.

Struggling to even see his opponent, he never saw the left hook coming. It changed the course of his life. After examinations by two specialists, it was determined that Harry's right eye retained only about one-fourth of its normal function. The doctors made it clear: He would no longer fight, so Harry asked himself, "What will I do now?" The answer came during his hospitalization, and his life took a necessary detour.

Though his fighting career labeled him a ruffian, Harry's heart was gentle and his faith was strong. The Rev. George Henning came to see Harry at the hospital, and was impressed by the young fighter's religious zeal and his astute observations on life. Through a sponsorship, Harry went from battling belligerent fighters in the ring, to being a light and inspiration to the sad and the weak. Five years in the Fortrain Seminary earned him a Doctor of Divinity degree, and he was hired as the assistant pastor at the First Methodist Church in Princeville, B.C. Occasionally, Harry would make the quip, "I'm not sure why they call this the "First Methodist Church" It's the only church in town." He would spend years in Princeville, a seaside community where steep coastal mountains plunged into the Pacific, and plentiful salmon often lay on his dinner plate.

Harry fell in love with Andrea Perelli, daughter of an ex-miner who befriended him while at the seminary in Vancouver. Her father, Mario, treated him like a son, and there were many weekends spent together, bending their fly poles and gracefully laying out lines on the river. They caught more than their share of feisty trout and landed salmon larger than their family retriever.

Mario became a sort of father to Harry, whose own father died of a heart attack when he was just a boy, and whose mother was taken by influenza when he was only twelve. With no other family, Harry was sent to an orphanage, and it was there that he received most of his early religious instruction. While the "orphaned" Harry would never be a "son" again, he would become the next best thing to the Perelli family. He became Mario's son-in-law.

Andrea and Harry married in 1888, and they moved to Princeville as newlyweds. For a while Andrea taught school, but the demands of being the minister's wife quickly became another full-time job and she resigned her teaching position at the end of her second season.

Life was good, but the richness of Harry's life was

transient at best, and there would be more than his share of tragedies in the years to come. He'd considered himself blessed to have lost the sight in his right eye, for it was that injury which led to his new life, and he understood that his calling now was to encourage others and comfort them in their times of pain, hardship, and fear.

When Rev. Ronson Lybbert, the minister, suddenly passed away, Harry became the shepherd over the Princeville flock. He would serve for over eleven years, and his sermons and kindnesses would become legendary. He became known as the local icon for applied Christianity, a person who always gave, and asked for nothing. The passing of the plate was always the least of his priorities. His passion was for the salvation and spiritual nourishment of those he served.

Just as Harry expected, Andrea was the ultimate wife, and the heavenly bonding, which followed, brought a warmth that Harry previously thought a mere figment of authors' minds. Andrea reached the mark in all areas of his hopes, and her wise, feminine intuitions and sensitivities made her the ideal mother of the congregation. She could "fix" things when Harry might have been a bit too severe in dealing with a church member's problems, and his flock looked to Andrea for help almost as often as it petitioned its minister.

With the pressing duties of his ministry keeping him passionately involved, it was almost two years before the bridal couple could get away. The Methodist Council graciously offered to pay a substitute minister so that the couple could take a much-needed vacation, and Andrea was delighted at the prospect of a real honeymoon. She threw her arms around Harry's neck. "I'm so excited," she whispered, "a real honeymoon." Harry arranged for coastal steamer passage to Vancouver from Princeville, and so the couple was able to take their first romantic getaway.

Harry and Andrea's excitement grew as the day drew closer. But the honeymoon turned into a nightmare, when horses pulling a beer wagon bolted near the Anderton Hotel. The next few moments would become a blur in Harry's memory as the din of hoof clatter, snapping boards, and shouting, filled the enveloping mist.

The beer wagon overturned, rolling six barrels like bowling balls down High Street, the main thoroughfare through the town, which descended steeply, from Vancouver's downtown, northward toward the harbor. The first of the barrels luckily lodged against a lamppost, hitting with enough force to snuff its light and bending it at a near-right-angle toward the ground. The second barrel bounced over a basement railing, falling to a downstairs entrance with such force that two of its hoops failed, leaving a foamy yellow puddle and a pile of slats in the doorway below. The third barrel continued down the steep grade, crashing through the left front wheel of a delivery wagon that was parked in front of the bakery, making a loud snapping noise and sending the wheel's steel rim careening toward the docks. The hackney in the wagon's harness was also hit, and the gelding lay in the road, thrashing and unable to get to its feet.

Barrel number four, turned as it was pitched from the wagon to the steep roadway, rolling harmlessly to the side of the street and stopping against a hitching post with no apparent damage. But the chance release of barrels five and six would have lasting effects--ones that would always haunt Harry's life. There was a rumbling sound, and then a sickening pop, as an eight-year-old boy was slammed to the roadway, clutching his leg, and screaming in pain. Harry dropped to his knees, saying a silent prayer, and grabbing for the handkerchief in his pocket. "You're going to be all right," Harry reassured the boy, "we're going to get you to a doctor." Harry found the handkerchief, doubled it up, and wrapped it around the crushed leg, holding it tightly to stop the heavy bleeding, which instantly left a large red puddle migrating down the steep roadway.

Later, Harry would find out that the lad's leg was damaged beyond help, and that it would require amputation. In the commotion of galloping horse hooves and screaming bystanders, Harry noticed nothing but the injured lad, and his immediate first aid would be credited with saving the child's life.

"Andrea," Harry shouted, "Run and find a doctor." A crowd gathered next to the boy, and a man running from behind them announced, "I'm a doctor. I'll take over now." At that same moment there was a loud report as the injured Hackney gelding was put down. But then the doctor stopped abruptly in his speech. "Keep the pressure on the boy's leg. I need to check this woman first."

The doctor leaned over Andrea, checked for a pulse and shook his head. "She's not going to make it." he said. "Do you know this woman?" Harry choked it out, "She's my wife. Andrea

Mills." Andrea lay there motionless. Still clutching the boy's leg, Harry touched her face with his other hand. There was no response, and the doctor went back to helping the boy. When the noise and excitement subsided, a chilling quiet draped over the crowd, and Harry sat in the middle of the road, holding Andrea's head in his arms and sobbing aloud.

After two years of blissful marriage, constantly enriched by Andrea's sweet and optimistic smile, the ensuing desolation changed Harry's life, and after that single, tragic moment, he would never be happy again. Still, his warm concern persisted for those he served, and that became the substitute sustenance of his existence, helping to fill the gaping hole that was once an idyllic life.

Nine years passed, and, deep down, Rev. Mills understood that his ministry would never provide him complete fulfillment. Though he'd continued to lead the congregation at Princeville, he was always subtly aware of the vacuum in his life. When the acute pain of losing Andrea faded into an aching, lingering loss, he began, once again, to consider the value of finding love and the rapidly fading hope of having a family. His dreams of children eluded him, and he understood that the tragedy of his loss should not define his future. Harry prayed that the right person and opportunity would find him, and suddenly there was new promise in his life.

It was only a few days after Harry's prayerful petition that the Methodist minister in Eagle City quit his job, summoned from the lord's work to a placer mining operation in the Yukon. Mills was invited to fill the post, and he had not hesitated in his decision. While Harry understood that his good fortune could be attributed to a miracle, he also knew that the opening in Eagle City could just as easily be credited to the departing minister's betrayal of God for the pursuit of riches. It was an unusual situation, as there were very few ordained ministers who jumped ship in search of material wealth, for, to most of them, the adoration of their congregations was a high enough wage. To summarize it in a parable of shepherding irresponsibility, one might say, "The lambs are in the pasture, and the wolves are all around. The Shepherd's gone and left them for a pot o' gold in town." Without looking back, Harry accepted the new assignment, and headed to Eagle City and a new life. But the bigger town and its populace were not the opportunity Harry expected, and his heart continued in almost resolute loneliness.

As a leader in the church and a noted influence in the community, Harry took little time to socialize, and, during his dozen years there, he realized that the prospects for romance and love in Eagle City were almost as bleak as the dismal absence of opportunity in Princeville. There was one eighteen year old girl named Priscilla Commens who actually caught the preacher's fancy, but he could not visualize himself with her. She was simply too young to be marrying a middle-aged man, and he understood that, while such a marriage might survive, she would likely have resentment looking back on the life she might have otherwise found.

Like a filly feeling her oats, Priscilla possessed a strong zest for life, but she too was frustrated by a poor supply of eligible mates. A girl of good upbringing, her eyes and heart steered her from the roughness of the local men, who mostly wreaked of body odor from the physical jobs they performed, smelled like salmon from the catches they brought home, or stank from their wild and irresponsible relationships with women of low repute. So, despite their difference in age, Priscilla actually considered the possibility that she might become Harry's wife. In a gentle parting, Harry had reiterated his affection for Priscilla, but he let her know, in the most certain terms, that he could not consider marriage with a girl not even half his age. After he'd spoken the words, Harry experienced a deep sadness, understanding that Priscilla had likely been his last chance at love and a family.

There were five churches of various denominations in Eagle City, and they all stood within a city block of each other. Though Christ was supposed to be at the center of each, and Christian religions should have been in joyful harmony with each other, the social and business circles of the town seemed to be defined by the invisible lines of doctrine and membership. Baptists didn't play bridge with Methodists; Catholics would not even stop to have a wee dram with any of their protestant neighbors; the Eagle City Lumber Company charged Lutheran carpenters two cents a board foot more than members of other churches; and the "community" dances, held once a month on Saturday nights, and sponsored by the Presbyterians, neither allowed Baptists nor Lutherans at the events. Though Rev. Mills delivered sermons on the need for acceptance and harmony between the various religious groups, he found himself unable to bridge the traditional barriers. But what did happen was an en masse jumping-of-ship from the other churches to his.

As Rev. Mills' popularity grew, the handful of Methodists swelled to a congregation of over a thousand, and Sunday services found as many attendees standing as those who were lucky enough to find a pew. Not surprisingly, other ministers became acutely jealous as the members of their churches flowed across the street to hear Harry's sermons. Lawrence Babcock, the Presbyterian minister, was suddenly horrified by the dwindling attendance at his church, and was even more alarmed by the diminishing Sunday collections. It was Mrs. Grandy Smithers who overheard Rev. Babcock's remarkably offensive language when she returned to the chapel one Sunday after services, to look for her purse.

Having seen the last of the congregation leave the building, Rev. Babcock immediately counted the money from that day's collection plate, and was enraged by the meagerness of the offerings. "That damned Mills," he stomped as he said it, and then let out the burst that caused an immediate rose color to flush Mrs. Smithers' cheeks. "That little fucker," he fumed, "He's taking all our money." As Rev. Babcock stewed upon his last festering word, he noticed Mrs. Smithers's mouth agape, and departed the church with an embarrassed look on his face.

George Ralliston, the Baptist minister, found his congregation so depleted that he took a job at Weldon's Mill, and he too started attending Harry's Methodist services. Winston Stowell, minister of the Eagle City Anglican Church was worried that the collections would be unable to provide him with an adequate income, and Albert Downs, pastor of the Eagle City Church of Christ, began to make inquiries about ministerial opportunities in larger towns. Never had the competition for precious souls been a more compelling concern.

———————

As the attendance at Harry's church soared, not all the newcomers were Harry's friends, and there were a few, despite his devotion to his calling, whom he didn't particularly enjoy. There was Zack Bonner, a smelly ne'er-do-well, who had done every job in Eagle City at one time or another. His unreliable nature closed the gates to most types of employment, and he was now making a bare living mining for gold on a small claim up-river. He was smelly, uncouth, and perpetually drunk, and, more than once interrupted the Sunday services at Harry's church. But, whatever Zack lacked in manners and sobriety, he was an enthusiastic and solid supporter of Rev. Mills, and it was only his noisy disruptions brought on by the flow of endless booze that made him secretly unwelcome at the church.

During the most reverent times, one could never guess whether Zack would suddenly rise with a boisterous "Halleluiah." or an unsolicited comment to the rest of the congregation. "Damn," he'd once howled in appreciation of a sermon, "Rev. Mills sure nailed that one!" And he'd clapped and whistled to emphasize his compliment. Mills never expressed his displeasure, and Zack was greeted by the preacher each Sunday with a sincere "Zack, it's good to see you here." When Zack was killed in the collapse of his sluice, Rev. Mill was actually somewhat sad--sad because Zack lived such a rough life, and even a little disappointed because there would no longer be those unexpected Sunday disruptions that stole the boredom from more than one church service.

One of the growing mass of newcomers to Harry's church was Miss Mary Garrity, a young woman of just twenty-eight, who initially purposely avoided all the churches after her arrival in Eagle City four years before. Her story held the familiar threads of Harry's early life, for as a child she too lost both her parents to illness, and struggled with the embarrassment and stigma of being an orphan. Though a kind aunt eventually took her in and raised her, there was irreparable damage to both her mind and her soul.

Mary was lured to Eagle City by stories of high-paying jobs, but only succeeded in becoming a hostess at a local dance hall, where she was paid a shabby wage to dance with its patrons. Will Graham was one of those patrons--a wild-eyed sluicer from up-river who often came in for some Saturday night fun. Will was mighty handy when drunk, and Mary found herself groped and fondled while they were dancing. Though she was a virgin, and a God-fearing one at that, she experienced a surprising excitement, just knowing he was finding her attractive, and, when he offered her a dollar for a kiss, she supposed it couldn't hurt.

Innocent as she was, Mary was, by no means, ignorant. She certainly knew what the other girls did with the men they took upstairs. But she, somehow, didn't see the inevitable complexities of Will Graham's request. "Just one little kiss." Finding a discreet spot on the balcony, she asked for the dollar. It was more than she normally made in a day, and the kiss that ensued was titillating. Another followed. She remembered her fearful aunt's words of caution as she was forced to the balcony's planks. Holding down her arms, Graham locked his teeth onto the neck of her blouse and, tossing his head upward, yanked off all the buttons. She tried to stop him, but then his hand was on her breast. She struggled as he ripped her knickers, and gasped as he entered her. Mary was no match for Graham's strength, and her embarrassment was far too acute to allow her to scream.

For some inexplicable reason, which deeply puzzled Harry, Mary, and others who were forced by men were often cursed by a shame which destroyed their sense of direction and self-esteem. Now, one would think that such a vile act would leave its victim incensed, but instead Mary experienced only hurt, and a dark depression fell over her. Inside her, there was a sense that she'd hit rock-bottom and that any effort to grab hold of her future was futile. Mary accepted two dollars from another customer the next night, and this time she understood that the money was simply a prelude to the inevitable conclusion.

Before Mary walked into Harry's sermon on the unconditional love of Jesus and the worth of every human being, she worked at the dance hall for over four years. It was vomit from a drunken customer soaking her naked body that provided the smelling salts for her unconscious soul. She regained "consciousness," and she never wanted to go back. Trying to make a clean transition from her past to a more respectable life, Mary searched for another job, but found none. At least, that was the account she presented to Harry the first time she visited his church.

There was something about Mary that reminded Harry of his beloved Andrea, and he found himself wanting her to stay. The emerald color of her eyes, her auburn hair, and the hint of a familiar eau de toilette merged the two women in his mind. He understood how circumstances sometimes seemed to dictate out of necessity the confining path of a life, and he felt joyful that he was so fortuitously placed in a position to help rescue Mary's penitent and humble soul.

The two wept as she related the bad choices she'd made, and as Harry offered his arms and his cheek to the distressed girl, she turned her face and placed a gentle kiss on his lips. "You are such a sweet man," she whispered, "and it is so good to know that someone cares." For the first time since Andrea's death, Harry felt himself being swept by the strength of his emotions and his desire to be close. But instinctively he pulled away, entreating her to limit the scope of their friendship, or they would not be able to talk that way again. "Mary," he blushed, "I simply cannot do that, but I'll do my best to help you." He certainly knew that there was a risk in befriending her, for he could immediately see that she understood her power over men.

Whatever gyrations and acrobatics Harry's mind performed in that moment, he was moved by what he saw as Mary's spiritual prostration and her commitment to making herself a worthy disciple of Jesus. Knowing that she had no place to go after leaving the saloon's employment, he felt inspired to offer her a position, cleaning the church and rectory, and setting up the Sunday service. Along with her new job, Harry allowed Mary to live—though he made it clear it was only a temporary arrangement--in a partitioned section of the rectory specifically built for the use of a housekeeper.

Some in Harry's congregation thought it improper to allow a young woman, particularly one of Mary's past, to even enter the church, and despite the worship of his congregation, the questionable living arrangements became a matter of gossip.

Yet Harry considered his commitment to the lost sheep to be a far higher priority than a few mumbling members. Much like the blood that kept him from seeing the approach of that devastating left hook, his mostly-godly concern for the green-eyed young lady made it impossible for him to anticipate what was coming. "Young women," he had been instructed during his years at the seminary, "are a risky business around the church." He knew it was true, but his love of humanity drove him blindly into the punch.

Violation

Everyone in Stella's Cove knew why George Murphy left, and it was the constant sting of guilt and embarrassment that kept the matter out of the town's conversations. To most of its two-hundred-eighty-eight remaining residents--now dominated by the aging and childless--George Murphy's departure was the immediate and direct cause of the town's economic demise. There were only a few townsfolk who did not in a sense bite the hand that fed them, and they all, secretly, wished they could have remained Murphy's privileged wards instead of provoking his heart against them. Though much of their actions—or inaction-- had been passive and not directed personally toward George, the behavior of the townsfolk infuriated his moral sensitivities and left him with an anger that would not subside.

I have mixed feelings over my own mother's role in the biting economic pain that followed in the wake of Murphy's yacht. While her actions played no part in evoking George's angry response, her inaction was a different story. Someone once said that, for evil to prevail it only requires the failure of good men to step forward and take action. I'd seen first-hand how there are sins of both commission and omission. Whatever culpability Mother bore, she came to understand that George was a good man. It was his generosity that provided me with a college education-- something a fatherless family could not have independently afforded.

Though completely mired in the unpleasant aftermath and resigned to the town's death, Mother was among those who halfheartedly opposed the inhumanity of her neighbors and one of the few who attended the funerals of the gentle Rev. Harry Mills and Miss Kimberly Hardwicke—who had been crushed, along with Junior, by a sudden, violent calving of the glacier. Though they died together there was a stunning disparity in the handling of the bodies.

Killed in the same accident--the most recent in a series of tragedies that helped perpetuate the glacier's evil reputation--one of the dead was given a fine funeral and a prominent grave with a polished granite marker. The other two victims were not buried until more than three weeks later, and that was only through the kindness and humanity of George Murphy.

Within three days of the accident, Junior was remembered in a lovely funeral service and was interred in the town cemetery. His grieving father had depended on his son as his most essential employee at the bakery. So the blackness of that terrible day and the sense that part of Mr. Clemmerton's own heart was ripped from his chest were compounded by the immediate burden caused by the shortage of help, and Bart Sr. wondered how he could replace the dependability and hard work Junior had so faithfully supplied to their business.

As for all the other funerals of the last several decades, Rev. Miles Cromwell officiated at Junior's funeral and provided an impressive sermon, completed with the words, "He was a fine young man who knew no vices and always chose to be on God's side. While it is sad that he died with two of the world's most depraved people," Rev. Cromwell prayed, "now the angels have borne him to you, Lord, and may he forever be welcome in your presence. Amen." There were a few in attendance who were offended by the Reverend's words, for they couldn't help but notice that such a pronouncement of guilt upon Rev. Mills and Miss Hardwicke was anything but Christ-like. Even more offensive was the postmortem treatment of the morally condemned pair.

Those deemed by Cromwell as the "depraved "--Rev. Harry Mills and Kimberly Hardwicke—were not immediately buried. Instead, they were stored for twenty-two days on a pile of ice, just outside the blacksmith shop. There was not even a sheet or shroud to cover the sickening blue pall of their faces. The grotesque display was, in effect, a substitute for a zoo, amusement park, or freak show--things Stella's Cove lacked--and it would have been a consistent and logical addition to the tragic scene, had there been hawkers selling popcorn and souvenirs. Almost all the residents went to gawk at the spectacle. The remarks of onlookers were cruel and insensitive--no better than a mob of ignorant school children joining in with the taunting of some fearsome bully, looming over a smaller and terrified schoolmate.

The natural compassion that generally affects all who view such a tragedy was totally missing, and Stella's Cove was ruled by the mentality of a mob. I passed the bodies a number of times on my way to my chores at the Murphy home, and I wondered why George Murphy, a man of great goodness and love--and who certainly possessed the resources to provide a decent burial—did not immediately act to end the gruesome spectacle.

I would later understand that each long day the bodies lay in their irreverent display was an additional chance for the town to save itself. It would have taken only one or two strong, moral souls to bring the show to its end but no one stepped forward. My mother, though seemingly disgusted with the town's behavior, was nevertheless one of the weak, expressing her displeasure in the privacy of our own home, while essentially doing nothing. Undoubtedly there were a handful of people like her, who felt incensed about the inhumanity but felt unable to affect a change. My head fell each time I passed the coal bin--wondering how the nightmare would be lifted--and I wished that my friends could be alive again. My secret crush on Miss Hardwicke would never be revealed, and I knew that she would always remain one of the great influences in my life.

Living in the Clemmerton home, Kimberly Hardwicke had become like family to Junior. All three of us were on friendly terms with the Rev. Harry Mills, and visited him many times at his cabin on Muir Creek. Besides Harry's affable hospitality, he shared his impressive collection of books. We all appreciated his gentle kindness and his willingness to forgive the people who hurt him so badly in Eagle City. He was like the biblical shepherd, feeling great concern for those who needed comfort and a friend, and we personally witnessed how he always reached out to help anyone in need. When he found himself in Stella's Cove, injured and hurting, he was immediately exposed to the harshness of the attitudes and moral insensitivities dominating the community. He saw the callous piety of the townsfolk, and he was shunned and marginalized by a population that was entrenched in the bad habit of judging others and that embraced the stories and gossip that gushed from unreliable mouths.

As the bodies of Miss Hardwicke and Harry lay there on ice, for that seemingly endless three weeks, I noticed that people did not merely glance at the hideous sight, but actually made the large, ice-filled coal bin the equivalent of the town plaza. I could not understand how anyone could endure such a tragic display, but I understood that decent human beings would have attempted to end it. Instead, the bodies were the focus of a sick community, the informal gathering place for the curious and depraved, and the damning evidence of a town's inhumanity and hate.

On the second day of the display, I overheard the conversation of two ladies who were standing in front of the iced bodies. "It serves them right," noted Dorothy Glower, "The little slut was pregnant, and there isn't any question who the father was." Melanie Horlock couldn't help but adding, "How could Mills have ever preached to anyone?" Then, lifting her hand to hide the movement of her lips, she whispered, "He was a pervert and a rapist, you know."

————————————

The following evening, I was coming around the corner of the mercantile and noticed Dan Tillop and Denton Blethers standing over the bodies and having a smoke. I despised Dan, who was a rampant bully with the foulest mouth in the town, and I hated him for the smirk on his face as he stared at the silent corpses of my friends. Waiting in the shadows at the edge of the building, I remained just long enough to get an earful and a sickening visual shock.

Blethers was a Mongoloid, a diagnosis that the medical profession conferred on him shortly after his birth, and it was mostly-quietly spoken in the homes of the town that either his parents had done something very wrong to have deserved such a damaged child, or that Mr. and Mrs. Blethers had been far too old for reproductive purposes. Even at the time of his birth, physicians and scientists had already noted that there was a statistical connection between late-life pregnancies and a variety of congenital defects, and Mongoloidism was known to be the most common.

Blethers was older than I, but he was the mental equivalent of a four-year-old, or so people said. Over his twenty years of life, Denton's body far out-grew his mental capabilities, and his physical development and size presented a growing problem. While much of his presence consisted of nonsensical "blethering"--something that fit his name so perfectly--there were some assaults on the girls of our town. While other boys of that age are all faced with their intensifying sexuality and the powerful drives that develop during the transition from boyhood to manhood, they possessed, at least, some rudimentary abilities to exercise control. Blethers, with his greatly diminished capacity, was not capable of such restraint, and, as he grew older, the families of the Cove--particularly those with daughters—grew to fear the oversized and oversexed child.

Faith Ingram was walking to school one day after her thirteenth birthday, when Blethers came up behind her, forced his hand down her knickers, touching her most private parts, then shoved his hands up her blouse and fondled her budding breasts. Screaming and scared, she ran toward home, with Blethers following her, laughing with pride at what he'd done. While Faith's father was ready to kill the kid, Faith's mother attempted to assuage his anger, noting that Blethers was harmless, and simply didn't understand the impropriety of his violation. "After all," Mrs. Ingram said, in an effort to dissipate her husband's wrath, "he didn't rape her." It was obvious to Mr. Ingram that his wife simply did not grasp how traumatic the event had been for their daughter, yet he set aside his murderous hate in an effort to see the matter ended.

The Faith Ingram assault was merely swept under the carpet, although there were several other girls who were, subsequently, improperly touched, whose families chose not to publicize the matter. And there would be no more talk of the Blethers boy's improprieties until the following year, when young Blethers' impulses caused additional trouble in the town.

───────────

As I stood there, just out of their view, Dan Tillop flicked the growing ash from his cigarette onto the bodies, and seeing no other folks around, he taunted Blethers. "You think she's pretty, don't you? Wouldn't you love to touch her? Blethers squirmed when Dan said it, for there had been repercussions and a beating from his father after the Faith Ingram matter, and the pain would not soon be forgotten. But, thinking about the pretty face and body lying there before him, Blethers became aroused. "It's OK. You can touch her," invited Dan, lighting up another smoke, "She's dead, so it won't make any difference."

I could not believe what followed. Blethers climbed atop the ice, lifted the hem of Miss Hardwicke's dress, and touched her. Turning for a moment to confirm that no one was looking, he pushed her legs apart, slipped her knickers to the side and inserted his finger. Dan Tillop, obviously savoring the moment, gasped, letting out a spontaneous "Oh, my God."

Once again, Blethers glanced around, and seeing no witnesses, he pulled down his pants and entered her. Blethers shuddered for a moment spasmodically, and his eyes seemed to roll back in their sockets. "Uh oh," he muttered, understanding that he was feeling an immediate, extreme sensation and that he would likely be in trouble over this. At the same time, Blethers recoiled from the cold of Miss Hardwicke's body. He pulled her legs together, and quickly straightened the hem of her dress.

Sick as it was, Dan smiled, obviously feeling some vicarious pleasure in the violation which had just taken place, taken another deep drag on his cigarette, blown a neat little smoke ring into the air, and tossed it onto the ice next to Harry Mills.

Dan Tillop hated Miss Hardwicke. She had given him the bad grades he deserved and expelled him several times, over a period of only several months, for his deplorable behavior in her classroom. After one of her chidings, he had grabbed his own crotch in front of the whole class. "You're just a sexy tight-ass who needs a good hosing," he'd taunted, and he rocked his hips back and forth to emphasize his meaning, while pretending to hold his oversized appendage, directed toward her with both his hands.

Dan Tillop's loathing of Miss Hardwicke was both undeserved and vile, but it had been fueled and supported by the growing anger of Stella's Cove's adults, who were infuriated by Miss Hardwicke's teaching of natural selection's effect on the creation of mankind and the creatures of our world. Some of the parents, not sharing Miss Hardwicke's respect for the principle of evolution, actively promoted anarchy in her classroom in an attempt to protect their children from, what they considered to be, blasphemous ideas. They did all they could to undermine Miss Hardwicke's tenure, and there were several who, if they'd believed they could get away with it, would have gladly ended her life. From Miss Hardwicke's first day in Stella's Cove's classroom, the townsfolk felt the immediate need to run her out of town.

I held my breath in silent shock as Tillop and Blethers--who was now frantic about his actions--parted. "See you, Denton. Gotta go now." Dan Tillop turned and walked away. Blethers did his typical idiot guffaw, accompanied by a worried, "Uh oh," and headed back toward his home, licking his finger and laughing as he disappeared into the night.

As I stood there, still hidden by the edge of the building, I could not believe what I'd witnessed, and my heart was aching at the inhumanity--not just what Denton Blethers had did, but the whole idea of putting the dead on display for the purpose of ridicule. No one deserved that, and the two human beings lying there on the ice, in particular, were worthy of respect. I was at first unsure of what to do, but my assessment of the situation was that I could tell no one what I'd seen. People would simply view the atrocity as the actions of that Mongoloid, who was incapable of acting maliciously, and was not responsible for what he'd done.

Dan Tillop was another story. He was certainly culpable. He never personally touched Miss Hardwicke, although he certainly encouraged Denton's horrifying actions. Deep down, I felt personal guilt. I should have said something but hadn't, and I understood that showing my presence would have immediately ended it. Then, again, it all happened so fast that I could not have anticipated the actions of Blethers. I'd been aware of a nauseous and disconcerting feeling inside me, and, despite my internalized excuses, I could not totally understand my inaction. Even worse was my realization that I too felt stimulated by the event. I wondered to myself, "Does everyone have a dark side?"

If there was one person who was more culpable than Dan Tillop in Blethers' violation of Kimberly Hardwicke's corpse, it was the Rev. Miles Cromwell, for it was he who vocally encouraged the inexcusable treatment of the dead pair, stating "All should behold the wages of sin and the consequence of Godless lives." In a sense, Dan Tillop and Denton Blethers were the hands and voices of the community's religious leader.

Stella's Cove residents considered the ghastly display, just two buildings down from the church, to be a statement of what happens when people ignore the Bible. After the pair was left on display for those seemingly interminable three weeks, there were a few people who became publicly vocal in their opposition. Largely at the pleading of Walter Young and Mr. Forsythe, George Murphy finally intervened, arranging for a modest funeral for both the Rev. Mills and Miss Hardwicke, and for their burials in proper graves on some land George owned just north of the town. There were only fourteen people at the funeral, and I was one of them. Rev. Miles Cromwell was conspicuously absent, but George Murphy himself gave a tender eulogy for the pair, revealing his great respect for the good they so valiantly attempted--Kimberly in her zealous pursuit of providing truth to the children of the Cove, and Harry for the inspiration he provided to so many, before his career as a minister was so abruptly terminated.

About one year before the sad deaths of Harry, Junior, and Miss Hardwicke, Mr. Jim Merriman was fired from his post as Murphy Salmon Company's CFO. His replacement was a Mr. Grant Ashley, who was the former vice president of the Eagle City Savings and Loan. Though I never heard the details, I understood that Merriman was let go specifically for matters relating to his dishonesty--something that I could have easily predicted after Mother's short acquaintance with him. Though it did not silence the memory of that terrible moment in Mother's recliner, I found myself pleased that his bad character terminated his career.

Murphy related to me, one afternoon, at tea-time, how Ashley had sat in Murphy's office, discussing certain improvements in the fish processing procedures, which Ashley believed could increase company profits. As a matter of association and knowing of Ashley's previous position in Eagle City, Murphy mentioned his own sadness over Harry Mill's rough treatment by the mob. "He's such a good man," Murphy reflected, "and I feel so badly about the twist of fortune that brought him here. After getting to know him, I cannot even imagine that he was ever guilty of rape. I keep thinking it may still be possible to find him a new congregation, but, without a complete retraction of the girl's allegations, the Methodist Council simply would never allow it. I've written to them twice, and they've told me it's impossible.

"It was a real tragedy," noted Ashley. "I attended Harry's

services during his last two years in Eagle City, and there wasn't any doubt: He was the most popular minister in the town. I realize," Ashley added, "that there's simply never going to be any real proof of his innocence, as much as I'd like to believe. If he didn't do it, it's a real shame that accusations are so often accepted as fact."

Murphy expressed mild surprise at Ashley's comment. "So you've heard all about it." Inquired Murphy. "Yes, everyone in Eagle City knew about the rape, and," Ashley recalled "though I didn't personally witness the event, the story of Harry's beating and expulsion from Eagle City were a matter of common knowledge. There's something I've never shared with anyone else," Ashley continued. "Mary Garrity was a customer at the Eagle City Savings and Loan, and I personally spoke with her on many occasions. She was a charming young lady, and not the kind of person a man would ever forget, so it wasn't surprising that several of the other churches in town tried to help her financially after her terrible trauma. She was very good at drawing sympathy, and all of us hoped she'd be able to stay away from the brothel that came so close to ruining her life. I don't know what happened to her after the furor subsided, and I only saw her a few times after the rape."

"Wait just a second," blurted Murphy. Go back a bit. What do you mean about the other churches helping her financially?" "Having lost her residence in Mill's Methodist rectory," responded Ashley, "she essentially solicited financial help to get her back on her feet and start a new life."

"Really!" exclaimed Murphy, for this was his first contact with a person who personally knew the victim. Murphy thought for a moment, feeling both jubilation and hesitation. "Ashley, I'm curious; you've raised a real question: Did you ever consider that Miss Garrity may have been put up to it?"

"You mean she could have staged the rape?" Ashley's face paled and a troubled look came over him. "I never thought that to be a possibility, but, now that you mention it, she certainly could have. After you put it in those words, it really does seem a bit suspicious that she cashed several fairly large cheques from the other churches in the community."

Both men's faces showed a look of profound enlightenment. "There was no question," continued Ashley, "that Rev. Mill's popularity created jealousy in the town's other religious leaders. He drew away so many of their members. I remember Miss Garrity coming into the bank—last time I ever saw her—and cashing a large cheque—it was over $200, as I recall--from the Eagle City Presbyterian Church. Because of the size of the cheque, I checked the signature, just to make sure it was authentic. It was signed by Lawrence Babcock, the church's minister, whose signature I was familiar with. Even though I was acquainted with Miss Garrity, I felt the need to ask what the money was for. She looked rather embarrassed, saying that she was receiving some help to get her started in a new life, far away from the dark memory that plagued her time in Eagle City. I accepted her at her word."

"Thank you, Grant." Murphy ended their meeting. "You have no idea how much this information means to me." After the meeting, Murphy tried unsuccessfully to find Mary Garrity, retaining a Vancouver detective agency to follow up on some rumors of her whereabouts. After two weeks, the agency came up empty. She seemed to have totally disappeared, and it was apparent, after running into multiple dead-end inquiries, that Mary Garrity wasn't even her real name.

Murphy was troubled, but paid the agency for an additional month of sleuthing. He desperately wanted to clear Harry's name, but, even if he could, the Methodist Church was adamant that it was unlikely to re-hire a minister whose life was so clouded by scandal. Understanding that finding Mary would not necessarily clear Harry's name, and that she would likely stick to her story when confronted with her lies, Murphy was forced to drop the matter. But in his own heart, he now knew that the rape never occurred.

Though unsuccessful in finding a new ministry for Harry--blocked by both Mills' tainted reputation and by the cold pronouncements of the Central Methodist Council--George and Harry became good friends, and, more than once, Harry was invited to have dinner with the Murphys at their Point Fay mansion.

The first time that Harry was a guest at the Murphy's, it was Norwood, Murphy's personal secretary, who pulled up in front of Harry's cabin in the Reo "S" and spirited him off to the Point. Eva Murphy at first showed a distrust of their proposed guest, asking her husband, "Do you really think it's appropriate to have such a man in our home. You know they say he's done some terrible things, and we need to be very careful for the sake of Celeste." George responded that the allegations of what happened in Eagle City were unverified, and that he did not believe the story to be true. After finishing his explanation, George asserted, "I think he's a fine man." Eva gently acquiesced, "I have great trust in your wisdom, George, and so, if you have that level of confidence in him, I will welcome him into our home."

And the Rev. Harry Mills found something at the Murphy's home that was not evident in the other people of Stella's Cove. He noticed that, despite the trappings of wealth, the Murphys were humble people who took nothing for granted and appreciated their blessings. Of course George Murphy himself would likely not have used the word "blessings," although he certainly appreciated the quality of his life and the warming presence of his much-loved family. Unlike the many pious people who saw their fortunes in life as rewards for their goodness, George regarded his remarkable success as a harvest, born of hard work, with the additional and undeniable component of some very fortunate good luck.

There had been an immediate fondness between Harry and George, who grew to love the gentle preacher, and there was more than one evening when George shared a bottle at Harry's Muir Creek cabin, leaving him so inebriated he fell asleep on the pony cart's cushioned seat during the ride home.

While seemingly so different in both their personal lives and their careers, Harry and George shared much in common, for each was the target of gossip and unkindness within the community, and each possessed a rare form of honesty, independent of orthodoxy and convention. During the furor over Miss Hardwicke's teaching of evolution, George showed curiosity about Harry's position. "As a man of the cloth," he inquired, "what do you think of the evidence that seems to link man to the lower forms of life…I'm just wondering if there's a place in your mind for the concept that men descended from the apes."

Harry paused for a moment, then took a deep breath before answering. "Well, we know Rev. Cromwell's position on that matter, but I certainly don't share all of his opinions. He thinks that evolution and religion are mutually exclusive, but I'm not so sure. Please understand, I do believe that God created man. But I refuse to conjecture on how He did it. The idea of sequential building blocks in the creation process is certainly a possibility." Then George witnessed something no one else ever had. Tenets of the Bible were temporarily lost as Harry actually judged another man. "From what I've seen," Harry spoke with just a hint of guilt, and then emphatically finished, "Rev. Cromwell's probably the best evidence we have for the concept of evolution; I'd say Cromwell was descended from a snake."

When ministerial opportunities proved to be unavailable to Harry, Murphy offered him a managerial position at the plant, but Harry graciously told him, "That's a sweet offer, George, but I actually like the simplicity of my present life--the chances to see nature at its best and the opportunity to pan for just enough flakes to keep me fed. Besides," he'd added, "the politics of the Cove are not harmonious, and hiring me would be another impediment to your acceptance in this town." "Well, "acceptance is something that could never happen," George answered, "They'll take my money but I'll never be one of them, and the reality is that they will always bite the hand that feeds them. Frankly, to be accepted in Stella's Cove, I'd have to forfeit my values, and that's not something I'll ever do." The offer of a job came up several times during those years of friendship, but Harry's answer was always the same.

Once, Harry mentioned the matter of "God" to George, and there was a rather brusque explanation of why Murphy was not a believer. Harry graciously accepted the explanation, while George made it clear he understood peoples' need for a belief in a supreme being.

"You know," asserted George, "that I don't share your faith, but, at the same time, I would be the last person to take away anyone's most precious beliefs. My only concern is that a person has to sacrifice some internal honesty, in order to have an absolute faith in a God." When George said it, Harry winced inside.

"George, that felt like a low blow, to me--pretty strong words." George immediately apologized for his comment, but Harry interrupted him, "What you said hurt me, George, because, of all things, my honesty and character are my most priceless possessions. I want you to know that there is a part of me that understands and recognizes the truth in what you said. I consider myself to be a man of God, but that doesn't mean I am without doubt."

George Murphy had been such a close friend to me. Starting when I was fifteen, he'd supplied me with an endless supply of odd jobs at the Murphy mansion, which gave me, despite Mother's relatively penurious circumstances, a little spending money. Perhaps he would not have been so generous with me if he knew that his own daughter Celeste was a focus of my infatuation during the difficult adjustment after my father's death. George did what he could to give me fatherly advice and looked over me at a time when a mere mother was not enough-- that time when there was a shocking change between being a wistful, naïve boy and a young man, attacked by the messengers of original sin, who tore at my underwear and made it difficult to look on any woman--even old Mrs. Crump--without thoughts of carnal knowledge.

George was the only person I'd ever discussed those things with, and I loved his understanding--that it was all part of the normal growing up process. "Billy," he' confided, "what you're experiencing is what I experienced at your age, and you needn't feel ashamed that you're a normal, red-blooded young man. These changes are dictated by nature, and they're essential to make sure that mankind doesn't disappear from our planet." With all George's reassurances, I'm not sure, looking back, if he could have accepted that Celeste was one of my most passionate and romantic fantasies, and, more than once, I imagined the ecstasy of being with her. Even with George's kind understanding of puberty and his fatherly encouragement, I often felt a pang of guilt. For I imagined Celeste in that most intimate context, and it was something I could have never told him.

Icy Deaths

The ill fit of Harry's front door groaned under the onslaught of the wind, and drafts chilled the cabin's stark interior as Junior and the minister sipped their whisky. Junior listened intently as Harry described how Mary surprised him in the rectory, as she stood there, covered only from the waist down; how he stepped back as she tried to embrace him, saying "No, I can't do that." Harry understood Mary's desperation as she'd let her bloomers slip silently to the floor. Grabbing his belt, she thrust her hand into his trousers, and he felt only compassion when she cried that he didn't find her attractive. "I do find you attractive. I do." Harry pleaded, "…but I can't have that kind of a relationship with you." What he said contained the strength of a solid resolve, and he turned to walk away.

What came next was even more shocking than the seductive attempt that preceded it. Mary's countenance turned immediately to one of raging anger. "You holier-than-thou-son-of-a-bitch," she practically spat as she snarled it. "No one turns me down." She ripped at Harry's neck and face with her fingernails and ran from the church still naked, screaming "Rape."

As the details enfolded, Junior thought it strange that Harry didn't blame Mary--how he talked of the tragic and often perplexing disorders from which rape victims may suffer--and how Harry expressed no ill will, but only concern for Mary's eventual well-being. As the defrocked minister told of the ensuing near-lynching and beating, Junior asked him why he didn't use his prizefighting skills on the men who thrashed him. "I would have hurt them." Harry confessed. It was obvious, in both Harry's words and attitudes, that he felt only sadness for the wrongs committed against him--understanding what happens when individuals fail to abide by their own values, and succumb to the evil nature of a mob. Though the events permanently hurt his life, he held nothing against those who injured him, and continued to have forgiveness toward them all.

But, now, Harry stood up abruptly. "Did you hear that?" he asked, and he placed his index finger to his lips, uttering a soft "Shhhh." Junior could hear nothing but the sounds of an approaching storm, but Harry exclaimed, "It's that singing again. I heard it when you first came in, but I figured it was only my imagination." Then Junior heard it too--not the glacier's typical song. It was more like the sobbing, hopeless, distant cry of a woman. Harry opened the cabin door. There was no sound but the wind, darting nimbly through the spires of the glacier and leaving resounding tones as it swept across the crevasses that dotted the surface of the ice. Harry sat down, once more, in the glow of the fire. "We must be imagining it," he'd smiled. Even then, he rose once more, and walked to the door, opening it slightly to conserve the room's heat, and finally closed it again. "I guess it wasn't anything." Harry resolved, and it was obvious he believed their imaginations were simply playing tricks on them. "Just the wind..." he finished, and pulled his chair closer to the fire.

With Harry's story finally told, it was Junior who, peering into the embers of the fire, was now reflecting on his own life— reviewing how the lovely Miss Hardwicke, who roomed at the Clemmerton house since the beginning of the school year, became the object of his love. He told how their intimacy developed; and how her departure now left him with a sense of both loss and guilt. Junior raised his eyes to Harry. "You know, she was pregnant with our baby. I need to find her and make it right." Harry was feeling the pain of his friend, and he poured them each another drink.

There wasn't much else to do, for the cards of life were laid upon that little table in Harry's cabin. When the bottle was empty, Harry and Junior drifted off to sleep in their chairs by the fire, only to be wakened around 4:00 a.m. by the intense cold which had now replaced the fire's warmth. Harry stuffed a few logs into the open stove, and then froze all motion, silencing the creak of the floorboards and wishing that the new logs would quit their popping and snapping for just a moment. He stood there totally intent on the faint sound that slid between the cabin door and its ill-fit frame. "I can hear it again." said Harry, now sobered by the chill. "It's that singing."

Grabbing their coats, the pair stepped outside into the wind. Stopping frequently to listen, they followed the trail along the milky-white stream. The night was dark as the soot in the chimney of a seasoned stove, but, as they neared the glacier, the clouds parted just enough to view a few stars and the Aurora Borealis, rosily ribboning across the sky. For a moment, the pair saw only the immensity of the glacier's face, but, as they arrived at the glacier's ominous tongue, they were able to make out the form of a woman, lying in the snow.

The moon, partially shrouded in a black cloud and surrounded by a gentle halo of blowing flakes, disclosed the unmistakably pert nose of Miss Kimberly Hardwicke. The singing seemed to intensify for just a moment, and a shiver ran through the two men as the wind tugged at Miss Hardwicke's dress, accentuating her willowy figure and revealing the fullness of a secret love that could no longer remain hidden.

Junior knelt next to Kimberly. "Kimberly, Kimberly. I'm here." Her hand was cold, and when he pressed his fingers to her wrist for a pulse, he was barely able to detect the beat of her heart. He pressed his lips to hers and, when he lifted his head, he imagined he saw a faint smile. "It's hypothermia," said Harry, sounding frantic, "We have to get her warm." Harry ran back to the cabin, fetching a wool blanket to warm her, but when Kimberly was swaddled in the blanket, her silence continued. Lifting her gently, Junior turned toward the cabin, stopping for just an instant to listen. "There it is again," Junior hushed, "I can hear something." He mistook it, first for the heartbeat of their baby, then for his Kimberly, alive. Harry heard it too--now a throbbing, ticking, cracking, breaking, thundering. Then, silence, but for the reverberating chorus of the glacier's song, echoing through the night.

Rejected by an entire town, nobody cared where Miss Kimberly Hardwicke spent that inhospitable night. No one cared whether or not the defrocked Rev. Harry Mill's cabin was still standing. But Bart Clemmerton, Sr., was concerned when Junior wasn't there for his morning bakery chores. Shortly before noon, a small party with dogs headed up the trail past Harry's cabin and his placer claim, and arrived at the silver-tongued siren of Stella's Cove. The dogs headed immediately to the streambed, where an eighty-foot slab of iridescent, opal ice had become the unexpected mausoleum for Harry Mills, Kimberly Hardwicke, and Junior. It took over three hours, but, with ice picks and sledgehammers, the party succeeded in freeing the bodies.

Next to Harry, wrapped warmly in Junior's protective arms was Kimberly Hardwicke, approximately five months along. The search party knew, at once, exactly what had happened, and any of the town's thousand residents could have told you-- including my mother--everything but why an innocent lad of twenty-four was unlucky enough to die with them. It was easily determined that Junior gallantly tried to shield Kimberly Hardwicke from the falling spire of ice. It was obvious, too, that Miss Hardwicke had compounded the sins of her heretical teaching in Stella's Cove, by becoming another of the defrocked minister's sexual conquests.

Besides Junior's tragic death, there was one more thing that none of the town folk could figure out---why the faces of all three, pinned in the deep cleavage of that glacier's heart, showed no terror. It was such a sudden and violent end, but reflected on their faces was a simple, innocent peace.

Curse of Justice

I was heartbroken when I heard of the deaths. Harry Mills was an important part of my life and education. He'd loaned me Homer's Odyssey, and I couldn't even give it back. Miss Hardwicke would leave a hollow place in my worshiping, infatuated heart, and I would always remember the change that she'd promoted in my feelings toward myself. It was puppy love that inspired me, but that love led me to a new vision of my own potential. And, when I went into Clemmerton's Bakery, I would never hear Junior's friendly "Hello" again, nor would we join each other for those walks to Harry's cabin.

Junior was immediately given a good Christian burial. The townsfolk, who looked at Junior as the best of Stella's Cove's sons, all attended. But Harry and Kimberly were irreverently displayed in that coal bin, lying on a pile of ice. A hastily-constructed lean-to was placed to retard the thawing of the ice, preserving the bluish tint on their faces, and the citizens of Stella's Cove lamented that there were no close neighbors to whom they could pass the buck for the cost of interment. Falling across the town was an infectious attitude of contempt--promoted vigorously by the Rev. Miles Cromwell. His sermon, the following Sunday, would include the words, "People of such low quality and morals deserve to be left as carrion for the hungry critters and birds that traditionally take care of the trash." Three of his devoted worshipers actually rose from their pews and exited the chapel in response to the preacher's offensive words, and yet the display of the bodies continued.

George, Eva, and Celeste did not immediately hear about the tragedy, and it was I, on the second day, who walked to their home and delivered the ghastly news. The four of us, embraced in the arms of love, wept together, and I believed that George would immediately step in to provide a funeral and burial for our friends. Instead, Murphy, appalled by the town's absence of Christianity, was in no real hurry to remove the bodies. As grotesque as the display was, he viewed the spectacle as the ultimate statement of man's inhumanity. There was no God in Stella's Cove, and George knew that the event would forge the town's final condemnation.

He hired a sculptor to create a monument to the three, and, when completed, it would be placed on the north side of the Muir Creek trail, a short distance from the glacier's tongue. Murphy gave the sculptor a hand written note, specifying the exact language of the inscription: "April 11, 1913. Three Died Here: Kimberly Anne Hardwicke, A Brave Educator; Bart L. Clemmerton Jr., A Good Friend; and Rev. Harry Haven Mills, A Living Saint."

After the grotesque three-week display, and in an effort to avoid publicly usurping Rev. Cromwell's position, George asked for the minister's help with the funeral arrangements. "As far as I'm concerned," answered Cromwell, "they can lie there and rot. Those two got exactly what they deserved."

So, securing the services of a Vancouver funeral director, and hiring a coastal launch to ferry its staff back and forth from the funeral, George gave Harry and Kimberly a memorial service that very much touched those who attended. Rev. Mills and Miss Hardwicke had no known family, and there were only fourteen residents in attendance, including myself. None of us ever heard a greater eulogy and sermon than the one George Murphy personally delivered, and each of us believed it was the warmest funeral we'd ever witnessed. Not surprisingly, Murphy's funeral sermon was not about God, but about the products of good works and kindness, which are all that remain when a person is gone. Also not surprising were Murphy's words about the matter of judging others--how mistaken the prejudice of gossip can be, and how no man can know another's heart.

After the funeral, George put Eva, Celeste, and Norwood on the Bountiful and sent them to their home in Vancouver, choosing to remain behind to wrap up some unfinished business. I shared a tearful goodbye with Celeste and Mrs. Murphy, understanding that none of us knew when we'd see each other again, and as the yacht faded into the offshore mist, I understood that the fortune of the town was about to change. The Bountiful had once brought years of prosperity to Stella's Cove, and now she was out of site.

Only two days later, the foreman at the Murphy Salmon Processing Plant reported that, because of a breakdown in the hydroelectric generator, the plant was not operating. The unprocessed load of salmon, delivered the week before, began to spoil, and the northwesterly breeze carried a putrid stench that descended on Stella's Cove. With its electric service abruptly terminated, the little narrow gauge ceased to make its runs at the normal shift turnovers, and the smug faces of a town's successful economic era sat in their homes hoping that their jobs would somehow be saved.

An electrician sent from Vancouver confirmed the mysterious absence of the generator's shaft and stators--all custom made and virtually impossible to replace without great expense. One week later, the rank odor of rotting fish combined with acrid smoke, as the proud plant burned to the finest ash. And, only days after the smoke finally slipped the bonds of the Stella's Cove sky, a deafening explosion rattled the windows of the town, and the cantilevered dock plunged into the sea.

But that was nearly seven years ago, and there have been no signs of the town's revival. Seeing only the specter of death and destruction around them, the hordes of townsfolk waited for passage on the Aniak, and, within two months, most of the town was gone. Despite the years of prosperity, none were smart enough to save, and, for most, the price of tickets for passage to new opportunities was all they could afford.

There were three businessmen from Vancouver who visited the site of the plant, only to announce that the costs of clearing the channel and rebuilding the hydroelectric plant could not be raised. Everyone knew what it meant. There was simply nothing left that could save their perishing town.

Memories

The warmth of the stove has cooled, just a bit, and there's a chill running through my mind. The memories of the tragic events that took place before I'd gone away to college are overwhelming. I'm not looking forward to my month here, because it is so hard for me to break away from the harshness of those recollections. For a moment I am imagining myself as a fly, bogged down in the black mire of a molasses jar and unable to get airborne again, but I know that I must try to be sociable during Mother's short visit with Celeste.

The cheerful words, "Lunch is served" waft from the kitchen. It is predictably delicious, and the two women in my life are talking up a storm and laughing like I've never heard either of them laugh before. I have been worried that Mother's mood would reflect the dismal disintegration of the local economy, but she's in the best of spirits, and the darkness of her existence seems to have parted at the entry of a new prospect in her life--that her boy will get married to the loveliest of girls and that Mother will become a grandmother before she dies.

It's obvious to me that my fears of Mother's mood were largely a matter of my own projection, for I find myself lapsing, once more, into a maudlin preoccupation with the abrupt transition from the prosperous times. I consider how the washing machines, having made their whooshing-whirring sounds for years, are now silent. Many have become yard "ornaments" in which the birds take morning baths in the collected rainwater. I think of the electric lights that brought bright rays to the town's windows every night, and how they've been replaced with the old oil lamps, which now cast their scanty glows upon the ripples of the bay each evening, and I'm lamenting how the monthly docking of the Aniak has become less reliable--that it has been missing some of its scheduled stops--and that when she does pull into the harbor, there are no longer any excited residents waiting for deliveries from the catalogue store.

My thoughts turn toward the outhouses, which no longer have rolls of toilet paper hanging from their weathered walls, and how each has a Sears catalogue, once more, lying there beside the seat, with a bunch of pages missing. And I can't help but dwell on those faces that emerge reluctantly from their quiet cottages--detesting the spreading gloom and noticeable deterioration of their town--with no smiles of expectation for a happier future. And I realize that there will only be that look of hopelessness for the few residents who venture past their front doors and from the security of their whisky bottles.

I have reviewed, over and over, all the tragic events in my mind, although I have never seen the destruction personally. So after kissing Celeste goodbye for our month apart, and watching the Aniak pull slowly away from the dock, I start up the little trail toward what is left of the Murphy Salmon Company. Though it's only been seven short years since the plant went up in smoke, nature has already begun to reclaim the walking path, and, finding it remarkably overgrown, I decide instead to walk the ties of the narrow gauge. About half way to the plant, the electric replacement for the steam locomotive stands in my way. It is a silent and motionless messenger from the moment that the hydroelectric plant failed, so I am forced to walk around it, carefully making my way down the steep ballast. As I pass, I can see two raccoons playing on the engineer's seat, and there's a residual acrid odor of burnt electrical insulation coming from the motor.

The walk seems much longer than I can remember, perhaps because there's something unnatural about taking steps exactly thirty-six inches long. Every eight steps, or so, I find myself getting out of sync, and I am forced to readjust my stride to the spacing of the ties.

It's been almost an hour and I know I must be close. Suddenly, there it is. The rubble looks much like I have envisioned it. The remains of the hydroelectric plant dangle from its anchors on the rock face, and there's water pouring over its eviscerated cast iron housing, cascading to the willows below. I cannot see it, but I take a moment to ponder what was the steady source of endless electric power--the beauty George Murphy surely saw in the moraine above me, and the crystal water of the lake he named "Celeste."

A huge pile of debris is all that's left of the plant, with rusting corrugated steel roofing panels appropriately protecting the burned trusses and the mangled remains of a cement foundation lying partially exposed to view. I can't help but marvel how complete the destruction has been, and I imagine, for just a moment, the smoking embers that fell from the sky for days, following the plant's collapse.

Looking toward the West is what looks like the prow of a ship--the wood, concrete, and steel remains of the cantilevered, deep-water dock--desperately clinging to the sky as it slides stern-first into its watery grave. I never appreciated how much material went into the construction of that dock, and I realize that removal of its remains would be a costly and near-impossible task to accomplish. Parts of the steel anchoring system still grow from their roots in the solid bedrock, and channel markers with their stringy green skirts still bob with each passing wave.

There is now no question about it, for everyone knows that the townsfolk's jealous accusations were untrue: George Murphy certainly did not worship money, and the plant's pile of worthless waste is a testament to his convictions. He destroyed the enormously profitable salmon processing plant to demonstrate his disapproval for the depravity of a town. He scuttled one of B.C.'s greatest businesses to make a statement, and, while George believed that no one should judge, he had, as the town's last savior, pronounced a verdict upon the town which would not be lifted. For a few days after that final fire, gentle smoke rose from a few remaining hot spots--the lingering trace of the Province's most lucrative business--and George Murphy regretted, only for one single moment, the death of Stella's Cove.

Within weeks, the stone monument commissioned by Murphy, in memory of Bart Clemmerton Jr., Miss Kimberly Hardwicke, and the Rev. Harry Mills, was placed only a few yards from the glacier's tongue, and, as I leave the scene of the plant's destruction, I stub my toe on yet another stone marker, a solid granite slab commemorating the spot on which the first cornerstone of the Murphy Salmon Company plant had been laid. It is not fancy or polished, but along with the pain it has inflicted on my toe, its inscription jumps at me with a poignant voice from the dust of better years. It is the terse summation of George Murphy's role in the creation and the destruction of Stella's Cove:

"He Giveth and He Taketh Away."

Return

Eighteen years have passed since that month-long visit with Mother after graduation. Despite my fears, my month-long visit with her had been remarkably enjoyable, and together we reviewed both the good and the bad of the past. While I had more-or-less expected some grand epiphany on the most tragic events--particularly some personal absolution of my own responsibility--it never came. I left with the understanding that virtually everyone in the community had failed in some way, and, while the culpability of Rev. Cromwell was at the center of it all, it could not have happened without what was, essentially, a pack mentality.

Anticipated by the happy laughter she and Celeste shared in the kitchen during their first meeting, the future has been all we could have asked for. Mother has a granddaughter, now sixteen, and despite Mother's immoderate drinking, her health has been good up until now. When we received the telegram, we were shocked, for we assumed that Mother would be with us still for a good many years. But the wire was startlingly blunt. "Your Mother is failing. She has acute cirrhosis and will not live long."

Celeste's teaching career in Eagle City was a short one. Married after her first season, we anticipated that she would be able to work for several years--something that would have helped us save for the purchase of our own home--but things had not gone according to our plan. Celeste's morning sickness disrupted her teaching responsibilities in the spring of her second contract year, and Elizabeth was born that November. An unexpected, fortuitous bonus appeared one day in our mailbox shortly after

Elizabeth's birth, which enabled us to buy the home we dreamed of. A letter from the Arnold University Press related the good news that "Carnivorous Sheep" was adopted by universities all over the world as an authoritative text on mob psychology, and had been translated into four languages. There was a cheque enclosed, and Celeste and I were both surprised and shocked by the amount. $7,500.

While there would be no better times for Stella's Cove, life went on for us. Elizabeth is beautiful and smart like her mother, and I am now the chief administrator for the Provincial Social Services.

The pain of past losses has never been forgotten, yet the hurt has gradually eased with the flood of providence that followed. Father still cries to me from the sea, yet, at the same time, I see him smiling, dripping, as he emerged from the harbor with that bass and my favorite fishing pole. The naked memories of Amos Johnson and Ivy Klaut still lie at the glacier's tongue, no longer the target of ridicule for a ravenous flock of carnivorous sheep. And my dear friend, Burdett, is still dancing, cheek to cheek, with little Miss LeGrande. I am wondering about his child. Was it a girl or a boy?

Though Stella's Cove has made no economic recovery, the foxes and mink have returned in greater numbers than before, and the vein of gold, ground from deep within the Muir Creek streambed by the advancing glacier, is releasing greater riches than it did during the first gold rush. Even the few survivors are unaware that the glacier has granted the wishes of decades, but there is no one there who is young enough to reap the rich harvest that could so easily be theirs.

The government launch pulls up to the dock where the Aniak has tied up a thousand times, and the three of us alight onto the splintered planks that have survived a near-century of traffic. Weeds and small trees grow through the faint tracks of the town's deserted lanes I followed in my youth, and there are signs that the forest, left to itself for years, is starting to recover from the long and incessant assault by the axes and saws of man.

"We'll wait here until you're done, Sir," announces the Captain, and I answer in appreciation, "Thanks, Connelly. We shouldn't be too long." As Captain of the official government launch, Capt. Connelly has dropped me at virtually every inhabited point along B.C.'s coast. I have been with him across miles of placid seas that mirrored the coastal hills, and across the menacing and raging swells that threatened to deposit us into Davy Jones's Locker.

The Stella's Cove dock still echoes with Mayor Culp's mindless faux pas, the articles that memorialized his words for posterity, and the three Italians who disappeared in the glacier's grip. And there's the lingering rumble of the surplus steam engine as it moved up the temporary rails to the track that would etch the history books and bring an age of healthy prosperity to the town.

As we walk down the dock, I am hearing the sound of the siren that faithfully announced the changing of the shifts at the Murphy Salmon Company plant, and there are echoes of both the heartfelt sermons of Rev. Willis Fox and the contrasting empty, hollow words of Rev. Miles Cromwell, accompanied by the bells that always rang faithfully in the steeple of the old Methodist Church.

There's a typical misty coastal layer as we walk down the lane to my childhood home, and I'm surprised that it's looking as good as it does. The old bungalow stands, solid as ever, but one of its decorative shutters is hanging, skeewumpus, by its corner, and the moss on the roof has grown an inch or more thick. Small bushes erupt skyward from the rain gutters, and there are watermarks where years of downpours have seeped between the gutters and the fascia. Though not one of my fond memories, I can't help but reminiscing about the regular raging of Mrs. Crump, with a mouth more foul than any other I'd ever heard, and I am reminded, for a moment, of how I found the old lady's breasts a turn-on in my early teens.

But my smile of amusement turns into a look of loss as I think about the sweet Rev. Harry Mills, Junior, and Miss Kimberly Hardwicke, the public school teacher I loved. I have just a glimpse of the schoolhouse as we climb the stairs to Mother's front door, and I am remembering the way Miss Hardwicke's dress draped over her willowy frame, and the waving of the sun's rays, bent by the wrinkled glass, as it poured, for that glorious moment in time, through the windows of our school. But there is an overwhelming memory of death that haunts my every footstep, for there is the immutable history of those who sought to arrive at, remain in, or escape from Stella's Cove.

My thoughts are interrupted by Mother's frail voice answering our knocking. "It's all right. Just come on in." After all those years, our daughter Elizabeth is visiting my Mother one last time. "Hello, Granny," she says as she enters my mother's bedroom. "I understand you're not feeling your best." Mother hugs Elizabeth with all the strength that remains, and Celeste is suddenly ambushed by the intensity of her own emotions. There are tears welling in her eyes as she thinks of this woman, her mother-in-law, whom she's seen more in photographs than in person. I'm emotional too, but I am momentarily unable to give Mother a convincing hug, for Mr. Merriman is still there, sitting, gasping with an acknowledgment of "God," in the living room's leather recliner, and I'm remembering the contrast between piety and humanity that created such a gulf between Mother and me.

There's an echo, inside our home, of my pleading voice as I repeated, over and over, "What have I done, Mother. Why do I need to repent?". I am confronted with the understanding that my hesitation to pour out my affection is selfish, for Mother, despite her faults, deserves and needs my unconditional love at this moment, and the ultimate endorsement that proclaims, "Whatever you did, I understand that you had my best interests at heart." I walk to the bedside and kiss her.

Elizabeth is still at Mother's side. "I love you, Granny," she speaks in a longing tone, wishing that there could be a return of both the better times and of her grandmother's lost vigor. There is no ceremony, no family prayer, and there is no Bible proclaiming, "And it came to pass." Mother understands that this is our last visit, and, as we say our goodbyes, we offer, once more, to take her to our home in Eagle City." She has not changed her mind. "This is my home," she softly insists. "It's mine and your father's, and I'm going to stay."

I am standing there, just inside the front door of my childhood home, with Celeste and Elizabeth by my side—the years of a mostly menacing history staring us all in the face, remembering the bright future the town once held within its grasp but threw away because it failed to follow the most important lessons of humanity.

For judgment is the one act that no one can assume to perform, and it was judgment, on the part of both the town and its benefactor, that brought the future of Stella's Cove to a close.

The Aniak still does its runs up the coast, serving as the only scheduled lifeline to the smaller communities, and because of the newest navigational equipment the captain no longer needs a special pilot to guide him through the little islands, rocks, and shallows along the coastal channels.

World War I, which was considered the "war to end all wars," never really ended, and, under the leadership of Adolph Hitler, the polarization--created by the notion of a super-race of Germans--is raising its ugly head for a second time. I feel both loss and frustration that the life of my dear friend Burdett made no difference at all. There will always be war. I find myself mouthing the words of the poem, "When will they ever learn?"

Motorcars are now passé everywhere, and even Eagle City's miserable roads are a terrifying domain for the horses remaining from previous years. The ah-ooo-gah of horns is an incessant din, and one would likely benefit from a wet bandanna tied over the nose as a protection against the oily mist that has replaced the coastal fog.

Mother is one of only three remaining townsfolk in Stella's Cove this year. There has been no minister for almost a decade, for no shepherd can be found to tend a flock so small and unprofitable. Were it not for the Human Welfare Commission sending a boat full of supplies each month, providing ample firewood, and performing routine medical checkups, the town's population would have reached zero several years ago, and I understand that soon there will be no one left. Considering the continuous assault on her liver, Mother has lived a long life. Mother has spent all those years with her bottle of whisky, contemplating the guilt of the town and the tragedy of its untimely demise.

Now, at age eighty-six, she looks up at our daughter, Elizabeth, with the shriveled, yellow face and wrinkled eyes of enduring love, telling her, "I know there is a God, darling." Then, as a sort of tacit admission, she adds, "I realize that my own fears caused me to look at religion in an unhealthy way. It should have been all about love, but I taught it to your father the way my parents taught it to me."

Mother's eyes have now moved from Elizabeth to me. "I'm sorry, Billy." she apologizes, "God isn't all about fear and punishment. He loves us and he wants all his children to come back to him." I feel almost sad at her words, for there is a subtle hesitation, and the hint of a question within her affirmation; I sense that Mother's own faith has changed over the years, and that she is facing death with an imperfect confidence. "Never forget, my dear Elizabeth," Mother labors, "that you cannot judge others or you will someday find yourself dying with my own words on your lips." And then Mother adds one more terse thought, "You cannot see into the heart of another person,"

While it is a new world everywhere else, Stella's Cove has continued its plunge into a fading history. As we walk back toward the dock, I realize that the town is likely destined for permanent obscurity, and that it will soon be no more than the pile of rubble still cluttering the plant site at Murphy's Bay.

Celeste and I still have not warmed up toward religion, nor do we believe that the world was created in seven days. But the advice given by Mother, on her deathbed, to our sweet Elizabeth, is still our creed today. For there are a few, simple words that can replace every religious work ever written:

"Do unto others as you would have them do unto you." and "Judge not that ye be not judged."

A Sterile Place

There is the typical, curious hint of antiseptic and ammonia. It is something that characterizes the empty sterility of such places. The rhythmic beeping of the heart monitor is a metronome for the slow dirge that plays, incessantly, and has for the past three days. Celeste glances up from her knitting. The muted TV over the bed scrolls endless stories of the miseries and catastrophes of a troubled world. The green, tiled walls, meticulously scrubbed and polished, mirror the peaceful scene.

But the silence is not to last. The beeping stops and alarms ring. Nurses rush into the room, and the PA system rings with the words, "Code Three." "I'm sorry," says the first nurse as she enters, "I'll have to ask you to step outside." Dr. Simms flies through the doorway, knocking Celeste's knitting from her hands as the two pass. Outside the room, she can't help but silently ask, "Why's everyone making such a big fuss?" In a sense, the whole crisis is like a school fire drill, for there is no fire—at least not one that can be knocked down. It is a matter of foregone conclusion.

Celeste stands outside the room, thinking about the good years that passed so quickly. She thinks about that spit of land, the idyllic home perched at the watery gateway to the outside world, and the majestic glacier that crowned the town of Stella's Cove. And she reminisces about her years with Billy and the wonderful life they created together.

Moments later, Dr. Simms emerges. "Mrs. Potter," he says, obviously trying to convey that this event is something of much more consequence than the daily routines of a doctor's life, "I'm sorry for your loss." There is a perfunctory hug which does, indeed, seem to have the warm presence of humanity within it, and Celeste watches him as he disappears into another patient's room.

The End

About the Author

Michael S. Robinson, Sr. has a diverse cultural and geographical background. Extensive world travel has given him an appreciation for the diversity of its people and cultures.

A Viet Nam era veteran and graduate of the U.S. Army Infantry Officer Candidate School, his life has been one of adventure and activity. He has jumped from airplanes, accumulated thousands of hours as a pilot, and has created poetry, music, short stories, and contributions to dozens of publications. His western poetry has garnered four, first-place national awards, and he's performed his poetry and songs in over 2,500 shows

Michael did both undergraduate and graduate studies in journalism-related subjects. Writing is his love. Father of five grown children, he resides with his wife Carol and one mongrel dog in Utah.